Spark
of
Death

SPARK
OF
DEATH

PART 1

Christopher Bates

Inquiries and Book Orders should be addressed to:

Great Writers Media
Email: info@greatwritersmedia.com
Phone: (302) 918-5570
16192 Coastal Highway, Lewes DE 19958, USA

ISBN: 978-1-955809-53-5 (sc)
ISBN: 978-1-955809-54-2 (e)

Rev. date: 08/11/2021

Contents

ACT 1

Chapter One

ᴇɴᴛᴇʀ ᴛʜᴇ ᴡᴜ-ᴛᴀɴɢ (36 ᴄʜᴀᴍʙᴇʀꜱ)

"Team eight, this is GSE1. I have deployed from the nest, ETA thirty sierras and counting," Sparks spoke into his altitude helmet which feeds him oxygen at the great heights he has jumped from.

He is free falling from a spec op cargo plane. The first few hundred feet left him dizzy, even with the oxygen being fed through his airtight helmet. This is his first high altitude fall, but this is not the first time he has been put in a situation that he is unfamiliar with and excels. His ability to naturally adapt to situations has earned him the honor to work these high-risk missions with the Agency. He was twenty-five when he joined the Navy, which is old for special operations, but he was physically in his prime.He is considered an alpha in physical standards which means that he excels in all aspects of Navy Physical Training.

Sparks stands at 6'5" and is 250 pounds, and his hair is cut in a brush fade with deep waves. He is well built, and his skin tone is a deep mocha. His ASVAB scores, the tests a person takes before joining the military, were extremely high. They are a combination of academic and engineering questions that help the assessors know what jobs to recommend the service member.

Sparks scored a ninety six percent, which could have placed him in the Nuclear program, but instead he chose to pursue an engineering job. His motivation was that he loved working with electronics and he was not going to be put in a sub; that was what he thought would happen if he went to the Nuke program. After boot camp he went to his respective A-school and excelled to the top of his class. When he got to his permanent duty station, he chose to join the ship's *Vessel Board Search and Seizure* a.k.a. *VBSS team*, which boards enemy vessels.

He was a natural at tactical maneuvering which made the seals that taught the class pull a few strings and land him a position in the Agency, a new team composed of noncombatants to assist the seals and various allied special force teams in operations. He was perfect for operations that the Agency were deployed on, oilers and riggers, or some sort of turbine-based vessel or plant. And having a guy with his set of skills that could handle himself in combat would prove valuable.

"Team eight, this is Sparks. My free fall has ended. The LZ is in sight, I have two tangos on the roof, two tangos on patrol roving on the ground. I will be entering from the south in eight sierras.""Roger that GSE1, Stealth is advised, you are alone on this one. Deadly force is authorized, although loud rounds are not. Establish coms once the LZ is secured. Over."

"Roger that, over and out," Sparks responded.

8... First thing is to breathe, 7... Now assess the situation, 6... The two watch standers on the roof are sharpshooters, they make routine checks outside the facility and on each other, 5... The two roving watches cover the ground keeping watch over what the two sharpshooters up top can't track. They rarely keep an eye on each other.

4... The two roving watches are the weakness, 3... Sparks thought he should attack the roving watch covering the south, then eliminate the second rover. Afterward he would quickly make his way to eliminate the top sharpshooters and gain access into the plant through the roof. 2... Quickly and silently, 1... Unleashing from the chute and free falling the remaining twenty feet.

Sparks navigates himself so that his landing will be cushioned by the watch stander's head, successfully breaking the rover's neck as all six feet five inches and two hundred and fifty-six pounds fall on top of him at ten miles per hour. This happens so fast that the guard has no time to draw his weapon or even make any other noise more than the quick, "*umph!*" that escapes his lip; more air than voice. Sparks drags the man's limp body under a large bush nearby then looks up. He is looking for his parachute, but as promised it has now reverted to smoke (in actuality it is Nano bits that dissipate in the air, making it look like chemtrails or smoke, a genius invention that will never leave this top-secret community).

Sparks' wonder and amazement is interrupted by rustling of leaves, it was the second rover. Sparks instinctively takes a stalking position. He becomes cat-like in his movements to get closer to his prey. It is an almost unneeded precaution since the rover is distracted and from the view behind, Sparks can see the dim light of his cell phone.

"This idiot is playing candy crush on watch." Sparks whispered to himself.With the silence and agility that a person would not assume Sparks would possess since he is so tall and muscular, he leaps in the air, unsheathing his combat knife from his hip midair and thrusting it through the back of the rover's neck with marksman-like accuracy. Sparks left hand quickly muffles the rovers mouth so that his gurgled screams never leave the intimate closeness of the two.

The blood-soaked blade protrudes out of the rover's throat as he stiffens in Sparks arms. The shock causes the guard to tense up and he never lets go of his phone. In fact, he grabs it with such force that he cracked the screen. Sparks then drags the rover's body under a close tree that is hiding them from the sharpshooters on the roof.

"Now for the fun part,"

Tactical thinking and maneuvering have always come easy for Sparks. Some of his instructors have said that he moves quicker and quieter than any one of his stature, but Sparks has always known it is not that he is quicker than others physically, but it is that his thinking, assessment, and reaction happens seemingly at once.

It is the middle of June, two years prior, when Sparks was asked by his instructors at the VBSS school to become a part of a joint force Spec Op initiative. This initiative will place individuals in the military of three different ally countries in field positions to support Seal and other Operator teams. The initiative is called The Agency. Sparks is given directions that will lead him to the meet up point and was told to be there at 2300 navy time.

"This seems easy enough... I am to make it to what seems like... San Clemente... with no boat or Helicopter in three hours... Whatever this ALPHA project is I think they are looking for a X-man or someone who can walk on water... I mean, I am a good swimmer but I'm sure that is thirty odd miles away, and that is after you get out of the bay,"

Sparks says to himself in a condescending tone while looking out from the San Diego shoreline.

In the distance he can see the strip of island he needs to reach, but there is no way he will be able to swim there. Let alone swim there and make it there on time.

"Hey, what's up!"

Unshaken, Sparks turns around to find the red-headed gentleman who was sitting two tables away from him at the restaurant that he just left.

"I'm IT1 Loch... I was..."

"Watching me eat?"

"Well, Not really. But I think we have the same destination. You headed to San Clemente?"

Sparks had been in the Navy for four years. He was well aware of the term and meaning of *loose lips, sink ships*. Op Sec is a term that is preached religiously to sailors aboard war faring vessels. Op Sec stood for operational security, simply means that if someone was not at the brief you were at, then they are not to be told what you heard there.

Sparks was a good profiler and judging by the dust that was caked on IT1's boots, the wrinkles in the front of his shirt from laying and shooting a M4 rifle in prone position, and the scent of gun smoke, he could see that IT1 had definitely been in one of the classes today. Not the class Sparks was in though because his class had graduated that day, but he could have been from one of the other classes that had just started.

That would make the most sense because the first week was when the class would shoot for hours and hours. That is when the instructors were not intensively training the student till death. The instructors loved pushing students to the limits. Sparks knew IT1 could have gotten the same invite to The Agency as he had gotten.

"But... why? Why so early in his training? Was he some kind of Super sharpshooter?" Sparks thought.

And judging by the way Loch's uniform hung off of his frail body, Sparks new it wasn't because of his Athletic ability. As if Loch heard his thoughts he interrupted sparks profiling."I know I'm not the prize candidate as yourself, I was surprised, and a little afraid when they pulled me aside after class was over. You see, I was never supposed to be at the class, but I hacked into the server and placed myself on the list. I was sure they were going to call base security on me, and I would see brig time, but instead... they gave me this offer. They said I would be a good asset with the ... Skills I possess." Loch said with a bit of an unconfident smile.

It sounded legit and besides Isis was not going to send this guy to kill a few "*support guys*" who don't even have real training.

Not to waste any more time Sparks moved on to the real issue.

"Okay, IT1. How are we going to get to San Clemente? Any bright ideas?"

"Well I overheard. Uhm... Well I kind of hacked into... uh... There were two guys here earlier. Officers..."

"You mean the two ensigns that were sitting behind me and to my left?"

"Yeah, those guys. Well, they were saying that they were going to take a boat from the shop they worked at, being the divisional officers and all. They are going to have one of their guys drive them to San Clemente and then return once they get on land."

"And you got that info from hacking into their phones and reading their text?"

"Yup!" Loch said with a huge smile.

"Well, that's interesting. So, where is this shop and do you think they will give us a ride?" Sparks asked.

"Maybe not."

"Maybe not? Why not?"

"Because there they go, right there."

Sparks looked to where Loch was pointing, and about two nautical miles out he could see an inflatable rigid hulled speedboat wiz pass with three guys inside.

"Shit, my bad. You know I probably should have started off with that… You know, like, 'Hey, I know where we can get a ride!'"

Sparks watched as the boat got further into the horizon until something caught his eye.

"Don't worry, little guy. I just thought of a plan. Well, technically, you had the plan. I just modified it."

"What?? My plan is eight Nautical miles into the horizon, what are you talking about?"

"A boat. Look, all of these boats on this pier are moored and locked to the pier, except this one. It has no lock and it is only moored down by one knot in the line," Sparks pointed at a small speed boat with only two seats.

"Okay, I am not understanding you. Are you saying we should steal this boat?"

"I wouldn't say steal. Besides, I think it was made for us to take. How else are we going to get to San Clemente? It's more like borrowing, and coming from a government hacker/iPhone intruder you should be all in... What, you know, the navy way... If you ain't cheating, you ain't trying."

Sparks gives Loch a mischievous grin and a shoulder shrug. Loch looked over his shoulder and down the pier, then unconfidently shrugs and follows Sparks on the boat. After unleashing the line from the pier, Sparks pops open the steering control panel. He then carefully yet skillfully takes a couple wires, cuts them, then cross connects them with each other, and like that, the engine roars to life.

"What the hell! How did you do that? I mean, how did you know which ones would work?"

"Simple, only one rule to follow."

"Which is?"

"Red you're dead."

Loch mouthing out the phrase., *Red you're dead.*""Wait, what??"

With a chuckle and a huge mischievous smile, Sparks smashed the throttle and took off to San Clemente. And in the background of the roaring engine, they could faintly hear what sounds as if someone is screaming for them to stop, but neither one of them looked back to confirm it.

Chapter Two

CAN IT BE ALL SO SIMPLE?

With both the ground rovers dead, Sparks could now move about freely around the ground level of the facility. It was a small complex, roughly two acres in either direction. The ground was spacious with a few trees and bushes, but not too many as to keep it unmanageable. The main building ran from east to west, and the entire length of the complex was ten to maybe fifteen yards between the building and fence.

Sparks thought to himself that it looks more like a government than a civilian-used electrical plant. The roof of the building was about 20 feet high and on top of the roof were two towers, possibly exhaust stacks with rails and walkways. This is where the two sharpshooters were placed. As he assessed earlier, he can move freely in the shadows but not for too long. He figured it would only take someone's mind, roughly ten minutes, to realize the rovers that were walking back and forth below have not been visible for a while..

And that is when things would get tricky and outright detrimental to the mission.

First thing that a watch stander would do is conduct a comms check. To try and verbally check on the missing rovers, which if they are on a stand-alone frequency would be okay, but if others can hear, like the base the Seal Team is breaching, and once the power goes down, it will set them on alert, killing the element of surprise. No, Sparks needed to get this done quickly and efficiently. He surveyed the surrounding terrain. The tree he was hiding under was perfectly even with the roof. If he climbed the tree and moved down the branch, as long as he didn't make too much of a rustle, it gave perfect camouflaged access right under one of the exhaust stacks.

He could then silently walk right up the steps and neutralize the first sharpshooter. As for the second sharpshooter, his plan was to throw a rock over the watch standers head; just far enough that it would land right outside the fence he was surveying. The falling rock would make noise loud enough to get the sharpshooters attention but not loud enough to cause a warning. The sharpshooter would investigate the noise, and that pause would give Sparks the time to make it to the second exhaust stack and neutralize the threat.

It was like Gunny always said,

"Sometimes in the field, imagination can be an operator's best resource. Other times..."

Well, Sparks could only hope that this was not one of the other times.

****

The boat ride to San Clemente took almost two hours, which would leave them around one hour to find the rendezvous point. It was a rough ride, not due to the sea state, but due to the fact that once Loch started talking, he didn't stop. Loch told Sparks every crime he had committed on the internet. Frankly, Sparks was slightly impressed at what Loch could accomplish with a computer. The awe quickly resided once he went on to tell Sparks what seemed to be a biography.

Loch had grown up as a silent kid in the Midwest, to no surprise he was a computer geek choosing to be on the computer than to be around all the other kids. He joined the Navy as an IT because it was the field he loved. He was smart, making first class rank in five years and earning navy commendation medals in the process. One thing that Loch was not good at was swimming.After accepting the fact that the boat was not left for them, Sparks had come up with the plan to leave the boat sailing full throttle away from the beach as they swam the remainder of the 100 yards to shore. With how strong the current was, it would take a strong swimmer around 15 minutes to make it to the beach. Loch opposed the plan after letting Sparks know with enthusiasm that he would surely drown.

Sparks pulled the boat to knee-level trying to be as silent as possible. They jumped out, then Sparks sent the rented boat out to sea. This caused more noise than Sparks intended. He hoped that stealth was not one of the requirements in this adventure.

"So, now what's the plan?" Loch said as he ringed out the bottom of his shirt.

"The directions that I have said that the rendezvous point is just around that bend and up the coast a bit. Roughly a thirty-minute walk from here." Sparks pointed towards the trees beyond the beach.

San Clemente has been used by the navy and marines for decades as a sea to land ordinance training site. The marines will mark an area and the ships will send cannon rounds to the spot the marines marked. That makes San Clemente's terrain look very war-like, there are craters on the beach where ships have sent their cannons, dusted with burn marks, and jagged edges.

"You know that people still live on the other side of the beach? And the houses are worth a good amount. I mean how good of a salesman do you have to be to get someone to buy property on a ship's gun range? I can hear the sales pitch now. Looking out your window you can see the view is amazing. Don't worry about the dust from the shell impact and the marines you see scurrying around picking up shells. Believe me the loud booms almost become rhythmic." Loch said while looking down as he walked through the trees and over a few branches that had fallen due to cannon artillery.

"Shut up!" Sparks whispers and put his hand up in a halting position still looking forward.

"Hey, what is it? You see something?"

"Yeah. And you talk too much."

Loch was taken aback a little and frowns at Sparks.

"I think we are here."

Against the rocks, Sparks could make out about 12 people in the darkness, two of which had stood up and were making their way towards Loch and Sparks. "Well, well, well. If it ain't Radio. Hey Phillips! Look who showed up to the party!" Hooper said while lightly bumping Phillips' chest with his right hand.

"I see they must be inviting anyone to this Agency program. And I think he has gotten John Coffee to be his bodyguard," Phillips responded.

Loch stepped behind Sparks slightly. Sparks could sense the real fear that Loch had for these guys, and that fear was not from verbal assault only.

"Hooper! Phillips! I see you guys made it here… Safely," the sarcasm and indifferent tone was unhidden in Loch's voice.

To an ordinary man, Hooper and Phillips would seem mildly intimidating. They had the classic military look about them, clean shaved, tone bodies but not that muscular, and the jarhead haircut. Hooper stood around six feet two inches whereas Phillips stood five feet ten inches. It was almost comical how closely Hooper and Phillips as a duo looked similar to Sparks and Loch; like a big brother and a little brother. "I don't know what type of *High School Musical* or *Back to the Future* nerd-bully shit you guys have going on but leave me the hell out of it. I am too old to give a damn." Sparks said as he walked right past the two guys, who at first refuse to get out his way, but fail to stop the huge mass of a man and they are both ran through while looking at each other as if to say why did you let him do that.

Loch took this opportunity to slip past them through the space Sparks had created and was back at Sparks' side within seconds.

"Friends of yours?" Sparks said without looking at Loch.

"More like assholes I would rather not have to deal with. By the way, thanks for having my back, back there."

"No problem." Sparks said with no emotion.

"Yeah, that was sarcasm... some type of friend you are."

"Who said we are friends?"

"Oh! I just figured... I mean, yeah, I guess..."

"Chill out. I can't stand those guys, and I just met them. So, in this situation it's the enemy of my enemy..." Sparks looked back at Hooper and Phillips.

They were joking with each other and mimicking Sparks and Loch. They both stopped and turned when they saw Sparks looking at them.

"Word Son!" Loch was smiling with a huge grin which made Sparks crack a smile at the sheer goofy expression on Loch's face.

At that moment, a large booming voice cracks from the pine trees to their right.

"ATTENTION!!"

In what took only seconds, the fourteen people composed of military personnel from three different countries popped to attention as if the presidents of their respective countries had entered the area."Form up in ranks and listen close, Mutts." The group did as they were told making two lines of seven.

Still at attention, everything was silent, a dead silence, it was quiet before, when everyone was just slack and holding under toned conversations, but now not even the wind could be heard. The marine Gunnery Sergeant before them had commanded all their attention and was the sole focal point and voice.

"Ok, mutts. As you may know, you have all been chosen to become part of a joint military support team. The war on terrorism has escalated, the terrorists are not just attacking by physical means, they have been using electronic warfare and more advanced methods to push their cause. The allies and special operative teams we have around the world are being outsmarted in the field, but *not* outdone."

"We have chosen to equip the teams with not only the latest and the best weapons, but also the best minds. That is where you mutts come in the equation. Our job is to make you ready to support in ways that best suits your ability. Some of you will be direct support, some will support a bit further behind the lines, and some of you will play espionage."

It was all coming together and making sense to Sparks. He had looked over the group and could find that military experience was the only thing this group had in common. This group was made up of very uniquely different people. There was Loch, a nerdy, flimsy, slack bodied computer geek, great for long distance support. Then Hooper and Phillips, they were crypto technicians, and very conniving, they would be great at espionage.

There was a tall, slim, blonde woman from Britain's air force, must be a pilot. There were three marines who could be used as body shields or whatever marines are used for, Sparks thought. Then there were five Israeli army guys and an Israeli female from their army. When Sparks caught a glimpse of the Israeli Female, he could focus on nothing else.

She was around five feet and eight inches tall; she was fit yet her uniform hugged every curve of her body in the most elegant way. Her golden-brown hair was in a military specific bun, and she had a desert tan with a tint of hue, as if she was ethnically mixed with another darker ethnicity. She wore hipster style glasses, that Sparks knew were for show. But what set her apart from other ladies he had found attraction for, was her green tinted hazel eyes, the ones that seemed to peer into a person's soul. The ones that were, in fact, peering into his soul that very moment.

Sparks broke out of his spell and snapped his head back to the front. He couldn't believe he was gawking at this female. He was much more reserved, smooth and outright cooler than that. And not to mention, the disgusted look she had given him as if to say,

"The F is your problem?" Sparks was flat out embarrassed.

If black people could blush, he would look like a freckled face redhead. He tried to kick the thoughts out of his head and focus on Gunny who was wrapping up his speech. "Your training will be ending with soft shot tactical movements and a field test. That will be the curriculum we will abide by. So, if no one has any questions.... Good... Now it's time to have a little fun.... MUTTS... ON YOUR FACES!"

****

Thanks to all of Sparks' stealth training and live combat experience, the climb and maneuvering of the large tree was easy. He had worked his way up and over in less than a minute and was currently hidden at the bottom of the steps.

"Okay, that was easy. Now for step 2." Sparks said to himself under his breath.

Using the sharpshooters shadow, Sparks studied the sharpshooter's movements. He saw that the sharpshooter would look past the borders of the complex then look to his left away from the other sharpshooter, then turn around and look to the ground, probably looking for the rover whom he had not seen walk past his peripheral for the rounds. "Good luck, buddy. That rover won't be continuing the rounds..." Sparks leapt up the steps in a few swift strides, knife piercing and dragging across the watch stander's throat in less than three seconds.

"You can join your buddy in hell to resume the watch." Sparks whispered in the watch standers ear as his life faded away.

Murphy and his damn law always have a tendency to peek their ugly heads up during a mission. (*Murphy's law: If anything bad can happen it will happen.*) The longer it waits to surprise you, the bigger the gift. The key to any mission is to minimize the damage and threat that the surprise brings with it. On this particular mission, Murphy decided to tap the other watch stander right on the shoulder, in the middle of Sparks sending his buddy to the big duty in the sky.

Time is relative, a perceived element. So, when people say that time slowed down, what they meant is that in the moment in question, they paid attention to every second of time and took note of its brevity. This is why you feel time goes so fast when you are having fun and seems to creep while you are at work. Sparks understood this concept early in life and would play around with it, practicing slowing and speeding time, or at least his perception of it.

The sharpshooter spotted Sparks just as his comrade's body was being eased to the ground. In what would have been three seconds seemed more like fifteen seconds. The pure instinct of training on both Sparks and the watch stander is what motivated the events that followed. The sharpshooter reacted first. The space between him and Sparks was roughly twenty feet; perfect distance for his sidearm, but to use his sniper rifle would cause too much unnecessary movement and wasted time.

In this situation, wasted time would lead to certain death. The sharpshooter lets his rifle fall by his side, hanging to his shoulder by a strap. He then quickly places his left hand to his side where his 1911 45-caliber handgun was holstered. Flipping the safety off as he brings it up to his two-handed pistol grip.

Pstsss... Pstsss...

Two muffled shots can be barely heard in the anticipated silence. Two exit wounds burst from the chest of the sharpshooter in Sparks' arms. Two exit wounds leave out from the back of the last sharpshooter in the exact same spot, and his eyes widen. There is a chilling still in the wind as no one moves for a brief moment. Then the surprise sharpshooter blinks one last long blink, drops his side arm and slumps forward against the rail.

"Team 8 this is GSE 1 Sparks. All Targets have been neutralized outside of the plant. I am in route to breach and disable the generators."

"All targets neutralized, aye. Good job, GSE1. ETA on when that generator will be disabled?" The communications officer replied.

"Five mikes tops."

"Five mikes, aye!"

Chapter Three

1-800 Suicide

It's been two months of nothing but physical training.

> *4:00am: wake-up run to the Mess decks 5.6 miles.*
> *6:45am: 500 push-ups, 500 eight count body builders.*
> *8:00am: Fifteen-mile swim up the coast one way. Then a fifteen-mile swim back down the coast after the confidence course.*
> *12:30pm: lunch*
> *1:00pm: R&R.*
> *2:00pm: Stretches.*
> *4:00pm: Weightlifting.*
> *And by 6:00pm, if you are not asleep, then you are most likely dead or have quit by now.*

The dropout rate was high in the first month. There were 28 people in the beginning, 14 on the day Sparks arrived, and 14 more showed up the next day. Within the first month, half the people quit. Most of the excuses were *"I have already gone through basic training.*

I don't need to do it all over again, besides I never wanted to be a SEAL anyways". But few had families, and having just gotten back from long deployments, they did not want to be away from their families an extra 6 months for training then have to be placed wherever the military needed them; which could be in any part of the world.

Phase one was completed and the beginning of phase two was in progress. There were only ten people left now, after two more Israeli soldiers quit due to a broken leg and fainting spells. There was the tall, blonde British airman named Alexis. There were three marines, two from the guys that showed up the first night and one from the next batch. Hooper and Philips made it through, and the dynamics between Sparks and Hooper had escalated a bit through phase one; both trying to surpass the physical trails and competing each other.

Loch had made it through, there was a LT from the Israeli army who had been made the divisional officer. Of course, Sparks had made it and he was made the leading enlisted officer of the division. There was another Israeli army guy who made it and then there was Kelia. That was the name of the Israeli girl that Sparks had noticed the first night. If at first Sparks had been attracted to her, he had surpassed that emotion and was infatuated by her. She was mentally and physically strong and was quiet, like a beautiful summer's day in a field of bluebonnets quiet."Okay, Mutts. We have now created a canvas, you all came here weak. But now, you have given me something to work with. Now, I can turn you into valuable team members that will be able to assist spec op teams without hindering them."

"In this next phase, we will learn how to take opponents or multiple opponents down lethally or non-lethally. That's right Mutts, we are going to learn hand to hand combat, we will beat the daylight out of each other till we can no longer beat each other. Literally!"

Everyone gave a chuckle at how outrageous that sounded and how seriously it was said. They were lined up in ranks of five, they were told to pair off in five groups of two. Ladies where to find male counterparts.

As Gunny puts it,

"The battlefield holds no fairness, only fate!"

Sparks had been paired off with Hooper. Sparks liked the idea of having the opportunity to put Hooper in a place of humility.

All of Sparks' life, he had trained in various martial arts. By the age of 26, Sparks had practiced 6 different styles and had mastered 3 of them. His favorite being Capoeira which was a Brazilian martial art brought by the slaves. Invented by the inhabitants of Angola and disguised in dance to confuse the slave owners and also the opponents. He used this art the most falling back on the other arts when needed.

The purpose of the sparring this day was for Gunny to gauge each person's fighting ability. So, he would know what their strengths and weaknesses were. They were to fight each other till submission or knockout.

"Sparks! Hooper! Front and center!"

They both sprinted to the position Gunny had pointed to.

"You two will be first in this exercise. The rules are simple, take down your opponent non-lethally by whatever means you deem necessary. There are no time limits but, *do not* waste my time by dancing around all day. We will start when everyone has surrounded you. We will be doing this Quote un Quote circle of truth every weekend to gauge how your training has progressed. So everyone, gather around with your partners on the opposite side of the circle. Once one match is over, the next two jumps in when they have exited. Good luck, Mutts."

Both Hooper and Sparks started to circle each other in the tight proximity of the circle. Hooper could not help but take this opportunity to open his mouth and talk trash. "Okay, big guy. I know you might be bigger and stronger than me, but you are way too slow... I will give you this one opportunity. If you can hit me once... *Umph!*"

As quick and precise as a viper, Sparks threw out a jab and caught Hooper midsentence, right smack on the chin. Dazed but still standing Hooper gathered himself, the strike was fast and powerful but not a finishing blow. It was meant to send one message and it did just that. The jab Sparks threw was to tell Hooper to *shut up and fight.*

Sparks sized up Hooper's demeanor. He noticed the slight favor that Hooper put on his left knee due to general wear and tear from the previous weeks of running, swimming, and weightlifting. He noticed that Hooper was right handed but chose to fight in a southpaw stance. He also noticed that Hooper kept his left hand slightly low as an obvious bait to get Sparks to throw a huge right punch lowering his guard in the process. Leaving the left side of his face open to be bashed by a counter from Hooper.

That was exactly what Sparks was going to do, trap the spider in his own web. Sparks threw an over aggressive and wild right, overextending intentionally and stepping in a bit closer to Hooper in the process. Hooper reacted as planned, he threw his left arm up deflecting and grabbing Sparks' hand then countering with a right of his own that was aimed at Sparks' jaw, and would have connected had it not been for the footwork of Spark that positioned him too close inside of Hoopers personal space for him to throw a precise punch.With a full step of his left foot, Sparks slid right through Hooper's hold. Sparks then twisted his body slightly to be parallel with Hooper. Hooper's momentum from the right hand punch he threw that never landed, made him overextend and threw his body right into the knee that Sparks raised toward Hooper's midsection.

"*Umph!!!*" as all the air that was in Hooper's lungs escaped.

Sparks then stepped back a half step to gain separation. He then spin his body to gain momentum as he swung his foot up and slightly downwards. He aimed at Hooper's right ear and with precision in his calculations, Sparks foot landed against its target. Hooper's head whipped downwards towards the sand and his body went limp.

In what could be described as five seconds of amazement, everyone who was there went silent. It all happened so fast. From the first punch, to now seeing Hooper's limp body being taken by the medical team. And all anyone could do was try and comprehend, and mentally replay what had happened. Unimpressed and impatiently, Gunny snapped everyone back to reality."Are you Mutts going to stand there with your thumbs up your asses? Or are you going to fight? Now to the left... SHARPLY!!!"

With that bit of motivation, the next two jumped into the center of the circle. The fights went on. Some of the fights took a while due to both partners being evenly matched. Some ending quickly due to the opposite. No one else was knocked out so Gunny demanded that each team fight twice. Keila fought so rhythmically and graceful it was entrancing. She danced around her opponent like a hummingbird and when she struck, it was as elegant as a jaguar on its prey.

As for her opponent, Loch, though he was stronger from all the working out the group had been doing, he was still not much of a fighter. He gave it an honest effort, but to have a woman submit him twice, it was easy for everyone to see that he would surely benefit from the training he would eventually receive.

"Mutts, listen up!"

Everyone raised their heads from their exhaustion to listen to their instructor, still in the circle they had been in during the fights.

"Watching your skills in hand to hand combat, or lack thereof..." he looked directly at Loch.

"Has given me an idea of methods and training we will need in the coming weeks. Everyone should have gone twice if I am not mistaken, except for you GSE1 Sparks..."

he looked dead at Sparks.

Using the rank before Sparks' name was surprising, but what was absolutely terrifying was the blank stone look in Gunny's eyes. And the humorless half smile painted on his thin lips.

"Seeing as how your partner will be in the infirmary for a while, you will be needing a replacement for the last fight. Just your luck, it so happens, I am qualified to fill such... Billet... Maybe overqualified you might find."

Gunny was an old marine, possibly in his late forties or early fifties, but his body did not reflect his age. He was in great shape. Every muscle was accented and chiseled. He was not the type to just bark orders, as everyone found out in the first phase. He was with them through every lap, every eight count, every push-up, and every mile they would swim. He was a lean, mean fighting machine.

Everyone was standing in the circle, but to say they were standing in silent anticipation, would be a huge understatement. It was more like silent fear and dread. They had all witnessed Sparks, and how he effortlessly handled and knocked out Hooper. Some of them had to wash off Hooper's blood, that was spat out when Sparks' foot connected with Hooper's face. Now, the way Gunny challenged Sparks with such enthusiasm said one of two things, either Gunny was tired and in need of a good forceful nap at the hands of Sparks or Gunny was truly unimpressed with Sparks display, and if none of Sparks' peers could do so, then he would have to step up and teach Sparks the lesson of the day.

Gunny wasted no time, as soon as he discarded his shirt, he immediately rushed at Sparks full speed. He started his assault with a three-strike combo, leading with a left jab, then a right straight followed by a front kick. All of which were either blocked or dodged by Sparks. Without hesitation, Gunny then came in for a couple of kicks. He threw a side kick with the opposite leg he had just thrown the front kick, and then a roundhouse kick that was aimed at Sparks left temple.

Gunny's footwork was impressive, and his speed was amazing. Sparks sidestepped the sidekick using his evasive skills he learned in Capoeira. He did a side handspring moving in the same direction Gunny's roundhouse was headed, and while still in a crouching position, Sparks used the momentum he had gained from the handspring and threw a leg sweep. Gunny quickly lifted his foot out of the way but was not ready for the second sweep that followed after Sparks was spinning from the first one. The second sweep was not aimed for his legs but hit its target which was the center of Gunny's chest."Ugh." Gunny stepped back a few feet holding his chest.

"So, you have studied Capoeira? Well son, dance moves won't stop this ass whooping!"

Gunny dusted off the dirt that was left from where Sparks boot had connected with his chest. He then charged at Sparks running full force, then leaping in the air while spinning his body in a half pike and bringing his leg around for a massive kick. With this surprise move, he got the jump on Sparks, literally. Gunny's foot collided with Sparks' upper brow causing Sparks to temporarily be stunned.

As Gunny landed, he was in a crouching position. From this position, he brought his left hand up in an uppercut which was aimed at Sparks' chin. Sparks was fast but not fast enough to not get hit. While still dazed from the flying kick, he anticipated that Gunny would follow up with an uppercut due to how Gunny landed, but the punch came just a tad bit faster than Sparks had calculated. All Sparks could do was lean away, not avoiding the punch but taking most of the power away from it, and only catching a small amount of the impact.

Sparks' quick thinking had given him a few more minutes to fight. Had the uppercut landed, he would have found himself right next to Hooper. The quick thinking also gave Sparks a little separation from Gunny. Which was a good thing, cause Gunny's lesson was not over. He pressed harder.

Throwing left kicks followed by right punches. He threw spinning elbows and flying knees. Sparks had only seconds to react to the next barrage and had no time to form an attack plan of his own. Gunny had begun to dictate how the fight was fought and that was a bad thing for Sparks. Sparks would find himself ducking under a punch just to be hit with a knee, or side stepping a kick, just to meet a well-placed back hand.Kelia watched in silence along with everyone else. Her face had its normal stone look of indifference, but with the battle that was fought in front of her, inside she was in a war of her own. She thought she cared very little for Sparks, as he was the typical American douchebag. She hated how he was chosen to be team leader over herself due to the fact he was a male. She hated the smug smile he always had on his face every time they would glance at each other.

She hated the richness of his voice, hard with an undertone of someone who had lived and seen things. She hated the sheer mass of Sparks, how his perfectly symmetric body came together to perform at peak physical condition, from the broad of his chest and the cut of his shoulders. How his arms and legs looked as if his skin was painted on to his muscles.

Okay, being honest with herself she really didn't hate that so much. A girl had to have her eye candy also and watching him rise out of the ocean with the sun at his back on their morning swims would really warm her blood. Kelia realized as she watched Sparks take a beat down before her eyes that she actually might have a slight crush on Sparks.

Her thought confused her, for Sparks was everything that she hated in a man and also everything she liked. Watching him effectively and precisely take down Hooper impressed her. Now she was concerned, for if he didn't find that same level of ferocity now against Gunny, then he would be in a world of pain. At that moment Kelia wanted one thing more than anything else, for someone to just stop the fight.

Sparks was fading and fading quickly. He had given up all hopes of landing a strike on Gunny and had focused all of his efforts on just surviving Gunny's onslaught. Sparks moved around a few punches, but it was the one he never saw coming that sealed his fate for the evening. The last thing sparks remembered was the feeling; the feeling was sharp, and it overtook his whole being then there was nothing. Quite a dreamless sleep, then white lights, what looked to be a corpsman and then the sharp pain again.

****

The inside of the power plant was dimly lit. Sparks had entered through one of the intake grates near the exhaust towers. From his high position along the rafters of the building, he could see the floor layout very well. There were two generators, a main generator, and a back-up. There were auxiliary pumps that were used for cooling, lube oil, and fuel tanks. Along with fire pumps that would aid in firefighting if a fire happened to break out.

There were tons of pipes and to the left, by the exit door, was an engineering watch shack with two engineers inside. The engineers were not armed; they were only there to provide the necessary support needed to run the plant. There were a few cameras set up throughout the plant that would give the watch standers a good idea of location if a fire happened to form or if there was a saboteur.

Sparks planned his moves out in his head, he would first strategically place the video scramblers he had to put the cameras on a constant loop, so he could move freely throughout the plant. He then would sneak down to the generator's controller and mix a few wires to kill the power and make the engineer's job a bit more difficult. The Seal team could breach the compound and his job would be done. Seeing as how the engineers were not armed, if one had happened to get in his way, he would take them down non-lethally. As Sparks made his plans, he moved to execute them.

He could shake the feeling that he was not the only one stalking around the small power plant. The shadows seemed to follow his every move. He would stop and look to see if he could find his stalker, but after investigating his hunches, and finding nothing other than a danger tag swaying from a vent on an auxiliary pump or an open cabinet door, Sparks decided that he should just make his way to the generators. And finish his part of the assignment so he could meet up at the LZ for extraction.

After placing the scrambling unit strategically between the three cameras, he was free to move around the facility and make his way to the main generator. The scrambler would loop the last three minutes over again to make the engineers feel that all was quiet on watch. The engineers would not know what was going on until they got the alarm from the equipment malfunction, but by then, Sparks would be long gone, and the damage would have been done.

All the seal team needed was five minutes of darkness to breach their targets compound and eliminate the treats, and fulfilling their mission directives. Even if the engineers were great at their jobs, Sparks would do enough damage to the generators that they would need at least 30 minutes to an hour to truly get the equipment back online.

Sparks was now at the local control panel of the main generator. He opened the controller door and began his sabotage when a familiar scent struck his nose. The scent hit him so hard that he felt dizzy. Amongst other feelings he had not felt in the last year, it was a scent of fresh flowers and damp soil. Not perfume or soap, but natural and earthy, rich, buttery, tasty, and womanly.

The scent was right on the tip of his nose yet so close he could feel its presence. Sparks' reaction was untrained and of pure instinct, he rose up to a stance and without hesitation mouthed and slightly whispered the name of the only person that was on his mind…

"Kelia…"

As soon as the name left his mouth, he felt pain. Then a dreamless sleep.

Chapter Four

Uzi

After Sparks woke up from his forced nap, things seemed to take a different route for him. For the duration of his physical combat training, he was paired up with either a grappling coach or a Muay Thai instructor. Everyone was taught Krav Maga. Then phase 3, tactical weapons training, and he was placed in charge. This placement infuriated Aviv due to him being the highest-ranking officer in the bunch, but no matter what a person's rank is, he had to abide by the decisions of his superiors.

The best thing that changed for Spark was Kelia, he had heard that while he was in medical in "*deep sleep*" she had asked about him and had even gone to see him asking the corpsmen if he was okay. After he had joined back with the division, he would catch her sneaking glances at him which would turn her bright red from the embarrassment. Then the day came, it was gloomy outside with sporadic rainfalls, the division was just beginning tactical entry and breaching.

They had split into two teams with Sparks leading one and Aviv leading the other. The plan that had been formulated by both team leaders was for Sparks' team to enter through the front going in loud and being the distraction while Aviv's team would climb on to the roof and clear the house from the inside out. Flushing targets towards the external team. The instructors were the targets in the house, and everyone was armed with sim rounds which are bullet rounds that have soft colorful lipstick material for the projectile instead of lead.

Also, they were informed that the instructors would not be surrendering if cornered and would put up a fight even without weapons. The division's weapons training and school overall, was coming to a close. With only two weeks of training left, this was now all or nothing or what Gunny liked to put it,

"Nuts or Guts."From the start of the plan, Keila opposed Aviv's suggestion. She knew that Aviv hated Sparks; she knew that his hatred for him was because of her and Sparks' position with the team. Aviv had liked Keila for as long as she could remember and if she was interested in things that most girls were interested in, then she would most likely have dated him, or at least taken him up on some of his advances.

He was handsome and smart, but she was focused on her personal mission, and her mission did not include falling for assertive and good-looking men. Aviv knew this, and though he hated it, he respected her goals. That is what infuriated Aviv about her sudden interest in Sparks. Kelia was now infatuated with Sparks. She would think about him constantly and she would have stomach tightness when he would look her way, and her heart would race whenever he got hurt.

When it came to Sparks, she would find herself thinking about dates and relationships, she even imagined what their kids would look like. Sparks was not part of her plan, but she didn't care. She was only waiting for Sparks to stop being shy and speak to her, and she would drop everything to give what seemed like fate, a shot. Kelia knew Aviv could pick up on her emotions so she knew that this plan that they made was a trap to get Sparks kicked out of the program.

Since the start of the last push, the last three weeks, the division was on a point program. Everyone was given three points. If in a combat scenario you were shot or taken down, you would lose a point. If you lost all your points, you would go to a review board and they would determine if you should stay in the program or if the last six months was just a paid vacation.

Aviv was going to flush the instructors right to Sparks guns blazing. She was on Aviv's team, but she wanted to tell Sparks not to agree to Aviv's plan. But Sparks, knowing it would more than likely not pan out well for him and his team agreed. Keila could not believe that Sparks was okay with this plan. It made her question his leadership abilities, because who would put their men in harm's way for nothing? Maybe Aviv was right, and he wasn't fit for leadership or any other role that was laid before Sparks.

The drill started with the breaching team advancing to the house full of instructors. Sparks knew that Aviv was jealous and that this plan that he came up with was a trap. He would have said no to the plan had it not made sense. He was angered by the way Aviv would risk most of his team's lives for this house and for an opportunity to get rid of him, but if worked out right, Sparks could twist this to victory without one person in his charge being shot.

Sparks' plan was simple. When Aviv's team started to make their way through the house pushing the instructors towards Sparks' team, instead of breaching from the front, Sparks would breach from the back with a teammate to cover him while the rest of his team stayed in cover, and shooting whoever came out the front door.

Everyone was in position and the breach began with a flashbang. As the smoke and lights cleared, Aviv's team was already on the roof and through the window. There was gunshots and team chatter, as room by room, the upstairs was being cleared.

Sparks' plan had worked because when the flashbang had gone off the downstairs instructors had focused on shooting whoever breached through the front, leaving the back door unwatched. Sparks and Loch silently crept in and took position behind the kitchen wall. After a count of thirty seconds, the front door was breached with a loud bang. The instructors were disciplined, and did not fire but that was expected, what was not expected by the instructors were the two flash bangs that flew in through the side windows.

Just as Aviv's team had made it to the stairs and was going to start downstairs, in what took maybe five seconds, the flash bangs went off and Sparks and Loch went into action. Brandishing their sidearms, they first knocked out the two instructors that were hiding closest to them holding their ears. Wasting no time, they then simultaneously shot the two other instructors.

This was when the rest of the instructors made their way out the front of the house thinking the breach team had flanked them and came in through the back. They walked right into a trap, as soon as the first instructor came out, the other members of Sparks' team lit them up. With gunfire coming from Sparks and Loch from the back, and gunfire coming from the stairs, and from outside. It was a quick end for the instructors and the scenario was over.

Kelia was in love. She knew for a fact that this would be Sparks' first point, but he had somehow turned this into a victory. As everyone cheered in victory, she made her move. She walked right up to Sparks without anyone noticing, not even Sparks initially. Once she got right in front of him, she looked him in his eyes commanding attention. Sparks surrendered to her gaze.

"Meet me on the beach where we first gathered at 2200." She smiled, turned, and walked away before Sparks could even comprehend what had happened, but he heard what she said. As she walked away Sparks could smell her hair, it was a faint smell, it was earthy like flowers, sweet, not like perfume or soap, it was buttery, tasty, and womanly.

****

Sparks woke to the sound of gunfire; the sound was distant and mechanical. As he came to his senses, he realized that the sound was in his earpiece. He tried to focus on what was being said, but it was frantic and jumbled. His team was in a firefight and by the sound of anxiousness in their voices, it was not a winning fight. A body ten feet away from him, snapped him back to reality.

It was one of the engineers from the control room, whoever had knocked Sparks' out had possibly killed the engineer when he had come to investigate the noise. Sparks moved to check on the engineer but was still groggy and bound by the hands. He looked around and he was next to an auxiliary pump a few feet from the generator. He crawled to his knees and slowly walked to the panel he was at before he was struck.

It was crudely jammed open. He opened it all the way and saw an amateur constructed bomb. The bomb had a timer and by the looks of things, he only had thirty-seven seconds to figure out his next steps. All at once, he caught the same scent as earlier and looked to his right. A woman in tightly fitting tactical gear was walking nonchalantly to the door.

Sparks was shocked, stunned, and might have had a small heart attack. This time when he mouthed out the name it came out loud and forced.

"KELIA!" The woman stopped and looked down. She straightened up her stance and walked out the door in front of her. Sparks mustered all he could to give a chase, but he was still disoriented and weak. He barely made it to the door when he was overtaken by the loudest sound he has ever heard. It was like thunder had struck right inside his ears, and the pain that followed was like he had fallen into the sun.

This had to be what hell felt like and in those few seconds he experienced this pain he thought,

"No, I have felt Hell. This is nothing..."

And that is exactly what he fell into... Nothing."

Chapter Five

BROOKLYN ZOO

All of Sparks' short life he imagined death like everyone else. He saw death as a man in a hooded robe with a sickle. This infuriates death, she, yes, Sparks was also confused, is beautiful. She has long bouncing white hair, she is neither black, white, Hispanic, or Asian. But is all of them, changing to which ever form Sparks preferred. She has a heart stopping body which shouldn't come to any surprise for she is the reason a person's heart would stop. She wears no clothes yet mist drapes over her body in all of the sensual places as to not leave her exposed, unless she wants to be exposed.

Sparks and Death lay entangled in a very large, bed. She is rubbing his chest and kissing on the part of his arm that is under her head. As they lay, Sparks couldn't recall how long he had been here. The comfort he feels with this beautiful woman cant be explained either. It is as if he has known her all his existence. She feels like home. Her skin is soft and her hair is silky to the touch. Her kisses taste like pomegranates, as if the fruit got its taste from her.

All around them is mist, as if they were in the center of a cloud. Hours go by as they frolic under the sheets and reacquaint themselves with each other. The passion between them is electrifying. The build up of their energy causes the space they are in to change in color, going from dark grey, to violet then a dark pink. He is in love. He has never been so sure of love till this moment. Her energy is intence, and he can see what he feels is shared. He lays back and rest. He is not tired, but from all the intimacy he has a feeling he should be. He also can't get out of his mind the idea of time. How long has he been here? Where is here? As if she could read his mind, Dethia rubs his hair along the grain of his waves.

" You are worrying about the wrong things love. How long, doesn't matter anymore... and where, is only a matter of perception. For me, where we are now, is where we should be. Don't you agree?" She popped her head off of his chest and looked him in the eyes. Sparks looked back into her eyes and felt that she could say anything, and he would agree. He did not answer her in words, instead he leaned in towards her perfectly lush lips and gave them a long kiss. As they lay, A loud trumpet sounded, and Sparks sat up. He looked in each direction. There was nothing but mist. This was the first time he really took note of his surroundings. They were on a bed, that was for sure. Yet they were not in a room. It seemed to be a void. The darkness was so dark that it had a light to it. He kept looking, now looking to find who blew the trumpet. In his confusion he looked to Dethia.

She was laying on her back with her left hand on her forehead. Smiling to herself while shaking her head.

" huhhh... Its ok... Its just my mother." There was exasperation in her voice as she shook her head. She rolled over in the huge bed and placed her feet on the floor. Sparks rolled over opposite and looked down to see if there was a floor... Just as he thought, only mist. He rolled back over to see Deathia putting on a robe that was deep purple and floral with different types of colorful flowers. He immediately looked around her to see where she could have possibly gotten it from. His inquisition faded as she walked a few feet. She was absolutely stunning and eloquent in her movements.

She walked a bit further in the mist and sparks could only see her silhouette. He sat up to look a bit closer. He could still see Dethia, but now there was a glowing orb just in front of her. It was only the size of a fist and it floated a few feet away from her, at her eye level. He watched it. It was as if he was it. He was mesmerized. Although Dethia was blanketed by the mist. There was nothing around this orb, as if nothing could ever block it.

Sparks could see it perfectly as if it was right in front of his face. He could see its perfect spherical shape and how it looked as if it was a planet, or better yet a universe. He was trapped in its beauty. He could see everything in it. He could feel everything from it. He almost felt a ting of fear as he realized that even he was part of it. The vastness of being everything left him with a feeling of being as small as nothing in the same breath.

This feeling was so intense that he broke his gaze from it. He laid back down and let his head clear. The intensity did not leave yet it felt that Sparks soon elevated to its frequency, and this brought Sparks a bit of comfort. He knew, without a doubt, what or better yet Who it was. A simple phrase came to mind.... I AM...

Sparks could hear Death speaking silently with God. He can only make out a little bit of the conversation due to the complete lack of worry and caring, knowing that worry, and caring is an emotion reserved for the living.

Sparks hears death say,"You have yours, you keep all of them. I have loved him forever!" Death hisses."..........."

Sparks could not understand God; it sounded like thunder or rushing water. Whatever God had said, it was enough.

"Okay, okay. But remember your promise," Death says while folding her arms and rolling her eyes.

God makes the heavens shake violently. Death, unafraid, rolls her eyes again in a pouting manner.

"I know you never go against the word for you are the word...blah... blah...blah... I'll do as you command, your grace." Death walks back to Sparks and gives him a long passionate kiss pressing her body against his as he lays on is back in the bed."I have and will always love you," she says in a serious tone.

"Now go and get 'em sexy. See you soon!" She blows Sparks a kiss and winks.

Then Sparks begins falling and falling fast. Or maybe he felt like he was rising, or was he going to his right.

"No," Sparks thought.

He was definitely going left, then as if he hit a wall, everything went dark.

......................When Sparks' eyes opened, there was nothing but blurred objects. The light was dull compared to the bright darkness he had just been in. He had seen death and he had heard the voice of God and now he was back in the realm of the living. But he felt as though it was better where he had left. Death was beautiful, so beautiful that Sparks felt as if nothing in the living world would ever hold up against Death's image.

As he gained more focus, he could make out a person directly in front of him. This person appeared to be staring at Sparks, and he could faintly see that the person's lips were moving. Sparks concentrated on this figure, trying to gather who it was and what they were saying, not that Sparks cared, he was more interested in making sure he still had his vision and hearing. Slowly, he could hear the voice of the man who was standing over him.

"Mr. Sparks, Mr. Sparks. Can you hear me? Blink once for yes and twice for no."

"If I couldn't hear you then how in the hell would I know to blink twice for no?" Sparks said as he slightly repositioned himself, wincing with every move.

"Ha! Well, I didn't figure that part out, did I? I see you can hear me. It might take a few hours to fully gain your senses back. You were... Well, for a lack of better words, dead.""Yeah, I could figure that." Sparks said, still curious to who this man was.

"Well, my name is Liam Williams. I work for a private interest group who is very interested in your well-being. They are so interested that they have asked me to validate your resurrection and recovery."

"Did they? What's so interesting about me that they would take the time to send you to make sure the hospital revived and resuscitated me? I mean, resurrect is such a... Large term.""Mr. Sparks, you are a very interesting man, such an interesting individual as yourself should have any questions answered by someone with a lot more credentials than myself. As for the term resurrection, well, that is a scientifically correct term when referring to the revival of a person who was legally dead for three days. Rest up, Mr. Sparks. I'm sure all your questions will be answered."*Three days.* Sparks tried to gather how three days had passed by him so nonchalantly. He tried to remember what death and him did. Sparks concentrated on how he had even got to death's embrace in the first place. He thought hard, and he could remember a loud sound. He saw the moving counter. He could feel the flames against his back. It was so hot, and he could remember her... *Kelia.*

Chapter Six

FOURTH CHAMBER

Going down one hundred stories is a long elevator ride, but going underground one hundred stories is absolutely agonizing. Agent 11 hated this base, she hated the elevator ride, and she hated the guards who granted access. They were always so gross with their wandering eyes and sly comments. She knew all she had to do was tell Profett about it and that would be the end of them, but she also knew she could very well just break their necks and that would also end them.

Agent 11 cleaned underneath her nails as the elevator reached its destination and opened. Without even looking up, she walked out the elevator and to the right, nonchalantly pushing past the three guards on their way up to relieve the other asshole on the surface.

"Woah, little lady. You don't have to get so physical. I mean, I don't mind getting physical with you but I think the words you want to say are, excuse me!" One of the three said.

"Fuck off!"

Agent 11 flips off the guard without looking up at them or the direction she is headed to. She gets to the end of the hallway to two huge gaudy doors, and reaches into her cargo pants pocket, and pulls out a thumb drive. She pauses at the door as if contemplating going in. Agent 11 has been busy in the last few weeks doing missions from one side of the world to the other. In order to complete all the task she has, there are always going to be *collateral casualties.*Something she hates explaining but she is sure the topic will arise. She takes a deep breath and with the exhale she pushes the doors open.

The inside of the satellite control room for Zion is clean, godly clean. There is a desk and a map with targets pinned out. There are two seats facing the desk, there are no lights or lamps but there is always light. Some say that the office is lit by the light God left on Profett when he stood in God's presence.

Agent 11 walks in and takes a seat, she can remember a time when Profett would scare and creep her out with his appearing in thin air tricks, but nowadays, with the amount of things she was witnessing in the field, it was no more than a mere pallor trick."Eleven, good to see you again, and in one whole." Profett was sitting in the main chair behind the desk.

It was amazing how he appeared. If one was not keen with their senses, they would assume he was sitting there the whole time, maybe camouflaged by the shadows, but 11 knew she had not seen him in the room and that he actually did appear in thin air.

When she first met him, she would think that maybe it was a holographic image that put him where he appeared, but feeling his cold yet comforting grasp on her shoulder from time to time she knew he was real.

"Profett, it is good to see you also." Her words were laced in cynicism.

"But I am not here for small talk. I have the flash drive. It was acquired through toil and blood. So, I hope it is worth your men's lives.""Yes, I am aware of the methods you chose going to get the flash drive. It troubles me to no end the amount of death you are willing to bring about in your... Methods."

The sheer mention of the name *Death* brought chills through 11's being. She could remember with detail the meeting with the being Death, and how much resentment and anger death had for her. "Yeah, well the things you and your "*interest*" want are not cheap, and most times, the payment is blood. I'm not here to defend my methods of acquisition, you give me missions, I carry them out. That's our relationship. I don't see you or ... Her... Doing what you task of me, or for that matter stopping me while I do what I do." "Well, I can tell you that She and I wish only for peace and we all know that peace is not free. And it is sometimes paid by the blood of innocence and guilt. But your actions and the actions of the others we task bring about a grey area. If we continue to go about our quest in this matter, people will not see the difference in our agenda and the agenda of the fallen." Profett sat calm in his chair.

"Noted. If there is nothing else you wish to scold me about; I have a few things I need to get in order." Eleven already turned and walked to the door.

"There is one thing. He has survived." Eleven stops, she felt pain and joy in hearing the words Profett spoke. "You do know that he is not our enemy but just another soldier that has been brainwashed by the lie." "Well, I guess he is lucky. On a side note, all though the ones that we fight with may be brainwashed. It never stops them from pulling the trigger and taking our lives and the lives of the innocents." Eleven walks out of the door. She was relieved to hear of Sparks resurrection but that was not new news for her. In fact, that was the personal agenda she needed to take care of. If Sparks was alive, she needed to talk to him. She needed to know for sure what side he was on. If he answered wrongly, then the next time he left this earth, she would make sure that there would be no body for him to return to.

****

The next three days for Sparks was antagonizing, Sparks was labeled SIQ (sick in quarters) and was put on bed rest. The only company he got was from the nurses that occasionally check his IV and shift his sheets, and from Mr. Williams. Mr. Williams was not a good conversationalist, he would ask a million questions, mostly about what Sparks remembered. He was mainly interested in what Sparks could gather about his death.

Sparks was vague in telling him about his experience, sticking to the story of white light and feeling at peace. Williams always just listened with a stone face. And Sparks knew Williams didn't believe that he couldn't remember and that he was hiding something, but he never pushed the issue, telling Sparks to just try and gather his thought and it would come back to him. On occasion, Sparks would ask William to tell him about his resurrection and the people that William worked for, but Williams would always say in due time.

From what Sparks could gather, Williams was from a private agency, that worked with government agencies, like the Agency Sparks was employed under. He did not trust Williams. There was something about his questions and lack of answers that annoyed Sparks. His look even said shady vibes. He wore the typical agent suit yet his movements were not uniformed. There is a type of way that service officials move. Due to the training, they go through and the meticulously taught attention to detail. Sitting down, for a service member, is a calculated activity. Williams was free moving, like a civilian.

Sparks took his head out of the book that was in front of him. He had stopped reading it an hour ago as he let his mind run with his thoughts. Williams had really irked him today. He had stayed in Sparks' room for close to ten hours... "Ten hours.." Sparks spoke aloud to himself. Most of the time it was silence and awkward looks at random things in the room. This was what prompted Sparks to pick up the book in the first place. As soon as Mr. Williams left Sparks called in and sweet talked one of the on duty nurses. He made sure that she was to inform everyone on duty that the tall, funny looking dude, in the suit could not return to Sparks' room that night... As he placed the book down he positioned himself comfortably in his bed and closed his eyes. Immediately he went to sleep.

It was a nice day and neither Williams nor the nurses had come into Sparks' room. Sparks had spent most of the day reading the latest X-factor comic book and staring out the window daydreaming about Death. She had haunted his dreams, well, not really haunted. She would come to him in his dream and tease him with her amazing body. A few times Sparks would reach out to hold her and she would fade away into the mud reappearing a few feet from him.

She would always say that Death and the living could not touch though she longed for him. He was having one of these dreams when he heard a voice that sounded like Williams.

"Sparks... Sparks... Wake up now!" Sparks opened his eyes expecting to see Williams standing right in front of him.

"Williams, is that you?" Sparks asked groggily.

"Sparks, you can hear me that's good." Sparks looked around his room, he could not see anyone there, but he heard Williams as if he were less than an inch from his face.

"Mr. Williams, I hear you, but where the hell are you?""I am not in the hospital. I am communicating via a coms chip we had implanted behind your right ear." Sparks quickly placed his finger behind his ear, and he could feel a bump."We don't have time for questions right now. I promise we will have answers for you but right now you need to get out of the hospital... Now!" Sparks was confused.

He sat up in his bed looking around for a threat but saw nothing. He tried to quiet his breathing and listen. He heard silence, then he heard footsteps. They were very soft and sounded like at least fifteen individuals. He listens harder, and he could hear what sounded like a muffled scream as if someone had placed a hand over another person's mouth.

"You need to get up now. There is a bag under your bed with tactical gear and a Glock 19. It isn't much, but it is all I could sneak in. There are about twenty Zion operatives in the west wing making their way to you right now, and I don't think they have come to talk."

Sparks had a lot of questions but from what he heard when he listened, he knew Williams was right about someone coming to get him. He hopped out the bed quickly. Quick and strong for someone who had been bed ridden for at least a week. He reached under his bed and pulled out the bag, just like he was told there was gear and a weapon inside. He put the tactical gear on, it was loose until he zipped up the side and like a vacuum it shrunk to fit him perfectly.

He grabbed the nine-millimeter and the three loaded clips, it felt light in his hand and perfect like it was made just for him.

"Okay. I'm suited, now what? Do I engage? Where do I go from here?" Sparks lightly bounced around feeling great.

"Okay, I hope the suit fits you. It is yours, fit to your body. There are twenty Zion operatives coming your way from the west wing; they are armed and loaded. There are at least double that amount on the ground and five on the roof. We have placed a one-man helo on the roof that will be your extracting vehicle. It has built-in navigation to a safe house. All you need to do is get to there. Focus and you will find that your resurrection has given you a few... Umm... Talents that can be helpful. I will remain on comms to give you a little extra help."

"Sparks, these guys are nasty and very well-trained. I suggest you use any means necessary to make it out.""Wait, again with the resurrection talk? And extra talents? I have a load of questions and when I make it out you *will* answer them. See you soon."

Sparks felt amazing. He felt as if he could lift a vehicle and there was a spry to his step he couldn't explain. He was interrupted by a door opening down the hall. He heard it as if the door was right in front of him and he quickly shifted into a tactical frame. He grabbed a clean silver tray from the table next to him and snuck it outside his door.

He angled it to see down the hall in the direction he heard the door. He could see men moving in formation towards his room and he quickly pulled the tray back inside. In what took maybe 5 seconds, he thought of a way to maneuver down the hall through his opposition and to the exit stairs."Okay, bro. Time to get out of here. Let's see what these resurrection powers are all about!"The team leader of the Zion death squad had seen something shiny slip into the room where the target was at. He had been part of his fair share of elimination missions, but this one was weird. First of all, the briefing was vague. They said nothing about the target just that they didn't want any casualties on this mission and that the target was to be brought in alive. And second, they wanted the target to be brought back not to Profett, but to Agent 11.

Whatever or whoever the target was, it was important and dangerous because why would they need nearly 50 operatives for a tag and bag?

"Agent 11, this is team 1. We have eyes on the target setting up position now." The Zion team leader said in his headset.

"Good team 1. The shock bullets you have should send 240 vdc through his body, but you will need a clean shot to incapacitate him. Proceed with caution." Agent 11 said while standing outside her tactical vehicle.

As soon as the team leader ended the coms channel with Agent 11, he saw the door slam open and a tall, and very built man move from his room to the room adjacent to his room very fast. He also heard four shots ring out, and in the corner of his eyes he saw four of his men fall with perfectly placed head wounds. Before he could gather himself, or his team, the door opened from the target's new hiding place and the same man came out gun blazing at inhuman speed right at his team.

Bang... Bang... Bang...

Three more of his team fell.*Bang... Bang... Bang...*

The target was too fast to register...

Bang... Bang... Bang...

There was not one round wasted. As soon as he heard a gunshot, one of the team members fell. Three more shots rang out and three more of his team died. As the team leader looked back at the target he barely got a glimpse of the target doing a roll over the receptionist desk to reload. In this brief minute, he looked to his team. Besides himself, there were only three more of his men left alive.

Whoever this target was, he was extremely fast and a damn good shot. The death squad had not even had time to take cover before they were picked off by this Super assassin. He motioned to the rest of the team to take cover and maintain their weapons in the targets direction. The tables had turned quickly, they were no longer stalking the target. In fact, they had become the prey.Sparks had not even begun to breathe heavily. He could hear the hearts and heavy pants of the death squad. This brought about a slight smirk on his face. He changed the clip in his gun as he had left the room, everything was slow and focused for him. He knew that he was exerting the amount of energy to move at his top speed, yet his vision was in slow motion.

Every shot he took, he could see the sweat beading on his enemies' forehead, and that is where he placed the round. Sixteen shots all on target with four more to eliminate. Sparks felt strong and he wondered exactly how strong he was. He holstered his weapon, focused his mind, and made a beeline to the snack machine directly in front of the desk he was hiding behind. He got there extremely fast and silently, the remaining four guys didn't even see nor hear him leave from behind their cover.

Grabbing the snack machine with two hands, he effortlessly picked it up above his head and threw it at the sofa where one of the men was using as cover. It slams into the sofa and crushed the man between it and the wall. The sound alarms the other three to come from behind their cover.

One of the men attacked from Spark›s right, weapon aimed. Sparks grabs the barrel of the man's gun, then the man's arm and flings him into the other guy to his left.

As soon as they made contact with each other, Sparks landed a front kick directly in the man's chest. Sparks could hear all of his ribs cracking and could feel the man's chest cave in around his boots. The last guard lets off the only shot that this "death" squad got off. As quick as the man's trigger squeezed, Sparks twisted his body to evade the round, the electric bullet hit the man's team members and they shook violently from the shock.

Sparks then jumps high in the raised hallway, twisting his body again, but this time swinging his leg outwards towards the last target's head. With a loud crack, the man's neck contorts in an unnatural direction and his body falls soon after. Sparks looks at the slumped bodies on the floor then to the exit."Time to get some answers!"

Agent 11 sat in her bulletproof command SUV fuming. She had brought fifty plus men with her on this mission and from the sound of things, she only heard one shot from her death squad. She tuned into the helmet cams, and all she could see was Sparks moving very quickly and the flash of his gun, before she would have to switch to the next camara.

"So, I see that you have realized the benefits of being resurrected Sparks. Now be a good dog and lead me right to your masters."

The tracking device that was placed on Sparks' one-man helo was sending the position right to her phone. All Agent 11 had to do was wait till he landed and this time she would take care of him herself. Her plans had changed, of course she wanted answers but he had proven with this fiasco where his allegiances lay, he must be eliminated. From what she could see, he had all her power, but the speed was new.

"I wonder what other gifts you have acquired since you have been dead. Time to find out."

Agent 11 signaled to her driver to get her out of the area. She had already given the order to clean up and to make this look like some government agency trying to apprehend a fugitive. But knowing how the news and how the Agency worked, it would be televised that a terroristic sect of Isis calling themselves Zion struck today in downtown DC and as usual her efforts to protect the innocence would be turned to look as if they were the ones trying to kill and drain the world of the most valued resource humanity has; which is the soul.Sparks sat in the helo watching the news. He was looking at a recount of the hospital in DC. He had just escaped and he knew that the news could be biased since he was on a seals team and saw how the truth would be twisted in order to hide US involvement. The story the broadcasters gave was that a terrorist organization named Zion attacked a VA hospital in downtown DC.

The group left twenty-five dead and many more wounded, or mentally distressed. Sparks had begun to get angry until he saw one of the faces of the dead before they zipped up the body bag. It was the face of the man whose neck he had broken in the east wing before he went to the roof and took care of the last five guys, and got inside of the helo. Sparks quickly turned off the screen and flew the rest of the way, to wherever he was headed in complete silence.

The helo was descending and a warning buzzer woke Sparks out of his sleep. Sparks looked at the terrain below but could not make out where he was, it could have been anywhere in the Midwest judging by the flat lands and corn fields. And he was headed straight for a barn in the middle of nowhere."Great, the safe house is in bum fuck Idaho."

The roof of the barn opened up and the helo navigated itself inside as the roof closed in around him. Sparks jumped out of the front door of the helo and placed his hand on his holstered weapon. Although he was supposed to be in the midst of allies, he still didn't trust Williams or his *"employers"*. The barn was empty with a dolly style elevator in the far most corner.

As the helo slowed its propellers to a stop, he made his way to the elevator. He pressed the button and it opened up. The inside was pure steel and looked as if it could withstand the shock of a nuclear blast. Sparks, without looking, knew that this elevator had only one direction which was down, and possibly a few miles down. He walked in and pressed the only button labeled LL for lower level.

"No shit. Lower level. Well, that's creative."

****

"Ma'am, the target has landed in Kansas. It looks as if he is going right to the gates. What do you want to do?" Agent 11's driver informed her.

"Shit. How did I know he was headed there. We are going to have to go after him. He is too much of a risk to let him get indoctrinated. I will call Profett and get authorization to pursue him. In the meantime, take me to the stealth jet and get me a few of the Elohim warriors for the extraction." She barked the orders while typing a few things in her laptop.

"Yes, ma'am."

Agent 11 slumped down in her seat. She knew what was ahead. She would have to convince Profett to let her and a few of the most elite warriors in this organization, go right into the gates of hell just to rescue one man. She even had a hard time convincing herself that this was worth it. God herself stayed clear of the gates, not out of fear, but mainly because of the treaty, and Agent 11 didn't believe in the treaty.

What type of treaty says that one side can kill, deceive, and steal? While the other side never attacks? To her, the treaty was meant to be broken. The only problem is if she was to lead an all-out attack on the Gates, then she would need more than a few Elohim. She would need Gabriel and the whole army. Agent 11 sat contemplating and waiting, then she sighed and pushed the coms button for a direct link to Profett.

"Here goes nothing. What's the worst he could say, no?"

Chapter Seven

I Got Ya Back

"HELL NO!!! Eleven, what are you talking about? You know the consequences to what you speak of?" Profett asked as he put his hands up towards the screen so Eleven could see his hand gesture.

"I know what could happen," she rolled her eyes.

"Will happen!""Whatever! I am the only one who has been in and out of the Gates and can speak about it in this world. I can get in and get Sparks out, but I need to do this now Before she can sink her teeth in his soul. You and I both know how hard it is to extract her venom once she had corrupted a soul.""She won't get him to bend. He has already been claimed and she knows this. Right now, I am sure she is taking the right precautions to make sure Sparks is not even within range to touch her. You must have faith, Eleven!"

"FAITH?!" Agent 11 yells while slamming her hands down on the roof of the car where the laptop was positioned so she could have this face to face with Profett."Oh, I have faith. I believe a lot of things these days. I also believe in what I see, and what I saw was a bloodthirsty killer leaving that hospital room. A killer who is enhanced and modified to kill with ease, and I have twenty-five dead soldiers to back up my belief. So, who am I to have faith in?"

"If God has a plan, I hope she can explain to those soldiers' families what part of the plan involves their husbands, fathers, and children dying with electric rounds in a gun while trying to apprehend one man?""WATCH YOUR BLASPHEMOUS TONGUE, YOUNG ONE!!"

As the words came out of Profett's mouth, the sky became dark and Agent 11 found it hard to breathe. This lasted for only a few seconds after his words were said, then everything returned to normal."I think we both should take a minute to relax and think this through. I have talked to Her and she has told me to equip you with ten Elohim, and twenty-five death squad operatives to make up for the ones you have lost. Then you are to go to the Gates with orders to wait there till they open, and report when you have Sparks. This is what She commands and so shall it be, establish coms with me when you get to the Gates. And Kelia, do me a favor... Please just have faith and do what you are told.""Deal, as long as you do me a favor. Remember Kelia died a long time ago, so stop calling me by her name." Agent 11 slammed shut the laptop ending communications with Profett.

She had got what she wanted. Not enough Elohim, but with her there in the thick of things, plus fifty death squad operatives, she could storm the gates and retrieve Sparks if they were quick and precise.

As the last of the equipment and men were loaded on the stealth plane, the sky lit up with an unusual amount of colored light. The ground began to rumble and there was a sound of a trumpet and then all was silent.At the bottom of the drop hatch on the plane, stood ten magnificent Elohim, don in golden body armor and armed with gold-plated Galil automatic rifles. Each one peering straight through Eleven's soul with their fiery eyes. She shook off the creepiness she always got when she was around them and motioned for everyone to load up in the jet; it was time to shut down the Gates of Hell.

****

Sparks could not believe how long of an elevator ride this was. He first thought he had been in the elevator for an hour but as he looked at his watch, time was moving backwards. He tapped the watch to see if it was jammed or broken. As he stood in the elevator, he felt as if he was losing sanity. He put together that he was in this elevator for at least three hours; and was just about to sit down and give up all hopes of it stopping when it did just that, it stopped.

When the doors opened, Sparks was face to face with Mr. Williams."Good to see you made it here, Mr.Sparks." Williams said in a dry voice.

"I hope your helo ride here was comfortable? We all know the elevator ride can be... Hell... For a lack of better terminology."

Williams snickered at his last joke and Sparks found his laughter quite creepy, almost like a child who knows he is wrong but gets amusement out of their vice."Yeah, the helo ride was okay. Good thing it flies itself, cause I sure as hell can't pilot a thing. But if you will excuse my abruptness, I want answers... Now!" Sparks grabbed Williams arm as he spoke.

William looked down at Sparks' hand on his arm in disgust and slight fear. Sparks swore he could see a slight billow of black smoke rise from Williams' suit sleeve before he yanked his arm from Sparks' strong grip. Williams took a breath in what seemed a calming manner before he spoke."I advise you to refrain from your physical nature, Mr. Sparks." Williams said in an undertone.

"What would you like to know? I will answer anything I am capable of answering. As for what I can't answer, you have gained the interest of the wisest being around. She will give you all the answers you need. So, ask away.""Okay, first, I want to know what I am doing here. And where is here? For that matter." Sparks looked questioning at the hall they were in.

There were no doors on either side of the hallway. The walls were painted eggshell white, and they were bare.

"Also, what is this resurrection? And who the Hell is Zion? And what do they want with me?""Well, that is more than a first of all. That is technically five questions, Mr. Sparks. And I do have an answer to your last question. But first I want to ask you, do you believe in heaven and hell? Good and evil? Satan and God?"

Sparks was becoming agitated with Williams' political evading, roundabout talk, and didn't see that he was now in front of an extremely large oak double door. The door had large brass handrails and had a carving in the wood. The carving was a depiction of a battle of some sorts. The battle was between two legions of what looked to be angels, with what looked to be normal men in between.

Sparks would see that parts of the door would move, and it would catch his eye, but when he focused on the part that moved, it was still. As he got lost in the artistry of this door, Williams interrupted him."Mr. Sparks, you should open the door instead of staring at it. She hates to wait."Sparks' attention was broken by Williams' voice, and he reached to open the door. Just as he grabbed the brass handle, one of the angels looked at him. It was death, she was alone, near the middle of the door and she looked at Sparks with sad eyes then returned to the position she was in. Sparks shook it off. Thinking that he had been thinking about her way too much and proceeded to open the door and go inside.

****

Agent 11 always hated being in proximity to Elohim. What most people don't know about Elohim, or what some people call angels, or deities, are that they are absolutely infatuated with humans. They love us with the same amount of love as a child has for a super cool uncle and are attracted to us like a school crush. They are always kind and gentle. A male Elohim will be attracted to a female human, and vice versa, and will protect them all of his or her life.

This is where you get a guardian angel from. Both male and female Elohim are warriors and great fighters, known to destroy whole cities and bring about destruction to armies when just a few are gathered in a call to war. Agent 11's Guardian was Seriah. He was a mighty warrior who took claim for 821 fallen in the war.

He was in love with Eleven and even wanted to give up his wings for a lifetime, just to spend time with her in a mortal body. As it was told to her, she had convinced him to remain in the ranks of angels, "*Because he was too good of a warrior to lose.*" She couldn't remember anything before the day she found herself outside a small hut in the desert.

Although she was convinced this happened, she couldn't remember much of anything before she died. Most things were like a blur or a faded memory and a lot of her childhood memories were lost altogether. She knew that the reason she had him stay in ranks was because of her complete lack of interest in Seriah. It wasn't because he was not good looking, all angels were molded in perfection, but Eleven was just plain not interested in him at all.

Unfortunately for Eleven, Seriah was two seats down from her on the jet. Every time she would happen to look his way he would, like a puppy, try to get in her vision for attention. This would cause her to sigh and look the other way, it was very annoying for her. She was only grateful at the fact that when the Elohim were in battle; they were focused on nothing other than fighting. The pilot broke the silence in the cabin."We are ten minutes away from the gates. We will do a vertical landing. So, everyone, get ready to exit via the cargo hatch." The pilot said over the communication devices they all had in their ears.

Agent 11 looked out on one of the small windows of the jet. The barn was visible from wherever you looked, at least in a 400-mile distance. That's what it seems like when you are running away from it; all in all. Most people won't see it even if they are a few feet away. But she can always see it, even in her nightmares. And here she was back again, and ready to waltz right back inside if need be.

She spoke to herself,

"I must be losing my mind."

****

The inside of the office was dark and ominous. Sparks took in the whole office and it was huge. Around the walls of the office were books, all kinds of books, old and new books alike in no particular order. In the middle of the wall behind a large desk, was a wall of surveillance monitors. The monitors were watching what seemed like everything that was happening around the world.

Sparks looked closer at one of the monitors and he saw what seemed like a homeless man somewhere in the middle east, and another one was looking at a child somewhere in Africa wearing army fatigues and an AK 47. The look on both faces was sadness and despair, in fact, all the faces on the screen looked as if they were in pain. Sadness over took Sparks and he almost was at the point of shedding a few tears when a voice broke his moment of silence.

"Mr. Sparks. It is an honor to meet you... Again." Sparks was confused at where the voice came from, he was sure that he and Williams were alone in the room, and although his attention was on the monitors on the wall, he was sure he had not heard nor felt anyone come in the room. Yet as he turned his head to the voice, he saw a lady standing in the far corner, looking down at a book as if she was studying the book for a while.

The lady Sparks saw was very astonishing. She was older, possibly in her late forties but her body was in great condition, a little thin for Sparks' taste, but she could definitely walk through a room and command the attention of every man in the room. She was dressed in a very tight business skirt with a slit that rose right above appropriate length and her demeanor demanded respect, like she knew the answer to every question a man could possibly ask.

As Sparks took in the woman standing in front of him, she spoke to him in a very nonchalant and slightly humorous tone. "You know, Mr. Sparks, when someone says hello, you should greet them back. Standing there looking at me could make a girl nervous. But I am no ordinary girl, so, I'll just introduce myself. I am Lucile Shatan and I am the sole proprietor of what you see here." As she spoke, she never looked up from her book. She just waved her hand as if this was a speech she had given before.

Sparks snapped out of his awe and spoke, "I, uh... Excuse me, it is nice to meet you also, Lucile. I don't mean to be rude, but I have a lot of questions and Williams here keeps telling me that you can give me answers.""I bet you have questions. And I will answer all of them, so, go ahead and ask away."Lucile closed the book she was reading and looked Sparks right in the eyes. As she walked to her desk and sat down, folding her hands in her lap and crossing her legs on the corner of the desk in a relaxing and unprofessional manner."Okay. I guess, first of all, I want to know what in the world is going on? I woke up after being quote un quote dead. And Mr. Williams, someone I have never met in my life, is bedside everyday asking way too many questions. I get attacked by this terrorist group Zion, and I learn that I am a product of some kind of resurrection?""Well Mr. Sparks to answer all of your questions, Mr Williams is a most trusted associate of ours, these Zion freaks are pests that need eradicating. Thanks to you they are 25 men shorter now. And believe me when I tell you that your resurrection had nothing to do with us. Unfortunately, other hands were involved with that. But going with the laws of the land, you still can make a choice at where your allegiances... Lay. As for what is going on, well, that is a story in itself. And seeing that we have a few guests on my lawn I will make it a quick story, well as quick as it can be. So, I think the best way to start is with..."

"The age old saying... In the *beginning*," as Lucille started the story her voice began to triple.

As if three different voices spoke from her lips. The dim light that lit the room grew even dimmer and, with what seemed to be a spotlight, focused on Lucille. The monitors that were behind her all focused on a large cargo plane that was landing and ushering out armed men and what looked to be ten, seven-feet tall models in gold-plated armor. Then the monitors switched to an empty screen or what looked to be space with no stars.

"In the *beginning there was existence*. The best way to describe it would be that there was and will always will be life. But existence was longing to be expressed, and for a long time this longing was there, until one day the longing grew. It boiled and it expanded so much that the only place it could go was back inside itself. Then bang! You have matter."

"Now, this matter had been the longing, the imagination of existence, and existence was its creator. So matter would bend its will to what the creator wanted. Gas, fire, and solids were formed, planets were formed and then eventually, beings were formed."

"Now, this existence had no name, no orientation, only an identity for she was existence, so he was. As of her own accord, she made herself I AM. I found it to be a little large, but they call me the vain one. Anyway, the I AM created a few sons and a few daughters. But her first daughter was her favorite. She created this daughter as beautiful as the morning star. And she gave this daughter reign over the angels as well as wisdom."

"The daughter was wise, so wise that she could see the pitfall of her mother's ways. The I AM created with no constriction. Letting her creations have free reign to become what they wanted to become. The daughter thought that the only way to have full control is order. The I AM, did not understand this order. She told the daughter that from life there is a journey and that everything must follow its path and then return back to her in the end and yada, yada, yada."

"The I AM gave birth to two more children. A son to rule over all her firstborn, and another daughter to claim the souls and return them to the I AM at the end of their journey. I am aware that you have met one of the siblings and know her intimately Mr. Sparks."

Sparks felt a warmth take over him as she talked about death. He was in love with her and it scared him, because to be in love with Death means living starts to become boring to say the least."Yes, she is gorgeous and sometimes over dramatic. But she is not the problem here." As she continued the story the atmosphere in the room heated up to the point where Sparks was getting uncomfortable and started to sweat.

Mr. Williams saw this and backed away from Sparks slightly but wore an evil smile on his face. The monitors were showing visuals of everything Lucille had been saying, Sparks was caught in the story. As he listened, he noticed that Mr. Williams was slightly shaking and his heart rate had jumped up. Sparks could hear the beating of his heart and it sounded like he was about to explode from the inside out.

"Mr. Williams, are you okay?""I find it rude to be interrupted, Mr. Sparks. Especially when you asked for this story. It is almost over by the way. Don't worry about Williams, he gets a little anxious when I get upset. Now, back to the story, the eldest daughter of the I AM tried talking to her. Explaining the flaws in her ways. But the I AM felt like the daughter was just jealous and dismissed her."

"So, the daughter did what anyone in her position could do, she talked to her peers, convincing most of them of her Vision of a better universe. She even tried talking to her brother, but he was tainted in perfection and would only cast her out of his sight. So alone, this daughter threw a revolt against the I AM. It was unplanned, and it was not well organized, but it almost worked..."

"Needless to say, it led to many deaths, and to the daughter being kicked out of the I AM's presence. Sparks, I know you can see where this lead to. I am that daughter, the Morning Glory, the Bright Star, Satan, LUCIFER!"

As Lucille spoke the last words, the candles in the room lit, and the fireplace lit up blazing and making the temperature in the room sky rocket to almost unbearable degrees. Williams doubled over on the floor screaming and holding his stomach. Sparks jumped up out of his chair moving away from Lucille and Williams and close to the double doors. The monitors returned to individual screen but they were not just of Earth, but of different worlds with war and misery on the screens. Sparks looked down at Williams, his face had a smile and agony on it, it was contorting. His whole body was contorting like a... Werewolf."You see, Sparks. I have been at war with God for millions of years. On different worlds and in multiple dimensions. She has been winning for the most part but today, one of her strongest soldiers has been delivered right to my doorstep, *the one who lays with death*. I would be a fool to let this opportunity pass me by. Sparks, killing you, would turn the tables in this war. Hanging your body from my barn will turn the hearts of your rescuers outside. Those pesky Zionist bugs!"

"I will do one thing for you before you die in the pits of hell. You see, Williams here is a hellhound and he has heard my call to change. If you can make it to the top before he is done changing, you could possibly get help from your friends up there and ward him and his brothers off. That is if they don't still see you as an enemy. You did kill 25 of them just a day ago. Sparks, it's been nice meeting you and when you see my sister, give her a huge kiss for me. I always loved Death."

With her last words, she turned to face the monitors and disappeared in thin air. But that was the least of Sparks problems.

Mr. Williams was quickly turning into a hellhound. His lower body had transformed to that of a canine, his knees had shaped inwards and his feet had burst through his shoes to reveal hind paws with long sharp claws. Sparks stopped looking at Williams, though it was hard to take his eyes away because of the sheer disbelief at what was happening.

He focused more on his escape, he grabbed the large brass handles of the door, which was actively engaged in the war that was carved in the woodwork; but it would not bulge. Sparks pulled with all the might he could muster, as he pulled, his body suit turned into armor, raised around all the vital parts, and all the parts he would use to strike. Focusing on nothing but the door, Sparks pulled it. He pulled as if his life depended on it, and frankly it did.

Him having to fight whatever Williams was becoming in these tight quarters would not end well for him. Sparks was giving it everything he had, and he was gaining ground. He got it opened just enough for his body to slip through. He made it through, and the door slammed shut behind him with unearthly force. He was now tired and thought he could take a quick breath, but the hellhound was fully formed, and now wanted to feast on blood.

With ease, the door opened and what was on the other side holding it open was astonishing to say the least. This was no werewolf, or wolf of any sorts, this was something out of an Egyptian hieroglyphic nightmare. Williams had turned into a man with a bottom half of a wolf; strong legs that would be hard to out sprint. The body was the size of the Rock, on steroids, who has eaten Arnold Schwarzenegger, and the head was like a dire wolf two times as large. The sheer size that Williams had grown was crazy, he was now standing at eight feet tall and his chest rippled with every breath.

Sparks expected the hellhound to act rabid, and erratic. He had planned on it, in fact that was the only thing he had hoped would happen. He would use the hellhounds craziness against himself. But the hellhound reacted in Williams' mild manner as always. He walked through the door as if he was going to have a conversation. He looked at Sparks up and down, and Sparks decided to make the first move, he jumped up head level with the beast, grabbed his gun and released four shots at the beast's face.

This knocked the beast against the wall. Sparks took this moment to take off and find a means to escape, but the beast rose off the wall and on his feet. The bullet wounds healed quickly and the beast spit out the shells with a little bit of residual blood. Now, the beast was angry, it let out a roar that was ten times as loud as a lion and he started to give chase.

Sparks made it to the elevator with a little time to spare due to his newfound power and his body armor. He pressed the button and then walked in, but as soon as he pressed the single button inside of the elevator, a large hand grabbed him by the shoulders and yanked him out. The hellhound slammed Sparks against the wall and then on the other one, and then back against the wall he first slammed him against. Sparks nearly went limp, but he was able to squeeze a few shots on the inside of the beast's palm and that got the beast to release Sparks.

Sparks moved quickly and shot past the beast to the elevator. Once he made it to the sliding doors, he quickly jammed his fingers inside to get a hold and ripped the doors open. Sparks then jumped inside the shaft and grabbed hold of the wires that were hanging down, avoiding the weighted wire that was moving towards the ground as the elevator moved up.God knows how many floors it takes to reach to the ground level.

He quickly made his way from wall to cable. Moving almost ape-like up the elevator shaft as fast as possible. The hellhound crashed through the elevator door and immediately looked up at Sparks. He saw his target and jumped. Sparks was an estimated forty floors up from the bottom and could now see the elevator car. It wasn't moving too fast, but it was better than nothing. He only needed to get to the car so he could get on top of it and sever the cords crushing the beast below it.

He moved faster towards the car. The beast gained on Sparks fast, with one more jump he would be right on top of him. Sparks could feel the warmth of the beast, he could smell the beast's foul breath, but he only focused on making it to the car. It was so close, yet he was afraid he would be overtaken before he made it. One more leap and Sparks was on the bottom rail of the elevator car. He looked down towards the beast, he knew that the beast was right on his back, yet it didn't attack.

As he looked down, he saw why. The beast was setting him up as soon as Sparks grabbed hold of the rail the beast turned his body so he could kick Sparks upward. The kick was so powerful it sent Sparks armor clad body through the bottom hatch and crashing into the ceiling. The beast climbed in the car with an evil smirk on its face. Sparks could see a brief sign of Williams' humanity in the beast, but it was gone as quick as it showed. The beast had the upper hand, close quarters with Sparks, and nowhere for Sparks to run or move.

✳✳✳✳✳✳✳✳✳✳✳

Agent 11 was getting anxious. She was never the patient person but her quiet demeanor led people to believe she was. She kept a constant argument in her head, she kept wondering why does an all-knowing, all present and all powerful God play by rules set up to seemingly protect a wicked, selfish, spoiled, and outright evil brat of a daughter. With just the few Elohim that were with her, she could storm the gates and make a large dent. If all the soldiers of heaven where with her they could end this war once and for all.

Lucille's forces were depleted. All of these millennia of war had not gone well for her. She was winning the souls, but she could not use souls she tormented. Her only soldiers were those who willingly fought for evil and the fallen who loyally stood by her side. Eleven abruptly slammed her hand down. It startled the death squad members but only caused the angels to raise a brow. "That's it! I can't wait any longer! I have already reported to Profett. What could hurt if I and a few guys took a look or peek inside that old barn?" She made eye contact with a few of her most loyal men.

They gave her mischievous looks of their own and that was all she needed for confirmation. "Ok we are going to scope things out a bit inside. The rest of you just stay in position and be ready for anything." As she left with the five men to check out the barn, she was already expecting one more to come, there was never a moment of possible danger that Seriah was not near her even when she couldn't see him. Agent 11 gave the order to breach the barn silently. The seven of them all made their way into the barn. As she remembered, the barn was empty except for the helo that Sparks was in when he made his escape from the hospital. She knew exactly where to go, the elevator that brought you down to the gates. As she made her way to the elevator, she paused.

She could faintly hear the car making its way to the top. There was a loud noise as if something big had shuffled inside the car. Then a very loud roar and then silence. The elevator made its way to the top and all of the agents and the one Elohim that were with eleven were now focused and aimed at the elevator's doors. Right before they opened, Sparks' limp body was thrown through the doors and on top of two of the guys who were not fast enough to get out of the way.

Eleven rolled over to her right and got on her knees in a crouched position with her weapon aimed at whatever tossed Sparks out of the elevator. As trained, the rest of the men followed suit. Seriah was the only one not aimed at the elevator. His eyes burned with fire as he stood confident and ready; he spoke to what was inside hiding in the shadows of broken lights and skipping elevator music.

"If you come out you will be willingly violating the treaty, and I have authority by the most high to use extreme prejudice in eliminating you."

The Hellhound spoke in a large growling voice but with great English.

"I have only come up here to deliver that, as a message and warning to all. THE DAY HAS ENDED, THE NIGHT HAS BEGUN. JOIN WITH THE DARKNESS OR PERISH ALONG WITH YOUR GREATEST WARRIOR!" The beast pointed down at Sparks lifeless body and then dropped down through the hole he had created.

Eleven was shaken, she had never seen such a foul and huge beast. Not only that, she also knew that whatever was in the elevator must have been serious for Seriah to speak with such force and intensity. The whole time he spoke, she saw him beacon for the other Elohim to arrive, and now they were all standing here. Their attention was on Sparks, they were talking in the language of the angels."We must take Sparks back with us before his soul reaches death."

"Well, that sounds good and all, but I think I need to take Profett the body. I have orders." Kelia said.

"I have orders that supersede yours. I am sure Profett will understand this is of utmost priority. Kelia, you know how much I would give to make sure you are safe and in the best shape possible, but this has come from the most high. I don't have time to explain further. Just trust me you will be in the know when the time comes. Tell Profett I said 'Hello.'"Seriah lowered his voice once he called Eleven by her name, because he knew she would not like it but it would gain her attention.Once he was done, the Elohim disappeared from the realm of men the same way they entered, lightning and trumpets. Eleven felt a pain in her heart, she was already confused and shaken up about the hound from hell. She had never seen one, but she knew that they were Lucille's personal bodyguards for a reason. They were vicious and dangerous.

All her life she was told to run if confronted by one, but what it had done to Sparks and what it said about killing the strongest, she was, for the first time in her life, afraid. She was also worried about

Sparks. She tried to hide and conceal her worry through the flight back, but it kept creeping its nasty little head up. She used the long flight to the Zion satellite base as a quiet time. She would tell Profett all the details in person, but for now she just sat back in her chair listening to Erika Badu's first album.

Chapter Eight

SHADOW BOXING

Sparks opened his eyes. His first reaction was to look at his hands to see if they were shackled, since the last time he had woken up somewhere, he was strapped to a hospital bed. This was not the case. He was instead submerged from the neck down in a purple gelatin substance. He moved his arm freely and waded in the goo.

It moved like water yet would form back solid once he was still. His attention was taken from the tub he was submerged in, by a flashing light. The light was unearthly bright but lasted only seconds and it was gone with no consequence to his vision. Standing a foot away from Sparks was a very tall model-like man dressed in a toga that latched above his left shoulder in a gold crest. His Skin was a radiant dark brown that seemed to glow with a gold tint and he had short hair that was grey and almost silver. His eyes were so black that Sparks was sure there was no pupil.

"Hello Ishmael, I am Ki. No need to be alarmed, you are safe and away from all danger."Sparks felt what Ki said was, indeed, true. In fact, instinctively he felt the safest he had ever felt before. He also felt very relaxed as if he had taken a Xanax."Hey, what's up? If you don't mind me asking, where am I? And what is this stuff I am in?""You are very far from Earth or even the realm of mortals. I guess you humans like to call it, Galaxy. Your galaxy is called the milky way by your species. But you are in the Nebula galaxy.

Or what we like to call the realm of Elohim."

"To be exact, you are on the planet Shilo in the rebuilding chamber of Zur. You were hurt very bad, no one has gone up against a hellhound and survived, except for you. Consider yourself very blessed. You truly have the most high looking over you."

Sparks turned his head from Ki. He could remember everything in his attempt to escape The Gates."Well, I am sure that is an honor. But I would have rather died and found some peace." Sparks responded to Ki.

"Oh, yes. If I was *'He who sleeps with Death'*, I would want to rush back to her arms as well. She is most enticing to say the least."

Ki wore a huge mischievous smile and Sparks could not help but smile, not at the joke but at the fact that Ki radiated a genuinely good persona. It was a refreshing feeling after having felt the sadness, anxiety, and despair of being in the presence of Lucille.

"Rest up, Ishmael. The substance you are in is what your world was built on, *Ashe*. It will revive you to your former glory and better. Tomorrow I will show you to your quarters and begin training for your return. Unfortunately, this will not be a time of vacation for you. Ishmael, there is a war that is happening, and we are the soldiers to fight it. It is time for your training. You will be trained as an Elohim to fight off the wickedness of Lucille's army."Ki said his peace then left the same way he entered. Sparks had so much to ask, yet as he calmed his spirit and relaxed in the goo, he found that the answers were obvious. Ki was right, there was a war and Sparks was not ready to fight against beings like the hound, so he was ready to be trained.

Sparks was woken up by the sound of water draining. As the purple goo gurgled down the drains, he looked to his right and saw a tunic and sandals laying on a raised part of the floor. Sparks felt strong and fresh as he stood up in the tub. He had no pain at all, even the nagging pains in his knees and left elbow were gone. When he stepped out of the tub, he was completely dry like he had not been in a tub of liquid.

As he stepped towards the floor, he was surprised that the floor actually raised up towards his foot to make steps. It kind of caught him by surprise and he tripped up a bit then regained his footing.

"That was weird... and kind of neat."

He went to the toga that was laying on the raised part of the floor and picked up the garment. "I was really hoping that they came already made. how in the world am I supposed to put on a toga? Besides drunken twenty-year olds at college, these things have not been worn in centuries."

Sparks put on the toga to the best of his ability and tied the sandals around the high half of his calf. They were surprisingly comfortable and besides the fact that his manhood was freely hanging in the breeze, the toga was extremely flexible and unrestrictive.

"Well, that is amazing. I never thought that a toga would be so comfortable. I am going to steal one of these before I leave. And these sandals got to be made by Jordan. Ha! Yeah, I could work somebody on a court in these."

Like time work as soon as he finished tying up his last sandal, Ki appeared in the room.

"Ishmael, I see you found the clothing articles I had sent for you. Besides the fact that your toga is backwards, I would say that it is a good fit for you. We Elohims are not a small race. So, we had to have your toga specially made to fit your body. You should fix yourself and follow me. I have some of your training partners waiting for us at your quarters. I also have some substance for you to eat. It will not be what you are used to, but it will help you through the hard training we will be putting you through."

Sparks took the toga off like a tee shirt and turned it around and put it back on the same way. "Okay, Ki. I'm ready. By the way, why do you call me by my middle name?" "The names a person is given are part of the person's destiny. You were given three names Ishmael. And it has a lot to say about your destiny. Plus, I like Ishmael."

Ki walked towards the wall and as he got near it, a door opened like a sliding glass. A door that was not there before Ki walked up to it. Sparks was amazed at the technology of the building they were in.

"What is this place made of? Nanotechnology?"

"No, everything here reacts to faith. Simply put, if you believe the wall should open and let you through then the wall will do so. It's quite easy, why don't you try." Ki stepped back, and the door disappeared.

He pointed in the direction of where the door was,

as if to say Sparks' turn. Sparks gave him an *'Are you for real?"* look, and sighed. He shrugged his shoulders and went for it.

Bam!

Sparks went face first in the wall. "What the?? Why didn't it open?" He asked, giving Ki an accusing look.

"You didn't believe," he said with a chuckle.

"We will be working on your concentration. So, don't worry you will be as right as rain." Ki stepped towards the wall again, and like clockwork the door opened again.

He motioned for sparks to follow and they proceeded out to the hallway.

The decor of the place was ancient like an old Roman or Egyptian ancient. Along the walls were paintings that were in motion like when he was at Lucille's office doors, except these didn't stop moving when he looked. The images in the wall were of war and love, they would depict things like births and deaths, but not sadly, they were always celebrations and dancing. Along the trim above the walls was an ancient language, Sparks could not make out what it said but the writings were still familiar to him.

"This wall... This wall is like Lucil..." he stopped himself.

"Uh... The devil, I mean. This wall is like the large doors at Lucille's office. And the writings, it's like I can understand it, but I don't know what it says. Like I can feel its meaning." Sparks had stopped and was studying the wall almost as if it was speaking to him personally.

"Ah, yes. The wall is very, very old. As old as the universe is. It was made at the same time as the beginning of creation and gives a live history and account. It has been said that those humans who are chosen, can also see into the future through the wall. I have only met one man who could see that. And as for the writing it is a dialect of old Yuraba that we angels speak, I find it quite interesting that you can see it, let alone understand it."

"Well, I see it as clear as I can see the painting but understanding it? Well, let's just say it seems familiar, but we will leave it at that." Sparks stood looking at the painting, he heard slight whispers and felt a magnetic pull toward the wall.

Sparks' head became dizzy, yet he felt fine. As the pictures played back their memories, he felt as if he was right there in time. Everything else faded from reality and he was focused on the scene that was in front of him; it was of a little child. She was being swaddled by her mother near a swamp down south during slavery times. The dogs and the men were coming for her and her family with guns and ropes.

A man turns to the girl and winks. Then leaves the hiding place as gun fire and dogs barking intensifies. Sparks is pulled out of this vision by Ki's strong grasp on his shoulder.

"Sparks, you will find quite a bit of time to study the painting while you are here, but I must get you to your trainers, they have been patiently waiting to meet you." Ki placed his hand on Sparks shoulder in a non-threatening manner as if to say let's go.

The size of Ki's hand was massive. His palm went to Sparks' mid shoulder blade and the tip of his fingers wrapped around to the middle of his chest. Sparks didn't feel rushed, but there was no way he was going to shake free of the grasp even had he wanted to. The two of them walked down a few more hallways, and through a raised hallway that was surrounded by windows.

Below, Sparks could see a handful of Elohim sparing and shooting assault rifles at targets that seemed to fire back some sort of lasers. The targets were quick, and their aims were true, the targets pinned down the Elohim and it seemed that they were in a pretty strenuous fight.

"As you can see, this is our training area. It is one of many areas we train at. In fact, the whole planet is a training area which you will learn. We used to live in peace, but this war has turned every angel into a warrior. And to defend the crown has become our only purpose. Hopefully that will change sometime soon, but for now, we train."

Sparks and Ki came to a wall, and as suspected, it opened to reveal two large Elohim, a male and a female. The male stood almost eight feet and the female was only inches under him. They were gorgeous and in very good shape. As Sparks approached them, he did not know that he was staring at the both of them with his mouth opened until the female spoke."Do all humans breathe with their mouths and stare like this?" Azeri asked, looking a bit disgusted.

Her question was for Ki."Be gentle Azeri, he is an honored guest in our home. I am sure Sparks has never seen this many of our kind. It can be overwhelming to say the least. Sparks, you have to forgive Azeri she has not been to your realm, and has only just finished her training. So, you are her first experience with humanity."

"I... Uh... The feeling is mutual... I mean, hello... Uh... My name is Jon.""Yes, Ishmael, we know more than you care to think about you." Seriah cut Sparks off as he looked him over.

"Okay, well, I don't know what that means but... Yeah?" Sparks replied.

Ki sensing the awkward aggression quickly stepped in.

"Sparks, let me introduce you to your trainers. This young lady is Azeri, she will be training you in the dance of the stars, which will help you with balance, and synchronize your body with your spirit. And this young man here is Seriah. He will be helping you with hand to hand combat and train you in a weapon of your choice. And I will train you to become one with yourself and to quiet your thoughts so you can hear Olorun's voice and be one with its power."

"Get familiar with this room, as it will be your housing for your stay. You will be here for what seems to you a year, but in earth's time you will be only gone for a few days, as our time is not like your time. If you don't have any questions, then I would like to start your training."

****

The heavens rumbled and shook with violent spats of thunder. There was a dark mist that had settled on all corners of the earth, and Death was infuriated. She had not collected any souls for the last day. So, those who were to pass that day all fell into a deep sleep. A kind of coma that doctors could not understand. Death had left the realm of men and was now at the throne in a passionate argument with God.

"I don't care about them. I was promised my love from the beginning. You told me to pick one of all creations to spend eternity with and I did. I waited for him and he for I, but now that he has left his realm and has passed, I seem to have misplaced him? You the omniscient, creator of life, cannot tell your own daughter, who has been faithful to you, where her love is? Or do you know and just won't tell me? Which is it? I demand to know where Sparks is!"

Again, the ground shook but even more violently this time. Death had to levitate to save herself from the crack that formed underneath her feet. A faceless body formed in front of her, a body that was formed of pure fire hotter than any sun was nose to nose with death. It floated for a while not saying a word just looking at death. Then it spoke, not of a human voice,also it wasn't the normal voice the I am choses, which was expressed by rushing winds or waters. This was her silent, whispering, soft voice; hat when heard, commanded fear and respect of all beings.

"My beloved daughter, I always hold to my promises and will always hold them. I understand your loneliness. You have been a faithful servant since I created you. Knowing only the feeling of grief and fear through your labors. This is why I gave you Sparks and when all is done, if it is his choice, he will return to you. But his job is not finished. He has to fulfill his destiny, as all things that I created."

"It is not for you to understand the ways of my actions, for my thoughts supercedes your comprehension. Do *not* become like your sister and be rebellious in your nature. I love you Deitha. I will always love you, and your siblings, but I cannot honor disrespect and contempt.""But, mom!" Death sounded like a teenager, and if you thought about it in the scheme of eternity, she was the youngest of her siblings.

"I love him. He is all that I want. I don't mean to wrong you and please forgive me, but I worry. The last time I saw him, he was walking through the gates of hell in his mortal form. And those who have died in the gates are cursed to spend eternity with Lucille. He deserves better."

Death was now talking with a more pleading and sorrowful tone and was now kneeling before her mother. The I AM was stroking her cheek and wiping the tears away. The heat of her mortal form was enough to evaporate the tears without a trace of steam, yet since Death was of the I Am, her skin was undamaged. There were only three beings that could survive this presence of the I AM."You know I have forgiven you my child, but I won't tell you where Sparks is. For he needs to focus without you interfering with his mind. Just be patient and faithful. Everything you want will be yours." Death looked up at her mother.

She could see, as always, the genuine love in her mother's eyes. A sight she had not seen in millennia, and it filled her entire being with joy. She rose to her feet and gave her a hug. She kissed her cheek then turned to walk away. She was, as always, beautiful and graceful in her movements.

Her form she chose was her regular slim body draped in dark purples and black silk. The garment was loose and long with two long slits that allowed her toned legs to show with every step. Her skin tone was brown, and her face was that of a beautiful Korean woman in her late twenties.

"Oh, and Deitha. Could you please stop harassing the girl? She has a purpose in this fight, and we need her to be focused. Besides jealousy is unbecoming of a lady as beautiful as yourself." Death stopped and dropped her head."Yes, mom. I'll leave her alone."

"As long as she keeps her hands off my man," she thought to herself.

Fully aware that THE I AM could still hear her. The I AM smiled and just shook her head as Death left in the normal mist she is shrouded with.

Suddenly, the air became cold, and wailing and snarling could faintly be heard. A howl broke through the wind and was followed by another howl in the opposite direction. Out of nowhere, an angel in all red body armor and giant black wings folded to his side appeared before God. As soon as he appeared, he bowed and kneeled; afraid to make eye contact with the I AM."Balile, I assume your queen is nearby?" Sitting on the throne was Lucille, her legs crossed with her hands folded in her lap. On her face was a slight grin."Your majesty," she hopped off the throne and gave a sarcastically gestured curtsy.

"It's always so precious to see you and Deitha interact."

"Lucille, I have warned you about sitting on your brother's throne. I will not repeat it again to you. What do you want with this visit?" The I AM said in her usual soft voice.

"Seems all of your children get your love, but I cannot gain any advantage or grace from you, can I mother?""As always, if you repent from this war of vanity you are pushing, I will in accordance to my word, forgive you. I will also restore you to your previous title of head of all Elohim. A simple 'I am wrong.... sorry...' would suffice." Lucile walked away from the throne towards her mother. She looked into her fiery eyes and for a moment, God almost thought she could sense shame in her daughter but that moment was brief."I am sorry, mom. I am sorry that you can't see the need for change. Can't you see that these humans are weak? You have sent numerous prophets, priests, and even your beloved son to teach and guide them. And each time, all I have to do is show them an illusion of power and their greed takes care of the rest. I only came here to...""I know why you came here child... For Vanity... Your feeble words have no purpose in my ears, and you have no purpose in my kingdom, so leave. I leave you to your wicked ways and the judgment that comes along with it."

With that, the I AM disappeared and so did Lucille and the fallen she was with. Lucille reappeared behind her desk in the same pose she was seated on the throne with. "I hate when she does that. So rude... All powerful huh? Well, I guess I will have the opportunity to test that. See you soon, mother."

****

Sparks body was trembling. His leg was raised in the air at a ninety degree angle, he was on his tip toes, and both arms stretched out shoulder level. Azeri was circling him correcting his form. At times placing his chin up a quarter of an inch or moving his leg at the angle that would make the pose even more difficult.

"Form, Ishmael. Clear your mind of distractions and meditate. Use the pain as a focal point and breathe." The last seven months of training had been great for Sparks. He would wake up early and meet with Ki who would take him through meditation exercises to open his soul and be at one with the I AM's energy. After that, he would then meet with Seriah and train with all kinds of weapons. He learned how to master the staff then sias.

He practiced tactical shooting with the drones, which was fun, but the simulated rounds would hurt. He was allowed to pick his favorite weapon, and he chose the katana. He would spar with Seriah for hours, but he would never get the advantage on Seriah. He was definitely getting better. Later, he would meet with Azeri and go through her celestial poses to improve his balance and gracefulness. And at the end of the day, he would always return to his room.

He had improved greatly on his concentration thanks to Ki's training and could now, not only open the doors, but set up his room just the way he liked it. It was getting embarrassing for him having to call in one of the Elohim so they could make a toilet or draw his bath. Before Sparks would go to sleep, he would spend at least an hour in the purple goo to heal from the injuries he had acquired throughout the day. When he would get out, he felt like a new man.

He contemplated how he was going to sneak some out along with the toga and sandals.

The weeks continued to fly by for Sparks. Nothing seemed impossible; he was receiving the training as if he was an Elohim. He woke up from his rest due to the fact that the planet he was on had a sun that never set and he never knew when it was day or night. So, he would just rest and sleep when he was tired. The bed he slept on was made out of the same material as everything in the building but contoured to his body; he could make it as firm or as soft as he needed it to be.

Everything in the building was amazing to him. He stepped on the steps that came to meet his feet and bring him to the ground level. He made his way to his bathroom and handled his morning routine hygiene. Sparks was in a great mood, he had figured he could get any music he wanted by just thinking of his favorite artist, and like Pandora, it would play as loud as he wanted it to without disturbing anyone else. He was listening to Stevie Wonder's superstition when Seriah's voice broke his jam session.

"Ishmael, is it okay to enter your quarters? It is an emergency." Seriah's voice was calm, he was always calm even in the midst of combat, but there was a tone of emergency and haste in it.

Sparks immediately opened the door.

"Hey man, what's wrong? You sound a bit distraught... I mean, as distraught as you can sound.""Things have been progressing on earth and have turned for the worst for our allies there. Ki wants you to come to the briefing room immediately." Sparks quickly put on his toga and sandals and followed Seriah to the briefing room.

In the few months that Sparks had been here, he had only seen half of the complex. He was free to wander where he pleased but with his training, he had little time. He mainly went to the library and would spend great amount of time studying the wall. According to Ki, the wall seemed to like him, and spoke to him its secrets that were only revealed to elder Elohims and one other human, a man named Profett.

It was said that Profett trained as Sparks did with the Elohim a long time ago, centuries, and was sent back to earth to protect and lead the children of The I AM, or as they like to call it the Church. Before Profett had left, it was said the wall showed him a vision that was so profound that it left him in tears and scarred his soul. Ki had not seen the wall as active as it has been for Sparks since Profett left, and it concerned Ki for he did not want to see another human burdened with the truth of the wall's writings.As Sparks snapped back out of his thoughts, he realized he was coming into the briefing room. And as the door slid open, he saw at least twenty Elohim moving and conversing with a purpose. This was the most Elohim he had seen in one room and it was amazing how such large creatures could move amongst themselves so gracefully. Everyone seemed to stop what they were doing except a few who seemed to be plotting on a chart and gathered around the table that Ki was standing at.

"Sparks, sorry to wake you but this is an emergency. We have gotten a distress signal from one of the remote bases that our allies Zion use to conduct their mission briefs. Though it is a remote station, and not a main hub, it is a place that Profett likes to use as his place of residence because it is off the map."

"This being said, there are a lot of secrets put away there and not to mention Profett and his daughter are there. We must make sure that we don't lose this site. We will send twenty of our warriors along with you to aid the Church with defenses. The agency has sent a few thousand demons and a couple hellhounds to take the base along with the regular operatives. it seems that they don't know how important the base is.""Sorry to interrupt, but if this base is as important as you say, and as remote as it is, why would the agency target it and bring out demons and hellhounds if they didn't know of its importance? I worked for them and I have never even heard of the demons and hellhounds till recently. I am sure that the other field agents are the same. So, why bring them out and expose the secrets of the agency for a small victory?" When Sparks spoke a few Elohim looked at Ki with shock.

As if to say why is this human interrupting the brief, but Ki simply raised a hand and allowed Sparks input."It did cross my mind that the agency might know of our secret location but what do you say Sparks?" Everyone including Sparks was surprised at how Ki looked to Sparks just now as an advisor to a mission so critical."I um... Well, I don't mean to step on anyone's toes.""Sparks, you came here as a student but now you leave here as one of us. You have as much of a say as anyone in here and I see you as my equal." Ki then looked around to all of the other Elohim in the room in a challenging posture.

"If anyone in here has a problem with the title I have bestowed on Sparks, may he speak now against me and against the throne and be cast down amongst the other rebels!"The room was silent and the look on the other angels' faces was that of pure obedience. Ki realized that no one would dare rival the throne and his judgment, so he continued."Now, that we have that out of the way. Again Sparks, what do you have to say about the situation?" Sparks was shocked, but he was also ready for some action.He had a great time training and pushing his limits but now he wanted to put his new powers to action."I was saying that if this is a coincidence, then why would the agency risk exposure of its secrets. The agency knows of this base and are willing to risk all in capturing it. I believe that the force we know is on its way, is a Trojan horse of some type. And the real force is probably going to flank and hit hard. I say we put a few Elohim at the front and the majority we hide them until the real fight starts."

While Sparks talked, he mentally placed the chart that they surrounded in position to show what he was talking about. His plan was received well and when he was done, everyone went back to what they were doing before only this time they were putting Sparks' plan in order.

"Very well Sparks, this was the last test for you. You have completed your training and now you are ready to defend the throne. I only have advice for you now , love with your whole heart, live with your whole soul, and fight with your whole being. That is the key to happiness... Ahh...with a few other things but that is the gist of it mostly." Ki smiled which made Sparks smile.

During the time Sparks spent with Ki they had become friends and developed a closeness with each other.

"Seriah! Azeri! Come here."

Both came with quickness.

"Azeri, you have become a great warrior and now I will give you your first assignment. You are now the guardian of Ishmael. Protect and follow him through this life and the next. Seriah, you have an assignment, but it seems that your assignment and Sparks' share joint fates so protect them both."

Azeri was extremely pleased and could not hide her joy. She jumped to give Ki a hug which he returned back with love.

As for Seriah, he looked almost as if he was given the short stick. Sparks and Seriah had become close through competition and until lately, Seriah had all but dominated Sparks. With Sparks training and raw talent, Sparks had been coming up with the victories.

Seriah never gave off that there were any hard feelings till now. Sparks put it aside because for now, the main thing was the mission and he was ready for a chance to kill one of those filthy smelly hellhounds, mainly Williams."Oh, and Sparks before you leave to go back to earth, the seamstress has a gift for you. So, stop by her quarters before you leave, be blessed and fight strong."All three placed their right hands over their breast and gave a bow then turned and walked away. Seriah and Azeri told Sparks they would meet him after they all armed up and went the opposite direction. Sparks headed to the seamstress' quarters. He had gone this way a few times before, when his training attire would be ripped to pieces from the androids or Seriah.The seamstress was very old, but one could only tell her age by her mannerism or vocal tones. Her appearance was that of a woman in her mid-twenties. In fact, all the Elohim except for Ki, looked to be in their 20s, with Ki looking to be at the most early 40s. As he arrived at her quarters, the seamstress was standing outside with boots in one hand and a brown package in another.

She smiled at Sparks and said,"These are yours. I just made a few alterations to them. Until I see you again, Sparks."She was always one for little words. Sparks only bowed and thanked her as he grabbed the equipment and turned to leave.

He made it to his room and opened the package. It was the tactical armor he had when he left the hospital; only now it seemed to glow. He put it on and zipped the sides. Like before, it contoured to his skin, but this time it seemed to be alive and it moved across his body. Sparks recognized what was different, the seamstress had woven the Ashe, what the building was made of, into the suit.

He thought of a sword, and in his right hand, a sword had manifested. The sword was the same color of the suit though the hilt contoured to his hand as a real sword would. At present, the suit was black. He thought of a shield for his left hand and it appeared. It was the same color as his suit. Whatever he thought of, it was made reality, guns, knives, clubs, chains, darts, all made possible by the material in the suit and his faith. Sparks wasted no more time and ran to meet Seriah, Azeri, and the other Elohim to defend the base.

Intermission I

He ran. He ran as fast as his feet could take him. His heart pounded and his breaths were short and labored but that could not stop him. Behind him he could hear the sound of the foot prints from the beast that pursued him. The beast was so grotesque and massive, and bigger than any living thing he had seen.

But it wasn't the fear of losing his life that pushed his legs to top speed. He had to reach the meeting point, he had to give the disk to the Church, and Zion had to prevail. He relied on his training, blocking out the fear of the beast and only focusing on evading capture. He flipped over a small fence then quickly leapt for the escape ladder hanging in the alley. Jumping rather than climbing, he made his way to the top of the three-story building.

All he needed now was to jump to the next building and hope that his rendezvous brought back up, and enough firepower to ward off the hound that was on his tail.

He stopped and waited; there was silence. Maybe he had shook the beast off his trail, he looked to the opposite roof and saw a glimpse of light. That was the signal saying his rendezvous was in hiding and ready to meet. And he let out a sigh.

Just as the last bit of breath exited his lungs, there was a sharp pain in his chest. He looked down and saw a large hand with razor sharp nails protruding through his chest. The hand grew smaller as he slid off of it and fell to the ground. In his last moments of life, he saw Mr. Williams reaching into his inner jacket pocket and pulling out a thumb drive."Tsk, tsk, Mr. Phillips. What a waste. You were one of our more promising operatives. Such a shame. Well, consider this as your formal release note. The agency can't

have you giving away all of our plans now, can we? The time for revealing secrets is soon but not now!" Mr. Williams said loud enough so that the Zion agents could hear him.

He then looked right at the agent who was hidden quite well. Mr. Williams waved and smiled, showing sharp canines. He then turned his back leaping off the three-story building and into the darkness. Once the coast was clear, the Zion agent ran from his hiding spot and leapt over to the building to Philips side."Philips... Philips... Hold on, buddy. We will get everything taken care of, just hold on."

He was holding him close and though he knew the hole in his chest was beyond repair, it was all he could say, and hope was all he had to cling to. He knew Philips was a good man just playing for the wrong team.

With the last strength Philips could muster he said,"It's... It... Okay... I... Am... Sorry for being an asshole to you. But... he... took the wrong drive... LOCH... Ump... Ahhh!"

As he died, he placed Loch's hand on his cargo pocket. There was a tiny drive inside about the size of a thumbnail. Loch smiled and with tears in his eyes said,"Damn it, Philips. You were always a tricky son of bitch, weren't you? Sorry I have to leave you here like this. May God have mercy on your soul."

Chapter Nine

ALL I NEED

Two years ago. It was spring, and as cliché as it sounds, love was in the air. Kelia and Sparks had not only jumped headfirst in love, they spent every waking moment with each other. Kelia had submitted to her feelings for once in her life. Ever since she had arranged the meeting with Sparks in San Clemente, and Sparks had grabbed hold of her midsentence and kissed her. She left all doubt and apprehension.

The two of them were now finished with the training, and had taken two weeks of leave, which they were spending in San Francisco. They would wake up late around 0900 (which was late for them after having to be up at 0400 every day for the last 6 months). They would order breakfast in bed which would lead to playful horseplay and them having to officially wake up again a couple of hours later. Then they would head out to see the sites.

Kelia and Sparks were two peas in a pod. They loved the same things and would catch themselves saying the same things at the same times. The two weeks seemed to freeze in time, and they enjoyed every minute together exploring San Francisco and exploring each other. Their leave was coming to an end and they were nervously waiting on their orders. They knew that they would be split up, being that Sparks was to be a field agent, working closely with the seals and Kelia was to be an espionage agent, a spy so to speak, which would more than likely put her back in the middle east and all over the world gathering intelligence.

"What's wrong, Kelia? Are you thinking about the orders again?" Sparks had a playful but serious tone of concern.

He did not want Kelia to worry about the future cause no matter what happens, he knew that first of all worrying would not change anything. And two, he would not let anything, especially a few thousand miles, come between them as this felt too right.

"How can I not? It is like a mixture of excitement followed by dread.""I know what you mean, after all that training, I am ready to put it all to use but this... All this week has been like heaven with you." Sparks leaned in to give Kelia a kiss, but just as they were about to connect they were interrupted by a phone ringing.Kelia looked down at her phone, it was a private number, it was the agency. Her heart raced as she pressed the answer button and raised it to her ear. Her clear green eyes never left the warm dark brown of Sparks gaze. She had not said but three words. *Hello, okay,* and *yes sir.* She then hung up the phone and a tear left her eye. Sparks without asking, knew what it meant. It meant that she had gotten her orders, and more than likely it was going to take her far from Coronado, where he was stationed."I...""Don't say it. We have three more days together. We can figure the rest out later. Just for tonight, let's lay and enjoy each other."

Kelia smiled, she was torn, she had always put her profession first, but now, she wanted nothing else but to stay right there in Sparks' arms.

****

Kelia broke out of her daydreaming. It was five months from the two weeks her and Sparks had spent together, but things had not died down. She was attached to her team now, she had a handler that she reported to and got missions from. She also had weapons and gadget specialist, and an IT specialist and partner that would work with her on missions and stay close by. Just so happened her partner was none other than IT1 Loch.

They had become good friends, her and Loch, mainly because of Sparks, but also because they were both excellent at their jobs. The duo was becoming famous amongst the secret community for their proficiency and cleverness. Missions that seemed unrealistic or time-consuming were given to them with the same result, completion. Kelia and Loch always gave it their all because they knew that the intelligence they gathered would put people's lives at stake, and more than likely it would put Sparks' life at stake.

They were on such a mission now, and the mission was to infiltrate a formal fundraiser hosted by a secret supporter of the recent terrorist group Zion. Kelia was to impersonate a news reporter from Israel. She would, once inside the fundraiser that was at the mansion of the Zion supporter, make her way to his study and copy sensitive info to a thumb drive t

hat would give locations of bases and importance of the bases so the agency could hit them and clear the world of the new terrorist group.

Kelia's limo was pulling up to the front door, only two cars down.

"Kelia? Coms check. Can you hear me?""I read you loud and clear, Killa. Also, I think you should maybe refer to me by my call sign rather than my first name on missions. Don't you think?""Yeah, my bad Blue Jay. Haha. It was my idea to have the call signs after all, wasn't it?"

"It was... And you made up the names, Killa."

"Well, anyways, if you place your finger on the brioche in your hair you can give me a live feed"

Kelia reached up and touched the brioche nonchalantly like she was fixing her hair."How is that?""Perfect. Now, look around. Give me a little op test and we are set."

Kelia looks around the limo and then to a reflection of herself in the tinted windows."Ooh La La... You are smoking! You look like an Israeli Beyoncé or Rihanna. Or who is that wonder woman actress?""Gila Godat.""Yeah!! The black or Israeli version of her.""She is Israeli. Okay enough flattery, you are horrible at it. I need intel on where this study is.""Okay keep it professional. I hear you. That's probably why I can't get a date. Anyways, we all can't be Mr. Smooth like Sparks." Adam Loch giggled at his own joke a bit.

"The study will be in the west wing, down the hall from the bath room. The hard part is that it will be guarded by the sheik's personal bodyguard. You know, highly trained secret service type."

"Well, as long as your invite sticks and I get in. I can handle the rest." Kelia said while touching up her make up.

"In that dress, there would be no way you won't get in, believe me."

Kelia rolled her eyes as she was helped out of the limo onto the white carpet that led to the entrance. The sheik had gone all out. There were media and movie stars from all over the world here to support the sheik's fundraiser. The fundraiser was for world hunger. A good look for any one of power, but Kelia was sure that the funds would never make it to help.

What men show in public rarely mirrors what they believe in private, and she was going to find out all the sheiks dirty little secrets and bring this little group, Zion, to its knees. She made her way to the door man, a large bouncer type guy in a tight tuxedo.

"And you are?" The doorman said while taking in the beauty of the woman in front of him.

"Liane Wells from channel 7 Israeli television." Kelia laid her accent on heavy to sell the cover."Okay Ms. Wells, I have your invite here. Would you like to donate to the cause?""Why yes, I have donated on behalf of the news team. We sent it over the site when we got the invite. You should see it in your notes.""Oh, yes I see it right here.

Oh, one hundred thousand. Well, channel 7 must run a lucrative broadcast?" Kelia just smiled at the doorman in a haughty manner.

"Well, if you're done exhibiting your grammar for the night, I have better things I could be doing inside, thank you." Kelia walked past the doorman rolling her eyes.

As soon as she got to a safe distance, she reestablished coms with Loch.

"Well, your invite worked. I would say you are a genius, but $100,000? Are you crazy? No news station has that kind of money to donate.""Don't worry, by the time they realize that there is no money being transferred, we will be long gone. Now, mingle for a while until the Sheik gets on stage to speak. That will be the perfect time to slip away and go to the ladies' room. I placed a little surprise in the stall that should help you with the second half of the mission.""Okay, well, I am going to go silent from this point on. I don't want anyone thinking I am the crazy that talks to herself.""Roger that. I will remain on coms to help if need be. Have some fun and mingle. Besides, it's not every day we get to rub elbows with the world's most elite."

Kelia was at the open bar. And under normal circumstances she would remain sober, but in this festive environment, she would stick out if she didn't at the least have a drink in her hand.

"I'll take vodka and soda, two limes please." She ordered from the bartender.

"Such a humble request, I see I am not the only one watching your figure."

A robust and deep voice said in Kelia's blind spot. She rolled her eyes then thought it would be better to not be confrontational. So, she turned to look at whoever this pig was, in the eyes. As she turned, she was taken back, he was handsome and tall, and not to mention dark.

"I am Kiader, nice to meet you." He spoke then placed his hand for a shake.

Kelia returned the handshake, her small hand was engulfed by his.

"I am Liane Wells.""Yes, yes. Ms. Wells. Thank you for coming out tonight. I would offer to buy such a gorgeous lady as yourself a drink, but as it is, I am buying everyone's drinks tonight. So, it would be an obsolete gesture.""Oh, so you are Kiader Mulhinder? The wealthy sultan and oil tycoon that is running this charity?"

"Well, since you put it that way. Yes, that is me. I would love to have an interview with your station, you know. Something a little more exclusive?"

Kiader was really putting it out that he was attracted to Kelia which threw her off a little. If she wasn't a great spy she would have politely but sternly said no in, maybe, a physical way. But sticking to the role she had to do what every $60,000-a-year, attractive news reporter would do and be flattered."Oh, that would be great," She said smiling as she brushed her hand on the back of his hand, "and here I was thinking I would have to flirt with a few bodyguards just to get a front row seat at the press conference after your speech."

She was laying it on thick with the body swaying and the eyes as she spoke, there would be no man in the world that could resist her and the sultan was definitely trapped. He was flustered a bit then said,"Well, I will be waiting for the interview after the press conference. Can you meet me in my study? I have to rub elbows with a few more people then give my speech.""Yes, that would be great. Just don't schedule any other private interviews tonight because I have a few questions on your.. position, if you will."

"Oh, Ms. Wells, you have nothing to worry about. I will let my guards know that you have access to the west wing, whenever you want to head that way and wait for me... Till then..."The sultan winked and left Kelia at the bar. She smiled back then turned to head towards the ladies' room. Once she was inside the bathroom, she locked the door behind her and established coms with Loch.

"Loch, did you get all of that?""Yeah, you are amazing. I can't believe you did that. Wow! That was like James Bond, but opposite.""Yeah, that made it extremely easy to access his study, as long as I can get out before he comes up to cash in on his interview. I no longer need the equipment you left here in the bathroom, but

I am going to take it just in case. You never know when you might have to shoot your way out of a situation. Or just plan to shoot a sultan for being grabby.""Well, I would have just bypassed placing the equipment there had I known you would be so flirtatious with him." Loch laughed and Kelia rolled her eyes at him.

"Well, I just went with the flow. Anyways, I am going to wait till he starts his speech to go to his study. That, plus the press conference should give me enough time to put his entire hard drive on the flash drive.""That is if he doesn't bypass the press conference just to get back to his one on one with the hot Israeli in his study.""He won't. As much of a horn dog as he is, he is business first and this is good on his image. He will soak up the positive press as much as he can. I am going to head up to his study. I just heard them begin introducing the sultan. I will reestablish coms once in his study, so you can instruct me on how to operate this high-tech thumb drive you invented.""Okay. But it is not that complicated. It is more powerful than complex, but good luck with the guards if they are anything like their employer then they will probably end up helping you."Kelia smirked as she nonchalantly made her way out of the ladies' room, two ladies were waiting outside, and gave her catty looks. But she brushed them off without even looking at them as she made her way down the corridor, away from the party, and towards the sultan's office. She rounded another corner and just as she expected, there were two guards in front of a double door that no doubt led to the sultan's office. Without breaking her stride, she walked right up to the guards who never broke their glance at her. In a commanding stature yet very feminine voice she said,

"I am Liane Wells, the sultan is expecting me after his speech.""Yes, Ms. Wells we were informed that you were coming. Please make yourself at home. The sultan has a mini bar and he said that you can have anything you like."The guard opened the door and motioned for Kelia to go inside. She nodded a thank you and walked in. The guard closed the door behind her, and she surveyed the room. Inside the sultan's office was very distinguished. He had mahogany wood tables, floors, and bookcases, and was decorated in a London style décor. Everything from the desk to the books on the shelves look to predate her by centuries but the laptop on his desk was very new and expensive and it was what she was there for.

"Okay, Killa, can you see it?" She whispered while adjusting the camera slightly.

"Yes, I see everything. Very impressive. I would read the heck out those books. Kelia, can you go back to the bookshelf on your left? I think I saw an original copy of..." "Focus Killa. We have a job to do. You can come back to this hell hole on your own time and see if he will let you check out a book from his library. Right now, I need you to tell me what to do in order to get past his computer security and then I'll install the thumb drive. Get the files we need and tell the guards I have to go to the little girls room and leave before the sultan makes it out of his speech, plan?"

"Plan. Just let me work my magic." Loch said while typing on the computer he was in front of.

"He has a firewall set up. It is a little complicated but I... think... I... can... got it! Whew, I'm good!" "Easy, rock star. Good job but let's stay ready. This is way too easy for me."

A concern crept up in Kelia. She had been on a few missions as well as being prepared for this mission, but the fact that she was now a few minutes till she completed the mission and she was still in heels kind of bugged her. It was all too easy. She was aware that a beautiful woman could get anything she wanted but this was uncharacteristic of the sheik. Everything she had studied about him said he was unemotional and calculated, and at the bar he acted as if he was a teenage boy.

She just wanted to get this over with. The thumb drive was at 90% and she scanned the room once more to see if she was looking over something that was important. The thumb drive had finished downloading and she took it out and moved towards the door. Just as she reached to grab the handle, the door was opened from the outside and she was face to face with the sheik. He had a huge smile on his face, yet his eyes held humor.

"Ah! Ms. Wells, were you about to skip out on our interview?"Kelia was surprised because she was sure that she had more time, but her face showed none of the shock she was experiencing. She took a step back.

"Well, I was going to the little girls' room, I thought I would have a little more time than this."

Kelia thought she should stick to the plan, if she could just get close to the front door, she would make it to her limo before the sheik could figure out anything was wrong. And even if he wanted to apprehend her, he would do so at the risk of all of his guests questioning his actions.

"I would not be a gentleman if I tried to stop you, but I would be heartbroken if you did leave before I could tell you more of my involvement with Zion, and what we are about... Ms. Wells or should I just call you Kelia?"

Kelia's heart jumped out of her chest as she slowly backed away from the door and the sheik. She was confused. Loch and herself were sure that they would not have their cover blown. Besides, the fact that the agency was so underground that only a handful of people in the government knew of its existence. She and Loch were so new to the agency that their own handlers hardly could remember their names.

She kept backing up till she was stopped by the desk she was just at. The sheik motioned to the guards that were with him to leave and closed the doors behind them. She could easily overpower the sheik since he was a diplomat more than a soldier, but the shock she was in was overwhelming. The sheik moved past her and took a seat behind his desk and motioned for her to do the same."Please agent Kelia, have a seat. Besides, I cut my speech for the benefit short so I could have this time with you cause it is of utmost importance. I am sure right now you are curious about how I know who you are, and I will answer that. But first, I need to know how much you and Mr. loch, trust the agency?"

Kelia came back to her senses and took a seat. She was way too far in the mission and was obviously compromised, that to escalate things would not work out well for her or her team. She knew that Loch would be transmitting her feed to HQ so now, she would just play whatever game the sultan wanted and maybe she could work this out for the best and have him incriminate himself right here and now."How much do I trust the agency? Well, I would say I trust them more than I trust someone who is working for a known terrorist group.""Terrorist... Well, that word can have many different interpretations. Zion is considered terrorist now in this age. But wouldn't America be considered as terrorist to the native Americans? or even the African slaves they enslaved? More recently, when a bomb drops from the sky and kills a family would not the Americans be the terrorist to the family that had no evil intent to anyone? I say this to you under the assumption that the agency you work for is even an American sanctioned organization. Ms. Kelia, you are in a war between two entities that are older than any world power or government. So, I ask you, would you like to know the truth about who you are and your importance to this war?"Kelia rolled her eyes but could not deny that something about his wording or even his conviction interest her. So, she nodded for him to continue."Great, now that I have your attention. I promise I will give you the short version of it all so you can leave here tonight and process what I tell you. Your father will love to hear about how much of a beautiful woman you have turned into... So...""You knew my father?" Kelia perked up in her chair.

"Knew and still know.""That is impossible! He died before I was born!" Her voice became a little agitated with the mention of her father."Well, yes and no. He did die before you were born, but he is far too important to the end to stay dead. Technically, he has died and returned 12 times that I know of, I mean the 90's was hard to track him and a very active time. But your father is very much alive and the main reason we arranged this meeting... Oh... you didn't think that the mighty Zion... the biggest 'terrorist' group of this century would let sensitive info just mosey on through your pipeline without a reason?"Kelia was once again in a state of shock and confusion. She had only heard stories of her father. He was 25 when she was born, and he was in the Israeli army on a mission somewhere in Peru. She was told his missions were always secretive and the little she was able to get out of his life. She had to bribe and steal from the records guys in the Israeli secret service.

Everything she had ever gotten or heard about her father was always covered in secrecy. The one thing she knew for certain was his weird name, Profett Shalom."I can see that struck a nerve. I know you have many questions. So, I'll try and tell you all I know up to date and then answer any question you might still have... Let's get started!"The sultan was excited to get into his story and he talked to Kelia with great passion. He talked and explained what he knew of the creation and from there he talked about Lucille and her role in the war and also her role in the agency. He explained to Kelia what Zions role was in the scheme of things and also had a few videos that proved their innocence with some of the attacks they were named in. But what caught Kelia's attention was when he spoke of her father.

He was amazing. The stories he told her was something out of an action movie. There was espionage and explosions and he was noted to have stopped a few nuclear fallouts by himself. She was mesmerized by him, and when the sultan was done, he answered some of her questions then he told Kelia that she should be going back to the hotel to think about what she had heard."So, that's it? No villainous speech and lengthy explanation on how you don't want to, but have to kill me?"

"Oh, Kelia... You watch way too many movies. I would never kill you. I owe too much to your father and plus I am your godfather. I watch you come into this world and have been watching you and supporting you through everything till now. Your mother was a great woman. I am going to let you leave and most importantly, I am going to let you decide your own fate. You and Mr. Loch have a lot to consider."

Kelia straightened up. She had forgotten that she was broadcasting a live feed to not only Loch but to HQ. She stood up and made her way to the door. As she did so she nonchalantly took the brioche that was filming everything and closed her fist around it to muffle the sound."You seem like a good man and you seem sincere. I would like to give you back the thumb drive with all of your info and plans.""Please hold on to it for me. If you are anything like your father, it is safer in your hands."

The sultan smiled and Kelia walked out through the corridor and through the mass of people still conversing and dancing in the main room. She got to the limo and let herself in the door. This startled the driver who had dozed off a bit in the front seat.

"Ms. Wells, I... uh... I don't see you step out ... ma'am.""It's okay, Mathias. You can drop the act. I just want to head back to my room. I have had a long night.""Anything you want Ms. Shalom. You're the boss. By the way, I never got a chance to tell you how beautiful you look tonight. But please don't tell Sparks I was hitting on you. Sparks would not be an enemy I want.""Thanks Mathias. You're a real sweetheart."

Chapter Ten

GRAVEL PIT

With a jerk force of stopping a car at 80mph, everything came to a halt. Sparks quickly unbuckled his harness and stood up from his seat. The room was spinning, and everything was without color. He looked around to get his bearings as Azeri reached over to console him from her seat. The kind gesture was late and as if someone had turned on a faucet, he spewed the contents of his meal all over the floor.

Seriah and the other Elohim laughed."I told you he was going to earl. All of the humans earl when they jump through space. Hey Sparks, I bet you didn't see that on Star trek?" Seriah was referencing when they left orbit and he had told Sparks to concentrate on his breathing and close his eyes.

Sparks had looked at him confidently and said, "Hey bro, I have seen star trek, I know how to warp."

Sparks, still dry heaving, shot Seriah a side glance and waved a middle finger that had little to no conviction. All his strength was focused on not passing out as his knees shook and darkness clouded his peripherals. As he gathered himself and walked out of the large tactical vehicle they transported in, he looked to see where he was. He was next to a large plateau of rock in the middle of a desert. They were at the beginning of a large valley with mountains and plateaus on each side.

The Valley was polar opposite than the surrounding desert, because of its green grass and trees, and water filled oasis that rested on the Valley's bed. There was a large tree that looked like it could have been oak, due to the large and winding branches that sprawled out from its thick trunk. It shaded the beach of a mile-long lake that looked man-made, in fact the whole scenery looked man-made and with its location it posed questions to the creation of the oasis.

"What is this place?"

Seriah and the other Elohim where busy talking about the next steps and the transportation issue to answer Sparks, but Azeri had not left Sparks side since they had prepared to warp from the Elohim base and had stalked close by ever since, as if she was a secret service and Sparks was the President.

"This is Shalom. It means *peace*. It is an Oasis we made tens of thousands of years ago to give humans, who went to war, in these areas a place to rest amidst the fighting."

Sparks was only more intrigued by Azeri's answer.

"So, this is a man-made oasis? What do you mean when you say war and fighting? Who were humans fighting tens of thousands of years ago?"

Azeri paused as if she had said too much and gave a frightening look toward Seriah and sighed,

"I am not sure if I should be the one to tell you this so I will be vague. The history you have been taught has been... rearranged should I say. It only gives you some of the truth. Humans have always been at war with the Fallen and its dark soldiers, Sparks. We, Elohim, have been called by many names, as well as God and the Devil. From Divas and Gods, to Orisha's and spirit guides."

"The war between good and evil has been a constant fight in this realm. Ever since the creator stepped out of the Chaos, it has been a constant battle between the two. That is all I will say, I will let Profett answer any other questions you have about that, and as for this oasis being man-made, We, the Elohim, chariot of the most high, Host of Host, created by the I Am, made this so it is far from man-made."

Seriah and the more experienced warriors were talking strategically amongst themselves, and they seemed really concerned about a few hand-sized markings that had been scratched out. The rest of the warriors were busy clearing the area and setting up a watch parameter. Seriah broke conversation with his peers and walked over to where Azeri and Sparks were standing.

"This is a sacred rest haven we set up a long time ago."

"Yeah, Azeri somewhat filled me in on the history."

"We were going to make camp here for the night. It is the only safe place to camp in these areas. The base where Profett is holding up is a day away on foot."

"Well, why don't we start setting up camp?"

"There is a problem. The holy markings we left to protect the oasis have been defiled. They are strong but whatever magic that was used to defile them was stronger. There are a number of demons that work for Lucille but only a few who are this strong. They are called Zuzebub and Areelle, they are known as the twins of murder."

"They are the ones that are in the hearts of serial killers, spies, and soldiers. They tend to stay in the fourth dimensional plane and use temptation and suggestion to get their evil deeds done. They were the first angels to rebel with Lucille and have trained some of her more hardened warriors that are humans. One of the souls they have trained and held captive is Jin. Have you heard of Jin, Sparks?"

Sparks thought of all the spies and assassins he had been briefed on in his days with the Agency. A little light came on when he recognized the name Jin.

"Jin... I have heard of Jin from feudal Japan. But that was centuries ago, he was the first ninja assassin."

"Might have been a long time for humans but he is far from human now. That is the same Jin. He has a sad yet interesting story, but that is for a later time."

"So, you mean to tell me that Jin, the first Ninja, is still working for Lucille?"

"Yes, and he is still very dangerous, Sparks."

"How can that be? I was told that Lucile cannot employ the souls she takes from men."

"That is true. If a human lives an unrighteous life, then his soul goes with Lucille for her to torment. But if a human was to give their soul to her before death, then they are hers to do as she bids. That is what happens when you sell your soul to the devil. You don't sell your souls per say, more like the intentions of your actions from that day forward. Actually, Jin sold his soul to the murder twins and Lucille bought out the contract."

"This sounds as complicated as the NBA. What does it mean for us right now?"

"Well, for us, right now we are in a catch 22 Sparks. On one side, if we decide to stay here for the night then we will be sitting ducks for the attack that the twins have planned. Although, if we were to muscle it out and make our way to the base, I am sure that we would be walking into another trap. What do you think we should do?"

The group of angels were silent. No one wanted to go against the Most High and contend with Sparks and whatever decision he was going to come up with. With all eyes on him, Sparks thought hard. If they stayed and battled the twins and whatever force they had with them, it would waste too much time. There would be the Angels and himself setting up a counterplan and waiting for the attack, then there would be the battle that would come from it.

Then upon victory, the Angels and Sparks would have to pack up their team and start to make their way to the base which would still be a day away. The plan was obvious for the caravan he was in. They had to push their way to the base, if the attack happened on the road then if need be, he and a few Elohim could break off and assist the base.

"I think the base is number one priority. We need to push on. If they attack us on the road, we can still send help to the base but if we stay here and allow them to box us in, then all will be lost."

Seriah looked at a few of the angels and pointed and they ran off. "I will send a few scouts ahead of us so we can still have some sort of tactical advantage, but I think that this is the right decision."

****

Keila was abruptly awoken from her nap by a loud alarm and flashing red lights. She quickly put on her combat pants and strapped her two .45 handgun holsters on her chest over her dingy grey taint top she was sleeping in. Due to her combat experience she was accustomed to sleeping in her clothes. She knew that trouble or duty could always come during times of rest. She was no lady; she was a soldier and a missed shower and or clean clothes meant nothing if you are not alive to enjoy them.

This was no drill, at least not that she could remember being scheduled, and being that this was such a small and lowkey base Profett would only schedule drills in advance as to not cause any alarm to the surrounding villages. The base was located in the middle of nowhere and surrounded by dessert. Kelia laced up her boots in no time flat and finished gathering her normal load out which consisted of two .45 pistols, a .380 that fit in a custom boot holster, four throwing knives, a large combat knife, and a few bobby pins.

"These things always do more than just hold up this unmanageable mop I have up here,"

she said to herself as she hurried and put her hair into a bun and walked out the door.

It always amazed herself how fast she could get ready. The whole ordeal took less than two minutes. She was now in a small hallway that led to the main corridor. As she got to the frantic corridor, she made a left while pushing past a few people who started to complain until they saw who she was. She walked a few steps then waived her badge against a card reader that was beside a large double door, when the green access light came on, she opened the door that accessed the large, equally frantic, control room.

As she walked in, there were those of lower rank and lower security clearances that were being ushered out by the four generals in the room. Some of them being so new that they paused to stand at attention and salute Kelia. Something she hated and would, under ordinary circumstances rip them a new one, but she was focused on the main threat and gathering info, so she just returned their salute and kept walking towards the generals.

"Generals! What seems to be the problem?" Kelia had been far removed from her military background, and being in this group for nearly five years, the generals were lucky she even addressed them by rank.

"Keila, we have an invading force at our doors." General Eve said looking around to make sure they were secure, the older, grey haired general continued.

"It seems that our little march on the Gates was not received well. We now have two legions of demons and a few Fallen right at our doorsteps. Do you have any idea where Profett is?"

The Generals words where full of blame and annoyance. Keila was not their favorite agent to deal with and that was for a few reasons. She was, in their eyes, unchecked. Being the daughter of Profett she could get her way, despite their advice. What made it even worse was that her way always seemed to be the right way.

The latest thing that made the generals angry was the little trip to the Gates for Sparks. The generals were big on respecting the treaty and Kelia's little excursion was a blatant violation of the age-old treaty.

"No, I was going to ask you the same thing, General. I haven't seen my father for a few days now. I am sure he is locked up in his room studying or whatever he does in there."

It took all of Kelia's strength and tact to not say what she had wanted to say to the older but still attractive female General. Kelia had observed the General leaving her father's living space numerous times during the years she was with Zion. No one else knew about her father and the General's little secret but her. The General at times seemed to try and act as a mother to Kelia which was endearing, save for the fact that Kelia had a mother whom she loved and missed.

The General was not quite her superior. She did not want to play the little war games with the general but now was not the time for pettiness. As if on cue Profett's voice broke the confused silence that was in the control room.

"Generals, Agent 11! It seems that the day which I have dreaded for years has finally come. I see that we have some visitors. Generals, if you could gather your men along the fortress' walls and have all non-combatants ushered into the fallout shelter. I need to speak with my daughter privately please."

The other three Generals made their way to the door while General Eve gave Profett a questioning look that he brushed off as he turned towards Kelia. As she walked out, the door closed by itself, and he gave Kelia a huge hug.

It had been way too long since he had hugged her, besides the hand on shoulder every now and again this was the most contact she had gotten from her father since she could remember. The hug was breathtaking and she could feel tears coming down her eyes as they parted. Profett used his thumbs to wipe his daughter's eyes.

"You know, I have never told you how proud I am of you. You are so strong and wise, and beautiful! It amazes me that you came from me. You remind me of your mother every day."

Kelia just stood there trying not to cry, with no smart remarks. In fact, she could not say anything past the silent sobs she had. "What I am going to ask of you will go against everything you stand for, but it is the right thing to do."

Kelia rolled her eyes. Even with this moment being so beautiful, only her father could make it into something she would regret.

"What do you ask of me?" She asked as she backed up a bit to take in whatever BS was coming her way. "Sparks and a few dozen Elohim have come back to earth and are headed this way. I need you to take a few men and meet them so they can go to this location."

Profett had pulled up the location of a nuclear reactor not far from their location on one of the control panels.

"It is of most importance that you stop whatever agent that is sent there. I feel that this is Lucille's plan, not to attack this base but to keep us from going out and stopping whoever is at this plant and whatever they are going to do. As you can see, they have some land to land missiles with them. I don't know what the other targets are but if those missiles get off, we could be looking at a nuclear level event."

Kelia looked at the screen but she was not convinced of the threat.

"But Father, why would they send so many demons here if they had other plans? They must know of the drive we have here. Let me go down there and get the truth from the leader. It will only take a bit then we can go from there?"

"Kelia, I have let you do what you please. Mainly because I am a fool for you and I want to make up for lost time, the other reason is that you are wise and will be the leader of Zion one day. But If I have ever made a command to you this would be it. Do as I say... Please... I don't have time to talk about this with you. I must go to Nebula and speak with an old friend... KELIA... I ask again... Please!"

Without any other comment or even another hug, Profett disappeared leaving Kelia standing in the control room alone. She wiped the remaining tears from her eyes and with a smirk, she turned and made her way to the door.

"I will obey father. Just as soon as I squeeze out a few answers from one of those demons!"

****

The caravan of angels and Sparks had been marching through the desert between the State of Israel and Jordan for most of the day. When they first appeared in the Oasis, the time was 0800 and the sun had just rounded the horizon. It was now 1500 and the Sun and all of its anger was now focused on the scorched desert sand. Although the temperature was well into the hundreds, Spark's suit and the material it was made from, surprisingly kept him at a comfortable 78 degrees. The Caravan had now stopped to recalculate their navigation.

Seriah and some of the high-ranking Angels were now huddled around with Sparks over an ancient map negotiating the next steps. Sparks was surprised at how in control and authoritative Seriah was. He had gotten to know Seriah well through his training. The constant guidance and support he received early in his training from Seriah had changed to genuine friendship and camaraderie. While on Nebula Seriah and Sparks had become close.

They would talk for hours about fighting strategies and who their favorite martial artist was, Sparks was at a disadvantage because most of Seriah's favorites were Angels that Sparks had never heard of. Through the use of the Elohim Technology and the Wall of Life, Seriah would show Sparks of epic battles and fights that the Angels had been in, unbeknownst to mankind.

One of Seriah's most favorite fighters was Profett. Sparks had to admit, Profett was amazing.

Sparks was entranced at the scene of Profett slashing and kicking, jumping and grappling hundreds of demons. But the feat that really astonished Sparks was that Profett was the only being to have ever fought with a Hound from Hell. As Sparks loosely listened to the plan, he looked at the map that was laid on the ground before him. The map like the wall on Nebula and the door at the Gates of Hell, was constantly animated. As they spoke and changed their course their decisions were reflected on the map as well.

The base where Zion was being attacked, also showed on the map along with the demons that were outside waiting to raid the walls. The truth that the map bypassed, was that the hoard of demons that were outside of the wall, were really people, possessed soldiers that truly believed that they were fighting a good fight against terrorist.

The Caravan of Sparks and the angels were on the map in the exact position and stances they were in presently. If one of the members of the caravan walked away his avatar also did so on the map.

In between the caravan's position and the base, was a village of warriors that were sworn to lend a hand and riffle to the Most High's will. They were two thousand strong. One of the lost tribes of Israel that were relocated thousands of years ago when Israel was oppressed under Assiran rule. The plan was to pick up a few warriors from the village and Sparks, the warriors and a couple Elohim would attack from the back of the base and try to catch the demons in a crossfire.

"Sparks, do you have anything you want to add?" When Seriah said Spark's name it gathered him from the slight daydream he was in.

"No. Nothing."

The Angels all gathered their gear and started back to march. Sparks picked up the map and looked at it a little bit closer. Although he didn't have any problem with the plan, something didn't seem right. The map, when referencing a position, would show the life forms that were in the area. Be it human, Angel, or demon, when Seriah pointed out a destination on the map it became animated with real time images of beings.

But when Seriah briefly pointed to the village it was as if no one was there, and what scared Sparks even more was the shadows that he would catch a slight glimpse of but could not pinpoint what they were.

****

Kelia stood on the top of the walls of the base surveying the massive hoard of demons that stood outside the base's gates. As men and women hurried along the wall to their battle positions, she slowly surveyed the attacking hoard. She knew exactly what she was facing. To the naked eye, the invading force looked to be a UN force of soldiers. Kelia looked deeper than most would.

She observed the mannerisms of the upper chain of command. She noticed how everything from battle formations to the smallest thing like having to relieve oneself went all the way to the general before being executed. This would not be anything to the untrained eye, since most believe this is how a military works. And they would be right if the latter of the two might have stopped with the lower chain. The fact that those minor requests went so high in the chain only proved one thing, these men were possessed, and the fact that so many were possessed in the same manner only proved that it was a legion demon who owned the possession.

A legion demon was a very weak and yet very powerful demon. If confronted by itself, a legion demon would rather run than to fight, but if said demon was to possess a number of followers then its power would multiply by its number of possessed souls. The legion demon was not only a war fighting demon, the legion demon was also responsible for mass ignorance.

Whenever people would come together in a time of popular insolence, then the root cause would more than likely be the product of legion demon possession. Born out of Lucille's spite for the most high's regard for Israel, the legion demon would max out its possessions to 1,200. From what Kelia could gather, there were at least 4,000 troops at the gates, that would put at least 5 demons at the center of the possession. Her assessment of who was behind the invasions was the simple part. The real investigation came with identifying who the demons originally possessed.

****

It was close to the later parts of the afternoon. The heat and the sun had resided at its western home and the men who were traveling with Sparks and the Elohim had been grateful for this progression. The caravan of Sparks and the warriors were now only a few miles away from the village of warriors that they were going to incorporate into the battalion. Sparks could sense something was wrong. It was a feeling of dread and a feeling of being watched. The dread part had only started once he was able to see the village in the distance.

He had been to numerous villages in the middle east during his time with the Agency. Because of his background within the agency, he was generally sent to small villages where Zion had been rumored to be hosted. His missions would be simple, he would always be needed to shut down the village's power supply so that the seal team could extract who needed to be taken and eliminate who needed to be taken out.

Every time he would go to such a village, he would notice many wanderers and or herdsmen a few miles out of the village. He suspected that these people were lookouts for the so-called "*terrorist*" group Zion. Not only had he not seen such people, but he could also not see any smoke or motion that would be normal coming from a village that had to eat at some point in the day.

The feeling of being watched was different. He had had a feeling that someone was watching them since they first left the oasis. Not only had he had this feeling but he also saw streaks of black in his peripheral for the same amount of time. These streaks had been random to the naked eye, but to Sparks, he noticed an organization to their randomness. The first time he witnessed one of these "shadows" was when he was daydreaming through the brief that Seriah was giving at the oasis.

He happened to be looking towards the mountain ranges when in the corner of his eye, he thought he saw a shadow move between rocks. He had focused on that area right at the moment Seriah had asked if he had any opinions and broke him out of his search. When He was done and packed, he looked back to the rocks where he had seen the shadow and observed nothing. So, he brushed it off. Throughout the day, he had seen other shadows but took them as mirages although his instinct told him differently.

Now, being only a few miles from the village and within eye distance, Sparks was sure that these shadows were not mirages. He could not see people per say, but he saw the shadowy shape of figures moving swiftly between the arches of the sand-built houses. At closer review he noticed the movements looking tactical.

"Seriah, halt the men!" Sparks said in a quiet yet commanding tone.

Seriah did as instructed, as if understanding the seriousness behind Sparks' voice.

"Men defense positions! Sparks what do you see?"

"I... Well, um... I think or I *feel* something is wrong." Sparks told Seriah while still looking at the village questionably.

"Ever since we left the Oasis, I have been seeing these... Shadows? And now that we are close to the village I see that I have not been seeing mirageS. There seems to be a welcome party waiting at the village, and I don't think they want to throw us a welcoming party."

Seriah's face became focused with more concern shown when Sparks told him about the shadows he had been seeing. He looked to the other Elohim, as if he had communicated telepathically, the Elohim moved to a few of the soldiers that were with them and in groups of fifteen; they branched off and headed to the village via different paths.

Seriah looked to Sparks, his face filled with concern and what looked to Sparks as a bit of fear.

"Ishmael..."

Sparks knew whatever came next would be most serious cause he and Seriah had been so close that they mostly called each other '*brother*' if not first names. For him to be using Sparks' heavenly name, this put a bit of fear in Sparks.

"Are you sure you saw shadows? Do you think you may be seeing things or maybe even dehydrated?" Sparks a bit confused that Seriah would question his mental competency and hydration.

"Yes, I have been thinking maybe I was seeing things before but look at the village!"

Sparks pointed to the village and the movement of fifty or so shadows that were now on top of the houses and buildings facing the advancing platoon of Elohim, Zion soldiers, and Sparks.

Seriah without ever turning to look at the village and where Sparks was pointing, put his massive hand on Sparks shoulder. He looked Sparks in the eye as if the next words he spoke were of grave importance.

"Sparks, what you see are ghost warriors. Shadow demons... The first Ninjas."

Sparks was confused .

"They are followers of Jin. He is the first Ninja. It is said that he sold his soul to Lucille, to become the greatest warrior the world has ever seen. No one knows exactly how old he is, but his first confirmed kill was 1586. He is the master of shadows and deception and a deadly opponent!"

As Seriah spoke to Sparks, their eyes never parted. Although Seriah was a foot and a half taller than Sparks, they were now eye to eye. Seriah spoke to Sparks as if to be his last will and testament.

"Jin has never lost a fight."

Sparks heard those words loudly. Seriah had not said them as a challenge but as a warning or decree. There was no sign of hope or inspiration in his words, only doom. Sparks broke their eye contact and looked to the shadows on the roof tops. He skimmed the figures till he got to one with yellowish eyes.

They pierced into his soul. Sparks couldn't make out what frightened him more, the fact that the eyes he saw where inhumanely yellow and told a story of murder, or the fact that he could vividly see them from miles out.

Sparks gathered himself from his fear. He always believed that fear was needed, he did some of his best work with fear racing through his veins.

But a person must always control how much they allow their minds to focus on fear. Sparks now looked at the men and Elohim that were advancing tactically to the village. As Sparks prepared his mind for battle, his suit started to transition from a loose flight suit to a tight bodysuit equipped with hard pads wherever he would use to strike.

The color was in sand digital camo with a glimmer of gold in each thread that acted as a bit more camo by creating a visual distortion as if certain pieces of his suit was invisible. That was a great piece of added angelic tapestry the seamstress added to his suit. As the suit conformed to his body from feet to the neck something unusual happened, the suit kept moving past his neck to his chin, cheek, eyes, and connecting at the top.

This was new and startling to Sparks. The suit not only went up his neck which made him raise his head and start to scream but it went up his chin and into his open mouth and in his nose and inside his eyes and ears. The suit muffled his screams and his vision and hearing was restored as if nothing had changed. He looked down and admired the craft work for a bit, then a familiar voice spoke within his head. "Sparks I see you have activated the suit I customized for you."

Sparks looked around a bit to see if she was next to him for the communication was way more advanced and clear than any form of comms he had previously been exposed to.

"Seamstress? Is that you?"

"No. Goofy, I am the communication and information device placed in your suit. Think of me as your personal processor. Ki wanted me to sound like him, but the Seamstress thought that her voice would be a bit more comforting."

"So, you're like my suits' Siri?"

Everything went dark in the suit and he could not hear anything. The weight of the suit was at least 400lbs, due to the Elohim's gold thread, and he could feel the heat from the desert combined with the heat of having a full body suit in the desert. Then the suit activated back on.

"Unless you want me to do that in the midst of a fight, I suggest you never compare me to a talking box again!!"

Afraid to speak out loud, Sparks thought to himself, "Great, a suit with an attitude!" "I can speak with you mentally and verbally. So, yes I heard that. Anyway, how may I help you Ishmael?"

****

Kelia surveyed and spotted the original demons. There were five of them in armored cars far behind the battlefront. The key to handling these types of demons is to try not to kill the host when getting to the main demon. Legion Demons were a small group of demons who could mentally control thousands of weak impressionable minds. Hence, the name legion.

Profett always told Kelia that to kill a demon at the expense of a human's life makes them no better than the demon. A part of Kelia agreed with her father. Most humans have no real awareness of the world nor the war for it. Humans were innocent, helpless, weak, and dumb. She felt sorry for them, she really felt sorry for humanity, but innocence is a choice. If the truth is findable and you choose not to see it, then you choose the side of ignorance."And the side of ignorance leads to death."

Kelia jumped from the ledge she was standing on to survey the battlefield. The Zion soldiers that were accompanying her looked in frightened awe. As she fell from the ledge, ten stories up, she brandished her .45s, one in each hand, and started firing into the front lines. Every shot she took was precise. Landing on a soldier's shoulder or leg.

She was surgical with her shots, making each one a debilitating yet non-fatal wound. She landed on the earth beneath her in a combat roll into a kneeling position. She reloaded her .45s and ran as fast as she could towards the demons. Shooting through the crowd to open lanes to her target. Thirty-two shot later she brandished her pistols and pulled her two long knives.

She then ran straight towards one of the possessed soldiers and right up his chest. Using the soldier's chest to propel her jump, she cleared at least forty or so soldiers landing only a few hundred square feet from the vehicle the demons were in. She loathes the demons due to the mindless hoard they command. In normal circumstances, she would need at least a few more of her own men and a lot more guns to get as far as she was but the more consciousness the demons controlled, the more zombie-like the people became.

This, and the fact that she didn't want to hear what Profett had to say about her killing innocence was the reason she was only injuring and not killing. The more people you kill, the smarter the ones that are left become.

Kelia leg swept a soldier, rose up and kicked the next in the chest. She was swift and powerful. Although these men were not as smart as the average man, they were just as quick and powerful.Once the possessed men realized what was happening, they gathered around the vehicle. They wanted to protect their masters. Kelia reloaded her .45 with the last magazines of sulfur-tipped armor piercing rounds. As the men raised their guns, she shot two rounds at the vehicle. The round penetrated the two men in front of the vehicle through their shoulders which sent them flying in separate directions. The rounds then penetrated the passenger side of the windshield and directly in the middle.

Most of the men who had their weapons drawn were now shaking their heads with confusion; trying to get the fog of possession out of their minds. Kelia rose her pistols to the driver side of the windshield. The driver side door opened and two hands popped out in submission.

"Don't Shoot! Don't Shoot!" Legion stepped out of the military vehicle in a surrendering posture.

"You are good. Damn."

Kelia trained her weapons at him.

"Okay, okay, okay!!! I know what you think but kill me and these men will just start firing at the base in confusion. Look around, some have woken yet they still keep their guns aimed at you. Let us just talk civilized, you know you can't kill me..."

She looked around and the demon was right. She would definitely have to kill her way back to the compound. And the truth is that the rounds she had loaded in her guns would not kill the demon, the round would only send the demon to hell.

"You are right... But I don't mind killing a few of these cows and I doubt when you get back to Lucille and report that I sent you there before your mission started, she is going to welcome you home with open arms!"

The demon looked back at his fallen comrades and back at Kelia. His face went from fear to a huge smile."Ha ha ha ha ha! I can't do it anymore. Ha ha! I mean, I'm no actor. Ha ha! I just can't!"

Kelia looked in confusion. Usually, these demons are not manic or crazy, but he was acting both."What the hell are you talking about?"

As she posted her guns more threatening at the demon and walked a bit closer."Ha! Whew... You think my mission is just beginning, but child... My mission is almost over. You could come down and kill the lot of us and still not stop what we have in plan. WE DID NOT COME TO ATTACK YOU. WE CAME TO KEEP YOU IN SIDE!!"

The last part of his sentence was spoken by everyone who was with him. Possessed or not, they all looked at Kelia with the same smile and wicked eyes.

Kelia backed up and aimed at the soldiers next to the demon. As she moved away from the demon, the hoard opened up a passage back to the fort.

"Bye, Kelia. You might want to secure the base, the earth and its inhabitants might have a bit of a fall out"

The legion demon waved goodbye as the soldiers repositioned themselves in front of him and in formation. Kelia aimed her gun at a few soldiers but they just smiled while they either moved for her to go back to the fort or repositioned themselves in formation. She soon holstered her pistols and turned towards her base walking with no emotion. Her only thought was, "*I want my daddy!*"

****

Sparks and Seriah made it to the front lines where Azeri and the other members of their battalion had set up an offensive front. As Sparks ran, he surveyed the tops of the houses. He saw with clear magnified view, at least twenty warriors dressed in traditional black uniforms. The warriors would phase in and out of view. The way they moved from one position to the next made it seem there was more than what he counted.

Sparks was fooled by the tactic at first but when he squinted, he was able to zoom in on the warriors. As he zoomed, he then changed his vision in the suit from regular to what seemed to be astral projective vision. The suit was amazing."Suit, what am I seeing?"

"I have changed your field of vision to 50/50. 50% the dimension you are currently in and 50% the dimension that the enemy is switching in. It seems that the enemy is using the shadow dimension as a way to camouflage their movements."

"What do you mean shadow dimension?"

"There are multiple dimensions that encompass reality. Humans are mostly in tune to the 3rd. Think of it as layers that overlap on top of each other. Each layer has a frequency, harmonizing to create reality. Without one, there would be nothing. The warriors have managed to vibrate to the frequency of the shadow dimension. The shadow dimension is the exact opposite to this one."

Sparks studied the movement of the warriors. What at first looked to be frantic movements now seemed to bear roots of tactical schemes. The warriors were outnumbered, but their movements from one spot to another made it seem like there were more of them. To everyone that was with Sparks, the jump between dimensions was too fast to notice, but to Sparks, he could see it without interference thanks to the suit.

It was as if the warriors were solid then with sharp shaking movement, unseen by the normal eye, they became shadow. They would then run to a new position on the roofs that they were perched on and become whole once more.

As Sparks broke his concentration away from the enemy threat, he looked to Seriah, who was making inaudible commands to Azeri and the other Elohim.

"There are only around twenty warriors in the village."

Seriah was mid command when he turned his head toward Sparks while still looking to the other Elohim. "Are you sure you are seeing the situation clearly?"

"Yes, there are only twenty warriors on the rooftop. They are moving back and forth from the shadows to make it seem like their ranks are larger, but I can see them clearly. They also don't have firearms; they are only armed with swords."

Seriah broke his glance with the other Angels and was now looking at the rooftops trying to count for himself. He then, unsurely looked at Sparks trying to gain a bit more understanding on what Sparks was saying. The look on Seriah's face told a story of confused trust.

"Brother, I trust you know what you are talking about. If you say there are only twenty then I believe you. The Jin have been rumored to be able to traverse through the shadow realm but I do not see it as you can. What do you think we should do? Even twenty Jin can be deadly to an army and if their leader is with them, which I am sure he is, then we are not only looking at a town that has been wiped of its inhabitants, but a fight that could cost many of the men and angels lives."

Sparks broke his eye contact with Seriah. He looked at Azeri. He knew that she and Seriah would lay their lives down for him. Sparks looked at every other man and angel that was with him. He knew that they would also fight and die at his side. With him was a total of seventy-five men and thirty angels. One hundred and five beings that were on a mission to help a base in the middle of the desert, now tasked with fighting their way through twenty of the most dangerous and feared assassins in human history. Spark thought aloud to his suit.

"If we are to fight today, what is the percentage of a victorious outcome?"

"There is an 83% chance that everyone here with you will die today."

The suit was factual and unemotional in its response, but this did not change the fact that what the suit said hit Sparks hard. Sparks looked to the village they were facing. His gaze went straight to the piercing eyes of Jin, the leader of the Ninja. Jin did not faze into the shadow like his followers. Instead, he stayed looking into Sparks' eyes as if he could see that sparks were looking into his.

His stare was intentional and blank. It was as if Jin had seen nothing, but war and death and his eye reflected all the horrors they had been exposed to. Jin's disposition was tilted forward as if he was always on the offensive and battle position. His hand never left his sword which was brandished on his left waist. He was dressed like the rest of his men except for his head which only hid his mouth, unlike the other ninja who only had their eyes exposed and were covered from head to toe. His hair was jet black and shined from the late evening sun that beat on his head.

Sparks thought to himself, *"What are they waiting for?"*

He knew that they were there for a fight, he knew that the village was more than likely massacred. He knew that Jin and his group of assassins were there to stop Sparks and his men from making it to help the base, but he just could not figure out why they did not attack. As he contemplated what was the hold up, his suit interrupted his thought.

"Ninjas do not engage in frontal formal combat. They are more than likely waiting for the sun to set."

"How long till the sun sets?" Sparks asked as he looked to the west.

"In approximately 10 minutes."

Sparks tried to think of a plan fast. His mind raced from thoughts of slipping a few men around the back to flank the enemy, to even leading a full-fledged assault. He was becoming nervous and anxious at the thought of losing so many of his friends and men who trusted him that he started to breathe heavily, and anger took hold of his emotions. As his anger grew, so did the sword in his hand. The sword was the same digital camo color as his suit with the blade's edge, a sharp silver.

The sword grew from his hand with the hilt attached to his palm. Besides the sword that grew in his hand, the suit itself began to produce plates that protrude from his body, protecting vital parts and his arms and legs. Sparks looked down at the sword and the armor before returning his attention to Jin. The village faced the east, which meant that the sun was disappearing behind the enemy. As soon as the desert's last light disappeared behind the earth's curve, Jin slowly raised his sword to a sword fighting position.

When he did so, all twenty ninjas moved to the shadow realm with only Jin standing, a dark figure in the darkness.

****

Screams broke the silence. One, then two men that were with Sparks ended up with a sword protruding through their chest. The scream was quickly muffled by the gurgling of blood. Then, the sword and the dark figure wielding it disappeared to the shadows. This happened twice or more before the group realized they were under attack. Everyone moved together in defense positions.

"Everyone, get into defense positions. Wait till they expose themselves then strike!"

Seriah and the other angels positioned themselves around Sparks in a circle. The men that were with them did the same around the angels. Now there were two circles around Sparks. Sparks was amazed at how protective they were, but Sparks knew he did not need the protection. He was a well-trained warrior with a suit of armor that was well beyond the current tech on Earth.

Sparks waited for the next ninja to attack and jumped high into the air. As he ascended, at least twenty feet, in the air he kept his gaze on the attacking ninja. The ninja was swift, raising his blade to slash with cat-like precision across the unsuspecting soldier's chest. Sparks was too late to save the soldier but as he entered into his fall from his leap, he was not too late to see the last place the ninja was before he vanished back into the shadow realm. Sparks thought to his suit silently that he should switch from 50/50 to 100% shadow vision so as to not confuse himself with what he was seeing.

"I sense you would like to switch to the shadow vision, but I can do something a bit more beneficial. How about if you can just go to the shadow world?"

"I can do that?"

"Yes, but..."

Sparks interrupted, "Then what are you waiting for!?"

Suddenly everything went without color. It was like everything that was in the world yet without color of any kind, and all the twenty ninjas were now visible. As Sparks looked at where the soldier fell, he saw the ninja finishing his swing. Sparks landed and he swung his blade down with tremendous force at the unsuspecting ninja.

His blade resistantly sliced through the ninja's body but with no more effect than smoke vapors following where his blade once was.

As soon as Sparks hit the ground, he followed his gaudy attack with faster more precise blows that had the same effect. The ninja just stood there tall and unaffected looking at Sparks with a bit of bewilderment. Sparks jumped back a few feet in a defensive stance. The ninja did not make a move. Sparks was now caught in the same bewilderment the ninja was in.

"What the hell is going on?" Sparks asked quietly in his suit.

"This is 'the but' I was trying to convey to you in the midst of that grand performance of moves. While in the Shadow realm you cannot use force. This realm is much like a mirror, only a mirror you can only see and can't touch. I fear that all other senses are useless in the Shadow. If you wish to eliminate any threat it must be done in the physical realm."

"Okay that might be a bit of a complication."

As Sparks circled his present enemy, he noticed how other ninja would phase a bit while making striking motions then become clear again with a black sludge dripping from their swords and the soldiers who were in front of the holding different parts of their bodies. Dull flashes of light leaving the remaining soldiers guns in vain attempts to shoot their shadow cladded foes. The circular formation to protect Sparks was well broken and although the soldiers and Angels that were with Sparks were very disciplined and trained, it was as chaotic as any close combat fighting could get.

The Ninja that was in front of Sparks wielded his sword very nonchalantly. The ninja would occasionally poke his sword at Sparks which would never break skin but would pass through him effortlessly. The ninja would then flash into the real world then back as if to taunt Sparks.

Sparks knew that he had to engage his foes in the real world, his only problem was how he was going to blink in and out as fast as he needed to be. As if his suit had been reading his mind, which it was, the suit spoke up with a solution.

"I am integrated with your thoughts Sparks, if you think it I can do it as fast as .0325 seconds of lag time."

"Okay... But why the lag time?"

"I have to run algorithms in ethics on any decision I am involved in."

"So, robbing a bank is out of the question?"

"I would advise strongly against any decision that might break laws whether man-made or universal, but ultimately, you have the overriding decision."

"Laws... Man-made or Uni... never mind. Just keep up and try not to get me killed. Also, I can't keep calling you suit. So, we need to come up with a name for you."

The suit gave a questioning *'okay'* then Sparks ran towards his opponent full speed brandishing his sword.

****

Kelia walked into the front gates defeated. All the soldiers that were within the base were looking with astonishment at what she had done only moments before her return. But she knew the truth. She knew that no matter what she had done or wanted to do, nothing she did would stop what was to happen. The demon had revealed the whole plan in his last sentence. A fall out, they were going to nuke humanity.

She had no emotions. She had no desires; she had no feelings at all. The only thing she could feel was defeat. She had fought the last five years against Lucille and her wretched hoard of demons and to no avail. The human race had met their demise. As she walked in her defeat, a soldier approached her and interrupted her thoughts.

"What are our plans of attack?" The soldier had a sense of confidence in his voice after seeing how resourceful she was in combat.

"Nothing. Move all personal to the fallout bunker and lock down the base."

Kelia said this without looking at the soldier. The soldier was late to respond due to the shock of what he saw and what he was now hearing. She did not wait for him to respond, she snapped out of her trance and looked him in the eye. She recognized him as one of the soldiers who would give her problems every now and again. She was not annoyed or angry, she was now in charge of the base and every life that was in it.

She said again to the soldier but with a pleading determination in her eyes.

"The demons wish to destroy the earth and we have failed to protect it. I have lost the fight for billions of souls. I will not lose the few who are close to me. Shut down the base and move everyone to the fallout shelters. Please."

The fact that she was now pleading to the soldier threw him off, but he could sense the severity in her voice. He rushed away and started the fall out procedure.

****

Sparks swung his sword at the ninjas mid-section. Blinking in reality at the precise time the ninja blinked into reality to block his attack. The sparks of clashing iron were all that could be seen of the exchange. As Sparks quickly went back to the shadow world, he was filled with excitement.

He thought, *"this is one of the best weapons he has ever wielded."*

Although the slash he delivered was blocked, the sheer thought that he could appear out of thin air and deliver a blow then disappear once again filled him with a vigor that was unexplained. As Sparks was gaining a true understanding of this newfound power, he looked over his shoulder and noticed that the ninja was now turned to him and in a ready position. It seemed that now the ninja was also aware of Sparks' ability to control and manipulate the shadow realm. The ninja had a new aura about him, a more deadly and serious look in his eyes.

Spark and the ninja had a brief stare down then charged again at each other. As both were about to strike, Sparks saw that the ninja was balancing off his lead foot. The Ninja raised his sword high above his head then blinked into reality to gain a quick advantage over Sparks. The ninjas plan was to already be swinging once Sparks phased in so that he could deliver a death blow. Sparks hoped that this would happen.

Once Sparks realized that the ninja would be committing all of his balance into this powerful swing he moved slightly to the left before he phased in and swung his sword evenly with the Ninja's belly. The result was that Sparks caught the ninja mid swing and sliced deep through his midsection. Sparks blinked back into the shadow world as fluently as his death blow. Out of the corner of his eye, he saw the ninja drop his sword and hold his stomach as he fell to his knees in the real world.

Sparks and the ninja had been just beyond the circle that was formed around him to protect him. He looked at the battle that was forming before him. After he had jumped into the fight with the ninja, the circle was being picked apart one layer at a time. The ninja were phasing into reality and cutting down the Zion soldiers very ruthlessly. Every once and a while the soldiers would be able to get off a shot or two, but the targets would disappear as soon as they appeared, leaving a fallen comrade in their wake.

The ninja, although crafty, had less luck with the Angels. Due to the angel's fast reaction, they were able to defend against the ninja tactics and even kill a few. This made the ninjas go after the soldiers more frequently. They were thinning the herd. Sparks had to use this new ability to get the drop on the ninja. He ran at one of the ninjas that were about to jab one of the soldiers in the gut.

Due to the simplicity of their methods, they were not even maintaining their discipline which Sparks would use to his advantage. As soon as he blinked in, he decapitated the ninja whose blade was just at the soldier's gut. Everything happened so fast that the soldier had only felt the tip of the sword break a tiny bit of skin then dissipate along with the rest of the body. Only the ninjas' fallen and severed head was left to fall at the soldier's feet, eyes still staring with a murderous look at the soldier.

Sparks was able to kill three more ninjas before a lot of them caught on to his method. Once the ninjas were aware of Sparks' ability to go from real world and back to the shadow world, six of them now focused on him in the shadow world. Sparks was just finishing one of their fellow assassins, as the six of them circled him. Sparks stood in the center of the six-stalking ninjas with a ready but calm stance.

His feet were shoulder length apart, his knees slightly bent with his weight evenly distributed through both legs. His hands and arms were by his side, but limber and his shoulders were tense and ready for anything. Sparks' head was lowered so that he could use his peripheral vision as far as it could span. Although most senses were not useful in the shadow world, Sparks noticed that he could sense every move that the ninja behind him made.

He could sense that the right foot crossed over the left foot as they circled. He could feel the weight distribution and their heart pounded through his head as if he could hear it. This showdown only lasted but a few seconds yet due to Sparks' concept of time and manipulation of it, everything that happened in those few bloody and swift seconds was very slow and precise.

The first ninja leapt up to the air tumbling forward and thrusting his sword down to Sparks head as another leap forward thrusting his sword at Sparks mid-section. Another moved into a position to counter, however Spark would react. As Sparks saw the technique that the ninja was using, he chose to address the ninja that was leaping at him to thrust his sword into Sparks.

He spun to his right, phasing in just as the ninja phased in, missing his jab as Sparks ended up slightly to his left and behind the ninja, thrusting his sword behind him through the ninja's back. Without phasing back, Sparks ran to his left with the ninja still attached to his sword. He put his weight on his sword and jumped as high as he could just as the ninja that was in the air was swinging down.

The ninja hit his target only to realize that it was his fellow assassin's limp body and as he noticed this, he saw a huge 6'5" desert camo cladded from head to feet Sparks swinging one of his size fourteen foot right at his head before it connected and he saw black. Sparks' angle of the kick sent the ninja's body to the third ninja that was just phasing in to help against Sparks. As both bodies fell to the ground, Sparks pulled his blade from the ninja who he had run through.

Phasing back swiftly, Sparks now ran directly at the three ninjas who were standing amazed at what happened to their buddies. As they ready themselves for Sparks' attack and phased into reality, they were struck with an arrow in the heart. All three assasins fell to their knees before killing over clutching at the arrow.

Sparks stopped his pursuit. He was in the real world and confused. As the ninja dropped, he quickly surveyed the battle, that was now just his men looking at the fight between him and the ninja. He turned and looked at where the arrows came from, in the distance, on top of the building and still in the same spot, stood Jin with a bow aimed at the direction of the last ninja that was hit. Through all the commotion, Sparks had forgotten about Jin, and it creeped Sparks out that Jin had just been sitting there the whole time watching everything.

Chapter Eleven

B.I.B.L.E (BASIC INSTRUCTIONS BEFORE LEAVING EARTH)

Jin stood at the roof, his long jet-black hair blew with the hot breeze of the desert night. As always, he could hear them. Whispering, moaning, calling to him from the shadows. He had heard them for hundreds of years. They call for the blood of his enemies.

They would beg him to send them more souls; they craved the company. But this time their whispers were a bit different. Ever since Lucille had given him the order to track and detain Sparks, the voices of the souls sang a different song. A song of vengeance and reparations.

They now whispered, "Jin, now you will pay. Now you will come to be with us..."

Jin took this assignment with hope. Hopes that this man, 'The one who sleeps with Death' Jonathan Ishmael Sparks, would be the man to send him to his love. That is if he is worthy to deliver him to the other side. Jin had all the motive to make Sparks prove his worthiness.

Jin jumped towards Sparks and the rest of the combatants. He phased into the shadow world as he did so. Spark decides to phase into the shadow world as well only to see what could only be explained as a bright light. The brightest Sparks had ever seen. As Sparks concentrated, his eye hurts from the light, he noticed Jin's body running towards him.

Jin's body was dark, like the darkness you see when you look at the sun too long, to say that the light was coming from Jin, would be false. Jin's aura was so dark from hundreds of years of murder that he drew in all the darkness and in the shadow world, the only energy that could be emitted was light; pure, blinding, white light. Sparks was suddenly gripped with fear. The type of fear you would feel if you came face to face with a tiger.

He could feel all the death and sadness that was this dark being. Jin's approach would have taken a very fit and trained warrior twenty minutes but it only took him 2 minutes to be standing in front of Sparks and all who were there.

Jin Spoke to Sparks, never moving anything but his lips and never breaking his gaze that pierced through Sparks' eyes and into his soul. Jin spoke loudly for all to hear.

"Jonathan Sparks! The one who sleeps with death! I have waited for centuries to find a man worthy of my blade. Many have fallen by it."

He raised his katana blade horizontally to present it to the soldiers, angels, and to Sparks. The blade was sharp, so sharp that even the slightest glimmer of light reflected off of its edge. The hilt was onyx and without a hand guard, it was fitted to form the hand with each finger having a place in what looked to be the tiny opened mouths of demons.

"This katana was forged by hell fire and thirst for blood. Today, I will feed it the blood of a chosen one. Then... it will dine on the flesh of the Elohim!"

As Jin spoke, he pointed the sharp tip of his katana at those his words were directed to. The commanding presence and emotionless demeanor of Jin was intimidating. All the ninjas he had brought we're dead and he was surrounded by the few remaining soldiers and the Elohim, as well as Sparks. By logic he was gravely outmatched, yet one would be hard pressed to tell such by the way he paced and spoke in front of his opponents.

Jin had been an assassin for hundreds of years; 626 years to be exact. The date of his birth was unknown, but the body count of his sword was infamous. He has killed Kings and common people alike. He was single handedly responsible for the turn of feudal Japan. There were even rumors that his blade was the last thing Adolf Hitler saw on this earth.

When taking on a contract, Jin didn't care for the cause. Jin's only concern was to feed his blade. His blade was insatiable. It was said that the demons on the hilt were put there personally by Lucille. She wanted them to motivate Jin's blood lust. And if he thought about putting the sword down for a normal life, the whispers would gradually grow to screams. The agony of having to kill just to keep sanity could be seen slightly in the murderous gaze that was consistent in his scowl.

Sparks kept his eye on his foe. He tried to remember his training. He watched for signs of pain in his enemy. Looking for a limp or a favor of the side at which Jin likes to move. Simple things like which way he turned when he paced could show a lot in the subconscious of a warrior.

Sparks tried to study Jin but the unease he felt by just being in Jin's presence was unnerving and kept Sparks from focusing on anything other than the dark, erie feeling of hopelessness he was feeling. Sparks was still fitted in his suit that was a desert digital camo, but his face and head were now uncovered. Jin pointed his sword, which he named thirst, at Sparks.

"Are you ready to lay with Death for eternity?"

The idea that he could be with his beloved at last was tempting, but Sparks was filled with a mission and purpose. He had to do his best at saving humanity."I have noticed that you are good with traversing the shadow realm. But I would propose we keep this fight in this realm. A shoguns showdown. If you may?" Sparks was not wasting any energy or focus on anything other than maintaining it on his enemy.

He nodded firmly and gripped the hilt of his sword, which was an extension of his suit and had now extended downwards for room so that it could be gripped by both hands. The angels and remaining soldiers had now cleared room for the two combatants in what was loosely a half circle.

The air was thick with anticipation. It was nighttime, but due to the clear skies and the full moon, there was ample light to see. Sparks and Jin started the preliminary rotation and sizing that combatants have done for centuries. Jin's eyes never left Sparks'. It was as if he was looking into the core of Sparks and not only judging his steps but the contents of Sparks' soul.

Jin stopped his rotation and closed his eyes. Sparks took the only advantage he had and used that moment to deliver the first strike. He gripped tight on the hilt of his sword with both hands. Stepping towards Jin, he planted his right foot slightly farther than shoulders length and swung downward and slightly horizontally at Jin's left shoulder. The time between his strike and when Jin closed his eyes could only be measured in milliseconds.

As Sparks' blade neared its mark, Jin let a slight smirk leave his lips. Faster than anyone Sparks have ever encountered, Jin slipped away from the strike. Jin's sword still hanging loosely in his hand he kept his eyes closed. Sparks being disciplined in one on one combat, never lost his balance.

He twisted his hips with his arms in tow. He aimed this strike at Jin's mid-section. Eyes still closed, Jin threw both arms high in the sky as he jumped back, barely missing the tip of Sparks' blade as it slid through the air.

Sparks angled the edge of his blade upwards as he swung diagonally. Once again, Jin evaded the strike, still relaxed. Sparks began to slash in controlled combinations at which Jin swiftly and smoothly dodged all strikes.

When sparks ended his bombardment, he thrusted his sword at Jin's neck. Knowing that Jin would most likely evade all of his strikes, the thrust to the neck was what he had hoped to land. Jin, eyes still closed through all the slashes, caught Sparks thrust with his pointer finger and thumb with such strength that it stopped all momentum and jarred Sparks a little in the process.

Trying to keep a smooth face, Sparks was undoubtedly surprised. He tried to pull his sword back but Jin's grip was too tight. Sparks struggled a bit more, then stopped. On cue, Jin's eyes opened slowly and a smile seeped to his lips. Between Sparks' blade and Jin's fingers, a black liquid slowly rolled down to Jin's wrist, and Sparks could only imagine it was his blood.

"That was slightly underwhelming."

Jin flicked Sparks' sword like a smoker flicks a cigarette.

The motion sent Sparks' two arms high trying to control his sword. Jin then took his sword with both hands. He raised the hilt to his face and whispered to the demons as their mouths closed around his fingers in compliance. He then stepped his left foot back still facing Sparks. Though his movements were smooth and graceful, when his foot touched the soil, the earth around his foot broke away.

He then turned his torso away from Sparks and raised his sword hand above his head with the tip pointed towards Sparks. Jin's right foot pointed in the same direction. His free hand was now faced towards the ground as if to balance. Sparks got into a ready position. Jin, who's eyes were opened, was looking at the ground.

"Sparks, now you will feed thirst, now you will die!"

Jin pushed off his left foot as he lunged. As graceful as a leopard, he covered the few steps between Sparks and himself quickly. He began to slash at Sparks and Sparks was able to block his attack. Waiting on a mistake, Sparks played a defensive position. The mistake was all Sparks'.

Without taking a breath or moment to rest, Jin moved through position after position and attack after attack. Sparks dodging and blocking was beginning to be overwhelming. Jin had pushed Sparks back quite a distance, yet Sparks was still able to evade. He wasn't as smooth as Jin's movements nor was his eyes closed, yet Sparks was still alive and not cut. As Jin swung his blade, he spun his body and landed a spinning kick to the torso of Sparks. As Sparks released the air he was holding and hunched over from the blow to the torso, Jin stuck his sword in the ground and grabbed Sparks by the face. Jin's palm pressed against Sparks nose and pulled him into an uppercut. Sparks was rattled, and once sparks regained his composure, he was just in time to position his blade to block a swinging attack from Jin who had grabbed his sword again, throwing dust along with the blow.

Sparks was 6'5" and 250 pounds, Jin was a foot shorter than sparks and over a hundred pounds lighter. But Jin's strength was immeasurable. Whether it was Jin's strength or just the unexpectedness of the strike was unknown. Yet the force of the two blades clashing sent Sparks' body flying back then tumbling awkwardly on the ground as embers from the two swords ignited.

Sparks' body armor, reacting to the impending danger, caused pads to rise around all of his vital organs. His helmet rose around his whole head. His body laid incapacitated on the ground. The suit was not quick enough to shield him from the initial collision from the ground and inside his helmet were alarms of body injuries. One of which was a broken arm.

The suit hardened around the fracture to make a cast. Sparks still hadn't moved. Jin once again lowered his sword in a nonchalant demeanor. He began to walk towards Sparks as a predator does to a prey that is finished and ready for the kill blow.

"Sparks!" He spoke loudly enough for everyone to hear, but not quite yelling.

"I thought that you would be my greatest challenger. We have all heard the stories of the one who will sleep with death, and now that I have had a chance to duel with you, I am greatly disappointed. I feel that I will have more of a challenge killing the angels you have brought then this little dance we just had."

As he talked, he slowly made his way to Sparks' limp body. He waved his sword around arrogantly while he taunted Sparks and the party of Elohim that was with him. The blow that sent Sparks flying had broken the blade of Sparks' sword. Jin stopped and picked it up, examining it. He placed it in his palm as if to weigh it.

"This is a pretty good blade. But it is not a great blade. That, along with poor training." Jin pointed his sword to the Elohim.

"... is the reason why I am standing, and you are lying!"

Jin flipped the fragmented sword in his hand so that the tip of the blade was between his two fingers then he threw it precisely between Seriah's feet. Seriah and the other angels had watched this duel in shock and anxiety. They knew how important Sparks was to the entirety of the plan. And not just the plan of attack but the plan of God herself. They had to abide by the rules of the duel and not interfere, win or lose this was Sparks' fight and Sparks' alone.

The anger Seriah felt was tremendous. Not only was the future of mankind lying helpless on the ground but Seriah's friend was laying there. No one knew the severity of Sparks' injuries, or if he was alive.

As Sparks laid on the ground, he mentally connected with his suit. He asked for a damage report so he would not cause any movement to find out what was hurt.

His right shoulder had been knocked out of its socket. His left forearm was broken in two places. He had multiple scratches down his back and his hip had a deep bruise. All in all, he was in operational health. He thought about just jumping up and continuing the fight but deep down he knew he was no match for Jin.

Jin had fought many combatants and had learned lessons from all of them. Sparks was superiorly overmatched and his only play that would keep him in this fight, or alive for that matter, was to use his mind.

Jin had slowly made his way to Sparks' limp body. He crouched down to take in the last of his fallen foe. As he stood up, he raised his Katana named Thirst and aimed the blade downward towards the throat of Sparks.

"You were a sad excuse for a warrior. Fear not my friend, at least you will be reunited with your lover!"

Jin thrusted his sword downward and just as he did, Sparks twisted his body towards Jin's body and thrusted his katana, that was no longer broken because it was a piece of his suit, into the belly of Jin. Jin's downward thrust was stopped mid-air as his body hunched over the now impaled katana. The hilt of Sparks blade was firmly held in his right hand and the tip of the blade was poking out of the back of Jin. Jin dropped his sword and his hand wrapped around the exposed blade of Sparks' sword.

Jin's eyes looked at the sword then made their way to Sparks'. A slight smile creased on Jin's lips as he silently mouthed a single word before life faded from his eyes.

"Aoi."

Sparks lifted his body so that he was now kneeling on one leg. He used the shoulder that was not hurt to nudge and push Jin's lifeless body off his sword. In pain, managed himself to stand. Sparks looked at Jin, he had so much respect for him. Not only did he respect Jin, he feared Jin.

Even as Jin's body laid on the ground bleeding out what little black blood he had left to bleed, Sparks still feared him. No one had ever given Sparks such a beating as Jin had delivered in just, what would have been, 2 minutes; no man had hurt Sparks as badly. If you could even call Jin a man anymore. He had lived hundreds of years. The black blood was proof that any essence of humanity that was ever left in Jin rotted centuries ago.

There was a deathly silence in the valley outside the vacant town. As the angels, and Sparks looked at the oldest assassin, Jin. They could not say a word as his soul now released to whatever hell Lucille would concoct for him. The silence was deafening. Then came a slow yet deliberate clap.

Clap... Clap... Clap...

As the clapping came to a rapid applause. A single applauding figure emerged from behind the Elohim. Williams, dressed in his usual business suit, walked right through the large gold cladded armor Elohim with a mischievous smile. His eyes never broke from the shocked and terrified gaze of Sparks. Even the Elohim looked at Williams with confusion. Williams walked within ten feet of Sparks and Jin's lifeless body. He broke his gaze at Sparks to look down at Jin.

"Pity... Lucille will not be happy when you go to see her. She was under the impression that you, of all her "pets" would never be defeated." Williams said in his dry and humorless humor as he once again looked at Sparks with a smile on his face.

"And you... Oh, how lucky you are to be alive after that little dance. It seems that you, Jonathan Ishmael Sparks have once again eluded death. Although, I don't see why a man that is in love with Death would want to stay away from her. She is after all, the most beautiful of God's creation. Don't tell Lucille I said that. She is very jealous of her favorite sibling."

Sparks' eyes never left Williams. He backed up a bit, as he did, his suit began to form protective padding reacting to his increased heart rate. Williams' smile grew wider.

"I see you remember me well, Sparks."

Sparks could remember all too well what happened between him and the hellhound that stood before him. He remembered the fear as he climbed up the elevator chute. He remembered the sharpness of the claws that grabbed and tore at him. He remembered the heat of the Hellhounds breath, the wretched smell. And the acidic burn as Williams sank his teeth into Sparks' flesh.

The Elohim that was with Sparks started to move on Williams. Williams held his hand up as to motion for them to give him a minute to explain.

"Wait a minute. I promise we will all have a chance to rip at each other."

As he said this, his hand that was held up turned into the beastly paw of the hellhound. It urged the Elohim to draw their weapons.

"But, I am here for one reason and one reason alone..."

Sparks was concentrated on the transformed paw as were the others that were with him. No one ever noticed Williams' other hand. A hand that had not transformed and perfectly human raised with a Glock 19 aimed at the center of Sparks head and fired...*Bang*!

ACT II

Chapter Twelve

TRIUMPH

The air was sharp. There was a slight sheen of snow that coated the northern Tennessee Mountains just outside of Elizabethton; the quiet mountains. Everything was quiet these days. Mountains, prairies, townships, cities alike. It had been three years since the explosions of the nuclear reactor plants that went off at random parts of the world.

The cities that were affected turned into modern day Chernobyl, and the remainder cities that had not got hit by the fall out were targeted by all manner of grotesque beings. The earth was scorched in most of the major cities, although it had been substantial time since the attack, fires still raged. Some fires were small and some were huge, but that was what differed city from nature. That and the others.

It had only been two months since Alex and her husband first stepped foot outside the fallout shelter. They spent the last two years and eleven months, twelve days, six hours, thirty-two minutes, and eight... no... nine seconds. But it wasn't like Alex was counting. The first thing Alex had noticed when she exited the fallout shelter was the sound. The deafening lack of sound.

She and her husband were not sure who or what had survived. While they stayed in the shelter, they continued to send radio transmissions to anyone who would respond, but to no avail. The fact that they were alone was frightening but not terrifying. She was with her best friend and love of her life, and as long as he stood beside her, nothing was quite terrifying.

Alex stayed still. Her movements, if any, were slow and deliberate. She was crouched down next to a thin tree whose canopy was sprinkled with snow. She clung to the handle of her Springfield M1A 308 scout rifle. She aimed down the iron sights and breathed shallowly.

Her finger traced along the trigger guard. Alex could hear the calm voice of her husband reminding her,

"Don't put your finger on the trigger till you are was ready to shoot."

He was lying right next to her in a prone position, as he spoke to her, his eyes never left the binoculars that were glued to his face. She closed her eyes one last time. In her mind, she could hear her husband scolding her for taking her eyes off the target, but she knew he could not see her eyes at the moment, and she wanted to pray.

She wanted to pray a conflicting prayer; she always prays before a kill. She wanted to ask the universe for forgiveness but most of all, she wanted to ask the universe to make this shot clean. This deer could be a meal for months. They had tracked this deer for a day, and it had led them quite away from their shelter.

"Open your eyes Al," Adam said without taking his eyes off of the deer and almost inaudible.

It always amazes her how Adam knew such things. She knew he was in the Navy. She met and married him while he served. She also knew he was involved in some clandestine activities a few years before the fall. Sometimes, she believed he might be some sort of Jedi or psychic the way he just knew things.

She opened her eyes, her sight was still down range and looking right where the deer's heart was placed. Alex stopped tracing the trigger guard and placed her finger on the trigger. In a slow fluid motion, just like she trained, she squeezed the trigger. Never anticipating the sound or kick.

Bang!

The sound made the deer move in fright. It took a good three full strides before the loss of blood pressure forced it to the ground. Alex released her breath; she didn't even realize she was holding it. Her and Adam both rose to their feet and looked around in different directions. They needed to make sure that the deer was the only other creature that was startled by the shot.

As they slowly made their way to the deer, Alex's husband grabbed her arm firmly. He was such a gentle person, that it startled her by how intense his grasp was. She froze in her steps. Without a word, he motioned that they get close to the ground. Alex followed his lead unsure of what or where the threat was.

As she lowered to a crouch, her husband firmly pushed her down to a full prone. He pressed the back of her head down but in the direction of his face so that they were eye to eye. She was just about to speak when he placed one single finger to his lips in a shushing manor. They laid there still, in the distance she finally heard the sound of leaves rustling.

As she turned to where she heard the sound come from, she could hear the loud sniffs of something large. It sounded as if the beast was only twenty feet away and by the way it was sniffing, it was searching for its prey. As if in sync, Alex and her husband slowly pressed their hands on their respective weapons. She was equipped with the same M1A that she used to kill the deer and her husband had his trusted AK47.

He always picked that weapon, and a quick smile brushed over her lips as she thought of his explanation of why. Out of the large, unnecessarily large, stockpile of guns, knives, and swords. He chose that gun. He would always say, *"I can't have my lady packing a heavier kick than me. I know it's the end of the world... but allow me some pleasures from the cultural insecurities I have become accustomed to!"*

Alex was brought back from her brief daydream by her husband's hand on her back. She focused on his face and read his lips. He was saying that on the count of three, they would crawl backwards to the tree he pointed to. She nodded then he grasped her arm. When she looked at him, he said,

"Quietly" with a very expressive facial expression.

She could not only hear the weight of the beast that was ahead of them as it slowly flattened everything under its paws, but she could almost feel the rumbling of its low growls. As it warned them, and any other animal in the vicinity, of its presence. Alex did not need to be reminded of their elusiveness if it was up to her, she would lay there in quiet and never move again. As if they were anatomically connected, Alex and her husband took turns moving slowly and methodically in the opposite direction from whatever was in front of them.

As they slowly reached the large tree that was very tall but weirdly thick for its height, they moved to the side that would block them from the creature's sight. Breathing a bit deeper, Alex let go of a small amount of tension. Still aware and in the situation at the present. Her husband got low and peeked around the tree trunk staying eye level to the grass line. He positioned himself back to Alex's side.

"We need to get out of the breeze then make our way to the bunker. We will go by the creek and cross at its shallowest part, it will be the long way, but we will make it home before dark."

Alex nodded. She was never a contentious person, but the trust she had for her husband went past any trust she had ever had for anyone in her whole life. She was alive not only because of him, but because she did what no one they knew had done. She trusted him unconditionally.

****

Loche ran into the house frantically. It was 1:42A.M. and the ruckus that he was making was sure to wake up his wife Alex; that was his intent. He had seen what was only considered a myth, and what he saw shook his whole perspective on reality. As the door slammed behind him, he didn't waste time to lock it. No one had followed him, he was sure.

He made the correct precautions and even went as far as parking six blocks away and creeping through backyards to insure he wasn't putting Alex in danger. Alex was the only thing on his mind. He had to get her as far away from whatever he had drawn them into. As he rushed up the wooden steps to their bedroom, he saw the lights flick on and he heard her soft but raspy voice call out to him.

"Adan? Eres tu?"

He rushed into the room bypassing her as she stood next to the door, and went straight for the lamp that she turned on that was sitting on the nightstand and turned it off."Grab a few change-of-clothes and meet me in the kitchen. We have to go NOW!"

He never meant to yell at his wife; she was his heart. But he needed her to know the seriousness of their present situation. Alex picked up on his haste and did as she was told without question. She knew that he was involved in some crazy things and he never kept secrets. She could remember the day when they talked about marriage and he told her about the Agency.

She recalled the fear in her gut the day he came home and told her of the lies he had exposed within the agency and how he had befriended a guy within another agency named Zion.

As she threw a few days-worth of outfits in a black duffel bag, she put on her most comfortable pair of jeans and a black sweater over the Navy tee she slept in. Adam was in the basement and she could hear what could only be described as chaos coming from his direction.

She grabbed her and Adam's toiletries and ran down the stairs. As she got to the kitchen, he was making his way from the basement. He grabbed her by the side of her face firmly, yet lovingly, and kissed her as if they had been departed for years. For a moment, she got lost in his lips, and as the kiss ended, they opened their eyes and made eye contact.

"Babe, I'm so sorry. We... we have to leave to your cousin in the tri cities!"

"Tennessee?" Alex said with her eyes wide in disbelief.

"Yes! I can't explain this now, but I promise I'll tell you everything once I feel we are safe"

He held up a thumb drive as if all the answers to the great mysteries of the world were on it.

"Do you trust me?"

Without hesitation and in her most purest heart, "Yes!"

They left out the back door with three duffle bags. One bag of her clothes, one bag of his clothes, and a third bag of whatever he grabbed from the basement. They went two blocks from their house, to a house that was empty with a sign on the lawn that said sold. Adam walked right up to the front door and lifted one of the rocks that were lining the path to the front door. He picked up a key and went to the door to open it.

He motioned with his hand for Alex to wait. She stood looking at the door for a few seconds, her head shaking in the disbelief of what was happening. The garage door opened, and she walked to see what was going on. Adam was in the middle of taking a beige tarp off of a 69 Chevelle. It was matte black with dark tinted windows and black rims. [

In fact, it was so black that it was almost undetectable in the darkness of the garage where it was parked in. She walked over and as she made her way towards Adam, she let her hand slide over the curves of the car.

"Is this... Papa's?" She asked, never taking her eyes off the car.

"Yes... I bought it from the guy, who bought it from your mother after your father died. I was going to tell you. There's so much to tell you!" He sighed.

Alex wasn't angry about anything. Her curiosity and confusion had all gone quiet. She was lost in memories of driving with her papa. "We need to go, babe." Adam whispered as to not jolt her out of her obvious daydream.

He opened the door and threw the bags in the back seat. As he placed his first foot inside the car, Alex firmly placed a hand on his shoulder. He turned his head to look at her, with a half-smile on her face, "I'll drive... bro." She said condescendingly.

Adam handed her the keys then walked around to the passenger side and got into the car; quickly putting on his seat belt. Alex adjusted her mirrors and buckled her seat belt as well. She gave a slight pause after placing the key in the ignition and turning it.

The engine rumbled inside the whole garage as it turned on. She unknowingly had a huge smile as she shifted the rebuilt manual transmission into first gear and released the clutch while evenly pressing the gas like her papa showed her.

The tires chirped then grasped the pavement as the engine roared and they sped off heading east to Tennessee.

Chapter Thirteen

C.R.E.A.M (Cash Rules Everything Around Me)

*T**hings change.* A simple reality for some, but for Kelia it was a hard truth to swallow. She had always been the master of her own fate, or so she believed. She planned everything out to a T. Her whole life had been one plan after another and was by her idea, perfect.

Even in the chaos of battle, the thing that kept her alive was that she knew, without a doubt, everything that should happen down to the tiniest placement of her footing to detailed placement of her weapon loadout. But the present situation she was in was not in any of her plans. The base she was currently trapped in was in close proximity of the nuclear fallout. All of the Zion soldiers, support staff and leadership, that was attached to the base three years ago on D-day, were accounted for except Profett; who disappeared hours before the blast. They had all made it to the fallout shelter miles under the base.

To call this a resistance military base would be a mistake. After D-day, most Zion fighters saw themselves as defeated. Their mission was to protect humanity from the evils of the world. As cities were burned and lakes dried, it was obvious to Zion that they had failed. In three years, the base slowly turned into an unorganized civilization.

With each passing month of their isolation, the base's military bearing dissipated. Uniforms slowly turned into just clothing. Signia medals were taken off as well as name tape. Most people walked around in civilian attire. The chain of command was cannibalized into a more simpler leadership.

The armory was locked, and only a few people had a key. Due to survival being the greatest enemy, no one cared. More useful skills were traded for battle skills. Generators need to be maintained, electrical circuits needed attended, food need to be prepared, the people need to be self-sufficient. Due to the fact that the world had end and missions were cancelled indefinitely, there were tactical wings in the underground fortress that were completely abandoned.

This is where Kelia isolated herself, in the midst of cobwebs, flickering lights, and depression.

Kelia sat on the right front side of a large rectangular desk. The desk was at least twenty feet long with ten chairs on each side and a large chair at the front where her father would sit. On the table was a holographic screen that would be used to plan an attack or whatever mission was being discussed. That was now just a dark screen surrounded by an oak trim.

On top of the screen were papers that had been placed down in front of the members of the last meeting before the demons had shown up at the front gates. The papers were either in a nice pile or scattered slightly. She wondered if she had done that in one of her anger fit,s she would have randomly, or if they were from the panic that the leaders had in the initial blast. The room she was holding up in was large and lined with various tactical terminals and informative equipment, that is normal of a remote command station.

Kelia had made this room her living quarters. Within the first few months of the fallout, when the chain of command still existed, she and the other leaders spent hours inside the command station. The first priority was to find out what had happened, the second was to find out casualties, then there was the issue of finding out the enemies' movements. But slowly at first, then quickly, everyone left her, and only her to worry about these things. Most leadership felt that it was becoming a waste of time and that they should focus on survival of the people in the shelter.

"Survival... Bunch of bitches... SURVIVE! That is all you are worthy of."

The words came out as a snark to herself and grew into a yell as she threw the plate that was in her reach at the large double glass doors in the entrance of the room. The plate broke without leaving even a dent on the large bullet proof doors. She slammed her hands down on the desk. The small pile of dishes to her right shook and clanked from the strike. She liked this room because of the space, well, that is what she told anyone that asked.

Her real reason was that the room still gave her purpose. It reminded her of who she was, who she still is, and most importantly it gave her a belief that she could one day return to that person.

Kelia put her head down on the desk and began to sob. Before the blast, she only remembered three times that she cried. After a year of living like she was living in this new apocalyptic world, she could only remember three times that she didn't. She felt weak. She raised her head with tears flowing from her emerald green eyes to look at Profett's chair.

"Daddy... I know I always rejected your advice and at times your voice was the most annoying thing I would hear," a slight smile creased in the corners of her tear-soaked lips.

"But I need you. I need you here with me... DAMN IT!! We all need you and where are you now? You disappeared at a really convenient time."

She threw another dish at his chair. And dropped her head down as the tears poured out and her sobs amplified.

"I... I just..." she sniffed up her sadness and straighten her posture.

Looking at her father's chair as if he was sitting right in front of her. She paused, thinking of what she really wanted to tell him. What she hadn't told him in years. As the words made their way from her heart, and the vibration started to form in her vocal cords, and the words started to form on her lips. A light buzz was heard from one of the terminals.

Kelia's sharp senses shook her out of her sentence and she quickly rose up and headed to the terminal which was now flashing a red indication light. As she approached the terminal, she saw that one of the safe houses had been activated. The terminal was only used to monitor the safe houses that were so incognito that only five people knew of their existence. To someone not in the know, this terminal was for tracking agents in the field. But she knew of its dual purpose.

She pressed in her security code and navigated the touch screen to pull up the location of the alarm. At first the screen did not comply with her request. The dust, and the fact that it was running on a backup generator that was stand-alone from the rest of the base, made the equipment's CPU very slow. After frustratingly tapping her finger on the location of the alarm multiple times, the screen finally opened up the image of the safe house. She first looked at the safe house's location.

It was in Kansas, Bunker 21. She then took manual control of the surveillance cameras and tried to find out who, or what, had triggered the alarm. Her first thought was that maybe an animal like a racoon had ran across a doorknob. But what the camera scan had revealed almost stopped her heart. She froze, looking at the image in front of her; not knowing what to do in that moment, she did what her body's reaction allowed, she swallowed a little bit of spit and a large portion of air in a gulp. Her head shot up in disbelief and determination.

"Holy shit! Get it together, Eleven."

Being called by that name sounded weird, even though it came from her mouth, due to her not being active in the espionage community in the last three years but she was in shock. She stood there frozen in disbelief for a little bit then she turned, grabbed her dirty dishes that were not in pieces and walked outside the double doors headed to, well, she had no idea who to talk to but someone else needed to know what she saw, someone else needed to experience the glimpse of hope that was revealed on the terminal.************

The air was brisk and sharp. It had been 3 hours of hiking the mountainous terrain and Alex was sure that an hour of the journey was spent circling the entrance to the bunker. She rolled her eyes, the thing she admired most about Adam was what annoyed her the most about him also. Adam was a methodical man. Everything he did had purpose and intent.

She loved this about him when it was describing the things he did to please her, but in a situation like this, it was so frustrating. Though his methods did keep them alive, so it was not something to speak up about.

The entrance to the bunker was well hidden, it was underneath a bush that was thick with thorns it camouflaged the barb wire Adam had laid down, and if you didn't know the right approach, then you would be tangled in the thorn bush and barbwire wishing you had minded your business.

As always Adam motioned for Alex to go first. He was always a gentleman but she knew that this was because if anything or anyone had followed, Adam could confront the treat while Alex secured the perimeter from inside. They had a secret entrance that he would use if he survived that only he and she knew about. She shook her head thinking that there was no way she would leave him, and she knew in her heart, he knew this was true also.

Once inside, Adam pressed the large red button on the side of the manhole cover before descending the 4 stories to the bottom entrance to the bunker. This button enacted the motion sensors placed all angles outside the bunker. When Alex first heard of the motion sensors she laughed, she thought that they would be going off constantly due to the animals that were sure to be roaming the woods. But that wasn't the case at all. There had only been one time the motion sensors had activated, and it was due to a high wind dust storm that was so strong they saw it uplift a few trees before it took out two cameras.

The dust storms were a product of the nuclear blast. Any plain lands that were close enough to the blast were decimated. Hell, most of the mountains that once were teeming with vegetation were left with shrubs and stable trees. The lack of vegetation allowed for winds to pick up the resting dust and debris. That wind would eventually get large enough to create a spiral of dust that was unchecked and begin to make a twister of damage; these storms would be accompanied by rainless thunderstorms and lighting, making them very dangerous and large.

The entrance to the main bunker that they lived in was massive. It had a large corridor that was wide and tall enough to drive a tank through. And from the entrance that Alex and Adam used, it was still a quarter mile walk to the large garage door. Once they made it to the door, Alex typed in the four-digit code, which was 3109 (March 1st 2009) their wedding day., and the large garage door opened from the bottom lifting up into the wall. They let it lift just enough that they could hunch underneath and pressed the green button on the other side to lower it.

Once inside, Alex immediately felt safe. She didn't notice how anxious she was until the garage door closed. She immediately grabbed hold of Adam and embraced him in a long hug. He was startled at first by the gesture. Not like he was not used to his wife being affectionate, he was just thinking of other things at the time.

The hug brought him back to the now. He returned the hug. He tried to say he loved her, but he was so used to not speaking while out in the world, that the words got caught up in his throat.

"I love you too!" She said startling Adam even more.

Their bond was strong. He and her were truly meant to be. They were like two versions of the same person to the point that words were not needed in most situations, they just knew what the other was thinking.

"That is so creepy, still." Adam gave a visual shudder.

"Why? I just knew you were going to say you loved me. I could tell by how you grunted that you just couldn't get it past those stubborn lips of yours. So, I said it back."

"Yeah, you know these lips of mine," he said with a mischievous smile, "I wish we would have gotten that deer. It would have made for a good addition to the beans and veggie mix you are so well at preparing," Alex slapped his arm.

"You love that dish! You haven't complained about it once since we been down here.""I tell you all the time how much I... Ouch!!" This time Adam jumped from the pinch she placed right under his under arm.

"You are talking big for someone who will have to eat that dish tonight!"

Adam slumped down in a sad realization for a quick minute, then cracked a huge smile.

"Well, I just like to watch you walk around and do womanly stuff!"

"Well, if you change that sour attitude, I might walk around in something that you really like and do 'womanly stuff'" She said the last two words while making air quotation marks.

In all her beauty, she was horrible at the art of seduction. Adam actually loved that about her. It made her extremely cute and innocent.

They walked past the Humvee and the Jeep that was parked along the other side of the garage. When they walked past her dad's old Chevelle, Alex lightly let her hand brush across the curves of the frame like she did as a small girl. She smiled thinking how her father would fake agitation and tell her that he would "*Use her little hiney to buff out any fingerprints she left on his baby!*"

There were only three vehicles in the garage area. The rest of the space was used to store canned food and nuts, and at least forty barrels of gasoline. Once they made it to the door and typed the same code in, it was more of feeling home. The bunker was huge. It was at least four miles in all directions but had sectioned rooms for at least one thousand people.

They only used the first room that was a main rest area. Through the few months they had to prepare for the disaster, they had made the place look like as much of a home as they could. The first month was used to get basic materials and food. Every day they would, box by box, move necessities to their bunker.

At first, they worked during the night, trying not to raise suspicion. But after Alex's family, that they stayed with, realized that they were taking boxes to the woods, they told the family of their plans, and proceeded to work at all times of the day, relentlessly. Alex remembered how her family would pull her aside while Adam slept and try to talk sense into her.

She was sure they meant well, but she trusted her husband to no limit. She even tried to get her family to join them. She came from a humble, two-generation American and Mexican family. They were prideful and cautious of any white people. The fact that Adam was the whitest man they had ever seen did not agitate them, but it did make them curious of the crazy gringo's mental health.

After the first week of the third month, she was wondering if the man she loved and trusted was crazy by her damn self. She just kept at it, faith is not losing doubt but keeping hope when doubt arises. They had managed to get all types of furniture and memorabilia. Adam allowed Alex to decorate the large room and their sleeping quarters without a word said.

He made a smaller room as his man cave and put up his favorite soccer team's paraphernalia, Manchester United. Their bedroom was what seemed a mile down a large hall that had doors on each side. It was the last door and the largest room. The room was more likely a room for a high-ranking officer. It was in an oval shape, which she dreaded, but it had a large bathroom with a shower and a bath.

They used a golf cart to get back and forth. One for her which she painted black, and one for Adam which he left its original color. Though she had a short time, she had made it as homely as she could with the few resources, they had available.

Through kissing and coercion, she convinced Adam to start the meal while she took a bath. She wanted to be clean for his dessert. She soaked in the tub of bubbles as she thought of Adam. She felt a slight ping of self-disdain, as she thought of the world outside the bunker, but it was short lived due to her mind returning to what she loved most in this world. The tall, manly, man of fire red hair, Adam.

****

Death to most is just a reflection of their lives. Some only see death as torment; their lives are wasted on what they can attain. They preoccupy themselves with material objects and comfort. Then suddenly they die, and they only feel the want that they had on the earth. They live wanting and trying to gain then boom, they have a heart attack, or have a fatal accident and they are dead.

Their immediate appearance in the world of the dead is shocking. No one is quite ready for the spirit world, and most people's souls are so connected to the material world they try to associate. An example of this can be found in dreams. The fact that there is no need to sit in a dream, yet dreams contain chairs and other objects for the mind to relate to.

Most people are not in tune with their spirit or the spiritual world, so they immediately try to create a construct of what they remember to bring them comfort. But these constructs are not divine. They lack the breath of the creator. The illusions they create end up turning into loops of horror, due to the fact that the soul that created it is fragmented with trauma. Eventually, the soul realizes the loop and the falsity of their construct and they are then approached by their ancestors, or guardian angel, Elohim, Orisha, and they are offered a chance at redemption.

Only after they realize their want is not material, but spiritual, can their angels come to their rescue. They are told that they can return to earth and try again for peace. The catch is that they will not remember who they are and that they have to work with other souls to gain their salvation. They then congregate with other lost souls and make plays and plans on how they will help each other in the next chance at life. When all the plans are made, they jump back into the darkness of chaos, the womb, and are born again; to try to fulfill their mission and become worthy of peace and rest.

For others who are more adept with their souls. Death is not as bad. The crossover is immediately assisted by their ancestors and angels. They are embraced and celebrated. Their souls are then taken to meet the creator where they are told the secrets of life and death.

They are then given a choice. They can rest with the creator and become one in the kingdom of what most would call *Heaven* or select another mission and become ancestors. Some choose to forget, then fight to remember as they return to a reality to help usher other souls into the light.

For Sparks, none of this pertained to his reality of death. Sparks was different, he was given the death of a god. This meant that his soul and body stayed intact. He could walk the spirit and natural world alike. What some have believed where Gods and demigods were only Angels and Men who were blessed by the creator to do marvelous works.

All the angels and forces of nature were given tasks in the beginning to help man and other life on Earth evolve. For most people that believed in religion, this concept would seem sacrilegious, but it was the truth. Some angels were for the animals, tribal people would call them nature spirits. Some angels were meant to help man. Throughout history and cultures, these angels were given different names and labels.

Sometimes they were called gods, sometimes they were called spirits, but they did their jobs without fail and always did what the creator required of them. Though they were different from humans they still die, although sickness and fleeting health would never be the reason, wars and violence were not above them. In fact, war was their main job since the defiance of Lucille. The truth was that although Lucille was not evil incarnate, she was an agent of chaos. And the war between good and evil was nothing more than the war that started once God spoke order in the chaos, and that chaos trying to regain its grip in the void.

Death was not the gloom that she presented itself to most people. For Sparks, Death was his destiny. Dethia would hold him and kiss him. Whenever, and it was a few times, Sparks needed space, she would leave him to himself. She didn't worry about him leaving because she had him for eternity.

Sparks, madly in love, would never leave Dethia. She was perfect. She held his lust and love in her hand. Yet she never held it over him for power, instead she held it close to her heart for protection. Sparks had never felt a connection to anything, as strong as he felt his connection to death; she was his life, as crazy as that sounded in death.

Anything or any place they desired they could manifest with a word. They would make love on a huge bed in the Bahamas, then in the next moment, watch the star's birth, die and be reborn on the tip of the great pyramids. They never tired, yet they would sleep for days in each other's embrace. They were never hungry, but with a snap, any dish they wanted would appear. For Sparks, the reality of the fight he once lived was just a vague memory.

Through all the love and wonders of companionship that Dethia had, until now, never experienced came a grave price. Dethia had one job in the order appointed by God. She was to take life from those whose time had come. Most might think that this job pertained to only human life, and most people would be wrong. This was her universal charge while she did her job well and efficiently, she was currently in the whirlwind of love and she needed no help or exit plan.

Dethia and Sparks were laying on a cloud that floated over present day Panama. They usually never visited Earth but Sparks had always wanted to go to Panama City. As they laid naked and unashamed, Death placed her hand on Sparks cheek. Sparks was deep in thought but the moment he felt her touch he turned his head to face her beauty.

"You haven't talked to me for hours, love. Are you already through with me?" She said with a mischievous smile.

As she spoke to Sparks, her hand that was resting on his chest moved to lower regions.

"Well, you see... You have your answer to that question in your hand." He smiled his own mischievous smile and moved closer as he embraced her small frame in his grasp.

They kissed passionately. As they parted, Sparks once again shifted his eyes to the place that had him deep in thought earlier.

"See, my love. There you go again. What on earth has you so intrigued that you would take your eyes off the very last, most beautiful, creature a man will see?" She smiled before bursting into a loud heartfelt burst of laughter.

"Oh, brother you are the only one that laughs at their own jokes... with or without company," he returned his gaze on his queen.

"I... just don't understand what is happening to Earth. I know Lucille blew up the reactors and a large chunk of humanity was killed. But, where did they go? I mean, you have been here with me the whole time."

He had a face of confusion when he looked into Dethia's eyes. She hated that he was always so cute. Everything she did was like magic to a child. She would teleport them to another world just for the amazement in his eyes. She even shared her "*magic*" with Sparks, training him in the ancient ways.

She looked up to the sky with the back of her hand on her forehead while she laid on her back. She pulled in a breath,

"Well, love... The ones whose bodies were destroyed by the blast are wandering aimlessly and confused in the shadow realm."

Sparks turned his head and looked back at Dethia. He remembered the fight with the ninja and Jin in the shadow world. He closed his eyes trying to calm himself from the traumatic flashback. Dethia, as if she knew he had gone to a place unpleasant in his mind, caressed his cheek as she continued with her answer.

"Others that died or for all those that will die from now on will walk the earth in pain and sorrow. They are dangerous cause their pain has driven them to madness. Their only objective in life is to make those that live, join them in their hurt," she paused then looked deep into Sparks still questioning eyes. "Why? Why don't you collect their souls like before?"

Dethia cracked a slight smile,

"Well, for now, that ain't my job!" She winked at Sparks before giving him another long passionate kiss.

"This place has gone to the rats!" She said looking down from on top of the cloud.

"Let's leave... I want to show you the waterfalls on Diel!"

"Diel?"

"Yeah, Diel!"

And like that they blinked away!

Chapter Fourteen

B.O.B.B.Y.

There was an unusual chill in the air. He sat in the main Wardroom on the Elohim base, lightyears away from his home planet. His cold aging hands looked pale blue against the light of the fluorescent map below him. He leaned in to get a closer look at the screen before him. His palms faced down on the screen and his hard, dimmed eyes looking intently at the image.

He was looking for movement, any movement. But as always nothing. No signs of life, not even a tumbleweed.

"Not even a damn tumbleweed?!" He said with raspiness just under his breath.

But as the words sounded, the anger and frustration were evident. For three years, Profett kept the same routine. He would wake up around 6am. He only knew it was 6am because of the Apple watch that he modified to run on earth's sun cycle. As for Nebula, there was only one sun, no moon, and the sun stayed at the highest peak.

It was a symbol of the Most High. Nebula was the home of the Elohim and the one God they served; without question, never left their presence.

Once awake, Profett would rigorously train in the positions and poses of the universe. He would dip low with his legs straight to give honor to the source, then he would slowly bend and twist his body. His movements were slow and intentional. Each position mimicking nature or the cosmos. After his intense stretching and core strength-building, he would train himself for hours of various martial arts and weapons.

His strongest mastery of a weapon was the bow staff and long spear. It was said that with a Spear in hand, even the hounds of hell feared him. His movements were quick and graceful. No one knew Profett's age, but some would say that from the fables he was involved in, he had to be in his late sixties and nearing his third century. Watching Profett move, no one would dare underestimate this old man.

After his intense training, Profett would have a very light breakfast and then head to his room to meditate. During his meditation, peace was seldom attained. He found it hard to silence all the doubts and regrets he harbored lately. The rest of his day till the evening was spent at the console. The console that he was at presently.

He wished, no prayed, for a sign of life. Yet all that he saw was sand. As he hunched over the map, he felt a large hand grasp his shoulder.

"Brother, I hope you have found some sort of peace in your stay."

Ki said as Profett turned slowly to meet his gaze. Ki stood almost eight feet tall and without any slouch. Profett looked as a child standing next to him even with Profett being six foot four inches and having a well-muscular frame, athletic and sleek like a Jaguar. Profett had been around angels for most of his life so he stood tall and looked at Ki with a stern but withered look in his eyes.

"I... How can I find peace?" The words left his lips with no life, "Everyone I love. The only thing I love..." his eyes once again made their way to the map.

He turned back to Ki, realizing his posture had mimicked his mood, he straightened up like a soldier.

"I am sure there is a good reason I was called back here, when everyone needed me on Earth. So, I came. That's what we do, we obey!"

The last sentence left his lips with more vigor but less strength then he thought it would have. Ki looked away so Profett would not feel shame. There was no need to feel shame. Following orders from the most High was guiltless and faith that the most high had the best interest in mind was the only challenge a man would fight internally.

"Well," he cleared his throat to indicate the segue, "I have orders for you that are bitter and sweet. Which would you prefer first?"

Profett rolled his eyes. He was in no mood to play any games and for that matter, no news or orders could take him lower than he was or bring him out of the mood he had been in for the last three earth years.

"I could care less what order you say it in, so, let's get on with it please."

There was no emotion in Profett's voice for the statement to sound rude. Ki looked into his eyes. The pain and guilt were strong. For a minute he thought of not telling Profett the orders and finding someone else. He not only thought that it could give Profett the time he needed to heal, but he also did not trust Profett in this current state.

A man hurt is an animal waiting to strike. In this emotional state, Ki knew humans were dangerous and unpredictable. Yet, these were not the orders from the Archangel that could be respectfully challenged. These orders came from the King himself.

"You are to head down to Earth, unattended. You must activate bunker 21 to create a diversion and then make your way to Lucille's base of operations in Arizona. We need you to get recon and plant a few devices near the complex for our final assault."

Ki paused to let that sink in.

"Profett, when you set off the alarm at bunker 21, it will not only alert an investigation from the enemy. It will also alert the few members of Zion held up in the base you commanded from. Kelia will know you are back,"

Profett's eyes shined with hope.

"You are to make no contact with anyone. Profett, ANYONE."Ki said the last part slowly and deliberate. Profett nodded his head as he walked away silently.

He briskly walked down a few hallways to the door of his room that opened up automatically as he approached. He changed into his most stealthy uniform he had. An outdated, black, fighter pilot jumper that was form fitting.

He wrapped his head and face in a black shamek, then lowered the cloth from his face. He laced up his black sound-resistant combat boots. The tailor had placed pieces of cloud inside the liner and once he slipped them on, he thanked her aloud. Profett then walked down the corridor to the weapons room. He would need a quiet but deadly arsenal and a few things that goes boom, in case things got a bit heavy.

****

Alex stood naked in front of the large vanity mirror outside of the shower. She rubbed the condensation from the mirror adjacent to her face. She leaned in and examined her face. She looked at her long hair that was draping down her shoulders and towards her back. Her curls were heavy from the wetness.

She would be amazed at times to see her hair so long. She wore it pulled back and in a tight neat bun most times. Adam called it a military bun. She hated it at first but after all the training she had been doing, she found it very practical and it eventually became comfortable. She returned her eyes from the split end she held in her hand and back to her face.

She had a beautiful cinnamon tone. Her tia said she carried the blood of the Aztecs and all the magic it held. She examined her eyes, she could see the years of stress that the last three years accumulated on her. But most of all, she saw something that almost startled her. Looking back at her were two fiery hazel eyes that commanded respect, they looked as though they witnessed, experienced, and survived much. She looked into them shocked but now with understanding.

She thought of the time when Adam had told her he noticed the change in her eyes. They were arguing about a certain exercise they were doing. The exercise was to breach a room and clear it. Adam had shown her what to do, and to be honest she had kind of blanked out due to the rigorous training they had already done during the day. When they walked through the exercise, she went the wrong direction causing Adam to accidentally shoot her with a sim bullet.

It hurt like hell, and her immediate response was to turn and shoot him back. They argued for a brief minute when Adam stopped while staring in her eyes. He looked away for a minute then said that they had done enough for the evening. Later that day, while they cuddled in their bed, Adam told her that she looked fierce and that he felt it was unwise to poke an angry tiger. They laughed and then made love.

Alex could now understand what he saw. She wiped the rest of the mirror with her towel then let it fall to the floor. Her body was in the best shape she had ever seen. Her breasts were full and taught. Her waist was thin, allowing the curves of her hips to show.

Her legs were muscular, and she was quite venous. Her admiration for her body was interrupted by a distant crash. As if Adam had dropped something in the living space. She quieted her breathing and opened up her senses. Paused, listing for anything that would raise suspicion.

Alex shook her head and returned her gaze at the mirror. She smiled a seductive smile at herself. She then turned and made her way to the closet. She picked out a pair of her favorite stretch jeans and a flannel style button down shirt that was also form fitting. As she tied her boots, she spoke to herself.

"Adam, you, clumsy man. You would kill yourself if I wasn't here to watch over you!" She stood up and made her way to the noise.

Alex was approaching the kitchen. As she turned the corner, she was in mid-sentence,

"Babe, what in the world did you break now?" She made her way around the corner, but Adam was not there. She looked around in confusion then spotted the dish on the floor broken. She shook her head and went to the cleaning closet to grab a broom and dustpan.

"I swear," she said with agitation in her voice,""I am more like your mother every day... And you sir, are one large child!"

She swept up the pieces and placed them in the trash. She then put the broom and dustpan away and started to make her way to the garage.

"Adam!" she said loudly.

"It would be nice if you cleaned up after yourself!"

She knew that if he had made his way down the corridor to the garage, he did not hear her. The statement was more for her than him. As she walked down the corridor, she saw something shiny along the path. She walked up to the object laying on the floor. It was a long drill bit.

As she looked at it, she noticed that there was some crimson liquid in a small coin size pool just beneath the point. As she got closer, she saw that the tip was also covered in the same liquid. She reached down to pick it up and her heart sank a bit; it was blood. She straightened up and looked down the corridor. There was a bit of freight in her stomach and she moved slowly down the rest of the hall trying to maintain silence.

Alex made it down the corridor and into the garage. She looked at her father's Chevelle Adam had been working on. He had been putting ballistic armor on the car. He had been working on the vehicle for days now, and had gotten most of it done. There were only a few screws left to fasten the rear plate along the trunk.

She searched around with her eyes. He was nowhere to be found. She looked to the large door at the entrance of the garage, and her heart sank. She walked over to the door and looked out to the entrance of the bunker, and both doors were wide open. Alex started to spin.

There was no way Adam would leave these doors open. Plus, he would never just leave without her, or at least telling her. She felt anxiety wash over her. Her stomach felt heavy, her palms felt cold just as she was close to fainting, she remembered what Adam would say,

"The first thing in any stressful situation is, don't panic!"

Alex closed her eyes and breathed. She had to think where could he be and what happened? As soon as she calmed herself, she remembered the tracking devices Adam had placed in their wedding bands. He said if they ever got separated, they could use the computers and tracking units to find the lost person. She opened her eyes and ran towards the ops room.She got to the room and pressed the code, and the door opened slowly. She tapped her fingers along the trim of the doorway in a very impatient manner. As soon as the door opened up enough for her to slide through, she sucked in her imaginary gut and slid in rushing to the main terminal. As she pressed the keyboard to awake the screen, she thought to herself out loud.

"What was the password again?" she thought.

Adam had told her that there were two very important passwords to remember.

"Was it Hermès? No... Hermès was the God of messages... that is for the coded messages to Zion if things hit the fan. I think this is a good time if any..."

She quickly typed a message to Zion using the code words Adam had taught her. Then she pressed enter and escape. She began to think again about the password for the tracking.

"Okay, Hermès is for messages. Ares is the god of war," that did not mean a thing, but it was helping her think.

"Aphrodite is the Goddess of love, but... I am sure it was... Artemis! Yes, Artemis the huntress!!"

She typed one the password and a giant map showed up. It was a map of the southern US with Tennessee, Georgia and Alabama magnified. Moving very fast was a red dot.

"Damn, babe. You are moving so fast! Who has you?"

She synced the map to her watch and headed to the armory. When she got there, she equipped herself with her M1A rifle, a Glock 9 for a side weapon, two snub nose 357 security 6 in a double holstered snug vest that acted as a bulletproof chest plate as well. She put her flannel back on and then grabbed her long hunter's knife.

She held the knife up admiring it for a brief second before sheathing it on her opposite hip as her side arm. Grabbing a tactical backpack, she put as many magazines as she could carry on each gun. Adam usually carried the lion's share of ammunition; she could only carry about six magazines of each weapon and four of each in her magazine pouches on her tactical vest since that was really enough for her.

Adam always said that if a fire fight had to be engaged then that meant that it was the last end. They practiced stealth for survival and she was very stealthy. She grabbed a few bricks of C4 and headed back to the garage.

Once at the garage, she opened the trunk of the Chevelle. Just as she suspected, Adam had another bag of ammunition and a few more M4 rifles and large caliber pistols in a duffel bag. Next to the duffel bag, was a shotgun with a box of slugs next to it. She closed the trunk and grabbed the drill.

She finished drilling the last part of the shield Adam was working on then looked at her watch. The map was small, but the red dot was still blinking. She pinched the screen to zoom in. Adam had moved at least 200 mile in the time it took her to get prepared. She thought that maybe they were in some fast vehicle.

She jumped in the driver's seat and turned the engine on with a roar. She pumped a bit of gas in the engine to prime it a bit then popped the clutch. As she peeled off to the main entrance, she gripped the steering wheel with anger."Babe, I'm coming!"

Chapter Fifteen

SHIMMY SHIMMY YA

Adam woke up with a pounding headache. His thoughts, other than the pain, were disoriented. Where was he? What happened? What is that smell? The smell was musty and damp, like an unkept dog. He needed to think.

He calmed his nerves and did an exercise he remembered learning in the survival course he took with the Agency. Gunny would water board or put the trainees in head locks and have them do calculus or Geometry for their freedom. Gunny would always say that in order to think under pressure, you had to free your mind from the stress of the situation. Basically, you had to literally restart your brain with the trauma being your new baseline of operation.

Okay," Adam thought to himself, "I am Adam. Adam Loche, former IT specialist in the Navy. My wife... Adam stopped. My wife! Holy shit!!"

Adam was hit with a wave of anxiety. What happened to Alex? Was she alive? Anger shot into his body. Without thinking, he kicked and violently flailed his body around. His movements were emotional, but they served a purpose.

He was able to feel out where he was. The constraints on his body were tight and his hands were bound behind his back and his feet were tied to his hands with a long rope that allowed just enough slack for him to stand and move his feet one foot apart from each other. He was blindfolded and gagged. He kicked around a bit more until he heard a low and chest vibrating growl. It was a warning.

Adam had been around enough animals in his life to know the tone and severity of a growl like that. He stopped moving, he had gathered all the information he needed with his movements. He could tell that he was laying on a cot of some sorts. He could feel the increase and decrease of altitude and hear the pounding of the propellers to know he was in a helo.

His kidnappers were seated in front of him. He calmed his breathing to see if he could catch the rhythm of movement in the cabin of the helo. He knew that there was at least a pilot, and by the size of the area he was laying in, a copilot. The growl was close, so maybe they had a dog with them of some sorts. He tried to think back to when he was attacked.

The back of his head immediately started to pound. That was it, he never saw a thing. They had hit him in the back of the head. He laid there in thought and confusion. The rhythmic pounding of the propellers vibrating his cot, and the sway of the helo's movements through the sky lulling the pounding of his head.

"How did they get past the motion sensors?" He spoke out loud but to himself.

****

Alex Swerved past an abandoned nissan. She pressed the gas and down shifted. Her anger now was roaring inside her like the engine of the fine-tuned beast that she was pushing down the abandoned highway. She looked down at her watch. The people that took Adam had to be in a helicopter.

There was no way they could be traveling that fast on the windy mountain roads. The tracker had them somewhere over Memphis and headed west. She figured that she would head in the western direction and wait to see where they stopped. This would make her behind, but it was the most logical since she could not physically follow behind a flying object. She had enough gasoline in the back seat and trunk to make it to San Francisco, but her only concern would be major cities and populated towns.

They had not really explored much besides the woods where they hunted food. Once, Alex and Adam had come up on a small township. They stayed away and used binoculars and her rifle scope to scout the town. From the distance, it almost seemed that the inhabitants were living a semi-normal life. Alex and Adam chose not to reveal themselves to the people, and even went as far as to move their hunting grounds, which was already twenty miles from the town, and twenty more miles south of the town.

The concern is that people create laws and rules in any type of society. Those laws are what binds the people to each other. It is like a group of people making friendship promises. Once those bonds of society are strengthened, anyone outside that society, inherently becomes the enemy or a threat to the bonds.

Alex was now crossing state lines into Missouri. She made sure to take smaller roads and avoid the big cities. A trip that should have been roughly, five hours, took her eight. Putting her back a whole state behind Adam.

"Damn!" she hit the steering wheel in anger.

Her frustration was boiling and when she looked back down at her watch. Something was odd, she slowed the car down to a stop. The red dot was not moving, so she thumped the face of the watch, but it still did not move. She moved the screen to enlarge the dot and she could see that it was just beyond the state lines of Missouri and Kansas. Alex grabbed the map in the back seat, and she mapped out the best route avoiding St. Louis and Kansas City. With a loud roar of the engine, she peeled out and headed for her course.

It took her from six in the morning to eight at night to cross Missouri, but she was nearing the state border. The road she was on was winding, with almost as many curves as the roads alongside the mountains. At certain points, if you looked through the trees, you could see where the road you were currently on would end up after the next turn. Alex was nearing just a turn. At the end of the turn, there was an intersection of the two smaller county roads.

In the distance to the right of the intersection, she could see lights. It appeared to be two vehicles, moving at a high speed. The vehicles were chasing each other. A few things Adam had upgraded were a switch on the tail pipes that reduced the cars sound by 85%. She flipped that switch as the car slowed to a stop just before the bend, and with enough vision space for Alex to see the movements of the two cars.

Another upgrade Adam had made was to spray the window of the car with a tactical spray that allows light to pass but not leave. This acted in dual purpose, the driver could see out without any lights, yet no lights reflected off the glass. So, along with the Matte black finish to the car including the armor augments, at night, the car was almost invisible. This meant that Alex could drive without lights and see fine but still be quiet and elusive when need be.

The two cars were nearing the intersection. It seemed that the first car, a bright red late-model Camaro, was being pursued by the souped-up pickup with armor plates. The car passed the intersection and Alex let out a breath of relief. The last thing she wanted was to be sucked up in some kind of back wood beef she had no idea was happening. She had to get to Adam.

She looked down at the watch again, and the dot still had not moved. The Chevelle slowly creeped around the bend. The two cars were now slowing down, and as Alex creeped to the stop sign, she saw why. There was a man-made roadblock that was made up of cars and broken trees. As the car stopped, the pickup slowed down and positioned itself to be a roadblock so the car could not reverse.

Breaking Alex's curiosity of the situation, another pickup speed by the intersection with two adult men riding in the back. This one was a Ford 1985 pickup that was tan with a white stripe along the side. It pulled up to the first pickup and positioned itself similarly.

Alex sunk down in the seat as if that would hide her from view. She was a Quarter mile from the stop sign and it was pitch black outside.

She was sure they could not see her. Yet even with the sound dampeners engaged, if she fed the car any gas at this moment, it was sure to be recognized. She figured she would just wait out whatever was going on and let it pass. Soon as they left, she would continue on to finding Adam. Just the thought of her husband almost made her forget any thoughts of reserve and gun the car, but she calmed herself and inspected the scene.

The first truck opened its doors and the two men jumped out with shot guns in hand. They were loud and celebrating as if they were on a hunt. From their movements they were not in control. That title was reserved for the man that exited the passenger side of the second truck. As soon as he took two steps towards the Camaro, the other men, five in total, made their way to stand beside him like hunting dogs.

"Quiet down, now! Quiet Down!" He said to his henchmen.

"We don't want to scare the two of them now, do we?"

"Boss, I really want the small one! Hu Hu!" One of the henchmen blurted out while making a stroking motion with his rifle towards the car.

"Now, Pete, that's what I mean by scaring them. We just want to talk!"

The Old man said loud enough for the people in the car to hear.

"Why don't y'all just come out of that car? There ain't nowhere to run now, is it?"

There was a pause and the driver side of the car opened up. Slowly, a leg came out followed by two small thin hands. The driver put her other leg out and stood by the opened car door with her hand up in a pleading motion. She was young, about twenty-two but no older than twenty-five. She had a slender body but was very curvy in all the parts that differ in male and female.

She had long blonde hair that she had tied behind her head with a few strains covering her face. She was dressed in brown boots and jeans that were tight. She had a grey shirt and a brown short leather jacket. She had tears in her eyes as she pleaded with the men.

"Please... Please just let us go!" she pleaded with the men.

"Please... We don't have anything valuable. We just want to get home!"

Her pleads amused the men. The leader looked at the woman emotionlessly.

"Now, this is the end of the world, young lady. And everyone has... something a man could use."

As he said the last part, his eyes swept greedily over Amy's body.

"You know, us men here could use a nice young lady like yourself and your daughter to... well, how should I say... Repopulate."

He said with a dirty smile building on the crack of his weathered dry lips. The rest of the men high-fived each other in celebration of the idea. One man raised his shotgun and let off a shot. The blast did not scare Alex but in response she grabbed the M1A in the passenger seat and chambered a round. Amy fell to her knees.

"Please! Please! I beg you. Don't hurt my baby! She is only 13 years old! Do whatever you want to me but leave her alone! Please!"

She was now on her knees with her hands clasped together.

Alex could not hear everything clearly, but she knew what this meant. These men were despicable and had all types of despicable thoughts going through their minds. Alex sat back and thought. As she thought, the men made their way to the women as they cheered and shot off rounds in their celebration. Alex had to help, she could not sit by and witness two innocent women get hurt.

The girl was only 13 but she had to get Adam. While the men were "*busy*", she could use the distraction to slowly drive away and be gone before anyone noticed. She looked at her watch again and the dot was not moving. When she lifted her head from her watch she happened to look where the cars were. The leader was standing over the blonde lady teasing her. He had pulled out his manhood, or what he probably called the little mushroom in his pants.

Alex turned away but as she did, she saw the child being pulled out the car by her hair.

"Okay, fuck this!" She opened the car door and got out the car with a rifle in hand.

Alex aimed at the man holding the child by the hair. She had put a 4x magnifier on the rifle before she left the armory. She really loved using iron sights, but in certain cases like this, seeing the drooling buffoons face fly back after she put a round in it was so gratifying. Like she had trained, Alex put her rifle at the ready and bent her knees. She aimed her rifle right to the side of the man's face then smoothly squeezed.

Bang! Bang!

The first shot went right to the side of the man who was grabbing the child's head. His body spun lifelessly to the ground. The man next to him watched for all but two seconds when his sight went from color to black.

The first shot got everyone's attention. It startled everyone involved and in the shock, they all watched the first man fall.

The second shot did exactly what Alex wanted it to do. When the men heard the second shot they all, except for the man who received the second well placed head shot, ran for cover behind the parked trucks. This was perfect and Alex used this to her advantage. With them hiding, they could not see her run full speed to their right, flanking their position. The leader looked at his men he had left.

"Y'all see where dem shots come from?"

The men shook their heads no. One man pointed towards the intersection. He was close to being right. The leader tapped the man next to him to look.

"Boy, take a gander and tell me what you see now!" The man looked at him reluctantly and the leader slapped him across the face. "What did I say?"

The man picked up his baseball cap that went flying off from the slap. He edged to the front of the pick-up he was hiding behind and looked towards the intersection. Besides the overgrown weeds that were swaying in the night breeze, he could not see anything.

He looked harder trying to adjust his eyes to the night and possibly see movement.

"Well, asshole?!" He yelled at the man.

"I... I don't see nothing boss!" He looked away to meet the leader's eyes.

Alex had made it to the other pickup and was now jumping on the wheel to the frame. Hands still gripping the rifle, she jumped from frame to frame across the bed of the truck, and then jumped straight in the air, spinning her body to face the unsuspecting man on the other end. The man spun around in fear. He was looking up at the barrel of a 308 coming down on him from the sky. His mouth started to speak,"Good mother of Je..."

His words were interrupted by the sound of a rifle and the impact of a rifle caliber close range. Alex slung the rifle to her back and grabbed her side arm off her waist before she hit the ground. Before the next man realized what had happened, she put five 9mm rounds in his chest. She then ran to her right where the child was crouched down hiding behind the car. The leader and the man next to him had started to open fire at her.

She hunched behind the car and placed the child behind her and also behind the wheels so she would have extra protection from a stray bullet. The shooting died down for a second and that was all she needed.

Alex first stood up and aimed at the henchmen. She put three well-placed rounds in his chest. In one quick and fluent move, she pulled her right arm back with her left one to copy.

She holstered the 9mm while unsheathing her hunting knife. As if working in perfect balance and physics, she used her momentum to fling the knife at the leader, hitting him just below the heart, piercing the rib cage, and rupturing the artery. The leader fell down to his knees. Alex walked slowly to the man. His vision was hazy and he grasped out to her for help.

Alex stood just out of his reach as he grasped out and fell down to the ground. He rolled over on his back, still grasping slowly, and trying to mouth out something. Alex kneeled over him like a deer she had shot. She placed her hands on the hilt of the hunting knife protruding out the man's chest.

"I would think, you, would see the perfect irony of all this. You like sticking things in women without their permission..."

Alex slowly turned the blade in the man's chest. His hands shoot up to grab her shirt. She did not flinch. She looked him in his eyes as they went blank.

"Now, a woman has fucked you to death!"

She ripped out the knife as blood spurted then drained from the wound in slowing rhythmic concession. Alex then wiped her knife off with the old man's shirt. She stood up and instinctually started searching the trucks for anything she could salvage.

****

Profett knew his orders from the king was to be taken seriously, and followed to a T. But this was personal. It was years of following orders that caused the distance between him and his daughter. His eyes welled up with tears thinking of all the times he spent, months if not years, in the field while his daughter was raised by friends of the family. He thought of birthdays and school events he missed.

If he had not already sacrificed everything for the cause, then there was nothing more for him to sacrifice.

His insubordination was subtle, but if he knew his daughter, she was definitely able to pick up on the clue. It would be obvious to her it was him. Although his detection by the cameras were brief and it showed no more than a man in a black jumper and scarf. Kelia would know exactly who it was and make her way to the states.

If the plan was to work, he would need her expertise in espionage and her tactical mind in field battle. Being honest with himself, he also really wanted to hold his daughter again.

Profett was just outside of the bunker's entrance. He positioned himself downwind but still in eye view of the door he had triggered.

In the distance, he heard a helo approaching. He knew that this was the agency and he had planned on it. Their main base was closer than Kelia and their main job right now was to squash any opposition left. The bunker was in a large wooded area, there were trees and brush everywhere. A perfect place to set an ambush, but that was not Profett's goal.

He was actually planning to wait the agents out and remain undetected. Any engagement of the enemy would agitate a beehive that was content and in belief that they were winning the war. The plan was to allow them that comfort while the few Zion warriors and the Elohim engaged in tactical assaults simultaneously causing confusion. Profett wanted to stick to that plan since he was the main one to fight for it to be used.

The helo's large searchlight lit up the clearing around the bunker. Only an expert pilot could land a helo in the clearing that left no room for error. With precision and grace, the helo landed smoothly. Profett was hidden there and had attached a few listening devices around the bunker and inside, just so he could eavesdrop on the agents. And maybe pick up a bit more intel.

The side door opened on the helo and two men in black tactical pants and sweaters hopped out. The first man looked up into the sky. Profett tried to make sense of his movement. He realized that the man was not looking up but rather using his nose to smell; he was a hell hound.While on Nebula, they had caught wind of genetically altered soldiers being created by Lucille. They were taking Williams' DNA and splicing it with some of the most dangerous and battle-hardened soldiers in her army. These men were ex Seals and Delta force. They were trained by the best to be the best. And now equipped with the DNA of the hellhounds, these men were the most dangerous men on the planet.

Possibly able to go toe to toe with an Elohim. But this did not scare Profett, he was a dangerous man himself. Yet, he did understand the advantages of being able to choose your battles. With the patience of a leopard looking to thin the herd, he waited.

"This is hunter 1 to the Pack, over."

"This is the Pack. We read you loud and clear."

"We have arrived at Bunker 21, beginning the search."

"Roger that, Hunter 1. Make it brief, the woman is only 45 minutes from your location. We do not want her meddling in our plans just yet. And she is to remain alive. Best course of action would be to remain unseen by her."

"Copy that. We will be in and out, headed back to the den in no time. Hunter 1 out."

Profett watched as the two men searched inside and outside the bunker. They were not thorough at all. They looked as if they were just checking by and had other engagements to hit. He looked more carefully at the helo. The helo was a military grade H175 airbus.

The sliding door was still open from when the men jumped out. Profett could see in slightly due to his angle and saw that there was a man strapped down to a gurney in the back. He leaned in to focus. He could see that the man's hands and feet were restrained and that he was awake. He must have been a captive and they were transporting him to a base.

Profett knew that the closest base with facilities to hold hostages was in Arizona. That was exactly where he was headed. As quick as the thought of him tracking this help to pinpoint their location came in his head, he realized that he was on foot. He moved quietly closer to the helo. Being careful not to get too close to the two men who were now checking the perimeter of the bunker.

When he was close enough to the helo, he pulled out a tracker and put a piece of gum in his mouth. It was a big chewing gum and it tasted horrible. He made it soft enough to be sticky but still firm and placed the small tracking unit inside of the middle of the gum. He then threw the gum hitting the helo close to the landing gear and backed away slowly.

Even if he could not drive there, he still needed to pinpoint the exact location of the base. As Profett was backing away he stepped on a twig. He felt the twig and heard the crunch and stopped in his tracks. He looked towards the bunker where the two men were searching. One man did something strangely familiar to Profett.

Although Profett was on the opposite of a helo whose propellers were still engaged, the man heard the sound of the twig. And although that was crazy enough, it was the way he moved that was familiar to Profett; like a hunting dog picking up on a sound in the woods.

The hellhound heard a noise and quickly looked at where he heard it from. It was on the other side of the helo.

"You see something?" He asked half-heartedly.

"I'll go check it out. You go back to the helo and get ready to leave. I think there is nothing here." He said while staring at the direction of the noise.

Both men headed to the helo then parted in different directions. One got inside and the other to check out the noise. He made his way around the helo in a safe distance and looked. There was not a bush close to the helo and the trees did not move other than by the wind. He raised his nose to the sky and took a huge sniff.

His eyes closed as if he could see through the smells. He stood silently with his nose flaring every now and again as if he was sifting through aromas. He lowered his head in the direction that Profett was now hiding. As he slowly opened his eyes he squinted as if trying to see through the undergrowth. He stood looking in Profett's direction and from Profett's perspective, looking at him.

Profett held his breath as if that could help him. A few seconds that felt like minutes passed when the sliding door opened and the other man yelled something at his comrade. Profett could not hear what was said over the helo but he figured it must have been important because the man turned away and jogged over to the door and jumped in. Before he closed the door, he looked once more in Profett's direction and slammed the door shut. The helo lifted up and elevated past the canopy, then with a lean, to make its way to its next destination.

Profett's body relaxed and he let out the breath he had forgotten he was holding. There was something abnormal about the two men. He closed his eyes and whispered the words Kamala. When he opened his eyes, he was looking at a huge screen that outlined his view. A voice only he could hear spoke.

"Hello, dear. Long time no see!" The voice was cheerful and sweet.

His heart skipped as he heard it and he quickly said.

"Kamala, disengage voice replies!" an audible chime confirmed his orders.

He shook the nostalgia from his head and got back to what he was doing.

"Engage the tracking map and place it in my upper right peripheral view."

A small map with a blue dot appeared in Profett's view. It stayed large for a second then got smaller and moved to his upper right peripheral view. When Profett looked at it directly, it became larger and to place it back, he just had to look up and to his right.

Profett climbed to the top of the bunker which was a small rock overview of a valley. In the distance he could see a small encampment that was surrounding a gas station that had a food mart attached. The sky was getting light and he thought that if he was to steal a car, he should probably use stealth and the little bit of night that was left. He leaped down and started to the encampment.

****

"Thank you! Thank you! Oh My God… Jess! Where are you baby?"

Amy was holding her ripped shirt together with one hand while she used the other to stabilize herself around the vehicle to Jess, her 13-year-old daughter. Jessica was still holding her ears and hiding behind the Camaro. Amy ran by her side and as she approached, she knelt down and simultaneously wrapped her arms around her daughter. Jessica's sobs became audible and Amy rocked back and forth telling Jessica everything will be alright.

Alex watched for a second still leaning in the driver side door of the black pickup. She could emphasize with the two, all she wanted right now was to get to Adam and wrap her arms around him and say it will be alright. As she thought about Adam, she hurried her search for supplies. She slammed the door shut and glanced down at her watch. The dot had not moved.

She breathed a sigh of relief but was still tense. Even though the helo had seemed to land, she was unsure if that was its final destination. She rumbled through her thoughts as she walked back to the Chevelle.

Did they stop for the night? Were they dropping Adam off at this location? Her pace quickened as anxiety from these questions built up inside her. She was close enough to her car to smell the fumes from the carburetor, when she heard Amy yell out.

"Hey, wait!" she ran towards Alex with Jess in tow.

"Please! Wait a minute!" she got just about ten feet from Alex then stopped. Alex stopped but did not face her.

"No need to thank me. Those men got what they deserved. I need to keep moving. I left some supplies on the front seat of the black pickup. Take what you need and grab one of those men's guns. Good luck and try to stay off the highways at night." She looked over her shoulder and then proceeded to walk to her car.

"No, wait. We have a township down the road. We were on our way there when these men attacked. Please we can help you. You don't have to travel alone, you don't have to keep moving." Amy said as she reached out to Alex.

"By the looks of things," she said as she looked back at the men lying dead in the street, "I can do just fine by myself. Besides, I am not alone. I am with my husband. I just have to find him." She said almost under her breath.

"Maybe we can help. Is he somewhere close?"

"He is somewhere outside of Kansa city near the Kansas Missouri border," Alex replied.

"Well, I grew up in the area. And my camp is right near there. Maybe we can travel together, at least to my camp and see if anyone has seen your husband?"

Everyone stood silently as Alex thought about the proposal. Alex turned around to face the two ladies. She looked at Amy, she was thin and blonde. Very pretty, in a down home girl next door way. Her body was in shape but not like Alex's.

Alex and Adam had trained hard for three and a half years. But Amy was thin where you want and thick in places you love. Jess was your typical teenage girl. She was sprouting into a woman but with the strong innocent child features. She boiled up a bit thinking of what those monsters would have done with this child.

She opened the car door without saying a word. She reached in the back seat and pulled out the shotgun and bag of shells that were laying there. As she emerged from the vehicle the two girls huddled even closer to each other when they saw the shotgun.

"Relax. Guns don't kill. Murder is committed from the intent of the heart." She copied Adam line for line.

He had told her this the very first time they went to the shooting range. Her heart sank a bit more as she put the weapon in the trunk. She shook the sadness out her head as she used the trunk door to mask her bewilderment from the two ladies. She slammed the trunk door shut and looked at Amy and Jess.

"Get in and let's go. I don't have much time!"

The two girls ran to the passenger door and Jess got in the back seat. Alex walked slowly to the driver's side door. She placed her hands on the door and looked at the watch. The dot had moved, and se took a deep breath. As long as she had the tracker, she could find Adam.

Maybe the attackers know people at the town she was headed to. She had to find out where they were taking Adam, and then why. She lifted the handle and opened the door. As she got in, she looked at Amy.

"I know there are no more laws, but I think you might want to buckle up." She flipped the limiting switch off and revved the loud engine.

❊❊❊❊❊❊❊❊❊❊❊

"I know what I saw! It was my father, in Kansas! I don't know what he is doing there but he let himself get caught on camera knowing that we would get the alarm. We all know just how elusive he can be in normal day to day activities. You are going to tell me that he would be that sloppy on a mission?!" Kelia was furious.

It had been ten hours of finding former council members who even care. Then rounding them altogether, and now arguing for them to allow her to take weapons and enough manpower to go to Kansas and investigate. She shuddered to think what would happen after they agreed, and she told them of the plan to get to America.

"Kels, please calm down. We can see nothing from this video. Sure, that looks like Profett but are we sure enough to allow valuable resources to leave this station on a whim?" Councilman Eve said.

"What do we need here?" Kelia said as she put her arms up in a questioning manor.

"We are in our own prison. No one is going to attack us here because we are not a threat to anyone." She rolled her eyes and sighed.

"That is correct! No one wants to hurt us, and we are safe!" councilman Evesaid with a smile and the elegance of a queen in her throne.

Kelia slammed her hands down on the large oval table where they were all seated. She stared into Councilman Eve's soul. The look was pointed at Eve, yet it was for everyone at the table. As she slowly let her eyes connect with everyone in attendance, she eased up the tension just a little to where she was now resting on her arms with her hands flat on the table.

"What have we become?" she said in a very low but very stern voice.

"We were humanity's last line of defense. We were the shield that stopped Lucille's plans. Now look at us." She waved her hand around the room to include everyone.

"We hide like roaches when the lights are on," her voice became more energetic.

"We, the protectors of the word, are afraid to leave the compound we call a fortress. We have enough ammunition and fire power in this bunker alone to bring the fight to any one of Lucille's bases, yet they are looked up in a room with at least three years of dust on them."

"If you don't want to join me in our...job, then, I will go alone! This meeting was never me asking any of you for permission! You can leave or stay, I don't care. I am going to Kansas to connect with my father and see how I can help turn this war!" she pointed to the door as she said the last bit of her comment.

Slowly, one by one, the council members left, avoiding all eye contact with Kelia as they passed. She rolled her eyes thinking how much of cowards they were. The last to leave was councilman Thomas. He stood there a bit longer as the others made their way out the door. Kelia thought, how could this pudgy man help her on a mission like this?

Most council members were older, high ranking generals and politicians that were at the base during the attacks. Thomas was one of the politicians they used to add sway in the UN meetings; he was no warrior. Thomas slowly walked over to Kelia looking in every direction like he had stolen something. He reached in his jacket pocket; it was a suit blazer that had elbow patches. It was colored off green from fading.

"I don't much agree with any of y'all," councilman Thomas said in a very indecisive tone. His voice was weak and nasally.

"But, I do hate seeing you mope around in this depressing funk you are in. You were always the most beautiful woman I had ever laid eyes on, but seeing you like this... Well, I'd say you are not even in the top ten on this base alone!" He smiled a joking smile and pulled out a set of keys from his pocket.

As he reached over to hand them to her, she could not contain the large smile that crept over her face. He was handing her the keys to the armory.

"I don't know whether to be thankful or offended? But thank you, Thomas!"

She grabbed the keys and gave him a large hug before running out the sliding doors.

Chapter Sixteen

Da Mystery of Chessboxing

The walk down to the small town was long. Profett moved at a steady pace and made it there in a few hours. His movements were elusive, he was not the only thing dangerous in the surrounding forest. He stayed low and unseen, sticking to the brush. When he finally made it close, he stayed just beyond detection of the town's guards, who were only recognized as guards, by the mix of weapons they carried.

The town consist of an assortment of caravans and campers parked in a spiral formation around the gas station. There was a large generator next to the station, bordered off with a chain link fence. The gas station was the center of town and more than likely the nucleus. He wondered if that was because they still had fuel resources. There were numerous fire pits going in front of most of the living spaces.

There was a tent section that was attached and covered with a large arrangement of tarps that had been sewed together. The tarp was fitted to four ten-foot polls. Then draped along a fence that bordered the back of the encampment. It was very close to morning and to the east, Profett could see that the sun was just about to peek over the horizon.

"It is probably best to wait till sunshine," he said to himself.

He was sure that any visitor would not get a proper greeting during the night. He would seem less threatening under the light of the sun. Profett had not been on earth for three years and in those three years, things had gone from turmoil to apocalyptic. Before he left, a middle eastern man, as himself, would always receive suspicious looks. Although he was; considered the world's top terrorist that was running the infamous Zion, Profett's identity was unknown.

The looks he got were purely discriminative. Being a person of middle eastern descent meant '*terrorist*' to most people. Even though most people's countries conducted a large percent of national commerce with middle eastern countries, or even the fact that most middle eastern people were in fact terrorised by the same terrorist. Profett scoffed a bit as he thought of the world's ignorance and fear. It alway baffled him when he would hear someone say that they praise Jesus and not Allah.

Allah only means God in Aribic, the same way as Jehovah means in Hebrew. What was even more amusing is that people create war and fight over their interpretation of God, the man they believe to be watching all while sitting on a throne. The whole time they are both right; God has presented herself or himself to numerous people for many reasons in the history of mankind. The way you can tell that this is true, is how all the stories of God are similar and the message is always the same, Love. Yet people and their ego see the differences and think about control and war.

As he let his mind wonder in this thought, he rubbed his chin. His hand stopped in a small amount of surprise. He patted his chin a few more times lightly and then giggled to himself. He had forgotten that he shaved his beard before he left the Nebula sector. Good thing he did, as he thought of his situation outside of a caravan or trailer park. There was no telling what the mindframe of these people were before the fall out.

The likelihood, through these few years of hardship and fear, that they gained a more diverse frame of mind was very low. He wouldn›t look like a normal American, but maybe he could pass as one of her former sub-culture subjugates. As he looked at the camp while eating a piece of dried fruit he brought with him from the training facilities in the Nebula sector, he saw a vehicle approaching roughly two miles from the town. He got lower as the vehicle came into proximity to his position. The vehicle was not easily detected and to the untrained eye, it would not have been visible when Profett first saw it.

He felt the energy, before he actually saw the vehicle. As he got a closer glimpse of it, he was amazed at the craft work. It was a matte black, late model car with ballistic plates placed strategically around the frame. He could see the craft work of the shielding. It was thin and placed so well that it didn't hinder the mobility nor the speed of the vehicle.

Every additional piece of metal was bolted to the frame just a quarter of an inch above the exterior. There were no lights and the windshields, at least the middle part that did not have shielding, were as black as the rest of the car. It passed by him speeding at what he could only imagine 80 mph. The engine was as quiet as an electric car. The guard that was nearby jumped back from the road he was watching and then ran after the car while making radio communication with the rest of the guards; warning them about the oncoming vehicle.

Profett stuffed the fruit bag back in his cargo pocket and jumped from the cleared patch he was seated in. He pushed past the brush. It was thick, but his movements were so fluid he barely made a sound. He briskly jogged towards the fence that was being watched by the guard. The whole town would be distracted by that armored vehicle and he would use this time to climb the fence.

He needed a vehicle, and fuel. This township would have to knowingly lend a hand, or unknowingly donate to his cause.

****

Alex eased on the breaks while revving the engine and down shifting. She forgot that she had kept the limiting switch on and was a bit disappointed from the lack of rumble her car gave when she downshifted. The drive to this little shanty was long and quiet. Amy and Jess said little, only giving the directions on how to avoid the cities they were getting close to in their travels. She was approaching a makeshift gate that was made up of two large dump trucks with even larger metal welded to their sides.

They faced each other and either backed up to let you in or pull forward to keep you out. The whole shanty was fortified well, there was a row of school busses that had the same metal shielding as the dump trucks. In places where there was no metal, they had barbwire or century holes for defense.

Three years, this shanty had been crafted to defend the people inside. Three years of trial and error. How many times had they held off against the wilds of the world? How many friends and family had they lost in their pursuit of some type of community and normalness in a crazy world? Alex took a deep breath. She was holding back her tears. Sure, she knew that nothing would be the same.

She was in her box; Adam and her whole world were with her. She never really saw the effects of what happened. She knew that she would never again tweet about her favorite show on Netflix or order her favorite drink at Starbucks. Things like that didn't matter as long as she was secure, and Adam gave her security.

She stopped the car and placed the gear in neutral. She was moving around trying to get a closer view of the gates. The guards around the top were pointing their weapons at the car, along with the guards on the busses.

"You should probably get out first." Alex said as she looked at Amy.

"Yeah, as soon as they see me it will be cool!"

There was a bit of happiness in her voice. It wasn't perky but it felt as if Amy felt safe. This made Alex relax a bit. Amy went to roll the windows down. She flicked the button a few times in both directions.

Alex sat and watched as she got agitated and finally just opened the doors. She raised her eyebrows and looked in the rearview mirror at Jess who was watching her mother with the same face as Alex. Jess happened to look up and saw Alex was looking at her. They both laughed a bit at Amy before Amy bent down in the car.

"Okay, they are about to open the gates," she paused.

She looked at both of them in confusion.

"What are you two laughing at?"

The understanding that you can't roll down a window that has metal plates welded to the frame never came to her mind. This made Jess laugh even harder.

"Mom! Geez... You are embarrassing! Just get in the car and roll up your metal windows!"

Amy got in, finally realizing what was funny. She leaned back in her seat holding her head and laughing. Alex was laughing and so was Jess as the large trucks parted. It was a refreshing release after the traumatic experience these three women shared.

****

Profett silently rummaged through the kitchen looking for silverwares. He needed anything that was pure metal, most people will have silver and gold. He grabbed a knife and bent it a bit then threw it down. Picking up a spoon and doing the same. He closed the drawer and headed to the bed area of the RV.

He looked under the bed and pulled out a small chest. He picked it up and grabbed his smaller knife inside his boot. He placed the blade through the lock and braced it along the wood beneath the lock. With two hands, he quickly and forcefully broke the lock. He opened the chest and smiled.

Inside was an older pistol and a few pieces of jewelry. He picked up the hand gun and weighed it in his hand before putting it back down and grabbing all the gold and silver pieces from amongst the nice jewelry inside. Profett closed the box and placed it back underneath the bed. He left the RV undetected and proceeded to break into the next one after checking to see if anyone was close.

****

After entering the shanty, Alex had to get out and show her face. Everyone was tense. They never relaxed their guns. Even after Amy told them that Alex had saved her life. They just got back inside of their trucks and motioned for Alex to follow in her car.

"Did I say something to them?" she asked Amy, sounding confused and condescending.

"No, we just don't see many strangers around here. Nowadays you are either with us or against us. It is survival 101 around these parts." Amy said unconfidently.

The two guards were now motioning her to park in a space by the gas station. The whole shanty was simply put together. Alex was no master tactician, but she was sure that this was like their city hall and final refuge if someone breaches the wall and the ten rows of RV's. She parked the car and got out. Amy and Jess got out and closed their doors.

The sun was just starting to show and the dew from the night before had not yet dried. It made the windows on the RVs shimmer and the way the RVs were facing, there were sun power panels directly in front of the RVs, wielded to the back of the next RV. She spun around and chuckled as she realized what this shanty was doing. The rows of RVs were not there as protection. They are placed there as a power generator like a coil. She looked at the ground and saw cords protected by rubber pipes.

Her amazement was interrupted by a voice.

"Hello!"

The voice had a bit more delight than Alex had been ready for, after driving the better part of two days.

"Amy, Jessica! Come give me a hug! We were worried about you!" Jessica ran to the old man.

Alex looked him over, he appeared to be well into his sixties. He wore a worn-out overall and a flannel shirt. His jacket was a hunter's jacket designed in denim but a bit darker than his overalls and camo print pockets. His face was weathered with a salt and pepper beard, more salt than pepper. He was slightly balding and where he did have hair, the strains were thin and wiry.

A few gray strands hung in his face and were agitated with the light breeze of the morning. His eyes were soft as he hugged Jessica. His presence, as well as his matured strong voice, was calming and Alex let her shoulder relax a little.

She still surveyed the other town folks who came out to greet them. There was a woman around the same age as the man hugging Jessica. As soon as Jessica finished hugging the man she ran over to the woman.

"Nana!" tears in her eyes as she ran over and hugged the woman."

Alex looked to the woman's left. There were two men who looked to be either late teens or early twenties. They both wore jeans over cowboy boots, tucked in shirts with dicky working jackets. The closest one to the woman had a dark jacket and red buttoned shirt and to his right, the other wore a grey jacket with a black Metallica tee shirt. The two guys looked on quietly.

As Amy was done hugging the older man, he stood with his hand still on her shoulder talking and looking with care in his eyes. Alex could tell by the sobs that Amy was telling him about their incident.

"Young lady. Alex? Right?" He raised his hand in a welcoming gesture.

"I am Sam. My daughter tells me you saved her life. Please come inside and have dinner with us!"

He pointed to a large RV parked next to the gas station.

"Thank you but..." Alex didn't want to be rude.

She had not been around people for three years, other than Adam. She missed her family. She had a large family with Tia's and Tio's and cousins. She missed her brothers and sisters and their children.

She missed the talks with her mom on how long her and Adam were waiting to have kids themselves; she missed Adam.

Alex realized she had trailed off a bit and straightened up, "I do appreciate the offer. And under normal circumstances, I would be delighted to have dinner. But I am searching for someone."

"Yes, your husband. Amy mentioned that you think he might be around here somewhere. Well… We haven't seen any new faces around here. Believe me, with the guards and Ms. Parker's nosey butt, nothing gets done without accountability around here!"

Everyone but Alex chuckled.

"I did see a helicopter land and take off last night. I thought it was strange that those company folks would come around these parts and not talk with us. But you know, they are busy rebuilding the world so…" He shrugged.

Alex was a bit confused.

"Company? And you said there was a helicopter? Where did it land?"

"Well, it landed a few miles up that hill." He pointed outside the town and away from the highway.

"Yeah, it looked to be some sort of military vehicle. And as for the company, young lady, what rock have you been sleeping under? Bable ring any bells? It is the only company still in operation and they are trying to establish a bit of order."

"Thank God, himself! If you ask me."

The older lady said while holding Amy in a hug. Sam had slowly made his way to Alex who was standing near the trunk of her car. By his movement, she realized that she might have had a threatening posture. She smiled at him and placed her hand up mid-way in a calming manor.

"I know it seems weird I don't know these things, but I have been inside a bunker since the fallout. It has been just me and my husband, Adam. He was taken a couple days ago, and I think he was aboard the helicopter you saw. I am sorry I can't stay for dinner, but I have to go to where the helicopter landed. He might be up there. I have to check it out."

She was walking to her car door and got it halfway open when Sam gently placed his hand on the door.

"I understand your rush. Hell, I was just about to rally the whole town if my daughter and grand baby had not come home. But, I can guarantee you that no one is in that bunker. It is not fitted for personnel or captives. Please stay . Later, I'll send my boys up to show you where the bunker is, and you can search around. We have a bed and fuel if you need. You can rest and head out tomorrow. Driving tired, although there are no other drivers, can still be dangerous these days."

Sam gave Alex a stern, yet sincere look and Alex closed the door. They walked towards the rest of the group, Sam's arm around Alex's shoulder and a huge smile on his face.

"Okay, everyone! Who is hungry? Ill get started on dinner and maybe Jean can cook her famous three mushroom casserole"

Everyone's eyes and posture perked up with excitement except Alex. She just kept a smile and nodded when someone looked at her thinking she would be thrilled as well.

"*Three Mushroom casserole?*" She thought.

White people will make a casserole out of anything. She shook her head to herself and chuckled as she walked behind the group. She looked and shrugged.

"Family is Family."

****

Profett fanned the flames of his fire. He was a few miles north of the town, yet still close to keep a visual of the road. He had created a fire pit that was mostly underground. He dug a sixfoot hole and placed grass in it. Then he carefully put the dirt back on top of the grass.

The hole was connected to the hole he dug to build his fire. Along the hole, he strategically placed smaller holes in the dirt he matted over the grass. This way, the smoke would not look as if it was coming from a fire. Someone way out would mistake it for fog. And at night, in a world where there are no lights, no one would see it at all.

It was mid evening around five, and the sun was close to setting. He emptied his pockets and bag. Jewelry was laid out in front of him as he sat on the ground next to the fire. On top of the fire, he placed a grill top that he stole from one of the grills inside the town. He reached in his flight suit and grabbed a piece of shiny metal; it was no bigger than a quarter.

He grabbed it on both sides and stretched it out. It responded as if it had a mind of its own. He cupped his hand and placed the longer disk in his cupped hand. He then made a fist and placed it on top while closing his other hand around the fist. He twisted his fist and pulled it out.

The metal agitated in this form a bit and then hardened. He placed this metal cup on the grill and started to sift through the pieces of gold and silver. He had done well and only stolen two pieces that were not real. The cup turned from a dull grey to a bright orange red. He carefully placed the pieces of gold and silver inside the cup.

As soon as the pieces touched the metal, they started to melt. The fire was not hot enough to do this, but the metal cup was made out of a metal compound unknown to earth. It has the ability to stretch in mass and be formed. It also is very subjected to heat. Turning low degrees into higher degrees on contact.

Profett could have used a lighter if he wanted. He kept filling the cup until all the pieces inside were melted. He put on a pair of warrior gloves from Nebula. He was able to pick up the hot metal without even feeling the heat. He had a few molds of .45 ACP rounds, and he filled them all.

There were a hundred in total. He set the molds in water as they cooled. The steam rose to his face and he took a breath.

"Only thing better than this smell is the smell when these babies burn through a hound's flesh."

There is only one way to hurt, mame, and kill a hellhound, you have to use angelic steel. Here on earth, the material to make angelic steel does not exist. For that matter, no one even cares because no one knew they existed. They were myths. The closest thing you can have that will do the same effect is the metal you get when you mix gold and silver.

This mixture is called *Electrum* and it is very strong and flexible. This is where the myth of the silver bullet comes from. Profett continued creating his ammo as he looked into the direction of the town. He had made his camp right in front of a little clearing in the canopy that he could see the front gates. They were opening and he could see a truck leaving.

He thought to himself about how he was going to get a vehicle and continue to Arizona. He could not steal one from inside. There was no way they would open the gates to let him out with their neighbor's truck. He could wait and hijack someone as they left but seldom people have left the town since he had been watching and only one, the truck leaving now, had used a vehicle.

He thought about the Armored Chevelle. The windows were tinted just enough so that if he was to steal it and drive out, no one would know if it was him or the girl who drove it in. She would be okay with these people. From their body language and possessions, Profett knew they were just people trying to find a little order on this world.

He thought intently on the matter, his mind wandered to a post brief he had had with Kelia,

"*Sometimes the lines between good and evil get blurred in a war.*"

She was right. Though he did feel that the everyday choices are what kept a person on one side or the other.

He shook his head at the whole scheme of stealing the car. As he wiggled the kinks out of his body and stretched, he noticed a large branch and reached over and picked it up. He weighed it in his hand and began to twirl it around his fingers. It was shoulder length tall from his feet, but still had twigs and leaves around one end. He broke off the twigs and grabbed his knife.

As he sat twiddling at the branch, he looked in his cup. He had a little of the Electrum. His eyebrows lifted. He thought to himself,

"Well, if I can't steal, I'll ask."

"I'm just an old traveler looking for a lift..."

****

Alex returned from the bunker slightly defeated. She was ready to charge in and grab her husband from Satan himself if she had to. As she slowly drove Doug and herself to the parking space, she gripped the steering wheel hard and let out a very audible sigh. This made Doug shift awkwardly in his seat.

"Ma'am, I am sure everything will be okay." He said in a shaky voice.

Alex looked at Doug with a blank expression. She took in the young man. She was more thinking of her next steps than of Doug. A slight grin appeared just in the corner of her lips as she thought about how shook Doug was when she opened up the trunk and pulled out the open bag of guns and ammo.

He was confused as hell, as she checked the perimeter for clues. The doors on the bunker were sealed from the inside. There was a code pad and she expertly hacked into the circuit using her watch. Adam had trained her on numerous skills in the three years they were locked together. She got inside of the bunker and expertly cleared each room, finding nothing to clue her in to where they had taken adam.

"Miho, listen to me. Nothing is okay in this world. Everything is bad."

She had placed her hand on his cheek. Doug sat there, eyes open wide.

"The best we can do is love and protect the ones that are close to us. You hear me!" She grabbed him by the cheeks.

Not too hard but firm enough to drive her point.

"Listen, Doug. First off, I want to say thank you for bringing me to the bunker. That took some courage in these days and times. Second, I want you to promise me that you will watch over Jessica and her mother like a hawk. What happened to them yesterday will never happen again!"

She was leaning towards him in the cabin of the truck. Doug was terrified but listening.

"Yes, ma'am!" He said as he mustered his courage.

They stepped out of the truck and Alex went around back to grab her weapons. She took them to the trunk of her Chevelle. As she closed the trunk, "Ms. Alex! I hope you find your husband!"

He waved as he ran off towards his RV. Alex smiled. He was a nice young man. She made her way to Sam's RV and knocked on the door.

Conversation and laughter could be heard as footsteps came to the entrance.

Sam opened the door still talking to someone. He chuckled at their remark as he faced the gloomy and slumped shouldered woman at the door.

"Come in, Alex. Please come in."

He stood out the way and motioned her welcome.

"I see by your disposition; you did not find what you were looking for."

"No, nothing but leaves and dust from the helo." She plopped down on a chair Sam had motioned to her to sit on.

"Nothing? Maybe you and I can go in tomorrow and look inside? I do have the code you know?"

"Well, I do now." She defeatedly waved a hand.

"No need. I hacked inside and checked already, nothing!"

She was expressive yet very somber. Sam raised an eyebrow at the fact that she hacked into the bunker and stared at her puzzled.

"Well, nothing will get you thinking better about your next step than a good warm meal!"

He jumped up from where he was seated as spry as a man in his thirties and playfully tapped Alex's shoulder as he made his way to the dining area. Alex stood up feeling just a bit better from his energy alone. She followed Sam to a small dining area in the middle of the camper.

The dining area had two tables that sat adjacent from each other with a walkway between them. The table sat two, maybe four people, each. At one table, sat Jessica with Amy across from her, they were playing Go Fish. Sam sat down next to Jessica and scruffed up her hair a bit. Alex sat at the empty table as the lady from earlier brought out plates of food.

She placed a plate in front of Alex first, then proceeded to place plates in front of everyone else. She brought her plate out lastly and sat across from Alex with a kind and soft smile.

"My name is Jean."

She said as she offered her hand for a shake. Alex took it and told her she was Alex, though she was well aware that Jean knew.

"I hope everything went well today?" She said in a positive voice.

Alex slumped a bit thinking of her findings, or lack thereof. Jean saw her reaction and looked over to Sam with an 'oops' expression on her face.

"Well, she didn't find much but there is always tomorrow!"

He said in a failing attempt to cheer up the mood. Jean grabbed Alex's hands and rolled her eyes at him.

"Sweetheart, what you are doing is coming from a divine place. Your love for your husband is strong. And one thing I know is, no evil in the world can oppose pure love! Besides, if the lug butt over there got kidnapped, I wouldn't even lift a finger."

Alex chucked as Sam threw his arms up questioning and acting surprised.

The food was delicious. It was a bacon-wrapped deer with fresh veggies they grew in their greenhouse or RV along with the casserole. Hunting had been good for them, they had enough people on a hunt party to bring in plenty of meat from different animals. As they ate, Alex asked questions about their survival and journey. She was curious about the corporation Babel.

Sam explained that a little over a year ago, a man in a clean pinstripe suit arrived at the gates. No one had seen him approach and he had no vehicle. After convincing Sam that he was harmless, he proceeded to explain that Babel was now the only corporation left operational in the world. He said that the CEO wanted to extend any help she could to restore order. The man told Sam that if he would help with the collection of sun power, then they would receive favor from Babel which would ensure the camp's survival.

Before his arrival, the town had had multiple attacks from raiders, like the one she met yesterday, and the Others. Sam agreed to the mans offer., In weeks they had transformed their rag tag shanty to the town they had now.

"So, all you have to do is maintain the solar panels?"

"Yes! Easy as cake. The wires go to a conductor room in the gas station's cellar then to their underground transmitters."

"They had an underground transmitter already built? That would take years to do and what are they powering?"

Everyone at the tables looked at each other in confusion.

"Well, I never saw them digging to create the transformer. So, that is a good question. As for what they are powering, there are tons of cities like this one that lead right to Arizona that I have heard from travelers. I think they are creating a massive power grid."

"Yeah, to power what?" She said under her breath and to herself.

"I am sorry. I didn't quite hear you?"

"I... I just don't know if this Babel is trustworthy." She sat looking at everyone for a second before standing up.

"Jean, the dinner was magnificent!"

"Oh, I didn't cook most of this besides the cassarole. Thank Sam9 dear!"

"Well, Sam I see you are a man of many talents. I should go to sleep soon. I need to get on the road early."

She bowed her head in respect, as she made her way to the bed that they had laid out for her. She laid down while holding her prayer beads. She prayed and let her body sink into the bedding. She was asleep in minutes.

Chapter Seventeen

DUEL OF THE IRON MICS

Sparks and Dethia were now back at Dethia's planet, Ike. It is a small planet if looked upon in orbit. In fact, the planet is not visible by telescope. In orbit, it looks as if it is a tiny glowing black dot. Maybe even a small black hole.

But upon entering its atmosphere, everything changes. The sky is fuchsia with light purple and pink clouds. The grass is lush and there are flowers everywhere. Lilies and roses, Amaryllis and orchids. Death stays at the only house on the planet, or better yet a palace.

The decor is a mixture of all cultures of Earth, and not of earth. It is mainly open with no roof due to the temperature that's never changing. There is never anyone moving around the palace but when needed, servants come from around the corner as if they were standing and waiting. Death explained to sparks that these were not people or souls, just figments of his imagination, brought into existence to fulfill his need. Sparks giggled like a teenage boy.

"I am parched. Oh RiRi, could you bring me something to drink?"

From around the corner of the room, Rihanna came out to him holding a glass of water. She was dressed in a silver swimsuit that only covered her most private areas. As she walked past Dethia, she gave her a confident once over, walking a bit slower and fluidly. Once she made her way to Sparks, she handed him the glass of water then traced his arm with her fingertips. She made it to his shoulders now standing behind him.

Sparks drank the water as if he didn't even notice her there. She made her way to his ear and just as she was going to stick out her tongue, she violently disappeared in a cloud of smoke. A dagger was lodged into the wall. Sparks looked at the dagger, and as if he was tracing its trajectory back to the hand that threw it, he looked at Dethia whose hand was still in the throwing form. She looked dangerous and beautiful as she stood in perfect form.

"Be mindful of your thoughts, sweetie," she gracefully recovered back to standing.

"If you were trying to show off, it only showed how objectifying you really are."

Dethia turned and walked out of the room they were in.

"Babe, I was joking!" He half-heartedly said as she made her way out.

When you are connected with a person for eternity, arguments don't possess the same amount of anxiety. Sparks was in love and so was Death. They would not leave each other, for deep down inside they were each other. It would be easier for Sparks to leave his soul than for him to leave Dethia, his queen.

Sparks could have ran after her and grabbed her by the hips, spun her around and kissed her, that would put this make-believe tiff to rest. Yet Sparks needed to think. All this time he had been away from Earth, things had gotten bad. At first, he didn't care, but as he looked on, he just felt uneasy for not caring. So many souls would never know peace due to his and Death's relationship. Lucille was building some kind of a mega structure in Arizona. Things were looking bad.

Sparks was deep in thought. He was walking around a rose garden when he walked right up to an older man sitting on a bench. Sparks looked confused. He was not concentrating on his surroundings while he walked, but he knew for a fact no one was on that bench a few seconds ago. He stopped walking and stared at the old man a second.

He was extremely old. His skin, which was almost onyx, hung from his bones as if it would melt to the ground. He was hunched over and looking at a few flowers on the ground in front of him as if he couldn't quite see them. He shifted his glasses up and back down like he was comparing the view then he laughed in excitement. The excitement of the weak old man's laugh made Sparks move back a little in surprise.

"I just love it when they do that, those little tricksters!" He said almost murmuring to himself.

He had an accent as if he was from some western Africa country. Sparks took it as an invite to speak.

"Are you real?" Sparks said while lightly poking the man's hunched shoulder.

The old man straightened up his back and sat very tall for a man his age. He looked up at Sparks with a wonderful smile. He was handsome and his ambiance was gentle and kind. Sparks looked into his eyes and a great weight fell over him. Sparks took a large breath and exhaled.

He felt as if all the air in his lungs was leaving him and going into the void of this man's eyes. If Sparks could have properly explained it, he actually felt like the air was just returning to its origins. As sparks felt the last of his air leave, the old man blinked.

"Real is relative. If everything was created, then the only thing real is what's imagined."

Sparks was brought back to the now when the old man spoke. He felt as if he had been close to losing himself. As if a part of himself, if not all, was being drawn into the man's eyes. Sparks heard the old man but was a bit shaken up from his illusion.

"Sorry, sir. I don't mean to be rude. But I don't feel too well. I think I am going to head back." Sparks held his head.

Still confused on the vision he had just experienced. The old man smiled again.

"Son, sit here next to me. You will feel much more focused if you rest here."

The old man shuffled over to make room for Sparks and patted for him to sit.

"Besides, what is waiting for you back that way may not be too restful..." He said with a mischievous smile.

"Please, son. Humor an old man."

Sparks walked over to the bench and sat down. As soon as he did so, he felt extremely better. As if he never felt, whatever that was, at all.

"See, all better." he said half condescendingly.

"Now, tell me what's got you so sick. You know, all sickness comes from here." he placed a finger on Sparks heart.

When he touched his chest, Sparks felt as if his heart pumped. It made him jump a little. For three years, Sparks had been in the midst of Death. He did not need to breathe, sleep, eat, or let alone had he felt his heart pump. The old man pulled his hand back as if nothing happened and Sparks rubbed his chest.

"Tell me, boy. Is it troubles in paradise?" the old man cackled at his joke.

He truly found it funny. He shook with laughter making Sparks huff with a few laughs himself.

"Well, that has been a learning experience. I learn new things every day. I just found out you should never bring imaginary women into a relationship without talking about it first."

They laughed a bit more.

"But seriously, I have been thinking of something much more serious." Sparks' demeanor switched to more focused.

"Ah, I see. You've been thinking about earth."

Sparks' head shot to the old man as he wondered how he knew. Sparks figured this was just a figment of his imagination, literally, yet there was something original with this old man.

"How do you know about Earth?"

"Oh, I know many things about much," he winked at Sparks, "There is a rebuilding going on there."

Sparks thought about Lucille's construction.

"You know, when things get chaotic to a point of boiling over, order always finds a way to even the tides. But the truth in that is the opposite."

Sparks thought about what he said. It made sense but he couldn't see how that pertained to his worries.

"I guess. But I think I should be down there helping. There is so much pain and torment. Lucille is out of control. Why is God doing nothing?"

Sparks was frustrated and had his head in his hands. The old man placed a hand on Sparks' back. Calm was blanketed over Sparks.

"Sometimes, a plan is the very thing that causes something to fail. Things are looked at in such a black or white construct. How you see things now is how they were meant to be and have always been, but that is not the case. I have been in existence for a long time Ishmael."

When Sparks heard his middle name, he looked up from his hands.

"I have seen the power struggle of order and chaos. I have watched as all life adapted and changed within the war. All things, like these flowers, had to adapt and change. They sweetened their pollen to attract insects so they could breed. They flowered their petals and twisted their stems to find the sun. Was this the plan? Or did God create them with every tool to survive, and then let them do what they were created to do?"

Sparks thought about what was said. Out of the corner of his eye, he saw the man stand up. Sparks was too focused on his thoughts as the man said his salutations.

"Have a good day, son. I have a few more things I want to accomplish." Sparks looked up at the old man who was surprisingly tall.

"Thanks, sir! Have a good day also..."

Sparks held the statement as an invite for the old man to give his name.

"Just call me Baba. It means father."

"Are you priest?"

Baba chuckled and placed his hands on his knees.

"Yes! But I minister to the heart. I trust you will make the right decision Ishmael. Just trust in the talents you were given!" Baba nonchalantly turned and started to walk away. He was whistling a tune that Sparks found oddly familiar.

Sparks stood up and headed the opposite direction, he had gotten a few feet and realized the whistling stopped. He turned to look at the old man, but there was no old man. Sparks rubbed his head, they were seated along a long path that went straight for quite a while. Unless the old man broke into a sprint and was very fast at it, he should have still been visible. Sparks thought about it then shook it off; he needed to plan his next steps wisely.

****

Profett made his way to the town before the sun rose. He had found a tethered piece of cloth along the road and threw it over his shoulders. As he got within clear view of the guards along the fence, he slowly started to hunch over and slightly limp; using the staff he carved out of the tree branch he found the night before. He didn't do to much acting cause he needed them to believe that although he was old, he was capable of traveling the road.

As he got to the gate, the guards on the top ordered him to halt. Profett rose his head and looked at the century.

"Sir, I am sorry to bother this town, but I am in need of a ride. Is there anyone going west? Doesn't matter how far, really!" Profett held his hand out in a nonchalant pose.

The guards looked at each other and discussed something before ordering a third guard to leave; the man ran off.

"We don't have anyone leaving west. At least they are not going anywhere your feeble old legs can't get you in an hour!"

The guard yelled with a cruel smile on his face because of the cheap shot he took at the old man. Profett lowered his head in humility.

"Anywhere closer to my destination can help these legs out. I'm just trying to make it to my family." Profett said in a calm pleading manner.

The door on the bus slid open after the pieces of board and metal was slid away on the inside. The third guard that ran away was on the other side with a huge smile."Sir, please come in! The guys up there are just jousting you!" Profett bowed in thanks and followed the young man.

The guard on the other side of the perimeter asked if Profett had any weapons. He consented that he did and pulled out a pistol from his bag. Before handing the gun over to the guards, he released the clip and slid back the slide to safely discharge the round in the chamber. He smiled at the guard.

"Well, you keep the gun and I'll keep the bullets?" He said as he slid the round back in the magazine then put the magazine in his pocket.

The guard gave a light protest but Profett acted as if he didn't notice. As he walked off, the guard grabbed his staff. Profett held it with force, still appearing as if he wasn't using any force. The immovability of the staff caused the guard to pull harder, but it did not budge. He looked at the old man, he looked at the ground to rule out a trick.

Maybe the staff was lodged into the ground, but it was not. It wasn't even touching the ground. The old man was holding the staff so firm that the guard was unable to move it.

"You wouldn't take an old man's walking stick?" He said with a smile.

This was hilarious to him because it was a quote from lord of the rings. The guard slowly released the staff. Profett bowed again in humility and made his way toward the center of the town.

When he made it to the gas station, he looked around to find the old Chevelle. The woman who was driving it was placing the last of her bags in the trunk. There was no one with her and Profett walked over to her.

"Excuse me ma'am, I am headed west. I haven't seen my family in years. Can you please help an old man out?" Alex closed the trunk and without looking at the old man.

"Nope!"

Profett played along with the game, "Please ma'am? I just don't know when I'll see them again!"

"Not my problem." She was getting inside the vehicle, Profett moved over to her door before she could close it.

"We can make a barter. If you can get me close to Arizona, I'll give you some food and provisions to get you along the rest of the way you are headed. I am also a fine mechanic. And it isn't safe to travel alone on these roads. All types of beast and fowl man lay in wait for a woman such as yourself."

Alex looked the old man over. He was hunched over slightly but she could tell by the way his shirt clung to his arms, that he was built. She didn't see anything malicious in his eyes.

"Well, if you think I'm worried about these roads you are wrong. I am headed west but I don't know if Arizona is in the direction I'm headed. You can ride as far as you need."

"Thank you! Thank you!" He clasped his hands together in gratitude and moved over to the passenger side of the vehicle.

He jumped inside and placed his staff alongside the door and against his shoulder.

He reached over to shake the woman's hand.

"I'm Profett!"

"I'm Alex."

"Nice to meet you! So, you are just wondering?"

Alex looked at him, she was just about to tell him the whole story about Adam but thought against it. There was nothing this old man could do to help.

"Yeah, something like that."

She started the car and headed to the front gate. As they arrived, the gate had already started to open. Alex had turned the limiting switch off causing the whole town to rumble with every stroke of the gas. As they got to the opened gate, Profett asked if they could stop and get his possessions back from the guards. Alex assumed by possessions, he meant weapons and just proceeded to speed onto the highway.

Profett looked back out his window and then questioningly looked at Alex.

"Hey!" he yelled, "They still had my stuff. We need to turn back!"

Alex ignored him and stepped in the gas. The inertia forced Profett back in his seat. This made Alex happy inside because it was something that her dad had done to her, and something that every guy she had dated that had a car with a powerful engine had done. Now, she was the driver of the hot rod and he better sit back and look pretty. Profett realized that she was not going to turn around, and sat back. He had a scowl on his face, but he said nothing more. The two of them headed west in silence.

✳✳✳✳✳✳✳✳✳✳✳✳

Kelia had left the control room and was ecstatic. The key was the most precious gift she could have gotten. It meant the freedom to follow her destiny, it meant that she would be able to once more get in this fight. She needed to get a team together.

As she walked the corridors of scattered people, she was headed East. She knew for sure she needed a second in command. That second should be able to lead and be a tactician so she could focus on the broad picture. There was no outside support on this mission. She knew of only one man that could fill those duties. Unfortunately, it would be hard to convince him to be anywhere near her.

The last time she saw Aviv, she had just broken his heart and he was walking away with his head down. She felt so heartless and sad for the man. They had become reconnected once she had started working for Zion. Unknown to her, Aviv had always been a double agent and when she joined the group, he and her started dating. They dated for a few months.

It wasn't that Aviv didn't make her happy, she was attracted to him and was even surprised at how handsome and sexy she found him once she gave him a chance. He was protective and kind to her. It was, at the time, she was still not over Sparks. She tried to communicate this with Aviv, asking him to give her time so she could process her feelings and be more focused on what they were building.

He was hurt and confused. He told her that she needed to choose at that moment, if she wanted to be with him. At the time Kelia wanted Aviv, really there was no choice since Sparks was out of the picture. She just needed time. She also didn't like the ultimatum and due to that, she told him it would be best if he left.

They never talked again. Profett seemed to station them on the same base as if he was playing matchmaker. She hated that, but Aviv made sure to navigate in a way as to not make unnecessary contact, and when they did, it was professional. She felt bad and sometimes when she was single, which was most of the time, she wanted to grab him and tell him how she felt. But then, as sad as it seems, she knew she didn't have the time for a love interest, so she just let it be.

Today, she would still keep her feelings to herself for the same reasons. She needed him for business and that was the only reason she was breaking the silence. As she came close to his quarters, she paused before knocking on the door. She always felt crazy for how seeing him gave her butterflies or how she wished he would just look at her and smile, like he did before. She closed her eyes and took in a deep breath.

As she opened her eyes, she knocked on the door. She exhaled a breath as the door opened up and standing on the other side of the door, was a tall blonde who was wearing a men's buttondown long sleeve shirt. She had no pants on and possibly nothing else on but the shirt. Kelia was releasing the last bit of the breath with her mouth open wide.

"Hello, can I help you?"

Kelia looked the tall blonde woman up and down before speaking. There was something familiar about the blonde. Like they had trained together somewhere before but she could not pinpoint where.

"Uhh, well, I was looking for Aviv." She stammered out.

The blonde made her feel a bit insecure. She didn't know if it was the blonde's beauty or the fact that she was the one wearing Aviv's shirt, possibly from the night before.

"Oh, okay. I'll get him! Wait for a second."

"Babe! Babe... there is a girl at the door for you!"

The long leg and very attractive blonde walked to where Aviv was, on her tiptoes. Kelia scoffed at the 'girl' comment. She thought, if only she had time, she would define what the difference is between a girl and a warrior. As she snickered from the idea of her wiping the ground with this girl, while holding a fistfull of blonde hair, Aviv walked around the corner of his bunker. He was still deep in the book he was reading as he looked up.

Once he saw Kelia, he dropped the book and they exchanged eye contact. The moment was broken up by Alexis.

"Babe, should we do spaghetti or lasagna?"

She walked up to Aviv holding two different MRE packages. She waited for the answer, still looking at the packages herself. When she realized that there wasn't anyone answering her question, she looked up at Aviv and then to Kelia.

"Wait! I know you. You are Profett's daughter, Kel... Kelia! That's it!" She said as she excitedly made her way over to Kelia.

"You don't remember me?" She asked as Kelia finally broke the stare between her and Aviv.

"Uh... No, not really. I mean, you look slightly familiar. Did we train together somewhere?"

"Yes! You remember. Haha! We trained at the Agency!"

As soon as she said this, Kelia immediately remembered the woman. She was the blonde British pilot.

"It was so long ago but I will never forget a face!" Kelia was a bit confused.

"how did you make it to Zion?"

"Well... ol' steal buns wasn't the only double agent in those times!"

She patted Aviv on the butt and winked at him. Aviv gave an embarrassing smile and bent over to pick up the book he had dropped.

"Well, yes. There were actually multiple agents that infiltrated the Agency. I didn't even know Alexis was an agent with Zion until I saw her a few years ago and we reconnected."

Aviv's tone was nervous, as if he had done something wrong. Kelia recognized that it was due to the fact that he still has feelings, but she shook it off.

"Well, I am happy y'all found each other, but I am here for something extremely important. Aviv, can we speak somewhere more private?"

She cut her eyes to Alexis as she asked for privacy.

"There is nowhere more private than where we stand." He had mustered some courage.

In his heart, he loved Kelia beyond bound. But to be logical, that love had no place in his or her world. Kelia rolled her eyes and looked at Aviv with a confused look before starting her plea for his help.

Kelia was surprised at how long her convincing of Aviv had not taken long. He was with the whole thing from the get-go. Apparently, Kelia was not the only one on the base that was antsy. He said that he was going to grab a couple other highly qualified fighters to join their efforts. He also invited Alexis, which Kelia somehow didn't like, but he assured Kelia that Alexis was the best fighter pilot he had ever known.

They made their plans and thought best that they went their separate ways seeing the plan out. They would meet in the hanger bay the next evening and take a plane. As Kelia left Aviv's room, she made her way straight to the armory. They would need a couple palats of weapons and even more ammunition.

****

Lucille looked at a schematic that was laid out on the desk in front of her. She moved the paper around to help better pinpoint what she was searching for. The office she was in was nothing like her office at the Gates. It was extremely modern and stylish. It was equipped with state-of-the-art technology, the fact that she had a physical schematic was redundant.

Anything she wanted to view could be pulled up on her desk. The whole top of the desk was a monitor. It could be positioned up and used as a desktop. It could project a 3D image of what was displayed.

Lucille hated this office. Although technology was her idea to give to man, she valued the process of things. She didn't need convenience because she was immortal. A little bit of the most high that had rubbed off on her. Besides the fact that she valued the process of things, she knew that technology was the disconnect that she used to distract the humans.

It was the thirst for her gift that made humankind disregard a more simple and healthy life and pursue frivolous and violent desires. She liked to turn the pages on her books. She liked to use pencil and paper to write notes.

As she shifted the schematic once more, she was distracted by a buzz.

"Ms. Lucille, you have a visitor. It is Mr. Williams." the young personal assistant said with a british accent.

Lucille rolled her eyes and continued to study the schematics for a few minutes before pushing the red button on the rotary phone, the only thing she actually liked in this God forsaken office.

"Let him in." She said in a nonchalant voice.

The door to her office swung open and Mr. Williams stepped through. He slowly walked to the desk Lucille was at. He traced the edge of the desk as he walked around to where Lucille was standing, his finger that was tracing the desk made its way to the hand Lucille was using to stabilize herself.

His finger lightly traced up her finger to her hand. The nail on his finger grew larger the further he made his way from her wrist to her elbow. It left a trail of crimson blood as it broke the top layer of skin. As he scratched, the wound quickly healed just before it bled. Only a few drops of blood left the wound before it closed back up.

Mr. Williams was now behind Lucille and he swung the few loose strands of hair, that had escaped the messy bun Lucille had on top of her head. Her exposed neck pulsating with life. Mr. Williams bent closer to her neck and took a deep sniff. His lips were close to her exposed skin.

She closed her eyes and bit her lip in anticipation of his lips touching her flesh. Her hand clinched the schematic she was looking at, causing the paper to wrinkle in her fist. His hands touched her sides roughly causing her to brace. She let out a sigh. Mr. Williams let out a low seductive growl.

The rumble of the growled shook the water glass that was sitting on top of Lucile's desk. In one motion, William picked Lucille up about an inch off the ground and spun her around. They were now eye to eye.

Lucille could feel William's breath hitting her face. She started breathing hard as he slowly leaned forward, his lips aimed at her own, and just as they were about to connect.

"Well, that was fun! Now heel."

Lucille slid from between Mr. Williams and the desk. She adjusted her skirt and blouse, and positioned the schematic back on top of the desk. She bumped Williams in the process of repositioning herself. Mr. Williams took the clue with an eye roll.

"My queen, you know that I can smell that you want me right now. Let me take care of your needs." He said as he calmly walked to the other side of the desk.

Lucille was thinking about it. He was an adequate lover, and she marveled at how calm and collective he was as he took a seat and crossed his legs. He was a beast, her little hound. She was looking at him over her glasses then went back to look at the schematics.

"I don't have time for any of that now... but maybe later. Right now, I need you to give updates on our progress."

Mr. Williams shifted from his relaxed, seated back demeanor to a more professional one. Placing both feet on the ground.

"Ma'am, well, there are more towns being developed in the midwest. We have engaged with all of them that have agreed. And we sent the puppies to deal with all the ones who have rejected our proposal."

Williams said puppies condescendingly and with a little bit of an attitude. He hated that his blood was used to make those filthy creatures. Not only did they seem like a waste of blood, they were weak willed and impulsive. The men who were chosen to be part of this new pack, were very disciplined soldiers. They were picked due to the fact that they could follow orders, but when his blood mixed with theirs, well their humanity, did not mix well with his beast; humanity was so easily corrupted.

Williams paused for a second before continuing."All in all, the intervention has begun and is well under way." Lucille looked back at Williams from above her glasses that hung just at the tip of her nose.

"Great! I don't need anything to stop my plans. We are just at the final stages. My mother will not win this time." she said the last part just audible enough to be heard by William's sensitive ears.

Williams took this as his clue to leave. He had hoped that Lucille was in the mood to make love, but he knew that that was a far stretch. For the last ten years, she had slowly turned cold and more concise. The only thing on her mind was this war. He had been hers for all 723 million years of his life since the creation of the immortals. She had mothered and loved him. And as their bond grew, she had turned him into her lover.

His whole existence was for her, she was his breath, literally, since he was only alive because she breathed breath into his lungs. As he walked out the sliding doors, he had a defeated slump in his shoulders. Lucille noticed his disposition and she thought for a quick second then called out."Darling, before you leave tonight, you should meet me in my quarters." She said with a slight flirtatious grin.

"Maybe we can find the motivation to be great!" She winked at him and Williams smiled. His disposition changed and he walked through the doors with a new pep in his step.

Intermission II

The wind blew the leaves of the large Iroko tree. From the orange hew of the leaves, it was definitely fall, yet not one leaf fell from its branch. There was no season or time where Seriah was currently meditating. The ground he sat on was most sacred. He was underneath the tree of life.

The trunk of this glorious tree was massive, from a distance, it appeared as a normal tree but when close, you would find that there is no way to walk around the tree. The silver tinted brown of the trunk pulsates with life. Crimson sap is pushed through veins that entangled the tree like wisteria vines. Although there are no seasons, there is a reason the tree is not its normal vibrant green.

There is a reason that the beautiful assortment of flowers are not blooming, and why the wind agitates the leaves now. Life was slipping. Most people, if they were to know that life was in a slow march to death, would think that existence was over. But life and existence only relate by a thin thread. Existence is God and life is only a creation of God.

Seriah sat, eyes closed, and legs crossed. His golden dreadlocks danced in the wind. He tried to keep his breath calm. Ordinarily, this was an easy task. Angels don't deal in emotional reactions, but that is not to say they don't have emotions.

He opened his eyes. The wind had stopped and standing before him was an older woman who appeared to be in her late 80s. She was standing in the midst of fog and a bright light that radiated intensely but did not hurt the eye. She was dressed in a long dress that looked to be Angolan with a scarf that appeared to be from some native tribe in the North Americas. She smiled at Seriah and all frustrations he was harboring released.

Seriah rose to his feet then went down on both knees and lifted his arms as he bent forward and pressed his head to the floor.

"Rise my child." She said in a voice that was as low as a whisper yet very clear and audible.

Seriah stood up and let out a breath that was followed by a single tear.

"Mom, I... I... I need you."

He let out a few more tears and a couple sobs escaped his lips. He hung his head down as he wiped the tears from his eyes. Grandmother walked to Seriah and placed her hand on his chest covering his heart, he broke down with more tears and sobs as she then pulled him close, wrapping her arms around his back. He cried into her shoulder and grandmother hummed a few notes and the breeze started back but much calmer. Seriah pulled back gently to gaze upon her.

"Grandmother, after all these millennia you still look as beautiful as your first breath."

"Oh, how would you know? You were just a thought then." She smiled as she wiped the tears off Seriah's face with a piece of her scarf.

"Child, I could play theatrics and ask you what has had you sitting here, and in pain... but there is no need for that between you and I, is there?"

Seriah looked down and smirked as he shook his head no.

"You are a young one compared to this tree."

She pointed an open hand at the tree as if she was presenting it to him.

"I have witnessed six seasons of life, death and rebirth. When I first planted the seed of life, I created a process that took off in its own distinct and wonderful way. Humans make a difference between creation and evolution. I have always found that funny. One side believes I made a man and a woman and from them all people came about. The other side believes that everything just happened due to a few gasses colliding and erupting. Yet, they both have only a clue of what the truth is."

She was standing facing the tree looking at it in awe and reverence. Seriah quietly walked next to her and tried to follow at where she was looking. Her eyes darted from branch to leaves like it was her first time ever seeing the tree.

"There was a time, a few hundred thousand years ago or so, when spirits of animals would play on the branches and rest in her shade," she sighed, "but I have learned to love this time as well. She almost looks golden. So, you want to help the humans? You want to protect Kelia?" She looked at Seriah.

He didn't respond and grandmother knew his heart.

"Well, I know of a young human that had the same intent as you."

Seriah filled up with hope thinking of Sparks.

"I'll tell you like he was told. Plans are guidelines but are not definite. I'm tired of Lucille and her games. I feel it is time we take a bit of action!"

Grandmother's voice did not raise yet it was the only thing that could be heard. All around them, the wind had become turbulent. It blew violently in every direction swaying grandmother's dress around her ankles and around her arms.

"I... THE LORD OF HOST, CALL UPON THE ELOHIM... ACT OUT MY WILL! The Almighty, do command thee!"

Seriah closed his eyes and thanked the I AM then turned and slowly walked away. Grandmother was still in the eye of the storm. Seriah turned and looked back at her. Through the dust that had been gathered up in the winds, he could see her dancing, she was praising herself. Thunder clapped with every foot stomp and lighting zapped by when she raised her hands.

Music played as if the storm was conducting an orchestra. It was drums and tribal instruments. Around the storm holding hands, as if they were containing it, were the saints. They were singing beautiful praise in multiple different languages. Their energy magnified the storm and Grandmother was now almost impossible to see.

Something caught Seriah's attention and he raised his eyes to the top of the tree. Floating through the storm, as if there was no breeze, one leaf made its way to the ground. Seriah teleported away.

He made his way right outside of Ki's room. Before he could knock, the door slid open and Ki was standing there in full battle gear.

"You are not dressed! We leave for Egypt soon. Get dressed for battle and meet us at the teleportation room!" Ki walked past Seriah.

Seriah had his mouth still about to say hello and shook his head.

"Of course, he already knows." he said to himself as he walked down to his room a couple doors down.

Chapter Eighteen

Liquid Swords

Kelia was looking at a holographic image of The Great Pyramid of Giza through the rumble of the engine and the light sway of the bomber. She found it easier to close her eyes, but she shook her head and kept focusing. The image was an old model and Zion has a base underneath. The base has a mass teleporter that connects with Nebula's base.

About a year ago, when the Zion bases kept communicating with each other, her base got a distress call from the base in Giza. They were being attacked. Through the gunfire, one of the high-ranking officers had tried to contact Profett. Kelia tried to urge the other generals to send help. The generals were terrified that if they sent help, the demons would find their location and their base would be next.

She shook her head as she remembered pleading to help while listening to Giza plead for help. She lightly pounded her fist on the console. Trying not to damage any of the sensitive equipment that was on board the *"Oldest bomber still active."* Well, to be honest,

Kelia thought, it was probably the only bomber still active besides whatever Lucille had.

Kelia snapped back from her daydream. Aviv walked in and stood on the opposite side of the hologram as Kelia.

"You know, studying that map will do us no good. They have more than likely created an additional compound surrounding the Pyramid." Aviv raised a mug he had full of coffee and took a cautious sip.

Kelia rolled her eyes. She knew Aviv couldn't see it but for him to think that she was looking at this map at face value was typical male behavior.

"Thank you." she said sarcastically.

"I think we should land here and make our way to the side, I assume where the hostages are."

"Why here?"

"I would think that they have created a compound," She paused to let the condescending remake weigh in, "at least a mile wide in each direction. Using this canyon formation, if they have a brig, it would be a perfect way to trap prisoners. You have convinced me of the plan to free and reactivate as many Zion soldiers as we can but the biggest mission is getting to the teleporter to contact the Elohim." Kelia looked into Aviv's eyes.

There was a commanding tone in her gaze and just underneath a bit of pleading. Aviv lightly blew on his coffee and took another sip.

"Yeah, having angels on our back seems logical." He smiled before taking another sip.

A bit of the hot coffee rolled off his lips and landed on his chest. He jumped from the pain and spilled a bit more, barely missing the console. Kelia shook her head and used the opportunity to walk away towards the cockpit.

She opened the door and peaked her head in. Alexis was piloting the plane, and one of the four men that Aviv brought was helping her. Kelia looked around, she had been trained to fly but she was grateful that Alexis was the pilot. It gave her time to plan.

"Alexis, how far are we from the coordinates I set?"

"We are only about half an hour away. I have already darkened the vessel and we are slowly descending now. Regardless of how dark we are, we are the only plane in the air. We will be noticed. So, things could start to get rough."

Just as Alexis finished her statement, an alarm blurted. The copilot jumped as if he had been asleep. He looked around frantically before finding the flashing button and pressed it. Kelia and Alexis both looked at the button he pushed, and their eyes widened. Immediately, Alexis looked out the windows searching for a light.

Her training kicked in and she flipped up the plastic covers for the plane's flares. Kelia watched the radar, and coming on the right of the plane were two missiles.

"To the right!" She screamed.

Alexis banked the plane to the left and let off the flares on the right wing. Kelia held on to the copilot's chair. The missiles found their targets and exploded in the air. The aftershock of the explosions shook the plane violently. Kelia sat down and put a seat belt on.

Alexis was now descending but weaving slightly as to not give a steady target.

"Well... there goes..."

"Save it."

Another alarm started and the copilot quickly acknowledged it. On the radar, there was six missiles approaching. Two from the same direction as the other and two more from the left. There was one coming from underneath, and one approaching from the front. Alexis pulled back on the controls and press the throttle to full speed.

She pulled to the right as much as she could without stalling the plane. The one from the front whizzed by. She then pulled the throttle back, causing the engines to sputter. Gravity took hold of the plane and pulled it down, and back for a while. Wrestling with the controls with all her might, Alexis got the nose to point towards the ground.

She then slowly pressed the throttle up to a third of power. The speed at which the plane speed to the earth caused everyone to rise out of their seats just a bit. Alexis slowed the plane down a touch more and looked at the radar. The maneuver had lost all but one of the missiles. She saw the stretch of land they were going to land on and positioned the plane to land.

She was going fast and if she slowed down now, the missile was sure to connect. She was planning on dropping the last flare then dipping and slowing the plane down just in time to drop the landing gear. She inched the throttle back a little bit more, her eyes went from the ground in front of her, and the radar that showed the missile behind her.

"Come and get it, you little son of a bitch." She whispered to the missile.

Kelia and the copilot looked at the radar then at the ground. They both braced their hands on the objects in front of them instinctively. Just in the knick of time, Alexis dropped the flare and pressed the controls downward while pulling the throttle to one third of power. The plane dipped and dropped back as the missile exploded above them causing the lights in the plane to flicker and a few proximity alarms to go off along the cabin.

Alexis pressed the button to drop the landing gear and slowly moved the controls from left to right causing the wings to tilt on each direction while descending. She then flipped a few more switches as did the copilot.

"Shit!" Another alarm went off.

It wasn't an encroaching alarm. Kelia could see it was associated with the landing gear.

"I think one of those explosions fried some circuits in the landing gear."

She pressed the button down a few times, as if it would help.

"We are going to have to dry land. Brace yourselves this is going to hurt."

The plane was now only a few feet from the ground, directly in front, about three miles away, was the base. They had built way more than what Kelia or even Aviv had expected. Alexis slowed the plane down, as much as she could without stalling and as carefully as she could, she dropped the back on the dirt. She gripped tightly. The plane naturally wanted to fishtail.

She placed the rest on the ground and physics did the rest. Dirt and rocks pounded the windshield cracking the glass. The wings broke and flew in opposite directions. The plane slid full speed into the walls of the compound, bursting through before stopping.

****

Seriah made it to the mass teleport room with inspiration in his step. He was young for an angel but that did not mean he was inexperienced in matters of war. He fought against Lucille and her legions during the fall. The bravery he displayed on the battlefield earned him much respect with his fellow Elohim. He was a general in the army of hosts.

When he stepped through the door, the angels that were nearby, tending to their battle gear, popped to attention. He thanked them for their respect and told them at ease. He made his way to his platoon.

"Okay, make sure your battle buddy is ready. We are going to be coming in hot. There are multiple demons, along with soldiers, on the other end of that portal. We must push through and reach Zion. We are on the offense. The humans that fight against us have made their decision and they will reap the consequence. No man is to be spared if he raises arms against us. This is NO covert mission. We are backed by the word of the Most High!"

Seriah's platoon raised their chest at the last mention of the Most High.

Seriah felt the feeling to find Ki. Most people think that the Elohim speak to each other through psychic speech. But the truth is, they communicated through feeling. This was how the creator spoke. It starts with a feeling or a slight need for something, like a crave, then the mind processes it.

If the person that received the communication was vibrating on the same level, then they would proceed with the feelings and respond with the right action. Right now, Seriah was feeling the need to find Ki and he left his platoon and started searching for him.

Ki was in the middle of the other top-ranking generals. They were watching a hologram that was projecting from the brace on Ki's arm. Seriah walked up silently and watched the hologram with the others. It was a scene from the compound that the Agency set up in Giza. A plane was lodged into the wall and men and demon alike were moving to engage whoever was inside the plane.

Ki looked at Seriah, he gave him a concerning look and Seriah knew his feeling were true. Kelia was somewhere on that plane. Seriah calmed his frustration that was building inside. He had a duty to protect her, and he needed all his wits about him if he was going to do a good job.

"These are images from outside the Great Pyramid. A few Zion fighters are on that plane, but I am sure they can take care of themselves." Ki looked directly at Seriah.

Seriah just nodded his head in affirmation.

"This is giving us a good distraction. We will go through the portal and eliminate the treats. Once we regain the position, some of you will stay behind and protect this site. It will be our base of operation due to the portal being open. We are using the portal because although Lucille will be well aware of us capturing of her base, she will not know how many of our legions came through. So, the element of surprise will not totally be lost."

The other generals nodded in agreement and started back to their respective platoons. Seriah stood in thought. What he was thinking about was disturbed by a cold that chilled him to his bones. It was a feeling of acceptance for Seriah. He did not worry.

Yes, he knew that his beloved Kelia was in danger, but he did not feel obligated. All his deeds were done. As he sat in his acceptance, a dark light radiated with hints of indigo. It started to grow from the size of an egg, but soon grew to the size of a medium tunnel.

Sparks walked out and the light ceased. Seriah shook his head. The feeling he felt was leaving and he looked up. Sparks was looking directly at him. He nodded yet did not smile, and Ki quickly walked over.

"Sparks, now that you are here, we can commence our attack." Ki was just about to turn around and give the order when Sparks grabbed his shoulder.

"Before you start, I should let you know I will not be joining youyet." Ki looked at him questionly.

"May I ask why?"

"I must help Profett in Arizona. Right now, he and Alexandria Loch, the wife of a dear friend, are headed straight to Lucille's main base. I can't let them go there alone." Ki placed his hand over Sparks hand that was resting on his shoulder.

"I understand. Do you want any warriors to go along with you?"

Sparks looked Ki in his eyes while taking very deep breaths. Ki felt at ease like he had no care in the world. Then the fear hit him, he was no more as he once existed, and now Sparks moved his hand off of Ki's shoulder.

"I am never alone, any longer." Sparks backed up and gave Ki a nod of respect.

Ki, still breathing hard, nodded back.

"Hold down the front lines. We will gather an army. The Cavalry will arrive just when you need us!" Ki turned around and raised his hand.

All the Eliohem stood at attention.

They were positioned in ranks with each platoon's general directly in front. Ki walked to the Teleporting device. It was shaped as the pyramid yet upside down. It was as large as the actual pyramid. The way it worked was the energy from the physical world was collected from the top and the energy from the spiritual world was collected from the bottom, located in Giza, the top everyone could see. The bottom was deep underground.

It was large enough that the whole army of hosts could walk right through in the ranks they presently were in. Ki made his way to the front. He looked at the portal, and it was a reflective mirror. All he saw was himself and the army behind him. This was symbolic while the shape of the pyramid drew the possible energy to move matter across the galaxy.

It was the journey of the self that actually placed you from one destination to the next. He looked into his own eye as he slid his helmet on top of his head. His helmet was solid gold with short curved ram horns. It tucked just below the jaw, but left the face open. Ki turned around and drew his sword.

He looked at the multitude of Elohim that stood in front of him. They were warriors, and today they are to dance as they have always been trained to dance. Ki took in a deep breath, he was not the one for long war speeches, or chants, or even battle cries. He saved all that energy for the battlefield, he then turned around and faced the portal. His chest heaving in the last few sweet breaths of peace; he raised his sword and the whole heavens and earth shook as the army marched in.

Sparks watched all of the Elohim march in. He looked down at his hands and they were covered in his suit material. His suit moved differently now, almost like liquid. Sparks also noticed that he could no longer change the camo in his suit. He even tried to ask the Seamstress, the AI in the suit, to help and she acted as if no file existed that could change suit settings.

It wasn't that Sparks didn't like the new matte black camo design, it was stealthy. Regardless of what terrain he engaged on, he would be a problem to see. Sparks made a fist with both of his hands and snapped out of his thoughts. He closed his eyes and the suit covered his head and face. In front of him, a tunnel of black light opened up and Sparks walked into it.

****

Alex swerved trying to avoid the broken road and falling trees as the ground shook intensely. She had witnessed earthquakes before when her and her parents moved to America,. They first lived in Chula Vista, California. They moved the whole family southeast for a job her father and uncle both received. But this was crazy.

This was, for a lack of better words, *apocalyptic*. Profett snapped out of his sleep looking around and immediately telling Alex to watch out for a crack in the road. Alex rolled her eyes, she had been fighting this earthquake for at least a few minutes while he was still asleep. Alex steered on to the shoulder avoiding a tree that fell from the opposite end and then, as quick as the earthquake started, it stopped.

Profett held onto the dashboard and looked behind them. The road looked like a bomb site. He turned around and looked out in front, and everything was unharmed. He shook his head in confusion.

"What was that all about?" he looked at Alex as if she had an answer.

Alex shook it off thinking it was rhetorical, then looked back at Profett, realizing he was waiting for an answer.

"We are about seventy miles from where I... am going." She chose to change the topic.

"If you want, you can get out at the next crossroad, or I can drop you off at the next shanty we find along the way?"

The closer they got to Arizona, they had noticed more towns built like the one they left. From the tracker Alex was following, it seemed that the place they were keeping Adam was right in the middle of Phoenix.

Profett looked outside and he recognized the terrain. It would be a far walk to Phoenix from here. He was just about to ask where she was headed when the temperature dropped drastically.

It was fall, but they were in the south west. It should have been seventy-two degrees, the temperature gauge on the complicated digital dashboard read 72 degrees, but it felt close to freezing. Profett looked over to Alex and she also started shivering and rubbing her arms.

"Halaverga. Is it me or did it just get arctic cold all of a sudden?"

As she spoke steam left her lips. Alex leaned forward trying to focus on something. She shifted and slowed down the car.

"Holy mother of God." Profett looked at where she was looking.

He could not comprehend what he was seeing. In the middle of the road, was a very dark tunnel. There was nothing above the tunnel or to the side. It appeared as a void, standing in front was a large figure covered from head to feet in a very black tactical suit of some kind. The suit was almost darker than the void he was standing in front of. It made seeing any features of who this might be impossible.

Alex stopped the car in the middle of the highway and still looking at the figure, she reached between the door and her seat and grabbed the sawed of shotgun. Profett clenched his staff but did not move. He studied the figure. As they watched the portal quickly closed, they both were blinded a bit by the return of moonlight and the smaller lights that were put up post-apocalyptic to help travelers find their way from town to town.

"You saw that too?"

"Yeah... maybe we should keep moving."

He looked out of all the widows trying to see if he could find the figure. He turned back around and looked at Alex. She nodded and shifted the transmission. Just as she was going to release the clutch,"Don't be afraid." he softly spoke.

The surprise caused Alex to release the clutch and the car jumped before turning off. She spun around and aimed the sawed off right at Sparks' face. Sparks looked at her through his mask. The material on the mask moved and shifted. The mask not only covered his face but it was contoured to every part of his face.

When he blinked, it was the mask blinking over eyes that were covered in mask. Alex thought, this is more like skin than a mask. She moved back a little in surprise, shotgun still aimed at Sparks' face.

"Who the... What the hell are you? And how did you get in my car?"

Profett studied Sparks and then gently placed two fingers on the barrels of the shotgun.

"This is no enemy."

"The hell he isn't! He just walked out of some black void and now he is sitting in my car! I didn't let anyone in... Did you open a door and let him in?!" Her eyes were expressive.

"Is this one of your friends?"

She pointed the shotgun at Profett he leaned back away from the barrel releasing an annoying sigh.

"Listen, this might be hard to believe." he paused.

"Well, try me!" she pushed the shotgun closer to his face then pointed it back at Sparks' for a little while.

"Well, everything that is happening is due to a war between Chaos and Order. I am a soldier of Olofi or Jehovah or whatever other name you call her."

Alex raised an eyebrow at Profetts mentioning of God at her.

Profett continued, "There is a base in Phoenix that I need to get to. Lucille, or better known by you as Lucifer, is using the people and resources to control all life on Earth. She has been doing this for millennials. I want to stop her and use the power grid to give back to the people that are supporting it."

Alex thought a little while still aiming the shotgun at Profett and back at Sparks.

"I am going to Phoenix. Do you think this Lucille lady has my husband? And I still don't know who this is?" She aimed the shotgun just inches from Sparks' nose.

"I am Jonathan Sparks. I know your husband, Adam and myself are close friends."

Alex was confused. She had heard stories of Sparks and even had seen him in a few pictures Adam showed her. Adam loved and admired Sparks, but Sparks was a man. He was a human that could do human things. Definitely not walk out of void tunnels and appear in back seats.

"What the fuck is going on?" she dropped her arm lowering the shotgun.

She looked at Profett and Sparks. Sparks'mask slowly removed itself and Alex could see his face. It most definitely was Sparks. He looked just like he did seven years ago when the pictures were taken. There was something different in his eyes, like a darkness that gave her a feeling of serenity and peace.

"To answer your question, your husband is at the same base that Profett is going to. Lucille is currently questioning him about some thumbdrive he has or knows where it is. It has the location of all of the Zion bases. She wants to wipe out her only earthly competition so she can rule uncontended."

Alex grabbed her necklace as she listened. Sparks looked at Alex then at Profett.

"Your daughter is in Egypt. She and the Elohim are freeing and recruiting as many soldiers as they can so we can bring the war to Lucille. The Lord has finally given the call to battle."

Profett nodded.

"Good... They should make their way to us just when we need them. I must do my job. Are you here to help us?"

"Yes. We will slip in sabotage what we can. Save Adam, and free the power grid for the people."

Sparks' face mask went back up and he placed his elbows on the back of the two front seats. Profett smiled and turned around in his chair. Alex was confused. She wanted to get her husband out but the way they just nonchalantly danced around that whole, ideal shaking truth was hard for her to comprehend. She turned around in her seat and grabbed the wheel with both hands while looking outside the car. She shook her head and started the engine.

"So where to, guys?"

They all looked at each other and smiles formed on their lips. Alex shifted the engine and drove off. As the dust settled over a sign, it was a mile marker that read Phoenix 25 miles.

Chapter Nineteen

IRON MAIDEN

As Adam sniffed the air, he could smell waffles and eggs. *'Oh bacon,'* his stomach rumbled at the scent.

He rolled over in his bed and clutched for Alex. He giggled to himself as he realized that delicious breakfast he smelled was not cooking itself. Oh, how he appreciated his wife. She was his everything. He sat up and swung his legs to the ground.

At his feet were his house slippers perfectly laid down at his side of the bed. He smiled; it was the small things that really moved him. He slipped his feet into the slippers and stood up. He stretched and yawned as he grabbed his robe off the dresser door and made his way to the kitchen. As he approached, he sleepily called out to Alex.

"Babe, I was wondering what we could do after we eat this delicious breakfast you are cooking?"

He turned into the kitchen door and scratched his head. He looked around but she was not anywhere near the kitchen or the dining space. The rooms looked familiar but almost like they were a combination of places he had lived. Adam went back in the kitchen and looked at the stove. There was nothing cooking, yet it still smelled as if there was.

He heard a gurgle in the sink and looked in that direction. The gurgle returned and this time Adam could see a liquid bubble and pop out. He walked closer and saw that the little bit that did not go back down the drain was red; a deep crimson red. Then it happened again, this time it spurted out with a bit more force. It looked as if it was blood.

Adam got closer, putting his two fingers in a puddle that formed from the last spurt. He raised his fingers to his eyes to inspect the substance, and as he rubbed his fingers together, it was indeed blood. He looked down the drain and thought for a second that he saw something move. So, he leaned in closer. There was a small gurgle, and just before he was able to back up, the sink spewed out more liquid.

Adam felt the warm gooey substance pour down his head, face, and neck. And as he lifted his head, he was no longer in his kitchen. He struggled to open his eyes, but the warm liquid forced him to close them once more. He tried to move his hands to wipe it off his face, but he couldn't. His hands were tied to the wall.

His arms were stretched out in both directions. He tried to move his feet and his ankles were also tied together. He shook his head violently and squirmed. Most of the liquid that was on his face shifted just enough for him to slightly open his eyes, and a little liquid seeped into his left eye.

He shook his head again, but this time he was trying to get the liquid out of his eye. He blinked frantically as the sting of the liquid produced tears. He blinked hard and long and opened his eyes slightly again. He looked at where he was at, and it seemed to be some sort of high-tech medical room with a one-sided mirror just to his right. And in front of him was a carcass of what seemed to be a pig.

He looked closer and saw that the body was heavily mutilated. It was not a skilled butcher that did this, but by the looks of it, it was done by an animal or a couple of animals. There was hardly any blood on the ground which was odd. The flesh hung on the bone and the only way Adam knew it was a pig was because the head, minus the eyes, was pointed directly at him.

He looked past the carcass and saw a door with no handle. He looked at the wall and ceiling. They were the same gray color with a dark blue band that went around the room near the ceiling. And just above his head was a bucket dangling on a rope. Adam traced the rope as far as he could before concluding that it was attached to him.

It must have tipped over while he moved in his slumber. Adam recognized the type of room he was in, it was some kind of a holding cell, he thought. And the pig is a scare tactic. In his time with the agency and his short time working as a double agent with Zion, he had heard of places like this. Torture rooms were where unsanctioned methods of interrogation took place.

He froze, he literally felt his heart stop. He knew exactly what was happening. The Agency still existed, and they wanted the thumb drive. Adam took a few deep breaths, as it was hard for him to calm down. He was near a full-on anxiety attack and his thoughts ran wild.

He remembered Phillips giving him the thumb drive as he died from a huge hole in his chest left by some strange man in a pinstripe suit. He remembered seeing the man's hand morph into something beast-like, and the evil smile he gave him as he turned and leaped off the twenty-story building they all were on. Most of all, he remembered that attached to Alex's favorite necklace, was the thumb drive. He hung his head as he sobbed.

"No! No! No! Why did I put it around the neck of the most valuable person in my life?" He said inaudibly.

He let out a few more sobs before he was disturbed by the door directly across from him being unlocked.

The lock slid slowly, and the door was pushed open. Standing in front of him, just on the other side of the doorway were two white males dressed sharply in black business pinstripe suits. Adams popped his head up in fear, his heart raced as they slowly and calmly walked through the door. As they entered, the stocky tall man stopped and took a deep breath, "Jones, you smell that?"

"Which one? The rotting carcass you left on the floor or the fear?" Jones looked right at Adam.

Jones was slender and around 5 feet 11 inches, and the suit he wore looked a half size too big and he wore glasses that were a bit too big for his skinny, weasel-structured face. He had a menacing glare. It was as if he was thinking of what he was going to say or do next, all the time. He walked closer to Adam and sniffed a bit more. A smile came over his face as he stepped back.

Once out of Adam's direct view, Adam could see the other man, Mr. Robinson. He was taller than Mr. Jones, his stocky frame was concealed in his suit, Adam couldn't tell if he was slightly overweight or just that buff. His arms helped a little with the evaluation. They rippled and made the arms in the suit cling on for dear life.

They were not the arms you wanted to have around you. Everything about Mr. Robinson was bloated and rounded. His chin was solid, and his neck almost matched the size of his jaw line. Robinson was kneeling over the carcass and digging in an open part of the flesh. He pulled around a bit more, and the sounds of bones cracking and flesh swishing in his hands made Adam feel slightly sick.

Mr. Robinson yanked hard one last time and smiled while pulling out what looked to be a rib.

"Rotten? I just found a good rib right here!" Robinson licked his fingers before biting on the rib.

Adam could hear the bone crunch under Robinson's teeth. He clinched his jaws, gritting his teeth.

"Mr. Robinson, if you are done with your snack maybe we can complete the job we came to do...." He looked at Adam again and walked up close enough that Adam could feel his breath on his cheek.

"We want the thumb drive and we are going to get it!"

****

Aviv awoke with a horrible headache. He placed his hand on his head then with both hands, he lightly patted the rest of his body to see if he had any injuries. Besides the headache and the numbness in his left arm, he was in good shape; he unbuckled the seat belt and looked around for the three men he brought with him. They were awake and groggy and were doing as he had done. He gave them a thumbs up which they returned.

He got out the chair but stayed low, he motioned to the other three to do the same. He pointed to one of the men closest to the back. He patted his head, telling the man to stay covered then he used his two fingers pointing at his eyes then sweeping the fingers outward to signal '*look*'. The man crept to the door and peaked out, he quickly ducked his head back and lifted all ten fingers multiple times.

Aviv stopped counting after the second time, because anything more than 20 was an automatic five flashes. He looked to the armory and it was still locked. He motioned to the guy closest to him to unlock it. He then crawled on hands and knees to the cockpit.

The first thing he felt as he got close to the door was a feeling of fear.

He feared that he was going to open the door and find death on the other side. Most of all he feared that Kelia would be amongst the dead. He grabbed the handle and pushed the door aside. The cockpit was destroyed, and there were electrical wires hanging and sparking. Both his man and Kelia were on the floor.

Good thing is that they were both in the middle of their safety pats. Aviv let out a sigh, and just as he did, he heard a moan; it was Alexis. He moved over a piece of rock that had been lodged into the cabin when it breached the wall. He was only able to tilt his torso through the mix of plane and building but he was able to see Alexis. She was pinned in between a rock and her seat.

Her legs were crushed, and she was in shock. She did not know the situation she was in, but Aviv could see that life was slowly slipping from her grasp.

"Don't move babe." He said calmly trying to remove any fear out of his voice.

"We are going to get you out."

"There... there is no hope for me. I can't feel my legs. I can't feel anything."

"Just hold on, Lexi!" he tried to move the rock that was in front of him.

He strained and the veins in his muscles looked as if they would pop. But nothing even shifted slightly. He looked on the floor and he saw a pole from the fence that they were currently protruding. He picked it up and tried to position it as a lift. He pushed down with all his might, lifting himself off the floor a bit.

But nothing moved. He moved back to the hole and stuck his body in once more.

"Grab my hand! I'll pull you out!"

"It won't work," she waved it off then smiled a bit, "remember when we were in the rec room after the blast? You told me that someone already has your heart..." a tear rolled down Aviv's cheek.

He nodded and forced a smile back that quickly turned to a sob.

"She might have your heart, but I got a chance to borrow it. And I loved every minute of it." She smiled with tears flowing down her cheeks.

Aviv slumped, and they held hands for a little while.

Theer was commotion outside; there were men and demons alike moving in their position. The initial impact took out the watch standers and a few more, but the base was now getting into defense positions. Kelia touched Aviv's back, she knew what was on the other end and that there was no way to help Alexis.

They needed to get out of this plane as it was a kill zone. Also, the landing might have been rough, but they still had a mission to do. Plus, a mission that just got added on, which was to find a new plane. Aviv slowly pulled out.

"Is she..." Kelia said with as much empathy as she could muster up in the position that they were in.

"Will be..." Aviv answered emotionlessly.

"I'm sorry, but we can't mourn for her just yet. We have to complete the mission. She would want that. And we will honor her by staying alive and freeing the prisoners!" She spoke with more authority as she finished the sentence.

Aviv who was looking at the floor still in shock, moved his eyes to her clear green eyes. Although she spoke with authority, her eyes held so much compassion for him and Alexis. She was right. Aviv sniffed and straightened himself up.

His partner, who was silently mourning for Alexis as well, grabbed his shoulder and pulled Aviv in for a hug.

Aviv returned it briefly before motioning for them to go outside of the cabin. The soldiers and demons outside the aircraft had stopped moving. Kelia knew this meant one thing, they were organizing their attack and it would happen any moment now. She moved over to the pilot seat and bent down to position herself to see the condition of Alexis. She was doing bad; she only half opened her eyes to look at Kelia.

Kelia felt so much empathy for her. She could tell that the young British officer was proud and kind. She knew this during their training together. Kelia reached out and placed her hand in Alexis. They did not say a word, just exchanged a smile.

Alexis grabbed the object that was in Kelia's hand, then nodded her head as she lightly pushed Kelia's hand away. She was too weak to say anything but Kelia knew what it meant. She pulled herself out of the wreckage that surrounded Alexis and made her way to the rest of the guys.

Aviv and the other four men with him were completely in battle gear and were loading up their weapons. Kelia grabbed her load out and then addressed the men.

"I will go out and create a distraction. You five make your way around the ridge and get to the prison."

Aviv was just about to address his concern of the plan when Kelia cut him off before he could speak."Don't worry about me. I am going to head to the mass transportation device and get the Elohim." Although Aviv was a high-ranking officer in Zion and was with the organization long before Kelia, no one but Profett had more authority than Kelia. This was not because she is the daughter of the original founder, but it was due to her skill and tactical mind frame. She was a genius at making plans of war. She was even better at improvising when those plans needed improvising. Aviv understood which situation this was.

He didn't doubt her abilities, he was more concerned for her safety. Losing battle buddies was the worst part of war, but to lose loved ones felt even more sorrowful.

There was a loud roar and the humans that were outside yelled an equally loud battle cry.

"That's our cue. Let's go out this way and take cover. We still have one more surprise!"

Aviv looked curiously at Kelia as she and the other four men made their way through a hole that was facing the opposite of their opposition. He looked one more time at the cockpit, dropped his head and prayed a quick prayer for Alexis. He then straightened up and quickly caught up with the rest of his team who were hiding a little away behind a large boulder.

Chapter Twenty

POISONOUS DARTS

Alex, Profett, and Sparks had been walking for the last 5 hours. They had to abandon the car since the closer they got to Phoenix's city limits, the more cars cluttered the roadways. Alex parked the car in an abandoned garage and placed a tarp over it. She wrote the address down on a piece of paper and then folded it and placed it securely in the coin pouch on her pants. Her and the other two gathered as many weapons and ammunition they could carry.

Sparks was able to fit almost all of the preloaded magazines in his suit, as the suit formed around the magazines. He thought it was a good idea because, although he probably wouldn't need all the ammunition himself, he could give the support when Alex and Profett ran out. While they were loading up the weapons, Profett kept making a stink about leaving his guns. Alex found it amusing and slightly annoying.

Why was he so upset about those guns? She had many guns with her, and at different calibers. He seemed to let it go once he saw that there were two Glock 19's in her stockpile. He pulled out two magazines and exchanged them with the ones that were already in the guns. He then grabbed one of the shot guns and wrapped it around his back.

She found it weird that although it was not needed, Profett clung to his staff as if it was a walking stick, and not a makeshift spear with a strange golden silver tip. Alex stayed with her regular load out, the M1A rifle with the .40 caliber handgun. She had her hunting knife opposite of her handgun, she put a light leather jacket over the flannel shirt she was wearing and then strapped the sawed off double barrel shotgun she wielded in the car, along with a belt of shotgun shells she wore across her shoulder. Sparks grabbed one of the Ar-15's and they were off.

The walk was long, but nothing really slowed them down. Sparks navigated them through the streets. It wasn't that he knew the city, they actually used Alex's watch to pinpoint the destination. Sparks just knew how to avoid 'the others' as they were more active at night and in dark places.

He had studied them for years. Every time he was lost in thought on a cloud above one of the major cities with his love, he would curiously watch how they moved, how they processed, and how they interacted with each other. They were far from any zombies Spark's had seen in movies. They seemed to still have a trace of humanity. They hunted and stalked their prey and they didn't just chase, they didn't try to eat a person, they just wanted the person dead like them.

Almost as if they were building an army or a new civilization. He felt that even though the others moved at night, they were being watched at this very moment. Every now and again, Profett or Alex or Sparks would see just one *Other* looking at them from under a bridge or from a dark abandoned shop. They would never be aggressive, they just watch, and when you take your eyes off of them and look back to where you saw them, they were always gone, like scouts.

The group had made it to the city.

"Alex, what time do you have?" Sparks was looking up trying to find the sun.

The fog was worse in the cities due to the fires that still burned. "It is 5:42." She responded.

Sparks looked to the west, and he could see the light of the sun through one of the clouds. It was setting soon. Sparks looked and saw an abandoned gas station.

"We should gather ourselves and formulate a plan for our next steps. Let's go to the service station." "Why stop now? We are only seven miles from their base. Like maybe an hour or so keep going." She looked at Profett trying to convince him to side with her.

"We need to get ready for the night. We are in a city, the Others are heavily populated in cities. The next few miles are going to either be done cautiously or all-out assault mode. Either way we choose, we are going to have to work our way to the base." Sparks said.

"I agree, we should take the path of the least resistance."

Alex rolled her eyes at Profett, not because she didn't agree, just at the fact that he didn't side with her.

"Okay, I don't know anything about these Others, but if you feel we should try and avoid them, I will agree. I just want to get to Adam. I think getting to their base without raising suspicion or their threat level, is a good plan."

She took the satchel from around the back of her waist and laid it down on the counter. Sparks walked over to the window, and he saw one other just a few buildings down.

He turned around and went to where the other two were standing. Alex had pulled out a few silencers and handed one to Sparks which he screwed to the end of his rifle. She placed one at the end of her M1A and handed a larger one for Profett and his shotgun.

"I think the only way to proceed is to go building to building, limit exposure to the streets and open spaces."

Sparks nodded in agreement, then looked at Alex.

"How good are you with that marksman rifle?"

Sparks pointed to the rifle hung over her shoulder.

Alex smirked, "I keep the steaks on the dining room table. I put this old girl to work."

"Good, I want you to watch over. Stay a couple buildings behind but on the rooftops. You will have to keep moving from building to building. I would only recommend three of four shots before moving. Make them count, these 'Others' are smart. If you overdo it, you will be exposed."

Alex listened and looked for the nearest rooftop she could perch on. She chambered a round in her rifle and looked at Sparks and Profett.

"I'll do what I can. I won't have a great shot if you are in the buildings. I suggest if it gets too heavy, you get into the streets where I can do more damage."

Sparks and Profett both nodded, and Alex turned and ran down the street.

****

Kelia jumped up in the air and came down hard with a knee to the head of one of the enemy soldier. The soldier crumbled while his buddy turned in shock. His hesitation cost him his life as Kelia thrusted her knife in his throat. She couldn't wait and gloat at her kill. There were hundreds of soldiers and demons trying to converge on her position every time she attacked.

She ran and slid past a jeep to a roadblock, the reaction of the enemies was instant, pieces of the block chipped from the enemies' fire as she slouched closer to the ground. There was nowhere to run. She had dug herself in a ditch that would soon become her grave if she did not improvise something quick, she then reached to her side arms. In the initial attack, she quickly exasperated her rifle's ammunition, but with great accuracy. Kelia quickly peaked through a hole that had formed in the barrier. The pyramid was roughly a football field away. As she pulled her head back a bombardment of bullets chipped more holes and then the roadblock split in two. Kelia pulled her legs in tighter and slouched down more behind what remained. She took a deep breath, and as she was just about to return fire and make her way to a building, the ground shook violently. The tremor was so sudden and had such force that it caused Kelia to fall to her side, exposing her to the enemies.

The men and demon alike did not worry about Kelia. They were busy trying to brace themselves from falling while dodging falling debris from nearby buildings.

Kelia moved her hand away from a crack that was forming in the ground. As it got bigger, she realized that it would possibly break through. She jumped up and back peddled away from the now a foot-wide and nearly six-foot long crack in the ground.

She looked at the enemies and they did not even care about her anymore. She grabbed her pistols from their holsters.

"This is what's wrong with men, they lack discipline and focus!"

Kelia aimed and fired at a soldier, hitting him dead in the chest. She ran towards where he had been standing. Firing a few more shots at more soldiers, killing them instantly. She emptied a magazine in one demon. The bullets she was using would do nothing to him but stun him for a brief time, but that was all she needed.

She baseball slid the final few feet to his position and quickly popped to her feet. In one motion, she reached and grabbed her machete spinning around, slicing off his head from his neck. The demon's body fell to its knees and its head rolled away.

Kelia hated how these basic demons manifested on earth; they were grotesque. Their bodies were shaped like a sasquatch, with long lanky arms and legs but with no hair. Their heads had no eyes or mouths, just a slit for where the nose should be. To the people under their charm they looked as if they were just really tall men, but Kelia could not be put under any charm, thanks to Profett performing a ritual years ago to repel any harmful magic she might come across.

Two demons flipped from opposite directions in front of her. Another hopped on top of a car in a stalking position from her rear. They all stood for a second in a weird three-way standoff. Two or three demons was nothing, but that is the limit. Unless you can get the drop on the demons.

A hoard would surely kill most beings. Kelia dodged the swinging attack from the demon on her right. She somersaulted over a kick the one on the left threw and jumped up in the air doing a backflip over the tackle of the third that was on the car. The three demons collided into each other and Kelia ran towards the steps of the great pyramid.

Everything shook around the pyramid, but once she stepped on the first step, she noticed that the pyramid itself was completely still. She looked back at the base surrounding the pyramid, the ground was breaking apart and buildings collapsing everywhere. As she studied the catastrophe, she noticed that the tremors were rhythmic; like the rhythm of marching. "Thank you, Holy Mother! The saints have come marching in!"

She turned and ran up the steps to the entrance.

****

Aviv and his men finally made it to the top of the ridge and were looking down at the prison where the Zion captives were being held. Between the earthquake that had only recently died down, and Kelia. He couldn't tell which was the greater catastrophe to Lucille's base. There were only a few men still standing guard within the prison gates. He and the four men placed posts in the ground and the posts mechanically hooked themselves.

They tied their ropes to the post then threw the remainder of the ropes down the drop of the ridge. They hooked the ropes to their harnesses then started to walk down slowly on the ridge face first. When they got closer to the ground, they eliminated the remaining guards and dropped in, unhooking their ropes and lining up in a straight line against the wall of the prison, just left of the door. Aviv was second in line and the man directly behind him moved to the front to place a small pack of C4 along the hinges of the door. Once he was complete, he moved against the wall opposite of the other guys and gave a thumbs up.

All the men crouched down and guarded their ears as Aviv pulled out a small detonator and pressed the red button that was underneath a plastic guard. There was a loud explosion and the door flew inside. The man directly in front of Aviv quickly threw a flash grenade inside, stunning the men who were guarding the doors. One by one, in a single file line, Aviv and his men walked in shooting the men who were dazed by the commotion they caused.

Once the room was clear, Aviv looked around to find the control room. Two of his men were standing ready, guns still smoking from having cleared the room of its occupants.

"Clear!"

Aviv let his rifle fall to his side hanging by the strap on his vest. He quickly walked into the control room. There were monitors and buttons on a console, and two empty chairs with two dead bodies lying next to them. Some of the monitors had blood splattered against them. Aviv grabbed a piece of cloth from his cargo pockets.

He always kept pieces of cloth to clean his blades of the blood that gets on them from his enemies. He wiped blood from two of the screens to reveal two large holding cells with the Zion operatives inside. There was a cell full of men, and a cell full of women. The cells held about 20 or so people. They looked defeated and malnourished.

He searched the console to find the buttons that would free them. The numbers on the holding cells were 4 and 7, he pushed the buttons 4 and 7 and the doors opened up. The men and women that were inside did not move, they only looked at each other confused.

"Come on, damn it! Get a clue!"

The people did not move to freedom, instead they stepped back from the doors cautiously. Aviv looked at his men and shrugged. "I guess if they will not run to freedom, we will bring it to them personally! You three find the armory and you come with me."

The men nodded their agreement and parted ways.

Chapter Twenty-one

WINTER WARZ

Sparks and Profett were back to back in the middle of the street surrounded by the Others. The Others were faster and stronger than humans, and the only way to kill them was to either pierce their brains or sever their heads. This made it extremely difficult due to the sheer multitude of their numbers. Sparks and Profett had initially thought that the best idea to go forward was to go building to building which initially worked.

On the first few buildings, they only had to deal with two or three Others, which they took care of silently. The problem came when they made their way to a movie theater, there were at least a few hundred Others just standing around. It almost seemed as if they knew their plans and were waiting on Sparks and Profett. As soon as they were spotted by the Others, pandemonium broke out. Sparks and Profett quickly got outside so that they could have more room to move.

Sparks sliced downwards into the head of one of the Others. He pulled his sword out quickly and swung it to his right decapitating the next one that ran up. To his right, another one which was dressed in a coverall, as if he used to be a mechanic, ran up too close for Sparks to swing another blow. The Other's hand grasped at Sparks, just when he connected with Sparks' shoulder, his head snapped back, and he fell to the ground. The Other that was directly behind him paused, as his comrade's brains splattered on his face.

Sparks quickly jabbed his sword into the Others' eye. He looked to Profett and was amazed at how agile and strong Profett was.

When he first met Profett in the car, he initially thought he would be a liability due to the feeble posture he held in the car, but he wielded his makeshift spear like a shaolin monk. Twirling it above his head as if it was a propeller, he navigated his hands to the base and swung it like a baseball bat cutting two of the Others who were advancing at him at the same time, heads off with the sharp point coated with electrum.

Another one ran fast at the both of them, he was lifted off his feet from a well-placed shot to his head. Sparks was impressed at Alex's marksmanship. Three more Others fell back as bullets whizzed through their skulls. Sparks and Profett followed the opening Alex was creating and disposed of the Others that were missed by Alex's shooting. Sparks pointed to the large gated building three blocks down.

"That's where we need to go!"

They ran inside a small jewelry store while the Others looked to where the shooting was coming from. They were attacked by a few that saw them escape, but they finished them swiftly. Sparks created a dark fog and they slipped out the back.

"We are drawing too much attention. The base will be on high alert if we move on it directly with all these Others chasing after us!" Sparks looked at him.

He heard what he said but he was currently listening to the shooting Alex was doing.

"She needs to move!" he looked around nervously.

"They are going to surround her if she keeps shooting from that same roof top."

"We can go back out and distract them but like I said, the base will know of our presence." Profett said.

They looked at each other. Sparks looked at the ground and rubbed his head.

"I can't get my best friend's wife killed! We have to do something!"

"Before we do anything, let's see what she is doing."

Profett placed his hand to the earpiece in his left ear.

"Alex, this is Profett. What is your position and location?"

There was a bit of a pause and then there was activity on the line. At first all they heard was what sounded like heavy breathing and running.

"I am on the street. They got smart to my location so I am taking the alley ways to where you are at."

The line went dead. Profett and Sparks got nervous, yet they stayed quiet for a little bit longer.

"Alex... Alex... are you ok? Come in, Alex!" Sparks was pacing back and forth in nervous anger.

"Shit man. We need to go back!"

****

Alex was hiding behind a 2009 Toyota. She hugged close to the bumper and moved to her side just enough to see the four Others who were also hiding behind a car, across the street. They were looking at the building she had just come down from. They did not speak but the way they looked at each other and how they responded and reacted, Alex was sure they communicated. One of them pointed to advance, and they all started to walk slowly and calculated to the place he pointed.

She quickly ducked back and quietly made her way to the other side of the car. Making sure to avoid the windows, she nearly crawled to the front of the car as they walked by. She didn't even want to breathe. The four Others walked by, never even suspecting she was no longer in the building.

As they got to a further distance, Alex stood up from her hiding place and looked down the street. She could see where Profett and Spark were fighting earlier, and she tried to pinpoint the store front they went in. It was across the street, and approximately four blocks away. She ran across the street after looking to see if there were any Others looking for her. After she made it to the sidewalk, she raised her rifle up to her eye to get a better look at the road ahead.

Her rifle had two optic attachments. One was a large scope and the other was iron sights. She liked the iron sites, and Adam had put it on the gun just to the left, which made it easier for her cause she was left-handed. She rested her rifle. There were only a few straggling Others lingering around.

That was strange, she thought. Only a few minutes ago the streets were flooded by them. Had they all gone to the position she just left? She looked back and there were no Others anywhere in front of the building she was perched on. This had to be some sort of trap. She raised her rifle and twisted it so she could see through the iron sights.

To her, the iron sights were just easy, put the little green dot between the other two dots, and the target on top. She moved like a cat of prey, placing one foot tenderly down in front, and feeling her balance before moving the next foot forward. From out of a dark crevasse to her left, another Other jumped out and grabbed her rifle. She reacted quickly and pulled down on her rifle, this made the Other pull her closer.

She used this momentum to step on his thigh and swing her leg up to his shoulder. She pulled the other leg up and now she was sitting on his shoulders behind its head. Still in the momentum from being pulled, she leaned to the ground which caused the Other to tilt over in the same direction. Alex tucked her shoulder in and rolled on the impact of hitting the ground. As she rolled, the Other ended up being underneath her looking down the barrel of her rifle; the shot was muffled but the damage it caused was not as quaint.

Alex breathed heavily and fast. She was trying to gather herself and avoid a breakdown. She looked at the corpse under her and then looked up. Walking towards her were three more half-dead men. They had not spotted her cause of the car just in front of her.

She laid herself on the body she was still straddled on. The three moved slowly, she could hear their steps and the low grunts they made to each other. She grabbed her rifle and slowly slid to her left, putting the dead body between her and the street where the Others were walking. She positioned herself so she was now resting her gun on its chest. She waited intently.

Pttss... Pttss.... Pttss...

All three of the Others fell in sequence. Alex rolled herself to her back, and in one motion sat up then stood. As she readied her rifle and walked down to Profett and Sparks.

She thought of how effortless and tireless all this was to her. She was only breathing hard due to anxiety, but she was not tired in the least.

All the training and working out not only made her body look amazing, it also was keeping her alive. As she thought about this, Adam popped in her mind. She hugged closer to the rifle.

"Ya voy, mi amor!" She stopped.

Another dead woman walked in front of her from out of a store. She swung her rifle down so it hung from the harness. She pulled her knife and jabbed it through the dead woman's ear. Another one walked behind it and she pulled her large knife from the head of the Other she just disposed of and jabbed the new one in the throat. As it clinched for the knife protruding from its neck, Alex pulled out her side arm and grabbed the back of its neck forcing the barrel into its eye.

The shot was not as muffles as she had hoped. Two more ran around a car they were hiding behind and looked to where the shot sounded from. A group of what seemed like ten walked out from around a city corner just a block of where Sparks and Profett were hiding.

Alex quickly pulled the gun from the falling corpse and aimed it towards the two across the street. She placed two well-aimed shots in their heads. As she started side-step towards the street, she laid down for cover and fired at the large group just down the street. Her shots were focused but not well aimed; she hit more than half. A few in the chest and a few in various other upper body locations.

One got eliminated with a lucky shot as she rolled to a cover behind a parked car. She pulled up her rifle and reloaded it. She heard the movement of the Others as they ran to cover. They were smart, they moved well under fire. She raised up as she heard the footprints of one of the Others who was trying to cross the street.

She shot him in the leg, and as he stumbled forward, she shot him again in the head. She quickly aimed at one of the Others she had shot earlier. It was a female and she was now moving to Alex from behind a car she had found cover from. Alex shot twice at her head. One bullet pierced her mouth and the other one just above it to her nose.

Alex used her peripheral as she kept her sight down range. She saw another Other try to cross the street, and she quickly moved the nose of the rifle in its direction. She squeezed out a couple more rounds. The Other fell lifeless to the ground. She saw in a window, and the reflection of a group of four kneeling behind a faded blue Dodge Stratus.

She could see one of them tell a few of the group to go around the cars to flank her. Before the two stood up to do as told, Alex laid down cover fire. The .308 rounds left large holes in the car as glass shattered on the ground around the Others. She kept moving past them while shooting the remainder of her magazine at the vehicle. When the last round ejected, Alex squeezed three more times before realizing she was out.

The Others also realized she was empty and stood up to move to her position. They would have got the drop on her easily. They all moved inhumanly fast to where they thought she was. Alex was smart, she had moved to the car behind them when she had laid down cover fire and was hunched down reloading her rifle as they ran into the middle of the street. She jumped up again and placed four well-aimed shots in the heads of the confused Others, and again, they dropped in sequence.

A few more jumped up, and she quickly ducked behind the car. She was now half a block away from the store Sparks and Profett had run into. She took a breath. She could tell by how the Others were pacing and grunting, they did not know where she was. She listened to see if she could hear if any more arrived.

It sounded like a few more were opposite of their comrades. She looked towards the store fronts. There was a large broken window were Sparks had kicked an Other through. She thought about going into the theater but then noticed that there was an alleyway down a few doors. She slowly creeped towards the alleyway and slid into its darkness.

She ran silently down until it crossed into another alley just behind the store fronts on the street she previously ran from. She aims her gun down the alleyway. There were two large men standing almost at the end. She switched on the night vision on her scope then quickly lowered her rifle and smiled before she took off in a full sprint towards the figures.

Chapter Twenty-two

DAYTONA 500

G ual was a medium level demon. He and his partners were basic demons that did basic things, which were the usual possession and low-level summon work. Every now and again, some fame hungry couple would offer their children to him. Beside the occasional fight during an exorcism, there really was not much combat in his line of work.

Gual had never fought with an angel, or even seen one for that matter. This was why he and the thirty or so other mid-level demons were waiting in the large office area on the other side of the steel doors that separated them from the battle going on in the transportation room. Gual was no longer a street demon, his days of possession and menacing activities with humankind were long behind him. He was in a supervisory role.

Before the Fallout, he would target major people within the human infrastructure. He would then send lower demons to possess them, or most times, bargain with them. They would offer the demons that Gual sent to them many things, but mostly their fears. Demons never want nor can they obtain a person's soul. The soul is the sum essence of a person's being, it is impossible to sell that.

But the fear that you have given up something as important as a soul, was priceless. That is energy that is concentrated subconscious worship.

Gual organized the remaining demons to defend against the Elohim should they breach the large steel doors. They put a barricade of desks and printers just beyond the door and they armed themselves with weapons tainted with dark magic. It was quiet on this end of the large doors, so quiet that they could hear the clashing of swords and the gunfire on the other side. Faint yells and roars of larger demons echoed through the doors.

Behind them, Gual felt something. It was like a feeling of being watched. He turned his head and looked into the darkness. The earthquake the Elohim caused when they marched through the transportation device had knocked out all the lights except a few that were attached to the frame of the large steel doors, and a few back up lights that flickered on very weakly.

The demon next to Gaul realized his distraction and moved in closer to him. He was very tall but was crouched down on his hunches almost like an orangutan. He nodded up to him as if to ask what he was looking at. Gual waved his reptilian hand as if to say nothing and they both returned looking at the doors. Dust fell to the floor, as what sounded to be an explosive device erupted near the other side of the doors.

Gual felt a breeze on the back of his neck and shifted around in his uniform. He felt another slight breeze, and then another. He looked up to see if he was under a vent. There was one right above him and he moved a few more feet up. The demons in front of him recognized his authority and moved to make room.

Gual got a row away from the front lines. He was greeted silently by a demon he knew from working in the field.

"These damn angels pick today to attack!" Gual whispered to Steve while letting out an exasperated sigh.

"Yeah. Three years and no sign of the jerks. Now all of a sudden, a full-on attack!"

"Tell me about it. I was just about to put in for a vacation. My family lives on Mars and I wanted to spend some time with the kids and wife."

Gual finished his sentence and shifted in his uniform again. He felt another breeze and he heard what sounded like a cough. He was about to turn around.

"Hey, I didn't know you had kids! I got two of my own."

Steve was handing Gual a photo of his kids and wife. They were standing next to a large building somewhere familiar. He handed it back to Steve.

"Is that the unholy metropolis on Xess?" Gual asked inquisitively with excitement.

Not many demons get to go to Xess, unless you were a top tier official. The only other way is to be requested by a royal family there. He felt the wind against his neck and this time he saw a flash to his right in his peripheral. He turned his head and saw the body of the demon he was standing next to earlier. The head rolled over to his feet. He backed up as he noticed that there were no more demons standing on the side he was looking at. There were just bodies on the floor.

He bumped into Steve and quickly turning in shock. He found Steve still holding the picture as if he had just given it back to him. His eyes were blank and then they blinked slowly. His reptilian lips mouthed out some words, but no sound was coming out. Gual looked at Steve in shock as blood started to ooze from the skin around his neck.

Again, Steve's reptilian eyes blinked and then his body went limp. His head fell in the opposite direction of his body. Gual once again noticed there were no demons alive now on this side. He looked around and realized he was alone. There were only headless bodies.

He looked down again at Steve. His head was looking away from him. The eyes had shock, or horror in them. Gual looked to where the eyes were looking. A very attractive human woman was walking her way with a large machete in her hand.

He tried to focus, and the ground shook once again as dust fell and the lights flickered on and off, from another explosive. The woman was gone, and he looked around in panic. Gual pulled out his short sword and held it nervously with two hands. He was supposed to be removed from danger. He had a family now.

"Damn it," he thought, *"this was supposed to be an easy detail. Work long hours at a desk and take long vacations on a beach."*

The pain was sharp. He had thought that a death blow would be sudden death. What he did not realize was, death was off work. He looked down at the protruding blade in his chest. A small hand pushed him on the back as the blade was ripped from the wound.

He spun around before falling to his knees. He looked at the woman standing before him. She was so beautiful, he smiled a toothy grin then his eyes floated upwards. He could see his beloved Yurri and their beautiful children waving. He raised his hand up to wave then everything went dark.Kelia kicked the head of the reptilian demon out of her way and went to the controller that operated the large steel doors. As she looked down at the buttons, she paused and thought about the war on the other side. She was ready, her blood was flowing, and her adrenaline was high. She made a fist and looked at it. She felt confident.

She opened her fist and started to press the button on the controller when she caught a smell that made her stop. It was musty and damp, almost like a wet dog but stronger. Kelia's mouth opened wide as she remembered exactly the last time, she smelled this stench. It was at the gates when they went to grab Sparks. Whatever had thrown him through the elevator doors smelled exactly like this.

"So, they send a mutt to play with the wolves?"

A booming voice broke the silence. Kelia froze as she recognized that voice anywhere. The tone in itself nearly made her want to drop down and do a hundred push-ups.

"I figured you thought you would just waltz in here and open that door? Let your little angel buddies in the realm of men? Haha!

Well, should I say the realm of Lucille cause the world belongs to her and we are better for it!"

Kelia gathered herself. She turned to face the gunnery sergeant. He was as she remembered. He had not aged, and in fact, he looked to be in even better shape than when he was her drill instructor in the Agency. He was wearing combat pants that were desert digi camo.

The pants were tucked into his tan boots. He had a tan brown tee shirt that rippled against his muscles. He smiled his same menacing smile, but his eyes were different. There was a slight bit of what looked to be crazy in them; like a rabid dog. He was breathing heavy, as if he was holding back pain.

"You see, you fight for a 'God' that wants us to have no power or knowledge. Lucille has given me both!"

He slammed a hand down on a desk that was just to his right. The other hand grabbed at his stomach. He winced.

"Looks like your gift is one that keeps giving. If you need to excuse yourself, be my guest." Kelia pointed to a sign that read restrooms.

Gunny laughed while still holding his midsection. He raised himself up to a tall standing position.

"That is what will always be wrong with you sniveling little mutts. When things get painful, you want to quit. But I know that pain is just the necessary part of transformation." Gunny yelled.

His body began to twist and contort. His muscles, which were already large, grew even larger. The shirt he wore ripped and his pants ripped as well. Dark hair grew on his head as his nose and mouth elongated to a snout, and his ears got bigger and pointed. He was at least eight feet tall now and when he breathed, he would let out a plume of smoke.

Kelia looked with amazement. She had seen way too many demons to be afraid of what the gunnery sergeant had become, but it was impressive. He was some sort of a werewolf or an anubis; Kelia didn't really care to ask. She grabbed the machete in her right hand and a .45 pistol in the other. She walked slowly to her right aiming the pistol at Gunny and the machete over her head. Gunny tried to laugh, but the only thing he could do was snarl.

The experimental hell hounds were not as sharp or intelligent as Mr. Williams, Mr. Robinson, and Mr. Jones. If the host was of a strong mind, he could at least control more of the primal rages. When they first started to experiment with the hybrids, they used regular soldiers to experiment on, and the lack of mental resilience caused the Agency to put many if not all of them down. They could not handle the beast and they would turn feral. Then the Agency got permission to use Special force operatives from various governments.

The US being their major supplier, these soldiers were perfect due to the conditioning they received. They were able to control their mind, thus mildly controlling the beast when they entered their new beast form.

Gunny was all mental control. He had controlled his mind for years after he had reached his prime, to be able to still perform at the level he expected his trainees to perform. He had very high expectations.

He snarled and threw a chair that was in front of him to the side. Kelia stepped back a bit but did not show any retreat. Gunny raised his hand as if to motion for Kelia to make the first move.

"No, I'm good. Be my guest."

Kelia said as she stopped moving and got into a wide stance, and bouncing up and down on the balls of her feet. The Gunnery sergeant dug his large paw into the ground and charged at her. He growled a thunderous growl. He covered the space between the two of them in a second, or maybe two.

Kelia jumped as high as she could and grabbed a support beam near the twenty-foot ceiling. Gunny ran underneath, smashing into the barricade of the desk and chairs that were set up by a lot of middle-class demons as a defense. He stumbled a bit on a few desks but the impact itself had no effect on the beast.

He looked up to Kelia, jumped up and grabbed on to the post above him. With the agility of a chimpanzee, he maneuvered himself to be directly in front of Kelia just fifteen yards away.

"You... have... got to be kidding me!"

Kelia swung herself to a position where her legs were holding her up by the beam. She straightened her legs to let go and she started to fall to the ground headfirst. Gunny moved to where she had been and Kelia opened fire on the hell hound. Six shots, center mass, and he also started to fall to the floor. In mid-air, Kelia twisted her hip and the rest of her body followed as she gathered enough momentum to land on her left leg and roll back to the right knee.

She looked to where Gunny had fallen. His body laid on the ground curled up but still in beast form. She walked cautiously towards him with her pistol still pointed at his body. She stopped and released the magazine in her pistol then reloaded it with another. She pulled the slide back and walked closer to the body and though its back was facing her, she could see the labored breaths it was taking.

The massive beast took in large inhales followed by labored releases ending in a high-pitched wince. She used her foot to pull Gunny's shoulder over and check to see how close to death he was. He rolled over and sighed. The entry wounds from the bullet barrage Kelia had given him were healing. Kelia backed up and started shooting the beast again.

"Oh, hell naw! I have seen this movie."

She emptied a magazine and reloaded it before putting her machete away and pulling out the matching .45 and unloading both clips in the beast. She made her way to the controller she was standing at before being interrupted by this large beast, who was now getting slowly to his knees. Kelia pressed the button to open the large sliding door.

Dust shifted and the large gear started to spin. The steel door creaked as it slowly opened. Kelia heard a loud grunt and felt the energy shift around her. She ducked the swinging right paw Gunny threw. He threw another hook and another one.

She ducked one and back stepped the last one. Gunny jumped up and kicked out his hind legs in a drop kick. It caught Kelia in the chest, the impact forced her to fly back a few feet into the steel door. The impact made her breath escape her. She rolled over slowly and pushed herself off the ground weakly.

Gunny walked over to her and wasted no time, back hand slapping her upward. Her head jolted back with such force that it caused her feet to kick forward and she was once again laying on her back.

The two back to back blows were hard but Kelia knew that times like these are when life and death decisions are made. She had dropped both guns in the initial drop kick, so she reached for her machete. She mustered up a bit more strength and got to her feet again.

Gunny was walking around, chest heaving and admiring the damage he just delivered. As soon as Kelia readied herself, he attacked again. He swung his paws again wildly at her. She parried a few and dodged a few more. Sparks flew when his sharp claws struck against her machete.

Kelia ducked a swing of Gunny's claws and uppercut him in the chest with her blade. She whirled her blade around and swung it horizontally at his stomach, and again across his chest. The cuts were deep, and if she had been fighting a normal man, they would have been deadly. The strikes did draw blood against Gunny's thick skin, but they were healing just as quickly as they were made. The moves gave space between Kelia and the beast.

She looked to the door. It was opening up so slowly. There was still no space for even her to slip her thin frame through. She once again directed her attention to her threat.

Gunny was not all that excited about her last strikes. He was rubbing his now healed chest where the opening used to be.

"You felt that didn't you? You big overgrown stray!"

Gunny snarled and attacked again. He ran and threw a flying knee, which Kelia was able to dodge, he then swung a backhand at her head. She could not dodge this one in time and she threw up her arms to absorb the impact. The blow sent her sliding back a few feet. Using her arms to absorb the impact might have saved her life, but it did have its own consequences.

Her right hand was numb, and she dropped the machete into her left hand. She was sure her arm was broken because she could neither feel nor move her hand or fingers. She let it hang as she got into a shoulder length stance, ready for the next barrage of attacks from Gunny.

Kelia looked behind Gunny, the door was now open enough to allow two normal size humans in, or in Gunny's case, one of him. Kelia took the opportunity she needed. She had been on the defense this whole fight, allowing Gunny to throw his attacks first. This was a good plan, but in lieu of the broken arm that hung to her side. She could not take many more hits from this beast and still survive the fight.

She clinched the weapon in her left hand and dug into the ground before darting full speed at Gunny. He grinned and widened his stance in anticipation of her attack. In four fast steps, Kelia was just at attack distance with the beast. Gunny swung his claws at Kelia and she, still at full speed, ducked and slid between his open legs. As she slid past his large thighs, she drag her machete across the femoral artery.

Instantly blood spurted out. Gunny dropped down to a knee with his hand also supporting his weight. Even with his healing properties, losing so much blood was sure to make him weak. He struggled to get back on his feet. The wound was still pouring blood, and Kelia could see that the healing was slower than the previous times.

Kelia had never faced a hellhound. She had studied them along with other demons in her training. She was told that there were only three hellhounds that Lucille created by blowing moon dust in the face of Anubis. The Egyptian god then sneezed three times, and with each sneeze, he split himself. In her studies, she learned that the only things that could kill a hellhound was a well-placed strike to the heart with a substance called electrum, which was the mixture of silver and gold, or decapitation.

Gunny was standing a bit wobbly. Kelia charged at him again and this time she faked like she was going to go low; running at him in a crouched disposition. Gunny was still groggy from the blood loss. His wound was still bleeding but was over 80% healed. He threw kick at Kelia.

This is what she wanted, she used his leg as a plank. Nibbly jumping on it as he extended it in the kick. She raised her machete, her right arm hung lifeless by her side as she swiped down wards. Gunny raised his hand to protect his face.

The blow was not meant for his face. In fact, she had hoped he would raise his hand and expose the inside of his arm. She cut deep into his arm, slicing the brachial artery. Again, blood spurted out and Gunny howled in pain and grabbed the arm with his hand. Kelia, still in the air from her momentum, kicked her foot out forward and landed a hard thump in the middle of the beast's chest.

With gunny being weak from the wound in the leg that was now completely healed and yet again losing more blood, the kick was enough to make him stumble back a few feet before collapsing on his back.

Kelia stood in exhaust for a minute. She knew that she couldn't take too long, but she was tired. Her arm was starting to feel the break.

The initial shock mixed with adrenaline was wearing off and it was starting to throb. She winced a little as she looked at the deep purple bruise on her arm. She looked back at Gunny, he was still writhing in pain and whimpering like a dog. She curled her lip as she started to walk to where he was laying. She stayed her distance this time as she walked around to the top of the huge beast head.

She was going to have to cut his head off. She crept closer and Gunny let off a low growl that was almost inaudible, but Kelia felt the vibration and paused. Gunny swung his hand and grabbed Kelia by the calf. His grip was so tight that Kelia blacked out a bit seeing purple in her vision from the pain. She swung the machete and Gunny who was now crouching with her leg in his hand, grabbed her arm before she was able to get the momentum in the swing.

With one leg in his hand and one arm in his other hand. He stood up slowly pulling Kelia. She grunted and started to scream before he stopped.

"Enough of the games," he half grunted, and half spoke, "You are so pretty."

He leaned in and sniffed her belly.

"And you are ripe for birthing. If I bite you, you become my personal beta."

The thought of being any man's Beta revoked Kelia, but this was horrible.

"How does that sound? Huh? You and me starting our own wolf pack in this new world!"

Gunny was coming out of wolf form just a bit. His head had gone to a normal size though his body was still the size of the beast. Kelia mustered all her strength to not show the pain she was in and focused on her breathing. She couldn't close her eyes, so she looked past the gunnery sergeant and took in one last breath and let out a scream.

As she screamed, she jabbed her broken hand at the face of the gunnery sergeant. She had grabbed a pen out of her pocket as he was speaking. The pen pierced Gunny's eye and he instinctively threw Kelia forward. She landed roughly twenty feet from the beast who was now back in full beast form grabbing at his eye and roaring upward towards the ceiling. Her body tumbled a few times and she laid there.

****

Seriah watched as the doors opened. He could not only see Kelia fighting with the beast, he could feel the connection. He nodded for one of his soldiers to follow him and she nodded back. He ran as fast as he could to the large doors. A tall thin demon jumped at him, Seriah cut him in two with a quick spinning slash while still moving towards the door.

Another one of his soldiers speared a hound in the heart as the hound tried to attack Seriah from the back. Seriah didn't stop, he bent down and picked up a spear from one of the dead Elohim and he threw it into the heart of another hound who was advancing towards him. A couple more reptilian demons jumped in front of him. They both had two swords each, they whirled their swords around in balanced form and attacked.

Seriah never stopped walking, he dodged the swing and placed his right foot between the demon's legs. Going low to the ground he shifted his weight as he nearly crawled between his legs. It was a capoeira move he had learned from sparring with Sparks. As he raised up, the demon fell over after having been pushed by Seriah's broad shoulders. The other demon swung downward at Seriah's neck but Seriah hit him twice in his armpit which stopped him from completing the swing.

He then grabbed his smaller blade from the sheath alongside his armor. He grab the demon's other arm pulling him towards Seriah, and now in front of him, Seriah slid the blade against the demon's neck and pushed its lifeless body away while still looking at the steel door.

He could see Kelia standing over the beast about to cut off its head. As he continued to walk, he saw Ki fighting a little way over to his right. Ki wielded two swords with expert discipline. He was the master of discipline and justice.

He was currently fighting off a few demons with a group of Elohim. The group was becoming isolated from the larger army of angels. Seriah knew he needed help soon, so he started towards him. Before he committed in going over, he looked over to Kelia to make sure she was still in control of her situation, but she was not. The beast now had her by an arm and a leg as if it was going to rip her apart.

Every guardian angel knows that their bond with their human is not romantic love. It is much deeper than that, they love everything about humans unconditionally. They mourn when their human mourns, and when their human dies they make sure they are there to guide them to their truth. For Kelia, that was not today. Seriah ran full speed toward the opening door.

A group of combatants were fighting a few feet in front of him and he jumped over them grabbing his sword from its sheath mid-air. He landed and did a forward tumble before getting back on his feet. He looked forward, Kelia was on the ground slowly getting up. The beast was grabbing at its face frantically. Seriah would put it out of its misery.

He ran full sprint at the beast swinging his sword back and then forward. Just as he was rounding his full swing, a hand touched a pressure point in his wrist and his hand went numb. He dropped the sword and a hand grabbed it just as it was about to hit the ground. Seriah's eyes widened as he saw Kelia take two long strides while swinging the sword at the beast neck.

Gunny's head flew off as the sword swung down and collided with the ground with so much force that it embedded in the concrete. Kelia stood breathing heavy with her hand still on the hilt of the extremely large sword. Seriah jogged up after slowing down from his interrupted attack, rubbing his wrist.

"Next time, ask if I need help first!"

She felt a little annoyed, but she was extremely happy to see Seriah and the other angels.

"You can have this back. It's a little too unevenly weighted for me!"

She patted the hawk head on the end of Seriah's sword, and he went over and easily picked it out the ground and flipped it in the air once weighing it in his hand. He looked at Kelia questionably, then he felt Ki calling for help.

He immediately looked to where he had last seen Ki and the Elohim that were with him. They were now surrounded by a horde of demons and hounds. Ki only had a few men with him fighting off the demons. Seriah immediately ran towards Ki, Kelia ran behind him. They got halfway to the fight when a couple demons jumped between Kelia and Seriah. She fought the both of them, but it was an even fight with her arm still broken.

"Go!! Help Ki! I got this!"

She ducked a strike from one demon and kicked the other in the face. Seriah turned and ran away. He is too close to the battle to see Ki but he can feel his general direction. He starts slashing away at demons as they realize his presence behind them. A few more angels arrive along with him, and they start to make their way to Ki cutting down their enemy in pace.

Seriah was in the middle of dealing with two large reptilians when he felt a sudden pressure in his chest. He had been stabbed before but this didn't feel like that. It was as if a part of his heart was dying, so he quickly looked towards Ki. Through the fighting, he could not completely see him, but he was able to see his helmet. He was looking to the sky.

An extra amount of adrenaline kicked in for Seriah and he literally pushed through the remaining demons who had stopped engaging. As he broke through, he saw why they had stopped fighting. Ki was standing with both arms to his sides and swords still in hand, his head facing up to the extremely high ceiling of the massive underground transportation room. Which was at least two miles long as it was wide. Behind him was a shadow demon, these demons, like Jin and his assassins, navigated through the shadow world and earth's dimensions

Their bodies were dark and smoky in both dimensions. They were powerful demons able to create illusions and fought well against any foe. The demon's hand was pushed through Ki's midsection with smoke raising up and Ki's blood dripping down. It pulled his arm out of Ki by dematerializing it and stepping back. Ki fell to his knees.

As he started to fall forward, Seriah ran and caught him. He was close to death, he pulled Seriah's face close and whispered something in his ear then let go of the life he led. Seriah was furious. His blood boiled and he picked up Ki's two swords. He was very efficient in wielding two swords and only did not out of respect for Ki.

Ki never minded if he chose to but respected the respect Seriah had for him. Without looking, Seriah reached back and stabbed the demon in the heart. The demon did not see it coming and simply fell to the ground. Seriah's anger turned to blood lust as he stood up and began killing every demon within his range. Most of the Elohim stood in amazement for a while before helping Seriah rid the battle area of the enemies.

Once every last demon was dead in the transportation room, the higher generals came to Seriah's side.

"I am sorry for your loss."

"Such is war!" He was cleaning his blades without looking at the general.

"Well, the generals have talked amongst us and we feel you should lead us till we get word from Grandmother on who the next Archangel is."

Seriah already knew this would happen. He loved leading but this was more than a passion now, he wanted all evil eradicated.

"So, what should we do now?"

The general asked as Seriah looked up from his blade. He took his time responding, looking into each general's eyes, although he did not have to think about his next move.

"Next? I'll tell you what we do next!"

Seriah stood up so that all the angels could hear him.

"Next, we free the rest of the Zion fighters all over the world. Next, we kill every demon, hound, or man that opposes us! Next, we end Lucille's games for good!"

The room shook from the cheers and Seriah looked to Kelia. She nodded before turning and heading out of the doors she entered in. Behind her was the army of the Lord.

Chapter Twenty-three

Motherless Child

Lucille and Mr. Williams laid in a large bed naked and uncovered. Williams was still in beast form and Lucille was lightly stroking his massive chest as she draped herself around the girthy hellhound. Williams was shifting back to human form slowly. His head was the first to change. Bone cracked as they reset to the smaller human size.

Lucille placed her hand on his cheek bones as they returned. His chest and arms were next, followed by his legs. Lucille's hands soothingly touched every part of his body as it transformed back. She reached over to grab the comforter that was balled up on the corner of the bed closer to herself. Williams always shivered when he returned to human form; it was what he hated most about having to be in this human form.

As the beast, he burned with anger and passion. Everything was simple, everything was carnal. If he was hungry, he ate, whatever he wanted. If he was mad, he killed. There were no rules for him in beast form except the ones his lover, Lucille, created.

Williams was the fragment of Anubis that was still closely linked. He was the head of the beast. His brothers, Jones and Robinson, were different. Although they also were part of Anubis, they were very different aspects.

Anubis was not an evil being, in fact, he was very indifferent.

He was the guide through the underworld, he used to work hand in hand with Death. Dethia would collect the souls then transport them to Anubis so he could guide them towards their fate. When Lucille enchanted Anubis with the moon dust, the split of his soul caused fractures. His persona was literally split in three. Robinson took his physical traits, he was a brute and intelligence was not his strong part.

Jones took all of Anubis' cunningness. This was why he always seemed to be analyzing. He was always thinking of the next step and how he could manipulate it. As for Williams, he took on everything else, mainly the memories and wisdom.

This is what made him the head. He was closer to the source of who the trio were and Lucille liked this about Williams. He remembered, he remembered who she was. He remembered when she was in her glory and gorgeous, although she was still beautiful, Anubis had always had a crush on Lucille, and her on him. That reason is why she was able to get so close to him to enchant him with the moon dust.

As she laid watching Williams complete his transformation, she slid her small petite hand under the comforter she had placed over their naked bodies.

"Maybe we can hold off changing everything right now." She gave him a wicked smile and he smiled back.

As he smiled, his face started to shift back to the hound. Lucile placed her other, unoccupied, hand on his chin.

"No. I want you."

They laid, wrapped around each other and stared in each other's eyes. William was confused because Lucile only showed him intimacy during lovemaking. Most other times, she treated him cold and harsh. She made him transform every time they enjoyed each other. She almost acted as if she was disgusted in his human form.

He loved Lucille but would never tell her. He remembered how she treated him as Anubis, she was so loving and kind. During sex was the only time she ever did that to him as Williams.

A tear fell from his eyes. His heart fluttered in his chest as Lucille warmly wiped it off his check and leaned in to place a soft wet kiss on his lips.

"Lucille, my queen, my lord. I... respect you with all my heart. And I will do anything for you!" he stuttered during respect as he contemplated saying the word he really felt.

Lucille looked at him with the softness of her mother, and she kissed him again.

"Shhhhh... I know... Now, prove it, Anubis!"

Being called by this name, although it felt foreign, felt good to Williams. He pushed the cover off them and rolled over on top of Lucille. He looked her in the eyes before placing a kiss on her soft rose-colored lips.

****

Sparks, Alex, and Profett had creeped to another building and were just across the street from the large fence that encircled the tall building Lucille was using as her base. After they got back together, it was a bit easier to move to the next few blocks due to the fact that the Others were looking for them on the streets. They stuck to the alleyways and only had to dispose of four random stragglers as they made it to their current position. Sparks and Profett were going over a schematic of the building that Profett had taken from the Nebula library of knowledge.

Alex stood by the window of the second-floor apartment they were holding up at. She looked at the building then at her watch. Adam was in there for sure. She was feeling anxious, angry, and worried. One thing she did not feel at the current time was fear.

"We go in through the sewer." Sparks was pointing at the sewer to Profett.

"Then I think we should make our way to this service stairway. You will get out at the control room on the 13th floor. Alex and I will go rescue Adam. I think he is being held here. This is where they held prisoners when this was an Agency base. After we secure Adam, I will head to the penthouse and finish this mess with Lucille!"

Profett agreed and he and Sparks looked to Alex for her input. She was still looking out the window as if she had not heard Sparks.

"Alex! Did you get that?" She slowly looked towards their direction but not directly at them.

"Yeah, I got it! Can we go?"

She looked up to them with determination in her eyes, and they all took in a breath.

Profett pulled out his guns and made sure there were electrum coated rounds in the weapons. Sparks threw Alex a few more magazines out of the makeshift holders that formed in his suit. He did not need the magazines anymore due to the fact that he had abandoned the rifle he brought with him earlier. After they all got reorganized, they went downstairs to make their way to the sewers.

****

Adam hung limply from the wall. The position he was hanging from made it hard to breath. He had to raise himself up to inhale, and this made his shoulders very tired. He imagined, soon, he would not have strength to breathe at all. He thought about Alex.

He hoped she was safe and a good distance from all of this. They had made plans in case of an emergency. He really and truly hoped she had followed all the plans. He also, selfishly, hoped she would find a way to save him. He shook his head a bit thinking about how selfish that thought was. If he was to become free, then he was going to need to do it himself.

"Think, Adam!" He looked around the room for a clue on how to get free.

There was a knife and fork, but it was too far for him to reach. Pulling and struggling against the restraints would only make him tired, and take away energy he could be using on breathing. There was nothing he could do, his posture slumped and his breathing was short and labored.

The door opened, and a well inebriated Mr. Robinson walked in. He stumbled just a bit then stood in front of Adam swaying. Adam did not look up, and it didn't matter what these two did to him, electrocute, beat, bite. He shook his head a little confused,

"*Did they bite me?*" He thought to himself.

He was not going to tell them where the drive was. He would never tell them about Alex. Mr. Robinson cocked his head sideways and walked up closer to Adam.

"You know, I didn't even get to pick my own name." He looked over Adams face.

Slightly admiring the scars that he left a few hours earlier.

"I don't remember much before the split, but there is this nagging little voice that goes off every time someone calls me by Mr. Robinson," his lip curled a little, "Mr. Robinson," he said condescendingly.

"Do I even look like a Robinson?!" He yelled and grabbed Adam by the face.

"Look at me! I hope you never tell us where that thumb drive is. I enjoy your company!" He back hand slapped Adam and blood ejected from his lips.

"Mr. Smith thinks we can find all the bases without your help. I kind of believe him. I mean we did find you!"

He looked over to the table and walked towards it. He reached down and picked up the fork. He looked over it as if it was an intriguing tool, and then he walked back to Adam and poked the fork into a large scar on Adam's chest. He dug in and Adam screamed in pain. Robinson chuckled as he pulled the fork out and licked the blood.

"Oh, quiet down. It was only a taste. Now how about you start talking about that thumb drive... or don't. Like I said, I am here of my own free will."

****

"Shit! This one is also locked! What the hell are we going to do?"

Alex stomped her foot down in protest. They had made their way to the fifteenth floor. All the doors exiting out of the service stairway were locked.

"We have to either break through one of these doors and hope it doesn't lead to a bunch of enemies or set off an alarm. Or go back down to the fourth floor and use the elevator." Profett said everything condescendingly.

Sparks looked at both of them for a while, thinking. "There is another way, but... it will be just as dangerous..."

"Great..." Profett threw his hands up, surrendering to whatever plan Sparks had.

"I can take you and Alex through the shadow realm."

"You mean that hole you walked out of on the highway? Hell no! Esta Loco Cabrone?"

She looked over to Profett thinking he would agree. He just stood there stroking the grey and black stubble on his weathered chin.

"No puedes hablar en serio... really?" she shifted her weight frustratingly to the other side.

"So, we walk through the other side and get to where we need to be, then reappear in the real world?" Profett asked.

Sparks nodded his head yes but with little confidence. Alex noticed it and raised her eyebrows questionably.

"Well, why didn't we just do that before? We could have walked easily right through the front door and then to where we needed to be." Profett seemed a bit joking and a bit annoyed at this news.

"Well, the problem is this... The shadow world has always had its share of ghosts, specters, and demons. But since Dethia, or you may call her Death, has not been collecting souls. Well, let's just say that the shadow realm is a bit crowded these days..."

Alex stood there listening, but it was evident that she was not understanding exactly what Sparks was saying. Death not working?

The Shadow realm? Three years ago, she would have surely dismissed these two as crazy.

"So, let me get this straight. You can take us through the shadow world, but it is crowded? I don't get the problem. I really don't understand much of this, but I am going with it due to the crazy shit we have already seen. But what is the issue? Let's go through this shadow realm and get Adam."

She had grown impatient days ago. Sparks looked at both of them and took a deep breath.

"Ok... But before we do this, you both will need to stay close to me. We will move in a line with me in front. Alex you will hold on to my waist and move as I move. No deviations."

He looked her in the eyes, and she nodded that she understood.

"Profett, you will follow closely behind Alex, also holding on to her waist. Both of you will keep your eyes closed. The entities will be afraid of me but will try and separate you two in order to gain access to this reality. You will hold your breath. If you cannot hold any longer, you will tap the shoulder of the person in front of you."

"Do not listen to anyone and I will not be talking to you. And neither one of you should have your mouths open to speak. Whatever you hear is not from one of us. I will take us to the control room then to the holding cells. Once Adam is secured, I will make my way to the penthouse as planned."

Sparks looked at both of them. They both silently nodded their affirmation and got into position. Alex was behind Sparks, holding tightly to his waist, and Profett behind her bent slightly over holding onto her waist.

Chapter Twenty-four

CHERCHEZ LA GHOST

M r. Jones walked into the muggy room. The smell of sweat, vomit, and blood was intense. Mr. Robinson was in the middle of a combination of hooks into Loch's ribs. He threw a few more and the sound of bones cracking satisfied him to give it a break. Mr. Robinson wiped the sweat that was dripping off of his forehead.

He looked at Jones and shrugged. Jones shrugged back and proceeded to walk towards the table. Robinson grabbed a wet towel and put it over Adams face, he then grabbed Adam by the cheeks and tilted his head back. Jones had made his way to the table and was sitting on its corner closest to Adam and Robinson and without turning around, Robinson motioned for Jones to pass him one of the water jugs on the table. There were three full ones and two empty ones.

Jones looked at the jugs.

"I see you have been having fun." He chuckled as he passed him a full gallon of water.

"Tons." Robinson said.

It was very dry, but it was the truth.

"When you are done, Williams wants us to hang around the penthouse. He thinks something could be happening and wants extra protection for Lucille."

Robinson started pouring the water slowly over the nose and mouth of Adam. Loch's body shook and then he started to cough and gag.

"Maybe we can have a go at her this time. I always feel there is a connection between us!"

Robinson, pouring the water out in a slow constant stream. Jones chuckled and stood up to leave.

"Five more minutes and meet me upstairs?" Robinson, still slowly pouring the water, nodded and looked back at Adam.

****

There was a whisper to her right and Alex shifted her head to hear. It sounded like sobbing. It was male and he was murmuring something.

"Please... Alex... Babe..." she stopped just a second before being pulled by Sparks and slightly shoved by Profett.

It was Adam; she was sure of it. The shock of hearing his voice almost made her gasp, but she held onto her breath. She figured she could probably hold her breath for twenty, maybe thirty more seconds before she would tap Sparks to exit this realm or wherever she was. It was cold, but with most of her senses shut off, the only other thing she noticed that was different from the real world was the low hum that was constant and the whispers. She pushed her head in Sparks back as they walked.

There was a radiant energy coming from Sparks. It was a feeling of hopelessness, but a comforting hopelessness. As if there was nothing to hope for because all is complete. She felt afraid at how comforting the feeling was.

Just as she was going to tap Sparks, she felt a hand brush on her shoulder. She jumped and took a deep breath. There was a force as if someone, or something grabbed her in a hug. The feeling caused her to scream. As she let out the terrorizing bellow, she felt as if a hand was shoved in her mouth.

The hand reached into her mouth and down her throat. She could feel the fingers as they crawled down her esophagus. Her eyes popped open to see a smokey figure standing in front of her with his arm down her throat. The figure was large and human-shaped but with yellow eyes that glowed. He was smiling with teeth that were a dingy grey, and sharp.

Strings of spit linked each of his top teeth to his bottom teeth. She looked panicky to her left and right. Sparks and Profett were gone. She could see grey smokey images of what looked to be computer consoles of some sort. The room was large and yet felt so small.

She was all alone with this demon. Tears poured down her cheeks as the demon moved to possess her. Then the Demon pulled himself from Alex's mouth. There was a loud screech and Alex fell to her knees. A large hand grabbed her shoulder and the space became dark, then lights blinded her eyes.

Alex puked, more bile and spit than food. She could taste the hand that was in her mouth and she spit with more force, to get it out. She looked around and everything she had seen in the shadow realm was here but with color and no demons. She took a few deep breaths before standing up. Sparks was standing to her right looking down at her.

"Are you okay?"

Alex waved it off as she hunched over with her hand on her waist.

"Yeah! So, I might have broken a rule or two in there."

Sparks smiled and looked at Profett. He was looking at a large computer console. It was a switchboard, or the main operating console, of one.

"It's all here! I can't believe they have all the towns wired and controlled from here! This will be easy. I can take control here and shut down all the doors to the building. I will leave the ones you need to get Adam and control the elevator for you Sparks and end this with Lucille!"

They all looked at each other with confidence. Alex was so excited that she let a few tears fall from her eyes. The rest she would save for when Adam and herself are safe in their bunker. Profett typed a few things onto the keyboard, and a screen with a grid of the building opened up. As he typed, doors on the screen either turned green for open, or red for closed. Most of the screen was now red and Alex traced the green to a part of the thirteenth floor that read *'Holding 1'*.

"Now that I have this room all to myself, I am going to install this virus. It will take control of the software that controls the grid. Kicking Lucille out and giving me access as an administrator. Then we will be able to redistribute the power back to the people!"

Sparks nodded at Profett, and Profett typed in a few more commands then placed a tiny thumb drive in the USB port. He typed again on the keyboard, and the lights went off leaving the red emergency lights flashing. An alarm came on and they all looked at each other.

"Figures!" They all said simultaneously, chuckled, and shook their heads.

"I still have access to the doors. They will be breaking them down I am sure, but it will give us enough time to do what we need to do."

Profett typed more commands as he spoke. Sparks and Alex looked at each other and then to Profett.

"Go! Save Adam and finish this! I'll Be fine!"

Alex and Sparks took off and ran through the door and down the hall. The red lights were flashing and the alarm was extremely loud. Alex led Sparks to Holding 1 since she had remembered the path from the computer monitors. She started to jog, and as she got closer to the final turn that she needed to make in order to get to the only room holding an occupant, she saw the door and slowed down.

She had no idea why she slowed down at first. It was more of her body reacting than her mind. But as she got closer to the door, she realized the cause of her hesitation.

"Por Favor, Dios." She whispered.

She reached out for the door handle and stopped. She was afraid that she would open a door that would lead her into a life of misery.

Sparks placed his hand over her hand, and they turned the knob together. The door opened and directly in front of them was Adam. Tied to the wall and hanging limply.

"Adan!" She said his name in Spanish as she ran to her husband.

She lifted her shoulder just below his armpit so he could breathe. Adam winced from the pain of his broken ribs.

"Baby! You're alive!" She burst into tears and kissed his battered face gently.

He raised his head as far as he could get it up.

"Al... Is that you?"

"I'm here, babe. We are here. It's over! We came to get you out of here!"

Sparks looked Adam over. He could feel how close Adam was to death. Well, he would not see death, but he would become an Other. Sparks had a feeling in his chest. Looking at one of his dearest friends hanging from the wall slipping from life angered him.

As he brooded over his friend's situation, Sparks noticed a weird smoke coming from Adam. At first, he kind of thought it was himself. While fighting the Others he noticed that the more he killed the more his body would emit a black smoke. Now that same smoke was coming from Adam, Sparks watched as a few plumes moved from Adam and danced through the air and right on to his arm.

They were greeted by plumes of his own. It was like they were being welcomed home. Sparks moved his hand closer to Adam. And the closer he got to Adam; the more smoke would transfer to his hand. Adam and Alex were either too busy or just could not see the smoke.

"Aye, yo! Y'all see this smoke?"

Alex looked up at Sparks to see where he was looking. She was a bit confused to see he was not only looking at Adam but was also pointing at him as well. She looked Adam over from top to bottom.

"¿Qué carajo estás diciendo?" She looked at Sparks frustrated.

"I think..." He scratched his head.

"I think I can help heal him. Do you trust me?"

Alex was a bit skeptical but still agreed.

"Yes. Just help him, por favor!"Sparks walked closer to Adam. And as he did, more smoke transferred over. At first it was just a few tendrils. Then, a wave started to flow at Sparks' feet. He looked down then looked at Alex.

She was still confused at what the hell he was looking at. She was now, even more suspicious. What had he taken? She had seen a Primo get naked and jump in the pool at a Quinceanera one time. He also was asking if anyone else was seeing smoke.

After the family got him to get out of the pool and put his clothes back on, his wife informed them that he had been dabbling in Meth and Pharmaceutical drugs.

"*Lord,*" she thought, "*don't let him be on Meth. Hell...*"

All this felt like a bad drug induced trip. Had she taken any drugs? Was she even here? She shook her head.

Sparks touched Adam's chest and all the smoke now poured into his hand. He felt strong as if it was power being transferred. Nervousness almost took over as he questioned if he was helping his friend or possibly causing more harm. His questions were answered as Adam raised his head feebly and focused his eyes on Sparks.

"Jonathan? Is that you?"

"Be still friend, I still need to do more work."

Sparks now bent into Adams chest applying more pressure. He was confident he was helping. Adam arched his back and screamed. For a second, Alex could see the smoke Sparks was talking about. It was going from Adam and all over Sparks, engulfing his entire body.

She stepped back. Adam's body stretched upwards, his chest never leaving the palm of Sparks' hand. Sparks' suit covered his face as billows of dark smoke blanketed him. The dark light that now accompanied Sparks was all over the room and emanating from him. Everything was intense for a few moments.

Alex felt as if there was a strong draft coming in the room from somewhere, but there were no windows. Then as if it never happened, everything got calm again. Adam hung again limp and Alex ran to help her husband. Sparks stood strong and tall. He felt so much energy, like when he fought the Others, yet it took multiple Others to give him just a third of what he just got.

Alex rubbed her husband's cheeks, and as she did, she noticed that the open wounds that were there just moments before, were more like a month old and a bit of scaring had formed. Adam slowly raised his head.

"Babe, let's get you down."

She immediately unlocked his feet then unlocked his right hand. Adam pulled it into himself. Just moments ago, he hardly had the strength to raise his head. Yet now, he was not only standing on his own, but he felt pretty damn good. He rubbed his wrist where the restraints used to be.

" don't know what that was, but... Whoa!"He wasted no more time and wrapped his wife up in an embrace, locking lips simultaneously. Alex fell into his arms as they stood there in a moment of love.

"Yo, I really do get it. But to be real, y'all need to go. Profett unlocked the service stairwell on this floor alone. Leave the way we came in and make your way to the car."

Spark's suit contorted a bit around his chest area then opened up to reveal a service beretta in .40 caliber. He pulled it out and handed it to Adam. Alex took off the shotgun and shells from her upper torso and also handed them to Adam.

"Just so you keep a little of that 'male pride'," she winked at him and he smiled back.

Alex bent down to pick up her rifle.

"Where are you going?" He looked at Sparks.

"I have a date with the Devil."

Everyone paused. Sparks laughed a bit, while Adam and Alex both gave him the still face.

"Man, be careful. There are these two guys up there. Mr. Jones and Mr. Robinson. They... man they are weird. Mr. Robinson really worked me over."

He stared away while rubbing his ribs.

"You will need my help! I want to get back at those two!" He slid two slugs in the barrels and cocked the shotgun.

Sparks put his hand on the shotgun.

"Chill, I got this. I know more than you think. Those three dogs can't stop shit. I am going to kill Lucille and end this. You go and take care of your wife."

He lightly shoved the shotgun back into Adams chest, as if to say *you got this*, and Adam nodded back. Alex walked up to Sparks and gave him a huge hug.

"Dios te bendiga. Thank you so much." She sobbed on his chest then stepped back.

"Go kill that Punta!"

Adam checked outside the room and then they both ran out the door and down the hall to the service stairway.

Sparks took a deep breath then quickly walked to the service elevator. He pressed up and the door immediately opened. As he walked in, he felt no fear, he didn't know what fate awaited on the four stairs up. But for him, the one who is wedded to death, he could be relieved knowing that the only death coming tonight was what he was bringing!

****

Profett switched the screen he was previously looking at. He closed at least thirty tabs that he had opened while memorizing all the circuit layouts of the towns that supplied the power. He was trying to get back to the upload screen. And as he closed the last tab, he saw it, 98% uploaded. He was grateful.

The reinforced steel doors that separated him and the mixture of demon and human soldiers outside was starting to become dented from the heavy banging. He reached in his bag. He had six C4 strips and if he cut them in half, he would be able to place a charge on the beams of this building. Even if he did not bring it down in its entirety, he would be able to create enough damage to key places that would deem this base inoperable.

The screen he was looking at read 100% and he safely shut down the thumb drive that uploaded the virus. The screen went red for a few minutes, alerting the operator of the virus. He then clicked the pop-up box and everything went back to normal. He had no time to check if the control was truly his. He was going to have to go on faith.

He typed in a few commands and a few more obsolete doors opened so he could get into the spaces he chose that had the greater amount of weakness. He looked around for an exit, he needed to make sure that when everyone on the other side of the door finally came in, he would still have time to set the charges. He went into the control command on the computer and changed all the passwords before turning the computer completely off. This ensured that they would not be able to undo what he had done.

He looked up and saw a vent. He got on his tip toes and pushed the vent cover to the side. Then he lifted himself using his arms to look around the vent. It was large and spacious enough for a man to crawl around and not be too confined. He lifted the rest of himself inside before closing the vent and proceeding to his next destination.

****

The elevator stopped at the top floor. Sparks wiggled the last bit of anxiety off and walked out calmly. The layout on the schematic was massive, but as he walked in, it was only a small room. There were a few chairs on both sides of the small office. There was nothing exceptional about the office.

The wall had a very sterile and professional finish with motivational painting hung up. The painting had the usual picture of a man climbing a mountain with the phrase,

"Determination: the ability to do what you want... regardless!"

Sparks chuckled a little. For one, he remembered that these were the first memes and on the other end, the phases were so twisted that only a being as selfish and narcissistic as Lucille would come up with them.

There was a desk just to the side of a stained-glass door. The door looked to be a painting like the one Lucille had etched on her door in her office at the Gates. Yet this one didn't move.

Sparks started to the door. But just before he got past the desk, a woman stopped him.

"May I help you? Office hours are posted on the door, and Lucille can only be seen by appointments." The woman sat in her chair typing as if she was always there.

"Well, I already have an appointment. So, thanks!" Sparks replied.

The assistant typed a bit more then looked at the screen studiously. She was a black woman in her mid-twenties, had short dreads and was very beautiful. She did not dress up to her beauty. She had a wool sweater that fit tightly and showed a bit of her figure but it did provide a bit more modesty than the tight suit dresses Lucille wore. She looked over her screen above the glasses that hung on her nose.

"I don't see a Mr. Sparks anywhere on the schedule. You are Jonathan Ishmael Sparks?"

Sparks gave a questioning look. How did she know who he was? He shrugged it off and reached for the door handle.

"Well, I don't have time for this. Schedule or not, Lucille has an appointment with death, and I am here to collect!"

He twisted the knob and the assistant jumped up. She did not dare to try and stop him. She was by all means a demon, but her job was to record, not fight.

"I would advise against that, but if you are so determined to go inside, I must warn you... she has her guard dogs, all three, at her heel. Good luck, Mr. Sparks!" She said dry and condescendingly. Sparks just looked at her then walked into the office.

The office was entirely different from her office at the Gates. It was new and smelled new. The desk was extremely modern, and the walls were bare, no books of any kind. Sparks was on high alert and as he looked all around this large office, no one was there. There was another door behind the office desk, and he moved towards it.

As he got closer, a monitor on the desk caught his attention. It was showing the roof and on top he saw a helicopter landing and coming out of the doors was Lucille with three men in black suits. He looked back at the door and kicked it in with one kick.

"Do we have everything we need?" Williams was yelling at Jones and Robinson over the propellers of the helo.

They nodded yes. He looked them over and then at Lucile, his love. She was so powerful and yet so delicate. He would do whatever he needed to keep her safe. As he thought about Lucille, he was brought back to reality by a loud but muffled bang.

His senses were extremely acute, but with Lucille this close to danger, they were heightened even more. Jones looked at Williams and he could tell that he heard something.

"Are you okay, brother?" Williams slowly turned his head to look at Jones.

"Just get Lucille on board and safe. I will have another issue to deal with before I can join y'all."

Jones nodded again, but there was something in Williams' eyes that confused him. It wasn't fear, but it was an emotion that was just as strong, if not stronger. Williams' eyes went back to Lucille as Robinson helped her on board. A bit of jealousy riled up as he watched Robinson place his large ogre hand on Lucille's butt. What made it a bit more harsh, was that Lucille flirtatiously patted his hand as she smiled, obviously liking the attention.

Jones looked to where Williams was looking and saw the same thing. He looked back at Williams, who was in the throes of jealousy and realized what he was sensing from Williams; he was in love. Robinson and him always knew of Williams and Lucille's 'rendezvous' but he thought it was just that. How dare Williams think it would ever be anything more than that. This was their mother in a sense, and on a greater level this was the entity that was in charge of all selfish desires. He shook his head in disgust, inside he had lost a little respect for Williams.

"Brother, don't worry. We will treat Lucille with the same respect as you would." He patted Williams on the shoulder and gave his cunning smile.

Williams looked at Jones and raised his eyebrow. He knew what Jones was saying, and most of all, he knew Jones knew of his feelings.

"Great, brother. I will meet y'all at the Gates. I have a bit of a pest problem right now. It seems Mr. Sparks and I have a bit of history. Unfortunately for Sparks, I feel history will yet again repeat itself."

It had started to drizzle a bit as they got on the helo. Sparks rushed out the door just as Williams was finishing his statement. Williams could smell that he was approaching and said the last part loud enough so Sparks would hear. Sparks stopped and stared at both Jones and Williams, then his eyes darted to the helo. Lucille was inside and getting secured.

Jones then looked at Sparks, "Well, you two. It looks as if you have some catching up to do. I will let you at it. My queen awaits!"

He jokingly patted Williams on the back, letting the sting of Williams' imagination run wild. He then turned and briskly jogged to the helo, keeping his head low and his hand on his tie. Sparks started to follow, but Williams sidestepped to regain his attention and Sparks gave it to him. He came to kill Lucile andthat plan looked to be failing, but as a consolation, taking the soul of this beast would be a very close second.

Chapter Twenty-five

PROTECT YA NECK

As Williams and Sparks circle each other, the rain had turned from a light sprinkle to a full-on storm. As lighting and thunder cracked in the sky, Williams took off his suit coat very methodically.

"So, I see you will not stay dead. I will have to help you with that issue."

His words were dry as usual. And there was a menacing and determined look in his eyes. Sparks felt ready; there was no fear in his heart. He had faced this man or beast, twice before. Each time resulting in a devastating loss, but this time was different. This time he had brought a bit of death with him.

Sparks stayed silent. He watched as Williams took off his suit coat and dress shirt. The man had a hard-chiseled body. It was a bit surprising since in his suit he looked to be of an average build. Williams then rotated his neck.

"What's wrong? The cat got your tongue? I would say it is fear, but I don't smell that on you. You seem confident. I like that, it means there is more of you to break."

Williams' body started to change. It was faster than the last time he and Sparks fought at the Gates. It seemed to be gradual yet quick. The pain was still evident in Williams' eyes, but he made no effort in showing it. Within a matter of a couple minutes, Williams was a large beast. His hair that ran from the top of his wolf shaped head and down the arch of his muscular back, was matted from the rain.

He heaved in a large breath then let it out, the steam from his hot body released into the air. Sparks had nothing in his hand. He stopped circling and bent his knees. He took up a defensive Muay Thai stance, and Williams laughed a bit.

"No weapon? Well, it seems you are ready to get back to your woman."

He looked Sparks over. There was a trail of black smoke coming from his body. Williams squinted in recognition.

"Or should I say wife? Either way, I will be happy to oblige."

Williams charged at Sparks letting out a large growl. He reached Sparks within three steps of his large beastly legs. He swung his sharp claws at Sparks' face, and Sparks ducked. Williams followed with another swipe at Sparks which he also evaded. He threw a kick and Sparks bent down placing his hands on the ground to his side and twisted his body, smoothly ducking away from the blow.

Sparks popped back up to standing and started to bounce around like Ali. Flicking his nostrils with his thumb and settled back into a defensive stance. Williams got a bit frustrated, which was his weakness in beast form. He was a ball of emotions, mostly rage. He threw another combination and Sparks moved around from each blow.

Then Williams threw a jab and Sparks spun away from it ending to his left, next to his extended arm. The opportunity was there to deliver a blow. But instead, Sparks shoulder checked Williams' side, knocking the beast to his right a few feet. Williams regained his balance and huffed a large tendril of smoke and faced Sparks.

He charged again, but his time, he threw a few kicks at Sparks. They were dodged expertly. In frustration, he reached out to grab Sparks. His hands got just at his shoulders when Sparks leaned to his left circling his arms around the beast's arms. He then jumped on the beast's thighs and around to his back.

As he landed on its back, he pushed off, back flipping in the air and sliding back ten feet due to the wet surface. This sent Williams flying into an electrical fan. Destroying it and leaving him dazed.

Williams slowly got back to his feet holding his head; he was now a bit dizzy.

"Are you going to dance all day or are we going to end this?" He snarled.

Sparks let down his guard and walked slowly to Williams.

"I could have ended this for you with one touch. But I want to prove a point."

Williams shook his head.

"A point? I have beaten you before. There is nothing you can prove to me except dying!"

"I don't need to prove anything to you. The point I am proving is to me. I need to see that you are nothing more than a figment of my imagination. Your power is only as strong as I let it be. You will die tonight."

Sparks' suit had formed into his sword. It was as black as his suit. Along the edge was a goldish and silverish tint; it was Electrum. The hilt formed around his fingers like Jin's blade. Little heads of dragons protruded around his knuckles.

"Is that Jin's blade?" Williams' eyes got a bit wider.

"No, it is mine. And you have the opportunity to meet it firsthand."

Sparks swiped his blade a few times in the air and the sound of it whistled. He stepped back in a wide stance bringing the sword to his side. In what could only be measured in milliseconds, he sliced in the air before him. A raindrop was cut in half. The lower half still falling to the ground as if nothing happened and the top half rested on the point of his blade. It stood there shaking till it was met by more rain.

Williams felt something he was sure he had never felt before. He swallowed the large lump in his throat. His massive paws began to get a bit chilly. He made them into fists. And for some reason, he felt unassured if he could even defeat Sparks.

He literally shook his head. He had not only defeated Sparks before, but he had killed him. This little man would not be a problem much longer. He cracked his shoulders by hunching his back. He was not smiling nor was he as calm as he usually was.

He thought to himself, 'Maybe Sparks should be taken seriously.'

"Okay, Mr. Spark. I am tired of playing with you!"

He growled again charging towards Sparks. This time he ran on all four legs in a bit of a zigzag formation. Sparks stood there in the same position, his blade never trembled. Williams approached and lunged out at Sparks. Sparks pulled his sword back while spinning out of the way.

As Williams flew by, Sparks swung his leg up and down, hitting the back of Williams. The force of his kick mixed with the fact that he was on his way down, caused Williams' body to bounce a few times before he rolled twice from the momentum. Sparks did not wait, he jumped up in the air as high as he could, slashing his sword down at Williams' chest. Williams who was regaining consciousness reacted as quickly as he could by placing his hands together deflecting the blade with his razor-sharp claws.

Sparks' blade was too sharp, the strike was too true, and with the electrum, he cut off the fingers of Williams' right hand. Williams gave a loud yelp as four fingers went flying along with embers from the contact.

Williams jumped up to his feet, holding his hand against his chest with his other hand. He licked at his wound, still whimpering. Usually, a wound or a loss of a limb would not be a problem as it would just heal or grow back, but this was not just any wound created by any sword.

The Electrum made sure that any regeneration efforts would fail. Deep crimson blood poured from his hand, down to his stomach and legs to be diluted in the puddle he was standing in. He looked at Sparks in anger and a bit of amazement. Thunder cracked in the sky as lightning lit up behind Sparks, leaving a daunting silhouette. Sparks flicked his wrist causing his blade to fling the excess blood onto the ground.

Williams now knew exactly what he felt, it was fear. He had never feared anyone or anything but standing here now with his hand mutilated, he was not sure he would live to see tomorrow. Most of all, he was not sure if he would make it back to his love.

Williams shook his massive head. A tear ran down his cheek as he thought about Lucille. He would never again get to smell her hair or feel her lips against his chest. She was always so soft to him, in private. He knew she loved him, and he should have told her.

"I have yet to name my blade. Maybe I'll call it *Fingerless* or *the Dog Whisperer*. What do you think? Should I call it *Cesar Milan*? Cause after I kill you, I am going to kill the other two dogs, and then Lucille." This infuriated Williams.

His only passion in life was Lucille and he would never let anyone hurt her. He let both hands down to his sides. Although the pain throbbed in his arm, it didn't stop him. And as much fear he was experiencing, it did not match up with the anger he felt thinking of this mortal even touching Lucille.

Sparks tightened his grip on the hilt and started to charge at Williams. As he started, there was a loud bang and the building shook. It was as if lightning and thunder had hit the building. Sparks, as well as Williams, looked around confused. Then it happened again, then three more times in sequence.

The building shifted as the last blast went off and Sparks knew exactly what had happened. Someone was detonating explosives inside the building. And by the looks of it, there was going to only be piles of rubble after they were done. Two more explosives went off right beneath them and the roof collapsed into Lucille's bedroom.

The pain in Williams' hand now had guests. His back was numb, and his head throbbed. There was a bedpost sticking out of his thigh, and a large gash was on his right side. As he rolled over to push himself up the gash began to regenerate, he rose to his knees and placed a hand on his knee as he grabbed the bedpost in his thigh.

He let out a large roar as he pulled the post out, blood spurting into the heap of broken ceiling and bed on the floor. He stood up, dizzy from the blood loss as he looked over his wounds. They were healing fast, all except his hand. Looking at his nub infuriated him, and he looked around for Sparks. He wanted to rip his throat out with his teeth.

Sparks was lying on the floor unconscious and almost looked lifeless. His suit had hardened to break the fall. Inside, the seamstress was speaking to him lightly.

"Jonathan... Wake up... There are no external wounds. I am reading the signs of a mild concussion... You need to wake up, Spark. Mr. Williams..."

Sparks woke up to a hefty hand tightly around his throat. He tried to breath but nothing. He tried to grab the hand, but it was too tight. Mr. Williams had the advantage.

"Now, here is the Sparks I know. Wiggling and squirming under my grip." Mr. Williams smirked a razor-sharp toothy grin.

Sparks still had not said anything. He kicked a bit more, then a thought came to his head or more like an image. The image was of a porcupine. He closed his eyes and envisioned he was the porcupine. Razor-sharp spikes formed in his suit in an instance, protruding through Williams paw. The hellhound screamed and threw Sparks.

The first attempt at throwing him was unsuccessful due to the spikes in his hand. He flung Sparks a couple times. Sparks gained his bearings and as soon as Williams flung him to the opposite direction, he released the spikes and flew feet first into the wall. The force was so strong that he broke the wall, leaving foot indentions in the reinforced steel under the stucco.

He then pushed off the wall, and as he did, his sword grew in his hand. He pulled it back as he flew to the beast who was now nursing his other wounded paw. Mr. Williams looked up to see Sparks hurling at him. He was able to get his arm up that just been hurt by the spikes. Sparks swung his blade and took the arm off at the elbow.

The beast hollered and quickly tried to grab the elbow then realized he had no fingers on his remanding hand to grab with.

Sparks rolled then got back to his feet and calmly walked to Mr. Williams who was now hunched over and in pain.

"Doesn't look like that's going to grow back anytime soon."

He placed his sword just under Mr. Williams chin, lifting it up so he could look Sparks in the eyes.

"You look so uneven. Let me help you out with that."

Sparks quickly pulled his sword from Williams chin, causing a cut. He then sliced the beast at his right knee. The sword went through smoothly and Williams screamed again as he fell on his side. He wiggled on the floor and Sparks kneeled down beside him. The building was on fire and still rumbled and wobbled from its instability.

Sparks looked around from where he was kneeling. Everything was broken or on fire. The rain from the hole in the wall poured in adding to the wetness of the sprinkler system.

He then looked back at Williams and grabbed the beast by its mangy matted hair on its head. He lifted him up, so he was on one knee and the stub that was slowly but consistently pouring blood.

Mr. Williams winced in pain as his weight shifted on the nub that used to be his leg. His body was starting to shift back into human form starting with his legs.

"Oh, no you don't. I want to keep the head of the beast. The beast that I was afraid of, the beast that I have now conquered."

Sparks stepped back and bowed at Williams.

"Be easy. At least you get the honor of a beautiful death"

He swung his sword in the same manner he did outside. This time it wasn't at a raindrop, but it had the same effect. Williams body dropped to the floor and his head rolled to the foot of the bed.

"That is more than you gave me." Sparks looked at the beast's head.

A tear fell down the face of Williams. His head stayed in beast form and Sparks kicked it as he made his way to the door. He would have loved to bask in this glorious victory but there was no doubt that this building was on its way down.

Chapter Twenty-six

INCARCERATED SCARFACES

Alex was speeding down the open highway, there was a loud sequence of explosions, and she looked into her rear view mirror to see the large building surrounded by dust that lit up orange from the flames. She stepped harder on the gas. The car jerked back and Adam, who was getting a bit of earned sleep, jumped up a bit.

"Wha... no... babe!"

He shot up a bit confused and shook it off as he saw Alex with both hands on the steering wheel.

"It's okay babe. It's all behind us..." she looked back to the road and placed her hand in his hand.

Her eyes shifted back to the burning building. Deep inside, she prayed Sparks and Profett were safe. Although she hardly knew either, she and Profett had said little on the drive up. What he had told her, she was sure were lies; part of his cover story. And Sparks, she felt she had known Sparks as long as she had known Adam.

He always talked about him and Kelia. She hoped that he was alive and that meeting Kelia would be a bit different. She laughed at the thought. Different was all there was right now.

She looked over to Adam and he was resting his head against the window. She couldn't tell if he was awake or asleep.

"Cómo te sientes?"

She patted his hand then returned it back to the gears to downshift as she slowed to a stop sign. She put the car in neutral.

"Babe... What was all that? Why did they take you? Is this about the Agency?"

Adam watched as the grass and hedges came to a stop. He reached his hand to his face and pressed gently on a spot where Mr. Robinson had punched him. It was still tender as it had happened earlier, but the wound that he was sure should be there was gone. He thought about Jonathan. Where the hell had he been?

The last time he heard anything about Sparks was that he was killed on a mission somewhere in the Middle East. When he dug more into the files, he had found out that he was in New York at the VA then there was an "*incident*" at that hospital.

He was brought back by Alex who had shifted her hand from his elbow. She was softly stroking his under beard, and this always grabbed his attention. He shifted in his seat to look at his wife.

"Babe, I don't know how you did it, but thank you!"

He sat up a bit, grabbing Alex gently by both hands.

"I know all you would love to do is go back to the hideout and to be honest, that is also what I want. And to be sure that we... you are safe is my one desire in these times. But we can't..." he paused to let it sink in.

Alex looked deeply into Adam's eyes. She knew it was true.

"Those people or, whatever they are. They are from the Agency I use to work for. I am sure of that. In my last few years of working with them and around the time I met you, I had become a double agent for a group of freedom fighters named Zion."

Alex shifted a bit when she heard the name. She remembered a news program where a terrorist group, by the name of Zion shot and killed innocent workers and soldiers in New York.

"You mean the terrorist group?!" she said with a bit more angst in her voice than she wanted.

Adam put one of his hands up as if to calm the situation.

"The world is way more complicated than what the news can ever cover. They were there to get Sparks. And I am not sure, but I think he or someone from the Agency killed a bunch of the Zion fighters. I don't want to believe it was Sparks but he was still working for the Agency at that time."

They both gave each other a dreadful look. Alex remembered how Sparks felt. The feeling of life being over, and she remembered how comfortable and yet uncomfortable it felt. She also had seen him in action. If he was part of all that back behind them, she really didn't know if she could trust him.

And as if Adam had read his wife's mind, "I don't know if we can truly trust him. But I do know Sparks and he is the most noble and honest man I have ever met. As for why they took me,"

Adam's hand moved to Alex's neck as he tenderly tapped the back of her locket three times then the front once. There was a blue light that lit up along the sides and the front slid open. Alex, not knowing that her necklace was even a locket, or that it was this high tech, shifted her head back a bit to get a better look. Once the locket opened, a small USB male port popped out the size of a fingernail.

"This is what they wanted. It holds the locations of all the Zion bases in the world. These bases have soldiers that would fight against the Agency as well as children and innocent people that would have sought refuge from the Fall Out. I never thought that they knew I had it or that they would ever find us. This is why we left for the mountains in the first place."

Alex briefly remembered that night when Adam came home and changed her world.

"They will not stop looking for this. I think we need to get in touch with Zion. They will know what to do... They can protect us."

Adam tapped the sides of the locket and it swiftly returned to its original shape.

"So, do we go back to our bunker? We can message them there."

"No, that bunker is compromised. We need to go someplace random."

Alex revved the engine then shifted it to first as she peeled off.

"I know just the place. It is outside of Kansas City. Plus, I know a few people that could help!"

Adam was curious, but he was far too into his thoughts to ask Alex anything. He trusted her and he sat back as they drove.

****

Sparks walked forward and the dark portal closed behind him. He could hear the alarms and minor explosions a few blocks behind him, but he did not turn back to look. It was already behind him, he had beaten his fears and nothing at this moment scared him. He stopped walking to think. He really wanted Lucille's head, and he knew she would be at the Gates. He knew she would be preparing for war and he needed to be smart about his approach.

He could attack by himself, but there were two other hounds with Lucille. Lord knows what other demons were with her also. He needed to find the army of the Lord and together they would be victorious. The problem now was that there was no way he would make it to Egypt before they left to set more of the Zion fighters free. He thought on how he was even going to get a plane to get there, or, for that matter, who would fly the plane?

His only way to make it to the Elohim, in time, would be to go to Iku. Time was relative there, and he would do nothing to the timeline if he just went directly to wherever Ki and Seriah are now in a few minutes.

Sparks rubbed his waves trying to understand the math of what he was thinking. He created another hole and walked through.

He was excited. Not at the fact that he would be seeing his friends again, as much as the fact that he would be seeing Dethia again. He bit his lip a bit thinking of how they would truly consummate their union. One last thing entered Sparks' mind as he was sucked into the void between existences, the Old man in the garden. Sparks felt something inside of him saying to find this old man again, Babba, he remembered his name was.

The void grabbed Sparks and the portal closed behind.

****

Lucille slammed her hands on the large Oak desk. She was back in her office at the Gates. Looking down at the computer screen from her hunched position, she slowly typed in the password. Making sure to type each word deliberately and using the shift button appropriately and pressed the 'enter' button.

She grabbed the screen and threw it against the wall, breaking the bookshelf and causing books to fall on top of the screen. The screen arched a bit, catching fire to a few books that laid on top. Lucille looked at it unconcerned and rolled her eyes.

"When I find out who locked me out of my own shit." She balled her fist looking around the office as if anyone was there.

"Cassandra!" She yelled for her assistant who immediately opened the door.

"Yes, your majesty?" Cassy answered with a very undetected bow.

"Why can't I get into my fu…" She caught herself.

Although Cassy was a lower demon, she did have a bit of an attitude. If Cassy felt disrespected, she would just disappear. Lucille had been without her for months over 10 mins of lunchtime.

"Excuse me…" she calmed herself and adjusted her skirt.

Cassy looked at her and huffed, "Yeah, Lucy you excused." Then rolled her eyes.

"Why can't I get into my computer? The password won't accept."

"Well, I was trying to tell you earlier. You know when you walked past me like you didn't hear me. Tell you the truth, I almost took an extended vacation just for that but I thought you might need me after you found out about Williams. Anyway, someone hacked into our servers and uploaded a virus. Our Tech says…"

Lucile raised her hand to stop Cassy. She knew she had felt something earlier. She thought of Williams and she had to hold back a tear. She thought that it was just some of the residual emotions she had from their fun last night and most of the morning.

But she stood there, she knew what was going to be said after she asked the question. She could feel it, or better yet not feel it.

"What happened to Mr. Williams?" Cassy looked shocked.

"Oh, you haven't heard. Ma'am, I am so sorry to have to tell you this… but Mr. Williams let Sparks get away. He is dead." Lucile looked off a bit then waved her hand at Cassy as to shew her off.

"I know you ain't shewing me off? No need. I'll see you when I see you. I could be with my man and not dealing…" Cassandra spoke to herself as she walked out the door and pulled it closed.

Lucille stood there; her breath became labored and her head hung a bit.

"Darling… My… Love… You were the only one who remembers me as I was. You, my sweet Anubis. I should have never got you involved."

She walked solemnly to the chair behind the desk. As she plumped herself down on the seat, she placed her hands on her head and elbows on the desk. Her body shook from her sobs as the short breaths slowly turned to wails. She felt something she had never wanted to feel; she felt alone. Although there were two more fragments of Anubis left in Jones and Robinson, they had no idea of who they were.

Williams was the only one who knew who she was. She was afraid that soon she would forget who she was. It was as if Williams was her only reminder, and now he was gone. Her sadness turned into anger. The small fire that was still burning from the monitor, had almost died down.

She raised her head. All the lights except for the small fire and a couple candles went out leaving a little light to illuminate the large room. She looked at the door, she wasn't looking at anything, she wasn't thinking about anything. She could only feel her pain; she felt alone. No one to understand, as no one will empathize with the devil.

She smiled a wicked grin. Her mascara had run down her rosy cheeks. She took a deep breath then sat up tall as she let it out, alone or not, no one would ever destroy her. A few strains of blonde hair fell in her face and she quickly pushed it behind her ears. She turned her chair and stood up looking at her bookshelf opposite of where she had thrown the monitor.

As she walked towards the bookshelf, she skimmed the shelf with her fingertips, looking for her book. She did not need to do this, the bookshelf was enchanted and all she had to do was grab a book and it would be the book she needed. But this book was different, it required a certain amount of energy and a spell to be found.

As she looked over the spines for her book, she quietly said the spell. Once she finished the spell, she stopped and reached out for the book her hand was over. She pulled it out and went back to her desk.

She slammed the large book on the desk and immediately started turning the pages.

As with the method of her finding the book, she had to recite a spell to get to the page of what she wanted. As she got to the last few pages, she stopped. And there it was.

"I am not the one, MOM!!! I know you hear me!!! You want WAR! Well now, here it is!"

She slammed her hands down on the desk and a bright light came from the book. Her hair unraveled and flew back, and her eyes shined with the same white light.

"I, THE BRIGHT MORNING STAR, CALL UPON THEE: PESTILENCE, FAMINE, WAR, AND..."

She rolled her white shining eye,

"Hell, I know you ain't coming Dethia... GO FORTH AND DO THY BIDDING!"

****

Time stopped for three seconds, a trumpet sounded in the skies as everything turned dark as midnight. Seriah was discussing the plan with a few generals along with Kelia and Aviv. It was a split discussion, a few generals along with Kelia wanted to go to the Gates. They believed that attacking before Lucille could put an army together would be the best idea.

The opposing side that consisted of Aviv, and one that Seriah was giving substantial thought to, was saying they would free more bunkers and recruit more Zion loyalist to help storm the Gates with the power of numbers.

Seriah looked at the other generals who looked back knowingly. He then looked at Kelia who looked a bit confused.

"I know that signaled something..." She threw her hands up.

"Yes, it does. It means that we may have no other choice but to free as many people as we can."

Kelia looked at him questionably. She noticed that he did not act as he usually did around her. Ever since he was made general of this army, he was very professional with how he treated her. She understood the dynamic, but it was more subtle than that. Things like; he never asked if she was doing okay; or she never caught him staring anymore; or he wasn't as quick to take her side in arguments. That was the Seriah she needed right now.

"Uhh... was that God talking through a trumpet? Telling you all that?" she rolled her eyes and crossed her arms.

Seriah paid no attention.

"No. That was the sound of the four horsemen being released."

The other generals took a deep breath. Kelia stood there with her eyes wide. She usually did not show expression, but this was one moment where she didn't care.

She thought to herself, *"who are the four horsemen? There is Pestilence, War, Famine, and... Death."*

"Wait! Death is one of the horsemen, right? How is that going to work? I thought she was staying out of this."

Seriah scratched his chin.

"Yeah, this will be interesting!"

CPSIA information can be obtained
at www.ICGtesting.com
Printed in the USA
LVHW080317050921
697006LV00016B/800